TRICK

TRICK

THE CUSTODIANS
BOOK ONE

CARA NOX

STELLA CHARTA PRESS

For my sister.

CONTENT WARNINGS

I've attempted to compile a list of prominent warning keywords to the best of my ability. However, since I'm only human, it's very possible I've glossed over something that could be sensitive to you. Please use your own discretion when reading and only continue if you feel safe to do so.

This story contains: Alcohol, anxiety, blood, childhood trauma, death, depression, discrimination, mention of drug use, emotional abuse, gore, grief, loss, manipulation, threat of murder, parental neglect, physical abuse, mention of suicide, violence, and mention of vomiting.

ALSO BY CARA NOX

For an up-to-date list of all of Cara Nox's books visit their website:

caranox.com/books

TRICK

ONE
EVIE

Time stopped the moment Evie teetered on the edge of the sidewalk, gasping as she stumbled backward and crushed the paper cup in her hand. The contents sloshed in its container, heating the tips of her fingers in addition to the rush of adrenaline shooting through her. The gust of air from the oncoming bus whipped her near-black hair around her face, mere inches away from disaster.

If she wasn't feeling awake before, she certainly was now.

She clapped a hand to the cardigan draped over her heart. Her palm now wet and warm with coffee. Evie grimaced. "Shit."

"I guess that's an appropriate reaction." A chuckle came from the girl standing next to her—a grungy twenty-something who stood a couple inches shorter than Evie with dyed, pitch-black hair streaked with electric blue. She pulled the coffee cup from Evie's hand, wiping off the dribbles with her thumb and flicking it onto the pavement. "Look, if college is really *that* bad, then maybe you should just—I don't know, drop out? Jumping in front of a bus seems a little overdramatic."

Evie shot her a glare while she dug through her crossbody

backpack. "Very funny, Serina. It definitely wasn't because I'm running on four hours of sleep or anything." She began swiping at her shirt with a moist towelette, trying to keep pace with her as they crossed the street on the signal change.

Serina smirked, tilting the cup to her lips when Evie wasn't paying all that much attention and gagged. "Oh *God*, Evie. What the hell?"

"Hey!" She carefully pried it from her grip. "I didn't think you'd *drink* it."

"That's disgusting. I think I'd rather be hit by that bus than drink *that*."

"It's black. I'm not looking for a sugar high."

"No, but you're clearly hoping it'll put you out of your misery. Now I need something to get that taste out of my mouth." She made a sound of disgust, rapidly shaking her head like a violent, involuntary reaction.

"I just need to get this project done, so I can take the weekend to relax. I think I looked like death warmed over last weekend after overhearing a couple remarks from my aunt. But honestly, what college student *doesn't* look or feel like death?"

"Why don't you just take a break *now*, and save the project for Sunday night like every other normal person?" Serina glanced over at her as she nursed the coffee, making her do a double take. "Would you stop drinking that sludge, and come with me to get a real drink?"

"I'm underaged," Evie said with disbelief. "And I'm sure as hell not going to get caught with a fake ID."

"Look at Miss Goody-Goody, not even willing to tack on a year."

Evie rolled her eyes, and Serina let out a bubbly, raspy laugh.

"Come on, live a little! Enjoy life in one of the largest cities in the world!" She threw her arms wide to the glittering windows of the skyscrapers. A sea of people undulated around them like the bicyclists weaving past yellow cabs. "Stop sitting around your apartment and talking to your houseplants."

"I have *far* too much to do for school to be bothered with balancing a decent social life." Evie huffed out a laugh.

"Then maybe we should hook you up on a blind date to fix that."

"How about *no*. I appreciate the offer, but that's probably the last thing I need right now. What I need is someone who won't text me all night and eliminate the little sleep I already cherish."

"You know texting isn't all a relationship is good for, right?"

"And we're done talking," Evie said with a hard, unamused smile. She stopped in front of the towering double doors to her apartment building and flipped her phone over, a glare bouncing off the screen in the evening sun. "It's seven now, so I'm going to pull an all-nighter and have this damn thing done by four. You have a good night with your parties, and I pray you won't be dead come morning."

"Same to you," Serina said with a grin mock tip of a hat. She jogged off, skipping across the street and turning back to wave just as the signal's red hand popped up, counting down in time with each alarming chirp.

Evie pushed open one of the glass doors, her flats tapping against the glossy white herringbone tiles. Her keys jingled as she flipped through to the smallest one and jammed it into one of the silver boxes lined along the wall. The mailbox's door swung open to a collection of junk mail, judging by the thin, crinkled magazine paper, along with 'urgent' and 'limited time' faux stamps printed on the envelopes.

She shuffled through the stack on her way to the elevator and shared a small smile and wave with the security guard camping in his corner booth. Her thumb mashed the button, and the doors slid open, welcoming her inside the wood-paneled brown box to tap her floor's button with an elbow.

The lobby doors swung open again with two shadowy figures brightening past the tinted glass—a man and a woman. The woman's dark ponytail swung over her shoulder as she jerked to turn toward the guard counter, her sneakers squeaking.

The guy, on the other hand, stopped. His blue-gray eyes pinned on Evie with a curious glint, and his tousled, light brown hair shifted as he tilted his head. The corner of his mouth tugged down in a thoughtful frown before the elevator doors slid shut.

"Okay then…" she whispered to herself, tucking the mail under her arm with another jingle from her keys.

The elevator opened again, and she strode down the worn, khaki carpeting and past each silver-plated number posted next to the doors. Every peephole might as well have been watching her, those haunting eyes lurking behind each one. She shivered and shook it off when she made it to her apartment, pushing the door shut behind her. The snap of the deadbolt and the scrape of the chain allowed her to finally release a breath.

Safety.

Evie set her coffee cup and mail down on the small square of kitchenette countertop before dropping her bag by the couch. She stretched and swallowed a yawn on her way across the studio to the bathroom, her leggings grazing the edge of her bed's powder-blue comforter. A beaded friendship bracelet hung tacked above her gathering of plants, along with printed photos, notes, and cards under fairy lights—all memories of a simpler time upstate, filled with confetti and jars of fireflies from birthday parties and summer camping with old friends. Flicking the bathroom light switch, she winced at the harsh fluorescent and tugged off her cardigan to half-toss into the sink.

The necklace chain flopped against her skin, its heavy, pocket watch pendant finally slipping free as she scrubbed at the coffee stain and grumbled. She tucked the watch back into place and sighed, deciding to let the cardigan soak for a few minutes. That was when she caught a glimpse of her reflection. Evie grimaced at the dark circles pooling under her eyes, making her olive hue look more sickly in the shabby lighting. Well, at least that probably explained the guy's weird reaction in the lobby.

She scrubbed at the poor cardigan a bit more, drained the sink, and tossed it over the shower door when she'd had enough, praying the stain would come out the rest of the way in the wash over the weekend. Evie popped a hair-tie off her brush, pulled her hair back, and hummed on her way back to the kitchenette. Instinctively, she reached for the coffee cup, but detoured back to the mail, flipping through it again to file it into the trash piece-by-piece.

College-targeted businesses like restaurants, apps, cheap gyms, bars, and a tattoo parlor down the street boasted their own colorful flyers. Half the envelopes held ads for cable and internet. It all flitted into the bin and took a couple steps back to collapse on the futon. Her head lulled back, and she stared up at the small brown stains on the ceiling. Her lids drooped, and the second of rest slipped into minutes, carrying her away with the white noise of water kicking on and her upstairs neighbor's TV trickling down to her unit.

Evie jerked awake to pounding against her apartment door, sending her heart slamming in her chest. She flinched at the second urgent sequence of knocks and pushed herself up. "Coming," she forced out, her voice catching and not nearly loud enough to cut through the noise. She jogged over and stood on her toes to look out the peephole, taking in two men in suits standing on the other side. One checked his watch, the other glanced up and down the hall, tapping his foot.

Cops? Detectives? Evie unchained the door and flicked the lock for the deadbolt. The *click* vibrated through her, signaling her mistake when the door immediately swung inward. She stumbled back, feeling a hand clap over her mouth. Full panic kicked in, and she aimlessly flailed in a pathetic attempt to try to defend herself as the guy spun her around.

A woman's voice rang out. "Hey, asshole!"

The jab was followed by a crackling sound and a cry of surprise—a man's voice—accompanied her immediate assailant's tightening grip. It was countered by a blur resulting in sudden, backward momentum. He finally let her go.

A hand firmly gripped her arm, steadying her before she

yelped and ripped free—a surprisingly easy feat that allowed her to take in the scene with wide eyes. The suits were on the floor, unmoving with a man and a woman in leather and nylon jackets looming over them.

The two from the lobby.

Shaking, Evie met the woman's gaze, taking a step back as the woman took a tentative step forward. "Wh-what the hell?" Evie asked, pointing toward the two unstirring forms.

"Do you know these two?" the woman asked, glancing over to her *friend*—or whatever he was—who crouched down and began rooting through one of the attackers' pockets.

"N-no!" She rapidly shook her head, hating how she stammered. "I-I thought they were investigators or something with the suits and—"

Almost as if it were an explanation, the woman lifted up the edge of her shirt, revealing a badge clipped at her belt. "Well, they're not because *we* are. Likely the only thing the four of us have in common is that we're looking for you."

"Me?" One of her own fingers pointed to her chest with a squeak.

"You're Evangelina Thatcher, correct?"

"E-Evie. Y-yes—Why? What's going on?" No one had her unit number except Serina and her aunt. But Serina had just left, so why… She swayed slightly, a memory resurfacing of how she peeked down one of the hallways when her grandfather answered the door. Back when she had thought it was her parents coming home. "Oh, no—" She shook her head, the image of her aunt springing to the forefront of her thoughts. "Please tell me she's okay. My aunt's okay, right?"

"Just calm down," she said, holding up a hand. "I'm sure your aunt's fine. We're here to protect you because you're in danger."

"I-I don't understand. What's going on? Who are you?"

"I'm Tarryn Fuentes." She jerked her head towards the guy now flipping through a wallet belonging to one of the assailants.

"This is my partner, Haven Bennett. Look, I promise to explain everything, but it's possible that they have friends lurking nearby. As for us, we need to leave. Now."

Tarryn offered her a hand. Evie stared down at it with so many questions tumbling through her mind. Then her eyes flicked over to Haven's hand, held up with a glinting, round piece that almost looked like a coin. But it wasn't metal. Instead, the gleam made it look more like a slick piece of plastic.

Tarryn grabbed her arm. "Sorry, but we don't have time for this." Pulling her towards the door, Evie dug the heels of her flats into the carpet.

"Wait—I need my bag."

Tarryn stopped and slackened her grip, and Evie scooped up her crossbody. After a glance back at Haven, she shuffled behind her to the elevator. Tarryn repeatedly jammed her finger against the button to go down while looking over her shoulder to the stairwell door until it popped open. Haven ushered them both inside, where Evie awkwardly stood hunched between them. She nervously shifted while her eyes darted back and forth from Tarryn to Haven and back again.

The doors opened to an empty lobby, save the security guard who was fixated on his book, unaware of her pleading looks on the way out. These two weren't really cops, were they? Nothing about them added up, and not to mention that Tarryn's badge could easily be a prop. She chewed on the inside of her cheek as they started down the sidewalk. Tarryn rattled something nonsensical off with her phone to her ear, and Evie cursed herself for missing what it was since she was so focused on where they were going. Her grip tightened on the coffee-stained bag strap as she tried to get another look at the badge again.

They turned into the parking garage at the end of the street, and Evie sucked in a breath. This was it. Now or never. If she didn't make a run for it now, then who the hell knew what they'd do to her. A slow, painful countdown from five rang out in her head. When she hit zero, her soles scraped against the concrete, and the other two continued forward for a couple more brisk steps. She spun on her heel, and ran—a full-tilt sprint, launching her straight toward the street. Shouts echoed in the garage behind her.

A fresh surge of adrenaline pumped through her veins. She gritted her teeth and forced herself to push past that imaginary limit before one of them caught up. Just as she was about to turn the corner and throw herself through the side entrance, a shadow filled the threshold. Her heart leapt into her throat, and she skidded to a stop. Perhaps she had made a mistake. The guy standing there took a menacing step toward her. Her own unsteady step back sent her falling to the pavement, and Tarryn dove between them.

Taser in hand, she stood her ground. "Back off." It was a calm, deadly warning—or maybe it was more a threat, considering the weapon.

Evie scrambled to stand, her vision swaying before she even noticed the two other figures step out from the row of parked cars. "Oh, shit," she whimpered.

Haven stepped between them and Evie on the other side, almost like he was patiently waiting for Tarryn to strike.

"You dumbasses have one chance to walk away before I lay you out," she said coldly.

The one in front of her grinned. "I'd like to see you try, little girl."

She should've just gotten in the damn car.

"Bring it, bitch," Tarryn challenged.

He let out a growl and lunged for her, the other two going for Haven at that signal. Evie heard a wheeze from behind her, flinching as she witnessed Haven's upper cut to another. The sound of a taser echoed through the garage as he grabbed the immediate attacker's shoulders and kneed him in the stomach, sending him to the ground with a gasp for air. Swift footsteps pounded against pavement, and the third was met with a taser as well.

"Okay, I am *begging* you not to run," Tarryn said, a little winded when she turned back to her. Haven firmly grasped her arm and steered her towards the back of the garage again. Tarryn jogged next to them, holstering her taser. "If you try that again, you're going to either get kidnapped or killed, and that's sort of the last thing I need right now."

"Killed?"

Haven's pace picked up, only halting when they reached a black SUV with tinted windows.

"Yes, *killed*," she replied, opening the passenger's door. "Now get in."

"And how do I know that you two are really cops?"

Tarryn's hand went to her face. "Please just get in the damn car, and I'll answer that."

Hesitantly, she complied, eyeing her wearily until the door shut. She clutched her bag on her lap, hugging it to her chest as they climbed in, and Tarryn started the car.

"For starters, it's called being under cover. We track or hunt people down, so looking like a cop kind of doesn't typically work in our favor." The doors locked, and she put the car in reverse. "On top of that, we have your information. I know your name."

"So, where are we going?" Evie tried to dry her hands on her pants.

"To a hotel." Tarryn accelerated towards the street, glancing both ways before smoothly transitioning onto the blacktop. "Unfortunately, no one's manning our safehouse besides security due to some scheduling conflicts. Everyone and their mother's taking a damn spring break vacation. But we'll get you there first thing in the morning."

Evie's eyes roamed the rearview mirror, fixing on Haven. He hadn't said a single word yet. "Um… does your partner talk?"

"Oh—No, he can't."

"O-oh…"

"You get used to it."

Haven's eyes flicked up to meet hers in the mirror, and she froze, reddening. "I'm sorry, I didn't mean to—"

"Don't stress over it. Bennett's an… *acquired* taste, honestly."

His head snapped towards her, holding up his middle finger rather discreetly near the console for Tarryn's eyes only. Evie pretended not to notice, gradually sliding down into her seat instead.

TWO
CADE

"This is by-far the stupidest thing you've decided to do this week."

"Oh, come *on*, Alyx," Cade replied with a roll of his eyes. "Cat-calling the rival girls near the Upper West takes the cake for the stupidest thing I've done this week."

Alyx hummed, shaking her head after a moment. Her cropped, dark, wavy hair swayed with the motion. At least, the side that wasn't shaved close to her scalp. She, like him, wore a fitted leather jacket, sans labels or elaborate designs over her gray tee-shirt, matching his gray hoodie. Twins in clothing, but that was all, seeing how her coloring leaned toward a cooler, lemon-hue to his warm peach and flaunted cappuccino-brown hair and cognac eyes in contrast to his ashy blond and cobalt blue.

"Nope," she said. "Still pretty sure that you're going to get your ass beat once we step inside. You know the Martellis hate your guts, right?"

"What? *No…*" Sarcasm bled into his tone, thinking of his arch nemesis likely waiting in the Martelli offices. He was probably cleaning his guns and carving Cade's name into a single bullet at this very moment, as if he could sense his impending arrival. "Look, I just need to talk to Emilio for a sec, and then we'll leave. Not a big deal."

"Gee," she said with mock excitement, "I can't wait to find my way back home by myself once Emilio shoves you in his trunk and dumps you in the river."

"Live a little, Lyx."

She groaned, but he strode forward undeterred. His hand wrapped around the brass handle attached to the heavy, dark-stained oak door, and held it open for her. He trailed in behind, basking in the soft, warming lighting and rich, earthy tones of the cherrywood countertops and high-backed booths along the windows.

Cade sauntered up to the bar, sliding between two taller patrons who shot him irritated looks as he flagged down the bartender. "Hey! Emilio around?"

The bartender—a guy better suited as a gym junkie with a tight black tee-shirt and half-apron—narrowed his eyes at him. "Who's asking?"

Cade chuckled. "You must be new here. I'm Cade Hart. I'm here to speak with Emilio. If I can't speak with Emilio, I'm going to have to go home, explain that some large moron wouldn't let me see him, and then my brother's going to send someone else out here to knock some heads together." He deliberately, calmly slid his hands into his jacket pockets, waiting for those two marbles in the tin can that was his brain to finally clink together. "So, are you going to take me to him, or not?"

After a moment, the guy hesitated, glancing from Cade to Alyx and back again.

"Vicente—"

Cade's ears perked up, and he spun on his heel to face a man in a tie-less suit. The guy grimaced and ran a hand over his slicked-back black hair. "Never mind, just leave these two to me. We'll talk later. Come on, Hart." He turned, motioning for them to follow him to the end of the bar and into a curtained-off hallway.

"Hey Roman," Cade said with a grin, bumping shoulders with him.

"Sorry about that," Roman said. "We have a few newbies that don't quite understand the ins-and-outs just yet."

The glint of sports-league photographs and plaques followed them through the tunnel of half-stucco, half-wine-colored-wainscoting. "These new recruits up-state, out-of-state, or old-country?"

"Out-of-state. Extended family that wants to try their hand in New Atlas for a while. I doubt most of them will stick around for long. But you know Marco. He'll use them up before they walk away."

Oh, did Cade know Marco, all right…

"Little rough for family, huh?"

Roman glanced back with his hand on the door handle, cocking a brow. "Watch yourself. Marco's been in enough of a mood as it is. You'll have to suffer each other while Emilio finishes up another item of business. It should only take fifteen minutes."

"Marco's just waiting for an excuse to kick the shit out of me in a back alley anyway," Cade replied with a smirk.

"Gee, I can't imagine why," Roman said dryly, shoving the door open.

A handful of fresh-faced Martelli crew members sat inside, some circled around the card table in the middle of the lounge while a few others hung along the walls with their phones. Cade counted eight, but he could only name four. However, Roman and Marco were the only two he honestly cared about. Roman was the one who kept everything running smoothly for Emilio, handling the day-to-day of their establishments, while Marco handled the more… *unsavory* portions of the business. Cade likened him to the snapping guard dog that wouldn't hesitate to go for your jugular.

Naturally, Marco looked the part too. He was a couple years over thirty, rough around the edges with scarred knuckles and cuts on his jaw that broke the seamlessness of his well-kept facial hair. He wasn't nearly as tall as Vicente, but he was still just as bulky. The main difference was that he hid it well under a suit that wasn't all that different from Roman's.

"It's been a while, Marco," Cade said the second his eyes flicked up from the green felt of the card table.

His face immediately twisted into a snarl. "Get this little bitch out of here."

"Marco, chill," Roman said sharply. "He's just here to talk to Emilio, and then he's gone."

"Oh, come on, Marco," Cade said with feigned disappointment. "Don't talk about my lady-friend like that."

Marco glared daggers at him, Alyx hit Cade lightly in the side, shooting him a glare, and Roman put a hand on his shoulder, squeezing it a little tighter than Cade had expected. "Now what did I just say about not starting shit?"

Cade bit into his cheek, holding his tongue until the hand was removed. He trailed behind Roman to the table, where his host collected his hand of face-down cards. Despite not being invited to play, Cade dropped into the seat next to Roman, giving Alyx a moment of pause before she took the seat on Cade's other side.

"Want to deal us in after this?" Cade shrugged, leaning back in his chair. "Seems we got some time to kill."

Marco's eyes narrowed at him, but Roman spoke instead. "*Maybe.*" He shot him a sideways glance. "If you're able to keep your mouth shut until we say this one's over, then Marco might be generous enough to let you play."

Cade thought it was more likely for Marco to go find his gun instead, but he was willing to hedge those bets.

"Hey," Roman called, half-turning to the wall as Marco and the nameless individual began to deliberate over their hands, "Angelo—Make yourself useful and get Hart and his friend some water."

Angelo's head jerked up from his phone with a start, nodded, and wandered off. He wasn't gone for long though, returning soon after with four glasses, his fingers straining from how they were barely tucked into the rim of each one. Cade first, Alyx second, and Roman and Marco's were set down in rapid succession as a sign of respect for not drawing out which of them might be third. The nameless player groaned, throwing down his cards and getting up from the table while fishing a pack of cigarettes from his pocket.

"See?" Roman said with a motion to Cade. "He *can* be quiet. He just chooses not to."

"I like him better with his mouth shut," Marco grumbled. "But this damn white boy still shouldn't be allowed in here."

"Well, that's not very nice." Cade mock scowled at him.

Marco slowly leaned forward, pointing at him from across the table with malice in his gaze. "If I were in Emilio's shoes, I'd take a swing at that damn brother of yours."

Cade scoffed. "Now who wouldn't want to do that? Try living with him."

Marco stared him down while Roman reshuffled the cards. He said nothing, though there was a glimmer in his eye that indicated he had *liked* Cade's answer. Maybe he had finally earned some points with his nemesis and would live to see another day.

"Fake bets or real?" Roman asked, beginning to deal.

"Real," Marco said without a chance for anyone to protest. "Make this brat pay some of his allowance toward that dinnerware Emilio wants."

Cade loosed a laugh. "Go easy on me Marco, I'm broke." He threw a twenty on the table, and Roman sighed, shaking his head slightly as if to say, 'Lord, help me.'

Alyx jabbed him in the side under the cover of the table before she tossed out a five. "Stop it," she hissed in his ear.

"Looks like your girlfriend isn't so confident about her cards." Marco nodded to her addition.

"I'm not his girlfriend."

"Sounds like someone's single," someone called from the corner of the room—a guy with a toothy grin who practically sang the words. He started to get up from his seat like it was an open invitation.

Instead of speaking up to defend her, Cade hid his smirk, ducking away.

"Sounds like you're a complete dumbass," she said in a sickeningly sweet tone.

"What? A Hart too good for you?"

"I might actually be interested if either of them were *women*."

He cleared his throat, awkwardly backing up a couple of steps, which got a chuckle out of Cade.

"That never gets old," Cade mumbled, peeking at his cards and patting them back down against the felt.

"Everyone ready?" Roman asked.

Alyx's distraction finally gave her a quiet apology and took his leave down the hall leading outside. Roman flipped over the three cards in the middle. Cade hummed while the others began to raise their bets, though Alyx folded with a huff, crossing her arms over her chest. He raised, deciding the press his own luck. Finally, one-by-one they flipped them over. Grinning, Cade revealed a straight flush, rewarding him with an eyeroll from Roman.

"Two four-of-a-kinds," he said, lifting himself slightly out of the chair to collect his winnings. "I win. No hard feel—" His eyes went wide as someone grabbed the back of his jacket, forcing him back down to his seat.

"Pot goes to Marco," a new voice echoed from behind him. Though Cade didn't bother looking back, his eyes immediately fixed on the cards Marco had laid out in front of him. Two sixes.

"What?" Cade demanded, finally twisting around to take in Emilio. "How the hell does that make—"

He snapped his fingers, pointing to the middle of the table, where two more sixes lay face-up. "Sixes."

Cade's shoulders fell, his eyes rolling. "Oh, *cute*. I didn't realize we were playing with special rules. I just got cheated out of a hundred bucks."

Marco cut him a devious, satisfied grin at Cade's sour expression, and Emilio tapped the back of his chair. "Come on, Hart. If you're here to talk, then let's talk." He started toward his office, and with a frustrated sigh, Cade got up to follow. Alyx leaned back in her seat, waiting for him with crossed arms. He secretly hoped that she'd deal in again to win his money back, though he knew that she would keep it for herself even if she did.

Cade dragged his feet into Emilio's office and shut the door behind him. Papers cluttered the desk and tops of the bureaus. Oak cabinets sat popped open under photos of past ruling Martellis. All Emilio's personal pictures rested on his desk, angled away from the door—a quirk Cade had once needled him about. He naturally came to the conclusion that he could be worried about those smiling faces might be used against him.

But Emilio had replied with a chuckle and a relaxed calm about him—something he hadn't really expected in comparison to how Cade's older brother might respond, despite the two of them being the same age and matching experience. He'd simply said that only a coward would go after his sister and her kid, much like how her ex-husband had beat her. It had been followed by a glint in his eye that told Cade that her ex had gotten off easy.

Emilio casually leaned against the edge of the desk, face-to-face with him, a stance that would've been seen as disrespectful to his brother. "Is this a check-up, or a delivery?"

"Just a delivery." He pulled out an envelope from his jacket, holding it out for him. "Jay said that it was for your eyes only, so I'm just ensuring that no one else sneaks a peek."

He cautiously took it with a raised brow. "And you didn't look at it?"

Cade shrugged. "Look, if he wants to tell me, then he'll tell me. I just do what I'm told so I don't piss him off."

Without breaking eye-contact, he grabbed up the letter opener on his desk, cutting the message free. He scanned it while Cade followed the interweaving pattern of the maroon wallpaper to the ceiling along one wall.

"Should I burn this when I'm done, or…?"

"Use your discretion, I guess. Not sure what else to tell you."

He folded it up and slid it back inside the envelope.

"You good?" Cade asked with a smirk. "Ready to kick me out?"

"You know…" Emilio started, absently tapping the edge of the desk. "Just considering all the times I've had just talking to you one-on-one, I feel like if things were different, you'd be able to run things better than Jay."

Cade guffawed.

"Just hear me out—Your brother is an asshole, and you might act like a dumbass, but you're smarter than some of these guys give you credit for. I can tell you know how things function versus how they should."

"Emilio, no one takes me seriously."

"Because you're not a threat to anyone, Cade. If you showed people that you're at least a force to be reckoned with, they'll change their tune. Hell, maybe they'll even show you more respect than him because we all know it's begrudging."

Cade shook his head. "Please don't try to start shit."

"I'm not. I'm being serious."

"I'm not going to turn on Jay," he said firmly. "So, if that's your goal, you can stop now. The two of us clawed our way out of the gutter when no one else bothered to look our way. We cried for help for years. I'm just the way I am out of necessity to survive. We only had each other, so we watched the other's back.

That's why we strategize the same way, but I decided to play the good cop to his bad."

"I wouldn't say that too loud, or else Marco's going to bust down the door and accuse you of wearing a wire."

Cade couldn't help but smirk at that. "Look, Emilio, I get that you don't like me—"

"Actually, no. I like you. I hate Jay. Admittedly, I hated the both of you in the beginning, but when Jay stopped doing house calls, I realized that you were far more reasonable. Marco may not like you, but Roman and I agreed that if you ever decided to step out of Jay's shadow that it would benefit us to welcome you into the fold. That is, assuming you'd take us up on the offer."

Cade rocked back a little on his heels in surprise. Hesitating, he forced out a nervous laugh. "I... appreciate it, but I don't think I'd really be welcome here, despite what you say. Not to mention that I already told you I won't turn my back on Jay. He may be an asshole, but I've dealt with him my whole life. It's nothing new to me."

"Just throwing it out there," Emilio said with a slight shrug, folding his arms over his chest with a glance at the photo wall. "There's been rumors going around that power is starting to shift, so I think it's best if you're prepared."

Concern gripped him then. "Shifting *how*, Emilio?"

"If I knew, I'd tell you. I'm just hearing people talk. Plus, there's a lot of power changing hands this year. Just remember that it's possible that Jay won't always be at the top."

"Why? Because you want that spot?"

"Not going to say that I *don't* want it," he admitted. "But I don't think that I have the power to back up that challenge. Not right now, at least." Things quieted between them, leaving Cade with hesitation to press for whatever might've been left unsaid. "I won't keep you. You should probably continue with the rest of your errands or whatever the hell else you do."

He waved a dismissive hand, starting past Cade to open the

door, and he followed him back out into the hall. When they arrived back at the table, Cade's eyes went wide at the sight of crumpled bills piled in front of Alyx. She began straightening them out tauntingly, one-by-one with a grin.

"Bitch," he whispered just as the rest of the table slowly turned toward him.

THREE
REN

A light rap on Ren's door ripped him from his concentration. He pulled a hand away from his forehead and rested it on his desk before it creaked open. Light trickled into the dim safe haven of his room, illuminating the clothes thrown over his bed's headboard, rumpled comforter spilling from the mattress, and creased posters tacked up along the walls. Bands, video games, comics. Things that had come and gone from his extracurriculars yet stayed up as a reminder of what once was.

"You studying, Lorenzo?"

"Just a bit of homework, Mom."

She leaned on the doorknob, her mouth quirking up in a small smile. Her heart-shaped face was further softened by the glow of the hallway, haloing her bronze hue. "You were quiet during dinner? Everything okay?" she asked, the lilt of her Italian accent slipping through her words.

"Yeah." He pushed the tip of his mechanical pencil against the notebook a little too hard, pulling it up at the sound of the lead snapping. "Yeah, I'm fine."

Her smile faltered, causing him to tense as she started inside. A hand ruffled his hair before she pressed her lips to his temple. "Take it easy, okay? Don't push yourself too hard."

He huffed out a short, breathy laugh. "Yes, Mom."

The second the door pulled shut behind her, his phone clattered against the desk with a notification. He sighed, digging the device out from under the scattered graduation preparation papers he'd thought would be *fun* to flip through now that the end was in sight, only to be left overwhelmed. Did graduating high school really matter at a time like this?

When he unlocked the screen, his eyes flicked from the message to the last sentence of the essay he'd unknowingly jotted down in his notebook:

The clock's started.

He swore under his breath, dropping the phone and rubbing his eraser over the last line so fast that it almost tore. The sound of lead rattled as the pencil dropped back to the paper, and he gritted his teeth at the catching of his chair's wheels against the plank flooring.

> What do you want me to do about it?

> Need eyes on the two I mentioned earlier.
> Dealing with another problem.

Forcing back a frustrated noise, he pinned his eyes on the bedroom door and counted. Counted his own passing heartbeats, the footfalls of a heavier presence jogging up the stairs, and the notes to every whistle that echoed in their wake. Ren sent his chair rolling back in his rush to open it, bringing the musical tune to a stop in his brother's startled retreat to the opposite wall.

"Holy shi—"

"Angelo, I need you to do me a favor," he said, ignoring the wide-eyed stare and delayed hand rising to his heart since both had been too tangled up in his jacket pockets.

"Can't you go bother Carmen?" he half-whined with shoulders dropping in exhaustion. "I just got home…"

"Carmen left like fifteen minutes ago."

A groan.

"Look, I need you to cover for me. I have a friend asking for some help, and their parents aren't going to be thrilled about it." Lie. "Plus, I know Mom needs to get up early, and I don't want to worry her." Truth.

Angelo bit his lip, glancing down to the end of the hall where a door rested somewhat crooked in its frame. No light poured out from under it. Sighing, he turned his attention back to Ren, running a hand through his mussed near-black hair—near-identical to Ren's. "Fine, I'll cover for you—"

"You're the best," Ren said with a too-confident smirk, beginning to push the door shut again.

Angelo shoved his foot in the crack, forcing it back open with a stern expression. "Promise you'll let me know when you get there, when you're leaving, and when you get back if I'm not downstairs. The last thing I need is for Mom to burst into tears because I let my dumbass little brother wander around and get kidnapped. Not to mention Carmen will probably kick my ass…"

Ren's smile dropped, slipping into something a little more somber. "I'll text you. Promise."

Angelo's foot slid back, but Ren didn't bother trying to shut the door this time. He pulled his hoodie off his chair and tugged it over his head in the midst of collecting his phone, wallet, and keys.

"Don't stay out too late."

Ren chuckled, shaking his head as the door clicked behind him. "Trust me, I don't want to be out any later than I need to."

The stairs creaked with each bouncing step to the living

room, ripping the breath from him in what he prayed was a quiet enough escape. He squinted from the waning sunlight's reflected remnants of the morning rain on his way to the subway.

Where to?

He pushed out the sides of his phone case with his thumbs, waiting for a reply. Tilting his face to the ceiling, he closed his eyes before letting it drop back to his phone. He tapped against the glass screen, torn away from the smells of piss and body odor assaulting his senses. When he opened his eyes, his map had the address marked, calling him to his destination.

And that's where the next train was headed.

It dropped him off two blocks away, and by then it was finally dark—both a mercy and a harbinger of dread. His pace slowed at the sight of a sleek, black sedan along the curb ahead, where a woman stepped out with the minor assistance of the driver. She was all tight-smiles with the lingering welcome staff outside the restaurant, far too preoccupied with her awkward gate in high-heels, smoothing down her silver, body-hugging dress, and fussing over her black hair falling from the bun at the base of her neck.

Ren yanked his hood over his head before the driver climbed back in and rolled past, leaving his charge to weave through the lush, fancy tables of French food and people in suits until she reached a man on the far end. Though he was well-dressed, he didn't wear a tie, leaving his neck exposed with an extra undone button. Same black hair, same dark eyes, that medium-toned skin a shade lighter than the woman's made evident when he pulled her into a hug.

All smiles. No kiss. A teasing twinkle in his eyes as he lifted his glass of water to his lips.

Siblings.

Ren continued past the windows, heading toward the crosswalk with his sights set on a coffee shop on the other side of the street. The beep of his thumb covering the sensor didn't bring him the satisfaction he'd hoped for, causing him to eye his targets with a frown. He bounced on the balls of his feet until the light changed.

A window seat and steaming coffee cup later, he went back to spying, jumping at the rattle of his phone against the wooden tabletop.

> Sorry. Had to play some hide-and-go-seek.
> They're at l'Ivoire.

> Already there. Caught Emmaline on her way in.
> Elliott was waiting.

> And?

> Working on it.

He swapped to the notes app, steadying himself as he mentally tuned into the table, typing out whatever flowed into it like the strokes of a brush onto a canvas through a blindfolded artist. But rather than revealing secrets of a tortured soul, he'd gain the musings of conspiring influential elites—at least, he *hoped*.

FOUR
EVIE

Tarryn turned into a hotel parking garage, where she pulled a ticket and slowly rolled past dimly illuminated pillars. Signs for reserved parking and lettered rows guided them through aisle after aisle. Evie swallowed when they finally found an available spot near the back, and Tarryn threw the car into park. Doors opened, and Haven waited just outside Evie's as she hesitantly tugged off her seatbelt. He offered her a gentlemanlywe hand, and she took it, her palm cresting the soft leather of his well-worn gloves.

She jumped down onto the pavement and adjusted her bag on her shoulder as Haven pulled his hand from hers, switching to clamp down on her upper arm instead. *Fair.* Evie tried not to drag her feet while they followed behind Tarryn to the alcove of elevators, where she spun around to check all the indicators before one pointed above the doors.

The classical melody filling the elevator escaped into the lobby the second the doors fell open. Evie's jaw dropped. Rich, dark oak and gleaming white marble offset sparkling gold accents, much like the gold-trimmed glass shards of the huge chandelier bolted to the third floor's ceiling, visible from the gaping hole down to the compass design set into the tile directly under it.

Men in suits shook hands at the bar walling off a restaurant, manned by a couple of hostesses looking like they were cleaning up for the night. Other guests waited in cushy, high-backed furniture and talked on their phones or adjusted their makeup. Some strode out in designer high heels or dress shoes to town cars idling on the curb through the wall of glass doors.

Evie glanced down at her knit, thick-striped, gray-and-white shirt and quickly shifted her bag strap over the remnants of a few coffee droplets. *Good job, Evie. Cover a stain with another, larger stain.*

Tarryn jogged over to the reception desk, immediately tapping a finger against it, like she needed to speak to the manager. Haven pulled Evie off to the side, continuing to wait by the elevators. His blue-gray eyes skimmed over the patrons with a huff of a sigh. Something about his presence was sort of comforting, and the way he half-sulked was sort of cute in an awkward way. Evie chided herself. She'd had an entire college campus of boys to gawk at, but of course she decided to unbury herself from all her work now to take in the sights of her young, dashing potential-kidnapper and his maybe-girlfriend-slash-partner.

As if summoned, Tarryn pushed away from the front desk and started back toward them. Haven glanced down at Evie, and she jerked her sights away, feeling the tips of her ears heat. *Embarrassing.*

Fortunately, he stopped eyeing her when he followed Tarryn, and they filed into another elevator car. She tapped the button for the eighth floor, and Evie tensed at the sound of a laughter-like snort from Haven.

"Shut up," Tarryn said with no shortage of annoyance.

"Was... there something funny?" Evie asked.

Tarryn shot Haven a glare, though he continued to smirk. "He enjoys irony."

A few quiet, awkward minutes later, they trailed down the hall to a hotel room, where Tarryn fiddled with the door. The indicator flashed green with a *click*, and she shoved it open, flicking on the light to reveal a plush king-sized bed, along with a small sitting area tucked into the corner between the sliding glass doors and what had to be the entry to the bathroom.

Evie followed Tarryn's motion for her to take a seat on the edge of the bed, so she did, dropping her bag at her feet and anxiously waiting for something to happen. Instead of receiving some grand explanation about why she was there and who might be trying to kill her, Tarryn began to pace and rub her hands together while Haven leaned against the door.

"Um… can I know what's going on now?"

Tarryn slowed to a stop and spun around with her hands on her hips and a grimace. "Okay, so… I'll be honest with you: you're going to laugh. That's just how this goes. You'll laugh, you'll demand our badge numbers, and then you'll finally come to terms that this shit is unfortunately real."

Evie's eyes slid over to Haven, who had his closed, almost like he didn't care to be involved in whatever conversation she and Tarryn were about to have—not that he'd likely interject.

"That… *what's* real?" Evie asked slowly.

Tarryn scrubbed at her forehead. "Shit, I'm terrible at this discussion," she mumbled. "Look, the short of it is that people are hunting you down because you're special. You're like us— sort of." She motioned between herself and Haven.

"I'm sorry, but I don't follow… A cop?"

Tarryn let out a breathy, amused chuckle, and Haven's eyes flicked open, dancing to match his quirked lips.

"No, no. Not a cop. Um… Have you ever noticed anything *strange* about your family? Like, where did you get that watch?" Tarryn motioned to her own chest, and Evie looked down.

Her pocket watch. Evie's hand flew up to it, rubbing her

thumb along the silver case's seam with the thought of it slipping out in the chaos. "It was a gift from my grandpa. He gave it to me when I turned twelve."

"Any particular reason why?"

"I mean… he made a joke that it was the last year he could give it to me because there are only twelve numbers on it." She laughed quietly. "It doesn't work though. It's jammed, and I can't get it to open. So it's only really good for decoration."

"You sure about that?"

Evie's bemusement quickly faded. She wasn't sure.

"Where are your parents? You said you had an aunt. What about the rest of your family?"

"They're… They're all gone. It's just me and my aunt now."

Tarryn hummed, biting her lip. "Well, unless she doesn't know, I believe your aunt's been keeping secrets from you."

Evie's eyes widened. "Excuse me?"

"The watch isn't just some family heirloom, Evie. It's something that's passed from predecessor to successor."

She gripped the watch a little tighter, glancing over at Haven for some sort of confirmation. He only tilted his head with a slight raise of a shoulder, as if to say, 'Well, she's right.'

"There are people in this city who aren't who they claim to be. It's all a façade because they're like us. Some of them may not realize it, but most of them do. Each has a gift or calling that— *usually*—helps the rest of the world along. We're like fate's little custodians, hard at work. We keep everything on track when it starts to shift off course."

Evie cleared her throat. "That's… uh… a little far-fetched, don't you think?" she asked with an uneasy laugh.

Tarryn pressed her lips together, as if she were waiting for something.

I'll be honest with you: you're going to laugh.

Her mouth went dry.

"We're broken into a total of nine variations. Everyone among us fits into at least one, but no more than two. For some reason, it seems that's the limit, and they're considered special cases. All of it is passed through family lines. Which brings me back to your aunt. However, since we have no real way to prove that, let me just start with a brief breakdown of each variation, starting with mine."

She held up her hand, ticking off her index finger. "The eighth faction—hence my partner's amusement in the elevator—are known as Keepers. We are considered to be the last line of defense between anyone 'normal' and those who are a part of the Custodians. We're protectors and peacekeepers, which explains the name. Most of us end up being shuffled into law enforcement or cybersecurity or anything of a sensitive nature that requires handling."

"Does that mean that all cops are Keepers?" Evie asked, her brows knitting together. So far, this didn't seem all that strange, but her gut was telling her that it was about to be.

"No. There are plenty of normal people working as police. We have a special division just for us. They don't know what we are, but they understand it's a special unit." She shrugged, ticking off another finger. "Anyway, let's move on by counting down to seven. This is the number designated for the Inked. They're the chaotic, reckless, starving-artist types that sometimes hang around tattoo parlors and manipulate people for fun. At some point in the distant past, they used to mark people for protection or temper those who might be a danger to others. The downside is that they enjoy that kind of stuff. They get a high off of lying, cheating, and stealing. Think of the stories about evil fairies, and that's basically them. Everything comes with a caveat."

Tarryn shivered. "And that's enough about them, so let's move on to Shade, the sixth faction. They can manipulate shadows in some capacity. Some can quite literally *become* shadows as well. It's the perfect type of ability for espionage, which is why they can be both valuable and *very* dangerous.

However, some can also slip into other people's dreams or pull you into theirs." She paused, eyeing her. "You still with me?"

"Like *actual* shadows? You're saying someone could be in here with us, and we wouldn't know?"

Tarryn surveyed the room. "After you've seen it enough times, I feel like it's a lot easier to pick out. To the average person, not so much. Not to mention that it's rather rare to find someone *that* good at it. A lot of them aren't very careful about concealing themselves that well. They like to treat it like invisibility, but it's not. Trust me, there's no one else in here."

Evie began to nod, anxiously glancing around the room while she continued with this bizarre imaginary system.

"That brings us to five, which includes my friend over here." She held a hand toward Haven. "They're called Mist. They're the secret keepers, but more along the lines of general, vast, universe secrets that we occasionally pull from to glean information about what needs to be done to combat certain situations. Some are hearing, visually, or vocally impaired, some of them act cryptic, and a good chunk of them can break down a person's mind and rebuild it to make them forget certain things."

Evie's mouth worked, unable to fathom how *that* was even possible.

"Outside of that, they're a bunch of tight-lipped assholes who think that they're better than everyone else because they just *know* things." She shot him a glare. He rolled his eyes. "But Haven's both Mist and a Keeper, so I guess that means he's okay."

She waved a hand. "Tears are number four. They're named for their remorse and mercy. They can manipulate water as an element, including blood to help the sick or injured. Most are typically in the health care field, and while they still use medicine, they can often help things along a little more efficiently. On the flipside, we have their counterparts at number three, which are the Animated. They can also help mend people with their affinity for fire. They're also fire-resistant and can often summon fire. Once again, medical field, firefighters, or excellent chefs."

Evie scoffed. "I think that's probably the most outlandish one you've mentioned."

"Oh, it gets *better*." Tarryn smirked, holding up two fingers. "Two is the faction currently at the helm of New Atlas, though other major cities have different factions in the primary spot. Ours is the Spirits. Some of them, true to their name, can commune with actual spirits, but most are known for this connection to the space around us and divining from the celestial heavens." Her voice turned into something akin to a preacher, somewhat mockingly with her face and arms tilted up to the ceiling. Her hands dropped after a moment. "They're basically glorified fortune-tellers. They're good at predicting shit."

She held up a finger. "However, the future is nothing without the past. Which is why number one is the Trick. They can pull from history, and they are very much able to manipulate time. Granted, I've been told that it's rather limited, but it still can impact things just as drastically. That's where *you* come into play." She pointed at her chest, straight at the pocket watch.

Evie's mind was already far away by then, taken back to a house miles away from here. To a workshop filled to the brim with clocks. "I can't turn back time," she said, forcing a nervous giggle.

They didn't laugh with her.

Oh, dear God. They think I can.

"No, seriously. There's absolutely no way that's possible." Evie shot up from the edge of the bed. "I've never done it. I don't even know how the hell I'd be able to anyway. I've never seen anyone else in my family do anything like that either. You have the wrong girl, so I'll just go ahead and see myself out." She grabbed her bag, starting for the door, praying Haven would step out of the way.

"I wasn't done yet," Tarryn said flatly from behind her.

Haven pointed his finger upward, moving it in a circular

motion like he was telling her to turn around. Despite her reservations, she did.

"Lastly," she continued, "we have our ninth faction. It's a catch-all of those who have decided they'd rather have normal lives, with or without the memory of their power. Some have committed a crime in which the council—a governing body consisting of one member from each of the eight main factions—decides for them to be stripped of their power. They're called Fallen. All of the guys we ran into were a part of that faction. It's likely they're very much aware that you're Trick, and they're hoping to silence you. It could very well be connected to why all of the Trick in New Atlas have disappeared over the past decade and a half."

"Wait…" Evie said slowly, the image of a car pulling out of a driveway playing through her mind. "Are you… are you implying that it wasn't an accident that my parents died when I was younger? That they were targeted because of something they knew about all of *this* nonsense?" She motioned wildly between Tarryn and Haven, her stomach dropping as Tarryn's expression turned sympathetic.

These people were insane. She was just kidnapped and told this entire wild story about a secret society of people that played puppet masters for the rest of the world. "Proof," she said suddenly. "I want proof. And I want it now, or else I'm going to call the cops." She pulled her phone from her bag. "The *real* cops."

Tarryn clicked her tongue. "All right. I already told you that we are, but if you insist." She jerked her chin toward Haven, and Evie spun back around to face him. He began tugging off one of his gloves, reaching for her hand. She froze, unsure of what he was about to do. He gently took it, and the world around her fell away.

———

Evie stood at the counter of her grandparents' kitchen again as a teenager, her hands coated in flour with her grandmother humming quietly at her side. No flicker of sadness welled up within her like she had braced herself for when she took in her soft, wrinkled features and wire-framed glasses resting on the tip of her nose. But she felt warm. Content. *Happy.*

She was *in* the memory, listening to the quiet chirping of birds drifting through the open window of the suburbs and her grandfather's quiet snoring in the other room. That need to break free of that moment and rush in to see him didn't happen, as if she were glued in place—trapped in her own, younger body forced to continue a task already done. It was already set. Everything continued on the way it actually had, and the memory version of her refused to yield to her will to change.

———

It disappeared as quickly as it came. Evie was back in the hotel, standing in front of Haven with a tear rolling down her face. She swiped it away, taking in a shaky breath while he pulled his glove back on. He mimed dusting flour off his hands, and her breath caught. "You—How did you—"

"He pulled a memory," Tarryn said. "If he really wanted to, he could change it, add, or remove a piece from it. He could also remove it altogether, but it would leave a pretty nasty gap. Probably something close to a drunken black-out, which I've seen in a couple of people before. That's usually what they chalk it up to anyway."

She shuffled backward, shaking her head. The backs of her knees hit the edge of the bed, and she buckled, her bag tumbling back to the floor as she collapsed. "I-I'm not—I can't—" Her head dropped into her hands. This wasn't real. It couldn't be. Things like this simply didn't exist. There was no way she could turn back time or else she would've been able to fix so much from happening, right? "I'm still back in my apartment, passed out on my futon. I'd like to wake up now."

Footsteps sounded, and Evie felt the air shift around her. Something pinched her arm, and her head jerked up to find Tarryn crouched in front of her. "I know it's a lot to take in, but it's real. I get it, it sucks, but people out there want to hurt you, whether you know what's going on or not. We're here to protect you. I promise we'll sort through this whole mess after we get you to the safehouse in the morning."

"You said that my aunt knows about all of this?" Her voice wobbled through her whisper. "Why wouldn't she tell me?"

"Maybe to protect you? It's a possibility since if you don't know what's happening, she would assume that you're not a threat to anyone, right?" She stood. "Get some sleep. This is going to take some time to sink in." She glanced over her shoulder at Haven. "If... you're uncomfortable with us in the room, we can stand watch in the hall, okay?"

Evie stared at a spot on the soft, gray carpeting for a minute before she spoke. "Okay."

So they left, Haven vanishing into the hall before Tarryn paused to look back. Then the door clicked shut behind her, bringing the small flash of a memory of her shutting the door to her grandpa's office with it—an office filled with clocks taking over the walls and littering every part of his mini-workshop's cabinets. An office where she'd held an envelope in her hands, a sticky note slapped on it with a now-forgotten sentiment she tried to conjure up within her racing thoughts.

Evie scrubbed at her face and let herself fall back on the bed, taking deep breaths while she combed through her memories like she might uncover one that was once stolen from her ignorant existence.

FIVE

CADE

FRIDAY, APRIL 3RD AT 8:23PM

"Oh, come *on*," Alyx teased. "You can't stay mad at me forever, Cade."

He shook his head and grumbled, "I can't believe you hung me out to dry like that."

"Well… if it'll cheer you up, drinks are on me." She jabbed a thumb at her chest. "And—*bonus*—Emilio didn't drive you out to the river. I'd call that a win."

Cade snickered, trying to push Emilio's offer to the back of his mind. Though, his talk of power shifts still had him bothered. His face must've given it away since Alyx's expression dipped to a slight, concerned frown.

"Is something wrong?" she asked.

"No, just—" He bit down on his tongue, letting out a bit of a low hum. "I guess Emilio thinks that some people might be out on a power-grab right now."

"What? You don't think someone's after Jay's seat, do you?" she asked, eyeing him wearily. He grimaced. "You don't think *Emilio* would—That's sort of ballsy, isn't it? To openly announce something like that to the man's own brother…"

"I think he was trying to get me to turn on him."

She guffawed. "Are you going to mention it to Jay?"

He bit his lip, balling his fists in his jacket pockets and tilting his head from side-to-side. "I'm… not sure yet."

"What a dumbass," she grumbled. "Let's… just get a couple of drinks and head back. We can pick up some Chinese or something."

She elbowed him in the ribs and jogged up to catch the door to the pub, holding it for him to lead the way inside, where he headed straight for a couple of open seats along the bar. The place was comfortably dim, which probably helped to mask any stains and rings on the wood countertops. After deciding on a couple of beers, Alyx mumbled something about the ladies' room and slid out of her seat, weaving through the crowd.

Cade lifted the bottle to his lips, absently watching the screens overhead. Commercials played for the usual mundane products like furniture and life insurance before a split-screen mash of sports reappeared. Then he noticed Alyx returned to her seat from the corner of his eye.

"What? Decided not to ditch—" His words halted, suddenly realizing that it *wasn't* Alyx.

A woman in her late-twenties or early thirties had taken her place, teetering on the edge of being a little too old for him. His wandering eye caught on her crisp, white blouse and pencil skirt over sheer stockings tucked into red-soled high heels. Her hazel eyes popped with the smokey, dark makeup around them, and her lips stood out with bright red stain, making her appear that much paler, along with tendrils of dark hair framing her face.

"You're not the person I was expecting," he said with a slight smirk.

A slow, seductive uptick at the corner of her mouth triggered something in him—like a sense of déjà vu. "You're right," she replied smoothly, leaning against the bar. "I just decided to drop by and introduce myself." She slid something from her mini blazer pocket.

The woman held out a business card tucked between her fingers in offering. He kept his eyes pinned on hers while he gently slid it from her grasp. There was something unnerving about her that he couldn't quite place, but he decided to let it go, coming up with the idea that maybe she was just some unknown new rival of Jay's trying to feel things out.

"I'm sure we'll be seeing more of each other," she said wryly. "When you finally decide you're done fooling around in little turf wars, I'll be ready." She slid off the bar stool, and the *click* of her heels sounded against the wood floor on her way out. Cade watched her until she vanished from the windows.

His eyes dropped down to the card in his hand, flipping it over from the blank side to find an address scrawled on the back. Cade scowled. There was no name, no number—nothing else. Just an address. *Not much of an introduction.* He shoved the card into his own pocket just as his phone vibrated in protest.

Alyx reappeared, sheepishly pardoning herself as she bumped into a guy trying to escape his booth, but Cade's attention was already glued to the phone.

> Where the hell are you? Get home. Now.

"Someone trying to get ahold of you?"

His head snapped up, catching her climbing back into her seat and tilting back her bottle.

"Yeah, Jay wants me to head back," he said, slipping off the stool and dropping the phone back into his jacket. "Feel free to get some Chinese without me. Just do yourself a favor and don't drink too much."

Her mouth tipped downward. "I can go with yo—"

"It's fine, Alyx. He probably wants to discuss Emilio or something. Just enjoy your night. I'll see you bright and early in the morning, right?" He flashed her a smile, but from her persistent frown, he could tell that she saw right through it.

"Okay… text me if you need anything, got it?"

"Yeah, yeah—" He waved a hand before changing it to a two-finger salute. "See you in the morning."

He pulled up the hood of the sweatshirt once he was on the sidewalk and tucked his hands into his pockets. The feel of the cardstock against his skin sent a familiar chill up his spine. It was like he was being watched, despite how he was drowning in a sea of people. A number. A nobody. Honestly, that was the way he liked it: being no one.

Cade shook off that unease, focusing on dodging puddles and fixing his eyes on the last glow of the setting sun. The glittering city lights took its place, ripping through the dark like a beacon, calling each lost soul home for rest. Much like how his own soul longed for it.

Several blocks passed him by, his shoulders sinking with each step. The rhythm of his pace slowly eliminated whatever paranoia had overtaken him, along with his many internal explanations. He was spooked about Emilio and the Martellis, about Alyx's dark jokes, about Jay's ominous text, about that strange woman's 'introduction'... He shook his head, turning to briskly jog up a few steps and push through a door to a quiet apartment lobby.

The security clerk didn't even look up from the monitors tucked under the tall desk as he pushed down his hood. That was a blessing in itself with how awful his sneakers squeaked against the glossy, black marbled slab tiles. It was finally silenced by the large, gold-trimmed royal-blue rug between him and the elevator banks, one that he needed a resident keycard for. Pulling out his wallet, he rocked back and forth some while he waited for one of the elevator cars to descend.

A chime, a tap of his wallet, and a number press later, he stepped out into the quiet, charcoal-carpeted hall to his unit. Keys jingled in his hand, slowing and sorting through them before he came to a stop in front of the door. He didn't have the chance to slide a key into the lock before it swung open.

There stood Jay, basically just an older version of Cade with a harder jawline, a slightly-crooked nose, and a near-permanent scowl. Still the same blond hair, still the same blue eyes—just a little lighter—and still that same slim frame but slightly taller. His black shirt had the sleeves rolled up to his elbows, revealing old scars and calloused hands, things that Cade had in far less volume. Twenty-two, meet twenty-eight.

Cade ducked inside without his brother bothering to budge. The door clicked shut behind him. "Is… something going on?" he asked hesitantly, too much of a coward to look back. His eyes roamed the apartment, a sleek, modern thing that was cleaned every couple of days by some middle-aged woman touting a fake designer handbag who occasionally left him a plate of cookies on the counter like she was his mother.

Jay didn't answer, brushing past him, down the hall, and disappearing into the spare bedroom that he used as an office. Anxiously, Cade let out a breath and followed him, like he had no choice but to diffuse one last ticking time-bomb before bed. He only got like this when he had hit his limit, nearly bursting at the seams with anger.

"I foolishly assumed that you'd come straight home after finishing your errands," Jay said, kicking the wheels of the office chair and sending it spinning off to the side. He wasn't shouting, but his voice rose, adding heat to every word that passed his lips. "Here I am, waiting to hear that you handed Emilio the damn message, but instead you decide to take some detours and not pick up your phone. So, now *I* look like a dumbass for calling around to find you."

Confused, Cade pulled out his phone, finally seeing that notification he hadn't noticed during his last check. Four missed calls. He winced. "Sorry, I must've had poor reception or something—"

A fist slammed against the glass-top desk, ratting pens in a steel mesh cup. Cade's grip instinctively tightened on his phone and stood uncomfortably straight. He almost never saw him this mad, at least not specifically aimed toward *him*. The only other time he could recall him lashing out was over his birthday last year.

He'd turned twenty-one and dipped out to spend a week with a group of people that he didn't ever really consider to be friends. They had been acquaintances, and friends of said acquaintances—all in to treat him to a nice time because they hoped to earn some brownie points. They'd bar crawled and eventually he ended up horribly hungover, laying in about an inch of water in a bathtub of some girl's high-rise apartment. None of the others had fared much better, but at least they hadn't later suffered Jay's wrath like he had.

"Did you read it?" he demanded.

Cade shook his head. "No. You told me not to. I didn't."

Jay's fist uncurled, laying his palm flat on the table.

"Why are you so pissed? Did something happen?"

"We have a job tonight." The words came with a deadly calm that didn't so much scare Cade as much as they confused him.

"I'm… not sure how that involves me at all. That is, unless you're putting me under house arrest since I only run erran—"

"Starting tonight, you're going on jobs."

His mouth worked. "Jay—" A sharp look made him snap his mouth shut.

"I was informed a few hours ago that we have a problem. Between that and the growing unrest of certain individuals— who are starting to push for change because of the next big over- haul—everyone's going to have their eyes on *us*."

Cade swallowed, stuck on the sound of the office clock ticking to fill the void.

"You realize," Jay began in a slow, deliberate tone, "that there will come a time when I will be dethroned here. And when that happens, they'll get rid of you too, one way or another. There is no more room for weakness. They won't care if you *seem* 'harmless enough.'" He pushed off the desktop, adding mocking quotations. "They'll make an example of you too."

Unsure how to respond, he opted not to. He waited patiently for him to continue after he slowly paced along the windows.

"I'm promoting Alyx to take your spot. From here on out, you run jobs. It's time for you to learn to be a threat. You're not just some kid anymore that gets to ride the elevator to the top because of someone else's hard work."

Cade's fist clenched, his jaw setting in turn. Like he hadn't sacrificed as much time as Jay did in all of this. Like he hadn't spent all of his free time during high school putting in hours of work before passing out at midnight or up to two or three in the morning just to do it all again. He'd propped him up for *years* without asking for anything in return. Getting to this point was his reward because he could at least catch his breath.

Jay didn't care though. He twisted a key into a nearby drawer and set a case on the desk, unlocking it, and pushing open the lid in a single, fluid motion. Sweat beaded along Cade's back at the sight of the tool Jay offered him. A gun. "You'll need this."

Well, whether he needed it or not, Cade didn't *want* it. But he stepped forward anyway, lifting it from his brother's hand. He checked the safety while Jay retrieved his own. Whatever was going to happen tonight would probably scar him somehow, but he had already come this far. There was no turning back now, not even if it left a bitter taste in his mouth.

SIX

CADE

FRIDAY, APRIL 3RD AT 11:49PM

"Fuck. This." Cade stared up at the building, his mouth part-way open as he took in all the floors towering above them. He ran a hand through hair, swapping out his disbelief for a grimace.

"Sounds like someone's backing out." It was a jeer from one of the two minions Jay had recruited. He was a few months older than Cade with wavy, reddish-orange hair that fell just past his ears, paired with dark eyes and a smattering of freckles on too-white skin.

"I'd like to watch you jump eight floors up, Declan." Cade flicked a wrist up toward the balconies with a scowl.

"I mean, I would if I could." That damn obnoxious, shit-eating grin again.

Cade glanced past him, eyeing Jay as he relayed something inaudible to the other Callaghan. Conrad was the taller of the two Callaghans, his hair a few shades dirtier than Cade's own blond. A cigarette rested limply in his fingers, held at his hip. He was maybe twenty-five or twenty-six, sans Declan's freckles, despite a bit of a tan he'd gotten during a recent vacation. Next to Declan or Cade, Conrad was *built*, though it was well-hidden by his hoodie.

Cade shifted in discomfort, returning his attention to the task at hand, though he wondered how much longer they'd be standing here. "Why the hell are we ever doing this? Who's even up there?"

"You're not supposed to ask questions, Hart. Get fucking use to it."

Gritting his teeth, he bit back his reply once he noticed Jay and Conrad start toward them. "Hey," Cade called. "Who's up there?"

Declan and Conrad exchanged glances, a silent ridicule of his sheer audacity to question orders. Conrad flicked the remainder of his cigarette into a puddle, and Jay narrowed his eyes at Cade.

"Go." Jay nodded toward the balconies.

"You're not even going to tell me who I'm going for? You're just going to say 'jump, bitch,' and send me on my way? What if I shoot the wrong person?"

"I was told there would be only one person in the room, so get your ass up there. You're the only one who can do it without going through the lobby. Now *go*, or I'll drag your ass down to the Callaghan's pub so you can explain why you blatantly ignored orders. Then I'll let *them* deal with you."

A short, quiet chuckle from Declan.

That echoing reminder from Jay telling him not to show weakness thundered through his thoughts. "Fine." Begrudgingly, he started for that column of balconies. When he glanced back to his brother, there was a frown on his face and his arms folded over his chest. A silent order not to embarrass him.

Conrad was already taking a couple steps away. "We'll be covering the doors, just in case. Make it quick, and we'll be gone. No one will know we were here."

So, Cade faced the wall again, imagining some old, rich, white bastard sleeping off a night of booze and wild sex with his mistress. He'd be doing the world a favor, right? Inwardly, he cringed at the mere thought of killing someone. Maybe he'd prefer having the shit kicked out of him by the Callaghans over this? At least then he wouldn't have to live with blood on his hands.

Rather than disobeying, he mustered up his courage, pulled in a breath, and threw himself against the brick façade. It was like diving into a pool—that sensation of being enveloped by something thicker than air. He propelled himself upward, gravity no longer applying in this fluid, shadowy state. Once he reached the third floor, he pulled himself from the inky black, hoisting himself over the railing just in time to watch the others split off in three different directions from the alley.

Cade leaned over the railing, eyeing the remainder of the jump. Four more balconies to go. He recounted while he tried to psyche himself up for the rest of the jump, hating how slick his hands felt. To shadow again, and reemergence on the eighth floor. The sliding glass door's curtain was half-drawn, allowing him to peer into the darkened room, barely lit by the moon and twinkling city lights at his back surrounding his own shadow. And a form lay in the bed.

Cade pulled the gun from his waistband, keeping it at the ready, and closed his eyes. He braced for the unpleasant sensation of passing through glass, cringing before diving in. Sharp, needling pinpricks swept through him, his body rejecting the transparent, reflective surface. He hopped slightly on one foot once he was finally through, regaining his balance after he assured himself that hadn't gotten anything stuck.

The gun felt even heavier in his hand as he approached the bed and squinted while his eyes adjusted to the dim light. Instead of finding some old bastard lying there, he towered over a girl—a girl around his age. Swallowing, he flicked off the safety, steadying his hand with a wince as he pointed it at her. He squeezed his eyes shut, telling himself it would be easier not to watch, only for him to reconsider how horribly he might miss and just cause more pain. An image of Alyx flickered in his mind, temporarily replacing her.

Cade's arm fell to his side. He couldn't do it. Alyx was like a sister to him. If someone had done this to her, he would be devastated. This girl meant something to someone. Flicking the safety back on, he just stood there, staring at her with contemplation. What a damn disappointment he was. A nuisance and a useless criminal. Another troublemaking Shade.

That's precisely when the phone on the night table buzzed, and the girl jolted awake.

SEVEN
EVIE

Evie screamed when she woke to a man towering over her bed. He jerked back and threw himself straight into the glass doors—*phasing* right through it. Her jaw dropped, and she sat straight up in horror as light flooded the room again, Tarryn and Haven bursting inside just in time for them to witness a shadowy form *melt* into the side of the building.

Holy. Shit.

It was real. It was very, *very* real.

Tarryn sprinted for the glass door, forcing it open and bending over the railing while Haven rounded the bed. He swiftly, but gently, pulled her to her feet, and brought her to the middle of the room. His eyes were glued to the hallway door, and Evie's heart dropped once she realized that he had taken her away from anything casting a shadow, minimizing their own by standing directly under the overhead fixture.

"We need to go," Tarryn said, shutting the glass door behind her with a little too much force. "Someone must've noticed we stopped here a few hours ago."

"He—" Evie pointed toward the balcony. "He was—"

"Yes, I know, and he could still be hanging around the building. We need to move." She made a shoving motion toward the door, and Haven began guiding her toward it.

He slung Evie's bag over his head before they spilled into the hall. Tarryn jogged past them to the elevators, repeatedly jamming her palm against the down arrow until one opened. "We get to the car. Don't stop. If there's anyone down there, I'll hold them off, and you follow Haven, got it?"

Evie rapidly nodded, shakily grabbing onto Haven's sleeve. Every ping of a new floor quickened her pulse on the way down, turning agonizing with every possibility of what might lay in wait for them at the bottom.

When the doors opened up to the garage, they maybe took four or five steps side-by-side until someone lunged at Tarryn. She struck like a viper, sending a blur of reddish hair stumbling back. Haven grabbed her hand and *ran*.

"Haven!" Evie screamed, catching sight of a bulkier man lurching toward him. Haven shoved her away, ramming his shoulder against him. A yelp escaped her with a tug on the back of her shirt, tossing her to the cement.

"Finish this." A hard, cold order coming from a man—the older of the two blond-haired, blue-eyed guys standing over her.

She scrambled to get up, her whole body shaking as the younger one stepped toward her with a gun in his hand.

"W-wait—" The word was barely a rasp, her throat closing up in fear. Her legs wouldn't move, despite getting this far. She was going to die.

Her executioner's face faltered, softening to regret, and then something else… "No," he said firmly, turning his back to her to face the other.

"You're making a mistake," said the older one.

"No. No, I don't think I am. I'm not some obedient dog, Jay. Give me a legitimate reason, and not a 'because I said so.' If not, then you can go fuck yourself."

In answer, Jay's arm flew to his own back, retrieving a gun from his waistband. The entire parking garage fell into a horrible, deafening silence with the single sound of a gunshot. She had expected to feel a sting or burning, but there was *nothing*. It wasn't until the younger man staggered backward that she realized she hadn't been shot. She hadn't been shot because *he* had shielded her from it.

Her eyes went wide as he fell backward. She rushed to catch him, the two of them falling to the ground. Her knees screamed as they collided with the pavement, and he gasped, his hand flying up to the wound. Blood darkened his already-black shirt around his chest. Everything was happening too slow and too fast at the same time, finding the gun pointed at her from her peripheral vision.

The chain of the pocket watch dipped over the boy's face, her focus slipping toward calm. This was real.

She closed her eyes, placing herself back in her grandfather's workshop. The rhythmic ticking from the room thrummed through her pocket watch, everything moving second by second. Her imaginary-self's fists clenched, willing all of them to start turning back. They protested, groaning to a stop. Unwillingly, they simultaneously released that first chorus of the hands moving back. Once. Twice. Three times.

She only stopped when she heard the tinkling of metal on concrete, releasing her mental hold on that visual. When she opened her eyes, she found the boy closing his. But the bullet was no longer in his chest. It was next to him on the ground. Her head jerked up to Jay still hovering there with a gun trained on her.

Tarryn threw herself against him, knocking it from his hand. It skittered across the garage while the two struggled against each other. Their other two assailants started for the exit, and that's when Jay broke free, bolting after them.

Tarryn rounded on Evie with wide, panicked eyes. "Holy shit —Are you—"

"He shot him," Evie said, her voice sounding lost and detached to her own ears. "But somehow I..." Her eyes fell to where the blood had been. It was gone now, but the hole in his shirt remained.

"Forget about him," Tarryn said, helping her up as Haven rushed to meet them. "Let's leave this dumbass if he's going to live."

"*What?* He just took a bullet for me!"

Tarryn hesitated, glancing back down at the prone form. They couldn't seriously leave this guy unconscious here.

"What if the others come back?" Evie asked, the question spilling out in a rush. "They'll kill him."

Tarryn made a frustrated noise. "Fine. Haven, carry this idiot to the car."

He made a show of sighing and heaving him off the floor. Ignoring it, Tarryn dragged Evie by the elbow to the vehicle. She climbed in, Haven carefully laid the boy's body across the backseat, and her bag was tossed in the footwell. Doors slammed shut, and the car started for the street.

"Let the record show that I absolutely *despise* this idea," Tarryn grumbled. "He was with the guys trying to kill you."

"Yeah, and I'd probably be dead since the others were occupying the two of *you*. That guy—Jay, I think. He was going to have this one kill me, but he said he wouldn't."

Tarryn's eyes went wide in the rearview mirror. "*Jay?* What the fuck? He's not—This doesn't make any goddamned sense..."

Evie's eyes dropped down to the boy again, his head lulling to the side where it rested at her thigh. "Who's Jay?" she asked, looking back up to gauge Tarryn and Haven's reactions.

She was rewarded with a glance toward the mirror from Haven, his gaze pointed toward the boy with a mask of uncertainty.

"You know how I said that the people back at your place were Fallen, right?" Tarryn began. "Well, I assumed that the guy making a run for it on the balcony was also Fallen with a little bit of shadow-shifting juice left. But if that guy was Jay, then the people who just attacked us are definitely Shade. I just don't understand how the hell they knew where we were, let alone why there are *two* different factions after us."

"Where are we going now?"

"A new hotel. One that hopefully doesn't have Shade breaking in at midnight."

She doubted that she'd be able to fall back asleep again, but after passing out around nine, she had at least managed to get *something* in. She leaned back, watching out the window while they drove. People were still awake, not that they ever really slept here, though it was a little quieter. A little *less* chaotic, despite how her night was going.

A while later, they pulled into yet another parking garage, and she felt the boy's head jostle against her leg again. She looked down, but this time he was staring back up at her. A hazy, somewhat incoherent smirk danced across his face. His dark blue eyes fixed on her. "Are you my guardian angel?"

The car door opened, ripping him out of the vehicle by his legs with a startled cry.

"Oh, good," Tarryn said, her voice dripping with sarcasm, "you're awake."

Evie jumped at the sound of her door clicking free to Haven, who offered her a hand. After grabbing her bag, she took it, and he led her to the back of the SUV, where the boy was now pressed up against the trunk with his arms pinned behind his back. Tarryn plucked a pair of handcuffs from the back of her belt.

"Are you going to at least read me my rights, officer?" he asked, playfulness seeping into his slight agitation.

"That would mean that you *have* rights, blondie." She shoved his head against the back window before checking his pockets. A wallet, a set of keys, a phone, and a pocketknife were set on the back bumper. Lastly, she retrieved a small, leather case, holding it up to his face with a raised eyebrow.

"That's not mine."

"Uh-huh… so you just happen to have a lockpick set on your person, but you have no idea how it got there?"

His lips pressed into a thin line.

"Haven, would you get me a plastic bag for all this shit?" She nodded to the front, and Haven huffed, starting around the car while Tarryn began searching his wallet. "Oh, you've got to be kidding me. All right, *Hart*, let's have a little chat."

The guy cringed, his head lightly thumping against the window in defeat. "Great…" He stumbled as she tore him away from the car, trading him for the bag Haven snapped open.

"You take our new punching bag and keep an eye on Evie while I get us a room," Tarryn said. "I'll make it quick." She started across the garage, grumbling as she weaved between the other parked cars. Her head swept back and forth for any stragglers while Haven dumped the bumper's contents into the bag. He looped an arm through Evie's with a tight grip on the new prisoner's arm.

"So, uh… do you always let her boss you around like that, or…?" he asked.

Haven's jaw set, narrowing his eyes at him with a firm shake of his head.

"He can't talk," Evie said.

"Oh… *Oh*. You're, uh, going to keep the gloves on, right?" He gave a nervous, sheepish smile. Haven ignored him, continuing to guide them toward the elevator bank. The guy's face fell, descending into slight panic as he looked to Evie for a reply. "He's going to keep the gloves on, right?"

She hesitated, trying to gauge Haven's expression as the corner of his mouth twitched to match a mischievous gleam in his eyes.

"I think he *might* be trying to scare you," she said. "But he's already taken them off once tonight."

The blood drained from his face, and he momentarily tried to rip free of Haven's grip. He snapped back to his side with a quick jerk of Haven's arm before they stopped in the midst of the elevator nook. She glanced past Haven, carefully watching every little nervous tick. His eyes were stuck to the indicators, waiting for Tarryn to return or for him to find an opening.

"It's Hart, right?" she asked, breaking the tense silence.

His head whipped toward her in surprise. "Oh—um, call me Cade. Last name's Hart."

"Why did you let yourself get shot for me?"

Cade squirmed some, looking away with a slight chuckle. "Well, I honestly didn't think he'd do it."

"Why not? I mean, you got between us, so—"

"Because we're brothers."

She didn't know what to say after hearing that hollow reply. Her sights set on the elevators again, absently staring while she tried to piece it all together. The piercing chime of one of the cars arriving disrupted her concentration before Tarryn appeared in front of her. She held the doors open, and they rode it up in uncomfortable silence.

Tarryn roughly dragged Cade down the hallway, his face tracking every numbered plate on the way there, like he was already planning his escape route. Evie thought back to the shadowy figure in her last hotel room, trying to match the silhouette to his. If that had been him, then why didn't he just do that now? They couldn't exactly stop a shadow, could they?

Nevertheless, Tarryn halted at their destination, tapping the keycard to the sensor and shoving him inside. By the time she and Haven stepped in after them, Cade had his cuffs looped through the spindles of a fancy, wooden chair back that had been pulled away from the corner desk.

"Take it easy—" he said, turning his head toward Tarryn while she secured his restraints.

"I'm sure as hell not giving you any wiggle room to escape. You're not going anywhere until you tell me what I want to know," she said, gripping the back of his chair to pull herself the rest of the way up. She began rounding his interrogation seat to stand in front of him. "So, let's start with why the hell you and your brother were hunting down Miss Thatcher." She jerked a thumb toward Evie, who awkwardly dropped her bag at the foot of the queen-sized bed.

"I don't know."

"Bullshit."

"I'm being serious!" he cried, his tone pleading.

Her hands dropped the arms of his chair, and he shrank back. "I'm pretty pissed right now because we've been attacked by both Fallen and Shade tonight. Not to mention that your name has been on my personal shit-list for a while with how often I hear you getting let off the hook."

His face screwed up into anger, narrowing his eyes at her. "I think you're forgetting the bit where I just got shot by my own damn brother, so I'm pretty pissed too. If it weren't for me acting as a bullet sponge, I think you'd be down a charge right now."

Tarryn's grip on the chair arms tightened, staring him down before he spoke again.

"He didn't tell me *why* we came out this way," Cade said. "When I discovered it was to kill *her*, I decided to back out. I may be a petty thief and a general annoyance, but I'm not a killer."

"Petty thief is an awfully generous title." Tarryn scoffed, pushing away from him. She paced across the room with a finger pressed to her lips. "So, here's what we're going to do." She slowed when she circled back to him again. "I can convince my higher-ups to let this slide if and *only if* you flip on your brother. If you don't, I'll have you thrown in a cell, and let the council deal with you."

He chuckled, shaking his head. "The council, huh? You're acting like I committed a grave offense."

Tarryn folded her arms over her chest, unmoving. His face slowly slid from amusement to slight concern, and his gaze drifted over to Evie. A pale hue spread over his features.

"Do you want to reconsider your statement, or…?"

"Is- is she *Trick?*"

"Seeing how you're alive, sans bullet in your chest right now, I think that's a pretty spot-on conclusion. Maybe you actually *do* have a brain."

"I- I didn't know." He began rapidly shaking his head. "You have to believe me. If I knew she was Trick, I wouldn't have been anywhere near here. I'm stupid, but not *that* stupid."

"Then roll on Jay," she said sharply. "Either that or you'll be sentenced to Fall if you're lucky. My guess is that they'll take your memory too, and I won't be able to do a damn thing to stop them."

He licked his lips, his eyes darting between the three of them in fear—a horrible, visceral fear that sent a shiver down Evie's spine. His pleading look vanished when his face dropped down to his lap, his shoulders falling in defeat. "Okay," he whispered, lifting his head again. "Just tell me what you need me to say, and I'll say it. I'm done trying to cover his ass."

EIGHT
CADE

Staring at the decorative, coffered ceiling of a posh hotel at 3:30AM hadn't been a part of Cade's original plan. Laying on the floor with only a pillow and his hands cuffed in front of him hadn't been a part of said plan either, but he supposed it could be worse. As much as he missed his bed, at least he hadn't had to scrub off someone else's blood before he crawled into it. Either way, he figured he wouldn't have slept tonight.

He pressed his thumb into one of the eight little marks engraved on the silver restraints. The sole anchor keeping him here. Then again, where would he even go? He fidgeted with his jacket zipper and his sweatshirt strings, rolling over to find Tarryn reading a book. When she slid him a sideways glance, he huffed and faced the ceiling again. He counted each page turning for a couple of minutes until it was interrupted by whispering, the sound of footsteps crossing the room, and the *click* of the door shutting.

Cade peered back to see Haven's arms over his head, stretching. No Tarryn in sight. Movement from the bed at his side told him that no one in this room was sleeping after all.

"Can't sleep either?" he whispered.

Those deep, velvety brown eyes peered over the edge of the mattress. "No," Evie replied. "I'm sort of just waiting for someone else to break in."

"Yeah, I'm… really sorry about that. I probably scared the hell out of you back there."

"I'll forgive you since you took a bullet for me."

He could've sworn he saw a faint smirk in the dim light from the desk.

"Do you know anything about the safehouses?" she asked. "Tarryn said that's where she's taking me later in the morning."

He hummed, worrying his lip at the recollection. "I think there are apartments near the council's headquarters maybe thirty minutes away from here? Those might be it since I heard there was twenty-four-seven surveillance and restricted hours. I've personally never gone near the place, but I know about it from a few acquaintances-of-acquaintances who've used it before. It sounds like a prison."

"Guess that's pretty fitting for you then."

He chortled. "Glad to see you've decided to join in on the bullying."

A quiet laugh escaped her, the corner of his mouth ticking upward. When it faded, he selfishly wanted to hear it again.

8:37AM

"Stop complaining." Tarryn slammed the car door on him, pushing up her sleeves as she ripped open the door to the driver's seat.

"Someone's cranky," Cade mumbled, taking note of how Evie covered her mouth. She faked a yawn, but he could tell she was suppressing a giggle.

"I can't wait to finally get rid of you," Tarryn said.

"You're assuming that someone won't try to finish the job before we reach our destination."

"Honestly?" She put her hand on Haven's headrest, backing the car up. "As long as Evie makes it there, fully intact, I don't really care. You're just a bonus turn-in."

He slid further into his seat, frowning. "When do I get my stuff back?"

"When the warden feels like giving it back to you. Now shut the hell up."

The car lurched forward, skimming through the garage. Once the tires hit the asphalt, Cade's eyes drifted over to Evie. She watched out the window, her head lulling against the doorframe. He wished she wasn't so… alluring? Magnetic? He wasn't sure of the right word for it, other than there was just something about her that drew him in. Or maybe it was white knight syndrome since she'd saved his dumb ass.

"Hey," Tarryn snapped, her eyes pinned on him in the rearview mirror, "stop that."

He scowled back. "Stop what?"

"Don't look at her. Don't talk to her. Don't even think about her. Leave her alone."

Evie's attention may have not been focused on him before, but it sure was now. Humiliated, he let his head thump against the window, keeping his eyes fixed on the driver's seat in front of him. The rest of the drive was met with a painful silence, combined with that longing to let his eyes wander again. The relief he felt once the shadow of the parking garage swept over the car, signaling they'd arrived at their destination, was truly immeasurable.

The echoed slams of Tarryn and Haven's doors led to the former's occupant opening his.

"Out," she said, leaving room for him to step onto the painted white line.

"Yes, officer," he said dryly.

She seized his arm, leading the charge to the bright, glass-boxed kiosk that sat in the middle of a vast wasteland of cement. Tarryn shoved him through the doorway to stand in front of a man fiddling with something behind the lip of the desk. She wasted no time tapping on the glass partition. His eyes finally lifted, catching on the cuffs around Cade's wrists.

"This isn't the station," came the security guard's crackled voice passing through the speaker.

"Trust me, I'm very aware," Tarryn said. "I need to speak with Annette Desrosiers. It's urgent. If she's not here, I need someone to call her."

The guard held up a finger with the promise that it would be a moment, sending them back into an uncomfortable silence while he placed his call. Pausing during his explanation to whoever was on the other end of the line, he unmuted his mic.

"Your name?"

"Fuentes."

Muted again, sending Cade's already growing unease through the roof. After maybe two more minutes—or potentially an eternity—he hung up and gave them further instruction. "She's already waiting for you in the lobby. Said she saw your emails this morning, so she's got a stack of paperwork waiting for you." The door buzzed, and they were let inside.

Inside was a white-painted elevator and a set of stairs, which Cade was grateful that she hadn't made him awkwardly trek up with his hands bound. Admittedly, the cuffs were starting to get rather uncomfortable, but the second he began twisting in them, Tarryn dug her fingers further into his arm.

When they reached the lobby, they were greeted by a tall, dark-skinned woman with thick-framed glasses. She wore a crisp, cream blouse and patterned, navy leggings with flats. A legal folder overflowing with papers sat at her hip, causing him to wonder if that was for Tarryn and Haven, or if it was for *him*.

"Detective Fuentes and Detective Bennett, correct?" she asked, looking between them with a pleasant smile.

"Yep, that's us," Tarryn replied. "We have Thatcher and Hart, so let's get this whole mess taken care of. I'm in desperate need of sleep."

The woman—decidedly Ms. Desrosiers—led them down a hallway, motioning toward the first room on the right. Tarryn pulled Cade into it, stumbling into what appeared to be some sort of lounge. Beige carpeting, soft-brown sofas, and a dark-stained coffee table took up the room. It had that feel of a therapist's office or counseling chamber that sent him back a step. He was shoved down onto the couch anyway as the others filed in.

"Well," Ms. Desrosiers said while everyone took their seats. "I have to say that I didn't quite expect the two of you to bring back a Trick and one of the Harts. Who would you like processed first?"

Tarryn pointed to Evie. "I want her in a room as fast as possible. I have some of my people dealing with a few of her other attackers at the station right now, but it's far from safe for her to go back to her apartment. I want her on lockdown until things are settled."

She nodded, opening her folder and tugging a clipped section of papers free. "For now, I just need the top one signed," she said, setting the documents in front of Evie, "The rest is registration information to get you ran and cleared in our databases. Once that's sorted, we can go over access. So, Miss Thatcher, I need you to sign here to consent to the rules of utilizing a safehouse apartment." She pointed a perfectly manicured finger to a line, handing her a pen.

Her eyes skimmed through the text as her hand drifted down to the bottom of the page. A moment later, she scribbled out her name.

"Now, as for you, Mr. Hart," she said, collecting the paper and setting her sights on him. "I'll need to keep you here for a few minutes. We'll need to fully detail out what occurred last night and into the morning, specifically in regard to your brother. While Detective Fuentes already summarized it for me, I'll need *you* to be the one to explain it in its entirety. If your brother is ordered before the council, then once you sign this document, you will have to testify against him."

She slid a paper free from the stack, pushing it in front of him. A protection form—a precursor to his own safehouse form. This could keep Cade here until they found Jay and had him tried, which could take *months*. His heart sank. He had been right. This might as well have been a prison. But it wasn't like he had much of a choice. Cade took the pen she offered him, signing his name without another thought.

Ren pushed the tattoo parlor door open, finding a bulky twenty-something wearing ear gauges and a littering of facial piercings, dyed-black hair falling over his face. His black tee-shirt had the sleeves torn off to show off his arms. Every square inch of sickly-pale skin covered in inked designs. They looked like the murals often pained on brick walls of old buildings.

"Got a permission slip, kid?"

"No."

"Then beat it and come back when you do. Can't serve every fourteen-year-old who wonders in."

"I'm seventeen," Ren said flatly.

The guy snorted, lightly chuckling as he did a once-over. "Sure, whatever. Still underaged. Now get out of here already. Can't you see I'm busy?"

"I'm actually not here for you." Ren held up an envelope, slightly crumpled from when he'd gotten it hours earlier. His friend had certainly been adamant that he didn't look at the contents.

"What's that?"

"It's a request for someone else," Ren replied, the words surfacing like he was reading off a script. "I want to talk to your boss."

"Sorry, kid, but the boss is busy." The guy shook his head, mumbling. "Not like we take special requests from kids anyway."

Ren *knew* this. This same scenario had played out before, like a small, misplaced fragment of time that he'd held until it slipped through his hands like dust. Something to reform elsewhere. To reform *here* and now. He stepped toward the counter, resting his arms on the layer of glass that protected hundreds of gridded designs like hearts, stars, and angel wings, all with numbers in the corners. "I'm not leaving until I talk to your boss."

The man's jaw clenched, finally understanding that he would be stuck with a nuisance. He dropped his tools back onto his cart with a clatter, starting toward the back curtain. "*Aiden*—There's some brat out here that wants to speak with the boss."

Ren smirked, satisfied that he knew the rest of the steps to this dance. The figure that emerged was another man, though he was a little taller and lankier in comparison to the first. He wore a black, unbuttoned suit jacket with a meticulously pressed black dress shirt underneath. Surprisingly, his hair looked to be a natural shade of chestnut brown, sheared on the sides with tufts from the base brushing the crest of one ear. While there were no tattoos to be seen on his visible, pale skin, multiple studs and cuffs adored his ears in their wake. It struck him as odd to find an Inked, well… *un-inked*, especially in a tattoo parlor.

"What's going on?" Aiden asked, his face creased in annoyance. He locked eyes with Ren, begrudgingly stalking forward when Ren flicked his wrist up, displaying the envelope once again.

"I have a request for your boss," Ren reiterated.

"Then make an appointment. We're booked."

"Something tells me you'll want to at least take a peek. You're the right-hand man, right?"

That damned curiosity got him. Intrigue lightly seasoned with malicious intent glinted in his eyes as he plucked the envelope from his grasp with a black-gloved hand. He bent it slightly, untucking the flap to retrieve the contents. It was just some slip of paper, folded neatly into thirds like a legal document printed on thick parchment. No money slipped out to bribe him, keeping true to his friend's word that they simply didn't need it.

After Aiden's eyes ran over the request, Ren was rewarded with a bemused chuckle. "Is this some sort of prank or something?" He began to refold the letter.

"Consider it a mutually-beneficial transaction," Ren said smoothly. "You win, the client wins, everyone wins."

Aiden thoughtfully tapped the envelope on the countertop, scrutinizing him. "What's your parlor trick, kid?"

"Fortune-telling." The phrase slipped out without a beat of hesitation, knowing that Aiden would give that feral, predatory grin. It still sent chills rippling through him, but he kept still, waiting for his next movement. The final act of this rehearsed play before he would be on his own.

Aiden walked over to the countertop off to the side—a black-lacquered plank with no base—and lifted it in invitation. With a brief, jerking motion of his head toward the back curtain, Ren followed, feeling both victorious and anxious over what might come next.

TEN
EVIE

Evie's hand flew to her heart at the reflection on her laptop screen. A stealthy, smug Cade peered over the back of her armchair, resting his chin on neatly folded arms. She twisted to face him, dropping her voice to a whisper in favor of not waking Tarryn, who had fallen into the cushions of the couch shortly after they were settled in. "You scared the shit out of me. I thought you were with Haven?"

The smugness vanished in an instant before he moved to crouch down next to her seat. "I've been here a whole three hours, and I'm on the verge of losing my damn mind. If I don't talk to someone who can talk back, I'll probably slam my head into a wall."

A hand went to her forehead, her shoulders falling even before Haven slipped into the apartment with a small armful of things to dump on the two-person café table just outside the kitchenette. Haven had already given up on dealing with his own charge, and now she still wasn't going to be able to get her project done.

"What's that?" Cade asked, pointing to the monitor.

"It's a marketing project for one of my classes."

His face scrunched up in disgust. "Why?"

"Well," she started, trying to push the impatience out of her tone, "it's due Monday. I had planned on finishing it last night, but that plan was hurled out the window after being incessantly hunted by a bunch of criminals." She narrowed her eyes at him.

"Yeah, you're welcome." He reached to shut the laptop, and she jerked it away. "Look, the project's clearly not worth it, so just close the damn thing and call it a day—"

"Don't you have some sort of job or coursework or something? How old are you? Twenty? Twenty-one?"

"Twenty-two, and *no*, I didn't go to college."

Evie hesitated, her eyes flicking over to Tarryn as she slowly closed the laptop. Perhaps it would be best to indulge him until he ran out of words *away* from her sleeping guard. Sliding the machine onto the coffee table, she rose and headed for the kitchenette. As predicted, he hopped up to follow.

"Why didn't you go to college?" she asked, pulling open a sleek, plain-white cabinet—one of those cheaper, overly modern ones you could pick up and assemble by yourself from a DIY warehouse-showroom. The cups had clearly come from there too since she recognized them as siblings to the ones she had in her own apartment. "Maybe you wouldn't be in this mess if you studied something that would get you into a good career so you wouldn't have to resort to thievery and potential murder."

He leaned across the counter from the living room, a breathy laugh escaping him. "Yeah—*no*." He shook his head dismissively. "As nice as that sounds, it wouldn't have done much for me."

"Why not?" Frowning, she pressed the cup into the fridge water dispenser.

"Well, it's… not exactly that easy for some of us."

She eyed him wearily, quietly pulling from her glass while he came up with the rest of his words. It was a little off-putting not to hear him come up with an immediate reply like he had done repeatedly over the past several hours.

"I grew up with nothing," he finally began. "My dad walked out on my mom when Jay and I were kids, and she wasn't ever really around either. She worked two or three jobs just to make ends meet. She wanted to make an honest living, rather than falling in line with the options you have as… well… one of *us*." He half-heartedly motioned between them. "I guess more of the options *I* have, but there's only so much you can do outside that role. She ended up getting pretty sick, and she was already so worn down… Jay had just turned eighteen when she passed, so he took care of me. I helped where I could, as much as I could."

"So, you two didn't have the money… You realize there are loans, grants, and other ways to pay though, right?"

He gave a bitter chuckle, shaking his head. "None of that really matters without a decent job to secure payments. And getting anything like that is restrictive because of the same issue my mom ran into: being Shade."

"What—*Why?* What does you being Shade have to do with anything?"

"Shade and Inked aren't trusted among the Custodians, Evie. There's a stigma there." He glanced over his shoulder toward the couch and eyed around the divider to where Haven sat with a book. "These two would love nothing more than to dump me in a cell until they catch my brother. It's why they didn't uncuff me until I signed the papers. They thought I'd just slip away and help him escape. Granted, I wished I could've done that last night, but I didn't exactly have anywhere in mind I could go.

"I could live a clean life, act like an upstanding citizen, and they'd still turn up their noses at me. They would already believe I'm a spy or a criminal, so what's the point in trying? No one was going to help us, so Jay and I helped ourselves. We dragged ourselves to the top and Jay took it by force. He put himself in a council seat." He sighed. "Now that's gone, so who knows what will happen to me after all this."

Evie thought back to Tarryn's sour tone when she described Shade and Inked. "That hardly seems fair."

"Life isn't fair." He still held a bit of a smile, though it didn't reach his eyes.

"If... if you don't mind me asking, how did your brother make it to a council seat anyway after so much was stacked against you two? Tarryn mentioned that some of you can become shadows and mess with people's dreams."

Cade's hand moved to the back of his neck. "That's, um... Well, he has a rather rare talent. Let's just say that it's best left to the imagination. It's not exactly something I enjoy thinking about him using, which is why most people just do what he says. He's personally never used it on me, but..." He grimaced. "Considering he didn't make a whole lot of friends, the rest of the Shade will likely gang up on him and turn him over if they find him."

"Do you think they'll catch him soon?"

His fingers drummed on the countertop while he chewed on his lip. "No idea. My unfortunate bet is that it'll take months, which means I'll be in here long after you're out. Either that, or some other Shade steps up to take that council seat, and they decide to claim me. They'd probably take some of their aggression out on me."

Evie gently set her glass down next to him, their eyes meeting in a horrible exchange of uncertainty. That overwhelming remorse pulsating off of him pressed on her, feeding her sympathy. "I hope they find him soon, and you're able to show the rest of the Shade that you're not like him."

"Nothing like a fun trial with you and I as star witnesses," he said, swinging his arm in front of him in mock-excitement before his smile dropped. "In all honesty, knowing that I'm going to have to start all over after this really sucks, but I can't imagine that you're taking it all that well. I'm surprised you even knew how to do that thing back in the garage. How'd you do it, anyway?"

"I… don't know," she said slowly. "I just kind of… started to panic, and then I thought about the watch I got from my grandpa." She tugged out the pocket watch from under her shirt, examining it. "After that, I just imagined myself standing back in his old tinkering workshop that he decorated with a bunch of old timepieces. It sort of *happened* after that. I guess it worked since I undid whatever happened to you."

"Your guess is as good as mine since you're the first Trick I've ever met."

She leaned on the counter, sighing and staring over at her laptop. "Do you think I'll be able to go back to class on Monday, or…?"

"*Seriously?*" Laughter bubbled up from his throat. "You just discovered you have superpowers, and you want to go to school? What the hell is wrong with you?"

"Look, Mister Badass," she said, narrowing her eyes at him. "I was just trying to live a normal life until the last twenty-four hours completely obliterated that fantasy. I'm also not really keen on the idea that I can do what I can do when I don't know why the hell I can do it. I'd like to pretend that nothing bad ever happened and continue on my merry way. So, as interesting as this whole dream-world is, I'd like to forget it."

Cade jabbed a thumb in Haven's direction, dropping his voice to a whisper. "I'd be careful saying that near *that one* over there. He could totally arrange that with the proper paperwork. Plus, I mean, you'd also probably forget me, and that would be a shame, wouldn't it?"

Her eyes rolled back in her head, causing his smile to drop.

"Fair enough," he mumbled.

ELEVEN
EVIE

Day three of the safehouse proved to be just as tedious as the previous two days, if not more so. It was Monday, meaning that Evie had finished her project, but she hadn't been allowed to email her professor to try to turn it in online. She wasn't sure why she was so hell-bent on lying to herself like this, but she attempted to complete the assigned reading from the syllabus anyway, knowing full-well that there was no way to receive any credit for any of the assignments. Maybe it had been because Tarryn had told her that she and Haven would be gone for the day with the promise of returning that she had automatically assumed it would be distraction-free, so she should use the time wisely. Cade had certainly made sure to pop that bubble at 11AM.

The light knock at her unit door, followed by sweet-talking that had eventually dissolved into persistent whining indicated that he was—once again—*bored*. She thought that she might be able to wait it out, but when she heard him fall against the door, sliding down to the hallway carpet, she shut her laptop. Tarryn had specifically instructed her not to let him in, explaining that the entire building was designed to prevent any of them from doing whatever weird magic tricks they had to potentially slip in and out. He was to stay in his apartment while she stayed in hers.

But the other problem was how the emptiness of the apartment had started to get to Evie. It felt too big compared to her studio and lonely, just like her grandparents' old house upstate. Cade sort of fixed that, though she wouldn't admit that to him. So, he made himself at home on the floor in front of the coffee table, his arms and chin resting against the black faux-wood while watching TV. She, on the other hand, had gone from attempting to catch up on assigned reading to working on the stack of paperwork that Ms. Desrosiers had given her earlier that morning.

"Do you think they'll let me go back to classes next week?" Evie asked absently, unable to really read any of the words on the stack of papers on the coffee table. Her head lifted to glimpse the flickering images on the screen with a frown. "Do my professors even realize I'm gone?"

"No, they won't let you go back," Cade replied without taking his eyes off the screen, "and yes, they probably realize you're gone. But, more than likely, some division of the Custodians will seize control of all your records and work their magic to excuse you from all of it for a month." He stretched, leaning back against the foot of the couch.

Her mouth opened, aghast. "A *month?* But I paid for those classes, they can't just—"

"Relax. You'll get reimbursed. Hell, they might even pull you out for the rest of the semester and pay for the entirety of your schooling up through this point. We're on semi-permanent house arrest, remember?"

"But they can't—" She shook her head, scoffing a little at the mere thought. "They can't seriously do that, can they? I mean, you clearly don't have anywhere to be, but they can't just expect me to shut down my whole life until they figure out what's going on with the Trick—"

"Um, yeah. They sort of *can*. I think you're forgetting why we exist. Our purpose is to control how everyone else functions." He held up a finger, drawing a circle aimed at the ceiling. "That's all there is to it. If they decide to lock you in here for a month, well, then you're here for a month. You'll have to wait until the Head council member says those magic words, *'you're free to go.'* Right now, I think that's the last thing on that guy's mind since he's out the door at the end of the month."

Her shoulders dropped as she panned away from him to blankly stare at the TV. An online college advertisement popped up like a slap in the face—probably one that she'd be derailed from if she even bothered to transfer to it. Would she get discouraged from certain paths like Cade had, all because she's Trick? "I'm going to lose my damn mind," she mumbled.

"See! Now *that's* the spirit!"

Her face fell into her hands. "I can't believe I'm stuck here. I just—*What?*" It wasn't so much directed at Cade than a general question directed at the universe.

"Odds on which of us will walk out first?"

Her hands dropped, shooting him a glare with her lips pressed into a line. Grinning sheepishly, he cleared his throat and returned his attention to the screen. Evie picked up one of the papers again with a sigh, helplessly reading through it while her hand went for the next one. There was no way to make sense of it all.

"I don't understand what any of this means," she said, flipping through a few more papers. "There's stuff in here about relationships. Just how personal and invasive are we getting here?"

"Eh." He half-shrugged. "I wouldn't think on it too much and sign them all."

"*Cade.*"

"Hey, everyone signs the same stupid documents when they

turn eighteen. It's just a legality thing that you're not going to run around and use your talents as party tricks or start telling a bunch of random people about the Custodians. Most of us know the general rules by the time we're about to be teenagers anyway since puberty can trigger a domino effect that forces your family to have that talk too."

He folded his arms at the back of his head, stretching out his legs from their crossed position on the floor. "I think I was twelve when I threw myself on my bed to pass out for the night and phased right through it. Scared the living shit out of me, and I screamed until Jay dragged me out. Got the talk. From then until eighteen, it's the parents' or guardians' responsibility to keep it handled until they sign that dumpster fire of paperwork and behave so the council doesn't have to drag your ass to trial."

Evie blanched. "*That's* how you found out? That sounds horrifying." The memory of a cheerful twelfth birthday party paled in comparison to the confusion and terror that came with doing something that defied all logic. She probably would've frozen up and screamed too, afraid to pass through something else like she was a ghost haunting the halls.

"Hate to break it to you, but an ethics case isn't going to get you out of signing," he said. "Do it and move on."

"But—" She made a helpless noise, a handful of papers buckling in protest in her grip. "I don't even know what I'm signing, Cade. I wasn't told any of this as a kid."

He sighed and scooted closer, tugging the small collection from her hand. He leafed through them before shoving the larger stack off to the side and placing a portion in front of her.

"So, these five are just *'don't tell, or we'll come for you.'*" He grabbed the pen and held it out to her. She cautiously took it, clicking it as he pointed a finger toward the signature line. "Sign here, and here—since that one's sort of just a disclaimer that you won't talk about us to anyone who you're not completely posi- tive is one of the Custodians themselves."

She went to sign, hating her hesitation as he continued the

explanation, "The only people that can't really prove it most of the time are Fallen, which is why they have these little black tokens with their symbol stamped on it. The ones who've had their memory wiped won't have one, but they're still in the system and get checked up on from time-to-time, I believe. If you slip up, they'll give you a slap on the wrist, but you *have* to tell the Keepers. They'll call the Mist clean-up crew to wipe some memories."

Almost immediately, she wanted to scratch out the signature. *"What?* Remove their memories how? *All* of their memories?"

"No!" His eyes widened. "Oh, no! Not anything like that. They'll just replace and rearrange what happened or anything leading up to that point, so it would've never happened, along with the chain of people they interacted with if they did..." Lightly humming, he skimmed through a few more. "Here's the general registration form. Check the box for Trick. Write in all your current information. Put any relations and what-not. All of that is usually kept so only other Trick can access it, but they've written in a recent clause for the council to be able to *apply* to access any specific records. It looks like it also needs to be approved by a majority vote of the rest of the council as well."

"To avoid people like your brother digging for it?" she asked hesitantly.

"Probably," he mumbled. "Though, Keepers can look most people up without a problem. Still, I think it's all based on access level and other shit they have to sign... Explains why it's taken so long to find you."

Evie began to write in the blanks, Tarryn's vague threat toward Cade in the parking garage surfacing to the front of her thoughts with that implication of tracking people down. "Didn't... didn't Tarryn imply that she had been hoping to bring you in?"

He snorted. "Her and just about every Keeper out there has probably been plotting to figure out how to get their hands on me and Jay for the past few years. You learn not to take it personally. It's like a hobby to them."

"How have you *not* been caught during all this time?"

"Oh, no, that's where you're wrong," he said, shaking his head. "I most definitely have been caught. The problem is that a council member will always trump a Keeper. Jay would walk in, say I'm coming with him, and then they have to let me out of the holding cell. They couldn't stop him, and I had to comply because I'm Shade. Disobeying the head of your faction is begging for the shit to get kicked out of you."

"Explains why you got shot…"

Cade grimaced, sinking down slightly. "Yeah, well… Tactical error on my part. Usually, I'd happily do whatever he asked, especially walking out of jail, but…"

She quietly tapped the pen against the signature line, re-reading all of that personal data with a dreadful, sinking feeling in her gut. "I… I don't mean to pry, but you said that Jay raised you at a certain point. Were you two close as brothers, or was it… different?"

Cade paused, his jaw working slightly while he stared at the next sheet of paper. Evie was just about to tell him he didn't need to answer that right before he did. "Yes and… no. It's complicated—*was* complicated—I don't know." He shook his head, a hand running through his hair. "We looked out for each other, but I feel like the further we climbed, the more he acted like I was a nuisance and a liability. I don't even think he realized how much I did for him to make him appear damn-near perfect. I was the scapegoat, but I didn't really care because he'd bail me out."

That horrible, weighty blanket of sadness fell over them, accompanied by its familiar friend of silence. His eyes started to scan the page again, like he was trying to let the entire topic drop.

"Cade," Evie said quietly, watching his eyes slide over to her, "despite the questionable things you've done, you still seem like a good person."

"Well, that's one upper-level member of the Custodians that thinks so," he replied with a mirthless chuckle. Divvying up the rest of the documents, he laid two more out in front of her. "This one's catch-all clauses and all that garbage. This other one is proof that you've received that packet with information about how our jobs work." He grabbed said packet off the coffee table, tossing it behind them to the couch. "Bunch of boring shit you can read later…"

"*Fantastic,*" she whispered.

"And then this last one is the Trick's archives document." He smirked, holding it in front of her. "It might just be your ticket out of here."

Frowning, she neatly stacked the other papers to the side before taking the document from his hand. "Well, there's an address listed, but how will this help if I can't leave?"

"You can request that Tarryn and Haven take you once it's signed and submitted." He tapped the page. "They'll probably even encourage it since you're quite literally the only person recognized as being able to access it in all of New Atlas. Only Trick can get in or admit others to it. It contains all of their records for meetings, historical data, rules, laws, and possibly the entire reason why everyone and their mother is hunting you down. All you have to do is wait for it to get processed and you're set."

"Do they give me a key or something?"

"No. Each archive was built so only that faction can unlock the door to it. I believe they were all crafted by Inked a long time ago. The registration is just so they're able to properly monitor who's going in and out via the station's archive security. You're also not allowed to leave with something from it without proper documentation—not even a copy of a page or something from in there."

"So…" she started, eyeing him before she scribbled down her signature, "I take it you've been to the Shade archives then?"

"Once. Jay went quite a few times, but it's more of a meeting hall to gather the heads of all the named Shade families."

"But you could still go there now, right? Do you think it would have information on why they attacked me?"

"Err… I mean, yes to the first part, and no to the second." He shook his head. "Jay made it seem like a normal job. I really doubt there's a record, let alone proof of him having a meeting there with the Callaghans beforehand."

"Callaghans?" Her brows furrowed.

He let out a long sigh, pointing a thumb back toward the apartment door. "The other two guys in the garage. They're two of his go-tos for jobs and high-ranking members of the Callaghan family. I don't care for any of them. They're ruthless, which is why I sort of prefer the Martellis…" He trailed off, like he had mentally disappeared somewhere else before snapping back to reality again. "They're different because they work in organized crime, by means of information trafficking. Not that you heard that from me."

"What about asking them?" she asked, quickly earning a grimace.

"I doubt they'll know unless it was mentioned in the letter I gave the head of their family yesterday, but I'm not sure how much they'd be willing to talk to me after all this. They probably think I'm a rat for saving my own ass." His back slid a little further down the front of the couch, melting closer to the floor.

"Trick archives it is," she mumbled, placing that paper on top of the stack.

Which meant a week-long wait for *possible* answers. Answers that Evie wasn't sure that she'd be able to make heads or tails of either.

TWELVE
REN

"You hear about Hart?"

Ren paused on the threshold of the tiled entryway at the sound of Angelo's question, pushing the front door shut behind him as slow as possible to keep it from squealing on its hinges. The clattering of dishes in the kitchen was followed by his sister's voice. "No," she mumbled, "but I've noticed Flynn's been acting tense the past couple of days…" The scrape of ceramic against newspaper-covered shelves.

He toed off his shoes, nudging them over to the side with a hand digging into his backpack strap. Every inch across the wood planks in the living room sounded louder to his own ears than Carmen's organizing of silverware.

"He's out."

Clanging rang out against the kitchen tile, bringing Ren to a halt. He bit down on his lip, nails digging into his palm. While he'd already known about this particular incident, he hadn't expected for Carmen to figure it out *just now*.

"*What?*" she breathed. "You're not serious—"

Angelo huffed out a short laugh, though it lacked any of his usual humor. "No, I definitely am. The Martellis are making a move for that seat."

"Shit..." Her voice muffled, like a hand had gone to her mouth. "And I bet the MacGuinnesses are too..."

"Likely."

"How many other Shade families do you think might be jumping into that power blood-bath? You don't think the Callaghans—"

"Oh, you bet your ass they're gunning for it."

"Bastards," she hissed, the scraping of metal on metal slipped into Ren's mind through the image of a bundle of forks clutched in her fist. Her dark hair fell loose around her face in tendrilled wisps, hooking through silvery hoop earrings. Dark, heavy eyeliner and mascara detracted from the circles under her eyes he poked fun at whenever she threatened or bullied him—both shots always in jest.

He shook his head, the vision fading in favor of a light ache pressing in the depths of his mind in protest. Grimacing, he closed his eyes and tried to will it away.

"They'll try to run the MacGuinnesses into the ground if—"

"If Emilio has anything to say about it, then—"

"Fuck Emilio, Angelo." Her tone hard and unyielding before the soft shifting of those death-gripped utensils against the kitchen island countertop. A sigh as a couple of things were tossed into the sink, releasing a tinny reverberation through the entirety of the bottom floor. "I don't think you understand how hard things are getting. Either one of them winning will inevitably cause us to suffer unless you happen to have some sway. Hart was taxing Flynn pretty damn hard before, but now that's in limbo, which means my paycheck is in limbo. I don't suppose you're due for some sort of thuggish promotion to make up for that, are you?"

Silence. Silence that gave way to a warmer, greedier ache that stole a wince from Ren.

"I'll figure it out."

"*You'll* figure it out?" She scoffed. "Angelo, in case you haven't realized, Mom's working her ass off to try to secure Ren's college money—Money that I've been trying to contribute to by tacking on extra to the mortgage and you've been chipping in to buy groceries." Her tone snapped to something deep and accusatory. "And don't you dare deny it because that damn lunchmeat didn't manifest in the fridge on its own."

"Yeah, you're right," he said, a chair screeching against the tile. "But I can start contributing more if it's turning into a problem."

"Do you even *have* more, Angelo? Or are you offering something that you're going to have to steal?"

Ren's ears perked at the slight catch of Angelo's breath, turning into Carmen's prey.

"I know you're trying, but maybe it's time you walk away from the Martellis—"

"No, I can make myself useful. You know I'm only good for intelligence-gathering shit. The Callaghans would beat my ass if I showed up on their doorstep to suck up after a loss unless I made the Martellis my enemies. That's assuming they'd even believe I wasn't double-crossing them. I'll push a little harder."

"Angelo…" Her voice wavered through a groan, like she was rubbing her face. "I'm just asking you to be open to jumping ship. I can try to pick up some extra clients at Flynn's, and if that's not enough, maybe I can convince him to let me breech our contract—"

"Or…"

"Or what?"

He cleared his throat, his boots creaking against the tiles. "We could… maybe reach out to—"

"Out of the question." Her words sliced through his suggestion like a knife. "That man can rot in hell. He's the last person I'd ask for help, and even then, I'd rather starve."

"And Ren?" he snapped back with more force than Ren had

expected to hear. "You're just going to let Mom's hope that he'll be able to do better than the rest of us collapse?"

The icy void that followed turned out to be enough to push Ren up the stairs, wobbling in the final few steps to his room. His pulse pounded in his skull, begging for release. He kicked the door shut and tugged his water bottle free from his backpack's pocket before letting the weight of the books inside fall to the floor with a thud. Shaking, he fumbled with his nightstand drawer, feeling around for the small container of pain relievers.

That spark of relief wouldn't come right away, but at least he knew it would greet him soon, despite how little it'd be. Ren crawled onto the bed, dropping into the embrace of his haphazard pillows and pushed-back comforter. His body began to relax until he saw the trickle of light cut through his eyelids, and he loosed a hiss.

"Sorry," came Carmen's apologetic whisper, the light vanishing in a mere instant. "I didn't hear you come home." The floor protested as she drew closer, the mattress sinking along the edge before he felt fingers combing through his hair.

Maybe if he'd just sucked it up and rode out the vision downstairs, he wouldn't be lumped in such a pathetic heap. Not that it had mattered since the last time he'd followed its twisting path that ended in him heaving over a public toilet and trying to find amusement in the crude graffiti scrawled along the walls.

"Can I get you something?" she asked, her voice gentle and understanding in all the right ways. He had to choke back a laugh at how ridiculous he must look.

"I took something a second ago. Just waiting for it to kick in..." Swallowing a little discomfort, he went for the reason she'd actually come up here: "The MacGuinnesses have card tables, right?"

Her hand stopped, jerking upward like she'd been burned. He cracked an eye open when there wasn't an immediate reply, finding her shoulders sagging.

"So you heard us."

"I can help."

She shook her head. "Ren—"

"I remember hearing you say Flynn likes rigging things. I can rig a card table."

"You're *seventeen,* and you're not Shade. You're better than Shade."

He gave a breathy, mirthless chuckle. "Faction doesn't equate to morality, Carmen."

"I mean you have better *opportunities* than Shade," she amended with a sigh, settling in next to him. "Which is why we want you to focus on your future, rather than slumming it with the rest of us."

As much as he wanted to let it slip that he was already 'slumming it' with Inked like Aiden, he kept his mouth shut. That extracurricular was a whole other problem that would send her into a tailspin, resulting in being locked away in his room until he'd hit thirty.

"And what if that's not what I want?"

He caught that faint frown as she dipped her head into the pillow, but she didn't seem to notice his stare since her sights were fixed on the ceiling. The glint of the trickling sunlight cut through the sides of the thick curtains, making her glittery eyeshadow turn into shimmering stars. "I think it's… hard to know what you want until you're older—not that there's some magical age for it, you know?"

"Do you know what you want?"

She snorted. "Hell no."

"Would you at least be willing to maybe take me with you during a shift?" he asked.

"Ren—"

"I won't know what's a good fit until I try it, right?"

She worried her lip and closed her eyes. That talent pressing on the back of his mind clawed its way out of its box. It worked its way into her thoughts, coiling around that careful plan of her leveraging her employer for extra money. Ren sat at the heart of that scheme—a trump card he found she didn't want to play.

But there was something more that pushed him to want to go—something on the edge of his mind he couldn't quite grasp. Like a word being stuck on the tip of his tongue—the vision's version of taunting him. There was a reason for everything, whether or not it meant anything in that moment was still yet to be seen.

"Fine," she sighed. "You can come along for *a* night, but not on a school night."

"Friday?"

"Saturday." She rolled her head to face him. "And you have to promise not to tell Mom."

"Deal."

THIRTEEN
EVIE

Cade groaned, lying face-down in the middle of the floor in front of the TV. They had made it to Wednesday, the two of them tired and bored, though Evie was trying to make the best of her time by working her way through her job information packet. Despite Tarryn saying that it would be the *three* of them going to the archives whenever they were permitted to, Evie was considering a way to frame it so Cade might be able to join. After all, he had managed to help her navigate through so much of everything up until this point that he might have a better idea of what to look for than she, Tarryn, or Haven would.

"I can't take it anymore." Cade shoved himself off the floor, dusting himself off in front of the flickering TV screen. "I have to get out of here for a bit, or I'm going to lose my mind."

Pressing her lips into a thin line, she panned back down to her packet. "Yeah… Good luck with that," she mumbled. "Have fun dealing with the security guards."

"I don't need Tarryn or Haven to leave."

"I don't think they'd let you leave even if you did have

Tarryn or Haven," she said. "Did you not read the entry paper? It stated that we can't leave, even with an escort, unless otherwise authorized, until Saturday. *But*, maybe if you're good, they'll take you to an amusement park." She gave him a wry, teasing smile.

His hand went to his stomach, feigning stumbling back with mock laughter. "*Funny.* Look, I'm leaving for a couple of hours. They won't know, and it's not like they're coming back tonight anyway."

"I think you missed the part about the guards—"

"Oh, no, I heard. Rather bold of you to assume I'm using the main entrance." He strode over to the sliding glass door.

Her stomach dropped, and she scrambled to sit up, tossing her packet onto the coffee table. "We're not supposed to open that or any windows until Saturday either and not without supervis—"

"Oh, *please*." He scoffed, waving a hand while grabbing the handle with the other. "We're not children, Evie. Not to mention that if you're actually worried about someone recognizing me, they won't, not unless I name-drop. We can't be tracked because we have no phones, and unless some Spirit jolts awake in the middle of the night with everything they'd need to tell on *us*, we're not going to get caught."

"*Us?*"

"Yeah, *us*. Come on, it'll be fun."

She hesitated, starting to shake her head. "That's a horrible idea—"

"And what are you going to do for the next two or three hours? Sit here, read your packet, and sulk?" He motioned behind her to that sad, cheaply bound document. There was a quiet pleading in his eyes, like he was some lost puppy to follow, rather than a potentially deadly shadow.

She twisted to glance at the packet, weighing her options. Admittedly, she was also very sick of sitting around this apartment, though she had her reservations about where Cade might take her. She knew the right answer here, but then again, what if he ended up getting hurt and never came back?

"Well, if you don't want to go," he finally said with a shrug, "then you can just let me back in when I return. Saves me the trouble of jamming the door." The sound of it gliding open spun her around, sending her speed-walking toward him.

"Two hours, *tops*," she said, swearing that his eyes lit up. "And if I don't feel comfortable about it, then we're leaving. Got it?"

"Got cash on you?"

Cringing, she remembered that she only really carried credit cards. "Um, no…"

"I guess it's a good thing I do." His smirk grew slightly devious as he braced himself in the doorframe. "It'll cost you, though."

"Excuse me?"

"Well, since you don't have cash, I'm willing to overlook everything I spend in exchange for a kiss."

She folded her arms over her chest and scowled. "Absolutely not."

In an instant, that sheer confidence deflated, his arms sliding down from their overhead grip ever-so-slightly. "Fine," he sighed. "Just pay me back whenever they let us out."

He pulled something from his pocket and jammed the door lock while Evie peered out over the balcony. Her stomach knotted as she counted the floors of the neighboring building, trying to estimate just how high up they were in a measurement that would put her at ease. "How are we getting down, exactly?" Her voice wavering. "I know you'll be able to pretty easy, but me…"

Cade motioned for her to step out, sliding the door back into place before wordlessly climbing over the side of the railing, hugging it. "You know how to swim, right?"

It was a strange question, considering there wasn't a pool anywhere in sight. As far as she knew, there might be one on the roof or somewhere in the basement of this place, but she didn't see how that was particularly relevant. "Yes, but…"

"Great." He grinned, holding out a hand. "Then it'll just be a little jarring. You… might want to close your eyes though. Everything moves pretty quick, so you might get a little motion sick since you're not driving."

She eyed him hesitantly, slipping her hand into his.

"Ready?"

Closing her eyes, she squeezed his hand a little tighter. The world tilted, forcing her to hold back a gasp at the smooth, fluid skimming motion. But just as quick as it came, it was gone.

"You good?"

Evie opened her eyes to find that they were mere yards from that tall, wrought-iron fence posted around the building. She looked back, craning to peer up at the apartment balcony, where the soft glow of the living room light filtered through the bars. "Yeah," she said breathlessly, awed when she turned back to him. With a flirtatious grin, he tugged her forward onto the narrow strip of grass, starting for the fence.

"One more hurdle, and then we're free," Cade said, stopping them about half a foot away from the bars. "I'll count down, and we'll step through together, okay?" She closed her eyes again and nodded, listening to his chant. "Three, two—"

She could *feel* herself pass through it, as if she were a ghost. Instinctively, she opened her eyes, finding the world around her colored in blurred, faded hues. It was like a dark watercolor or an ink diffusion spreading that sense of wonder through her. He pulled a little further from the fence with a slight, gentle jerk, and then the world sharpened again.

"And just like that, we're out." He grinned, still holding her hand. She didn't feel the urge to rip it away either, letting it naturally fall free when they started for the street. "Now, let's go have some fun, shall we?"

They walked a few blocks, passing by faceless and nameless people that she used to be one of. Barely any of them paid her any attention, and when they did, it was probably because she was walking with Cade. Her in her thick cardigan and him in his leather jacket. He walked with confidence while she glanced around, anxiously waiting for someone to ruin their escapades.

Finally, Cade hailed a taxi, instructing the driver to take them across the bridge to a place she'd never heard of—a place called *Teal*. When they arrived, she found a large, fluorescent sign boasting colored letters true to its namesake hung outside an opulent, double-doored entrance. Checkered black-and-white carpeting spilled out from the inside of the vestibule as fragmented tiles sunk into the concrete. It was large and boxy, like an old warehouse or factory with the high-up windows angled open. The line to get in wrapped around the block, giving her pause of whether or not she should ask Cade if they should give up and go back to the apartment.

He handed the driver a folded bill and pulled her out onto the curb with him. The taxi wasted no time taking in new, desperate pedestrians in search of a ride and vanished. His hand in hers, he bypassed the line, heading straight for the door. *Everyone* was watching them, whispering with intrigue or annoyance. Evie felt her cheeks heat with the attention, keeping her head down until they stood in front of the bouncer.

All it took was the flash of a card from Cade's pocket—a black-on-black inked thing with a weirdly shaded three-dimensional-looking cube printed on it—and the door was opened. Music thrummed on their way to the second set of doors, deftly pulled open by a man in a simplistic, all-black uniform with 'TEAL' written in large, block letters across the front.

A burst of sound ran her through, nearly staggering her backward if it weren't for Cade's grip. Soft, glowing lights drenched the walls along the edges of the club, slowly transitioning from a pink to purple as they started for the frosted glass steps fanning downward toward the pit of people between them and the bar. Her body jittered from the clash of noise, ratcheting up her anxiety.

When they reached the bottom, Evie's hand was ripped away from Cade's. Spinning around, she pinned her eyes on the culprit—a woman with deep purple, straight-cut hair and a wicked grin—who loudly 'whispered' a suggestion to stop babysitting and join her instead. He replied with something Evie couldn't quite make out, but the woman's face dropped the flirtatious expression in favor of something a little more pissed as she turned her gaze to Evie. Huffing, she pushed through the crowd.

"Do you know her?" Evie half-yelled over the music.

"Just some Inked girl," he yelled back. "I'm not really in the mood for a spiked drink." Her eyes went wide, and he quickly scrambled to explain, "This is a Custodians-only club, so we can talk about that kind of stuff here."

"About her *drugging* you?"

"Oh, *that*."

She gaped at him in disbelief.

"They like to get a little *too* loose sometimes, so you have to draw the line. I usually follow the rule of only talking to them during the daylight hours since they turn into psychotic gremlins after dark."

She glanced around, suddenly noticing that just about every other body in the place had at least a single tattoo on them, most with hair streaked or completely dyed some wild color or pitch-black. A guy at the bar was lamenting to the bartender over a detailed, penned napkin mural he'd made, causing Evie's jaw to drop. "Then why are we in a club *brimming* with them?"

"Because they throw great parties, okay?" He grabbed the sleeve of her cardigan on his way toward the bar. "It's how I woke up hungover in a bathtub on my twenty-first birthday. Just some harmless mischief."

Her eyes caught on the passing people, roaming over the murals of artfully crafted ink on skin. It reminded her of a couple of students she had class with, wondering for the first time if they were Inked or simply *inked* by Inked. Tortured artists took on a new meaning here, keeping her tense with every person she slipped past.

Cade signaled for the bartender, already pulling out his wallet to flash his ID. A carefully placed finger covered part of his name, though the bartender only really appeared to glance at it before taking his order. A look over at Evie, and she shook her head. Cade's brows knit together as the guy left. "I thought you wanted a good time?"

"I'm *twenty*, Cade."

"Oh—I didn't realize..." He awkwardly fidgeted with his wallet, clearing his throat. "Um, I mean, I could probably brib—"

She tilted her head, shooting him an incredulous look.

"I'm kidding—" He gave a nervous laugh. "Of course, I'm kidding."

Evie stifled a groan, hugging herself while he leaned against the bar and waited for a beer that was set in front of him on the bartender's way to the next customer. As he lifted his bottle, she peered past it to a guy standing at the end who stared at the line of bar patrons. At least, that's what she gathered until she realized he was staring straight at *them*.

A short glass was held in his gloved hand, barely filled with a ball of ice resting against the edge. He wore a black, open suit, a black dress shirt, and no tie, causing her to question if he was Inked as well. Oddly enough, he didn't have dyed hair like most of the others, but a natural-looking brown. The only part of his appearance that gave her pause were the studs and cuffs lining his ears. His dark eyes locked with hers, and she reactively elbowed Cade in the side.

"That guy down on the end is staring at us."

Cade's head whipped toward the Inked-in-question. Evie was aghast when she witnessed Cade give the guy a sheepish smile and a small wave. The guy mimicked it, though his smile was a little closer to what she would consider disturbed or feral. She grabbed Cade's jacket sleeve.

"You *know* him?"

"We've met, *yes*."

"I thought you said we wouldn't run into anyone you know—"

"Anyone I know that wants to *kill me*," he corrected.

Evie eyed the guy at the end of the bar as he set his glass down on the counter, straightened his suit jacket, and made his way into the crowd.

"Look, he's Inked, and we don't have bad blood," Cade said. "He's not going to tattle on us either unless people start asking around. We leave him alone. He leaves us alone." He pushed away from the counter, beginning to wade back into the crowd himself.

She hurried after him, feeling someone brush against her just before they cut in front of Cade. She stumbled into him as he skidded to a stop, avoiding colliding with the new body. Evie was being jostled in the crowd like the bottle that nearly slipped from Cade's hand. "Hey, watch it—" he snapped at the guy dodging in front of them.

"Sorry—" Evie called over him, shooting Cade a glare. Staying under the radar was apparently far too big of an ask.

The guy stopped, eyeing Cade. She was shocked to see that he looked like a high schooler, a teal wristband with a mark confirming that speculation.

"No, no—" the boy said, holding up his hands in a placating gesture. "That's my bad. I'm not too great at watching where I'm going sometimes." His smile was somewhere teetering between sheepish and smug, though none of that emotion reached his dark eyes as they slid over to Evie. He took a step back, turning away and stepping back into the throng.

"Stupid teenager," Cade grumbled.

"Evie?"

Her heart dropped at that voice, and she whirled around to find a horribly familiar face. Wide eyes, blue-streaked hair, chipped, black nail polish, and all. Serina stood there with an awestruck, open-mouthed smile on her face. "Oh, my *God*—"

She threw her arms around her, squeezing a little longer than was necessary. "I wasn't sure where the hell you were. I was beginning to wonder what happened."

"Er, um—Yeah, sorry. I—"

Serina *knew* about all this. She was one of them, and Evie would've never known.

"I'm just glad to see you're all right!" she said, pulling away with stars in her eyes. "I didn't realize you were one of the Custodians either. Which one?"

It was then that she wished she knew exactly how to freeze time, wishing she had more of it to think of an answer or grab Cade and bolt for the stairs.

Cade threw an arm around her shoulders, acting a little *too* casual with a suave grin in Serina's direction. "She's a Spirit."

Serina tilted her head, glancing between them with a creeping, wry smile. "Seems that's not the only thing you've been hiding from me. Don't have time for a relationship or parties, huh?"

Evie forced out a nervous laugh, pushing his arm away. "Oh, no, no—He's just a friend." She ignored that muffled, disappointed noise from Cade. "And this is just a one-off thing. Never been, so I thought I'd take a look."

Serina nodded slightly, her eyes drifting back to Cade. "Uh-huh…"

The second Cade flashed her a charming smile, lifting his beer, Evie grabbed his wrist and gave it a death squeeze.

"We were just leaving," Evie said.

"Wha—" Cade protested.

"I'm glad to see you're okay too," she continued, undaunted. "You'll have to actually show me your talent sometime." She gave her a brief hug goodbye before dragging her unfortunate baggage toward the exit.

"Hey, I'm not done—"

"Oh, yes you are. Either down your beer or dump it because this is getting far too real for me right now."

"Just because someone you know is one of the Custodians doesn't mean that you should freak out and run."

She rounded on him, stopping along the wall. "Cade, I don't think you understand that she was normal in my eyes a few days ago. I don't want to believe that everyone I know has been in on this world-altering secret this whole time while I've been sitting in the dark. God, I should've just read the stupid job packet and stayed in the apartment." Her hands balled into fists, resting on the top of her head. Her vision blurred, focused on some other part of the cavernous room.

He set his bottle down on the small ledge on the wall. "If you want to go, we'll go, but let's go somewhere else first."

Her arms dropped. "Where else could we possibly go, Cade?"

A grin danced onto his face. "Let's show you around the invisible New Atlas."

FOURTEEN
EVIE

Evie stared down at the fountain—an ornate, white-stone centerpiece in the middle of the hotel lobby. Water bubbled out from the cascading, sea-shell levels to the blue-and-white patterned tiles at its base.

"Why are we here, Cade?" she asked, looking over at him.

"For a secret." He winked, grinning with a tug on her sleeve toward the elevator.

"Are we talking about another underground club, but with a bunch of hookers, or…?"

He chuckled, pressing the call button in the alcove. "No, nothing that loud."

An arrow blinked overhead, doors sliding open for them to step inside. Cade retrieved his keyring, selecting a smaller key that he inserted into one of the locks before pressing the button for the fourth floor.

"Is that maintenance or something?" Evie asked.

"Numbers, Evie," he said wryly. "Think of the numbers."

"Like… the fourth group of the Custodians?"

"Yep. You remember what that is?" he asked, pointing up to the screen indicating the floors. "Hurry, before the doors open."

"Umm…." She bit her lip, counting through the ones listed in the packet Trick, Spirits, Animated… "Tears?"

Cade grinned. "Ding, ding, ding—" He moved his finger to point toward the doors as they opened to reveal a room decorated with floral-woven trellises and hanging gardens. Quiet trickling of water could be heard somewhere through the dense indoor foliage. The large windowpanes along the sides were speckled with dark dots to keep out prying eyes.

"It's a sanctuary, sort of," he said, leading her into the walkway. "More of a mediation garden, and there's a spa on the other side if we go a little further down the hall. I don't think there's anyone working this late though, so there's not much point going that far. Enjoying the garden, on the other hand…"

He guided her through an archway, bringing her to the water fixture cascading down one of the center walls of a lobby filled with benches.

"Sort of wish I could've brought you here during the daytime, but I sort of like how peaceful it is at night. Though, I think you'd like some of the tricks the spa workers do—they sometimes make the water go in reverse to entertain the kids that tag along."

"Did your mom bring you here when you were younger?" she asked, pacing along the wall and gazing at the flowers hung above them.

"A few times. She joked about how it was magic when we were too young to know any better."

"So… this is only for the Custodians too?" she asked, pointing a thumb back toward the elevators.

"Yep. One of the many little hidden nooks and crannies just for us to unwind or have some privacy away from the rest of the world. Everyone has a key. You'll get one at the end of the week with everything else, I guess. You'll always be able to tell if it'll work before you try it because there'll be nine marks around the lock—kind of like the eight-marked one next to the sliding glass door in the apartment. The ninth is for the Fallen, so it's like an invitation for them to use it too."

"Aren't the marks back in the apartment wards?" she asked. "Did one of the Inked make them?"

"I think so... Probably." He waved a hand in dismissal. "I mean, Inked have done a lot of that stuff in the past, but they're not commissioned all that often anymore since most everything we need is already in place. Inked just do whatever they want after that."

"Wonder if they can ward my apartment after this whole mess," she murmured, cringing at another realization. "Or maybe my house..."

"You own a *house?*"

She sighed, turning to him. "It was my grandparents'. They left it to me when they passed, and it's paid for, so... I just kind of assumed I'd keep it and live there after school. Get a remote job. Do my own thing for a while. Maybe settle down with someone I met at college." She scoffed at the absurdity of that idea, that sad, far-off memory of standing next to her grandma in the kitchen resurfacing in her thoughts. "Now my life is just a total mess... I miss them."

He gently nudged her arm. "Cheer up. They'd want you to be happy. Even if they didn't want you to know you were Trick. I think there had to have been parts of this they would've wanted you to see. You're special, and yeah, it's overwhelming, but once you get the hang of things, it'll seem like second nature."

She stared down at the floor, trying to imagine walking away from all of this. To go back to the life she had days ago—one where her biggest problems were turning in a project on time and catching up on sleep. "Have you ever considered becoming one of the Fallen? I mean, like... wouldn't it just be easier to ask to forget everything and go back to a normal life?"

He hesitated, putting his hands into his pockets. "I can't say that I haven't thought about it, but… I *like* what I can do. Even if I choose to Fall, it wouldn't get rid of the stigma attached to me, and I don't know that I'd want to forget if I did it either. I'd be missing a part of myself to live a supposedly normal life."

"I guess I just don't know if I'm cut out for this. I've been thrown to the wolves without a way to protect myself."

He grabbed her hand, pulling her back toward the water fixture. "What did you think about back in the garage? Think back to that."

Her brows knitted together, and she glanced up at him for a brief moment before fixing her sights on the water again. She reached back to that feeling, holding her breath for about ten seconds. She blew it back out. "I got nothing."

"You can't just think it," he said with a chuckle. "You have to *will* it to happen."

"Will you let go of my hand, then?" She motioned to it.

"If you stop time, then I won't know unless we're touching. It's like when we descended the balcony earlier."

Evie groaned, tilting her head back. "Fine." Closing her eyes, she drew in a calming breath. She imagined herself back in the workshop, surrounded by ticking clocks. She reached out with her thoughts, *willing* them to stop. A nudge. "I'm trying to concentrate, Cade."

"I think you did it," he whispered.

She opened her eyes, finding the water wall frozen, droplets sputtering outward and still. "Huh…"

Cade reached out with his free hand, making a gap through the water by running a finger through it. A childlike giggle of wonder escaped him, splashing it toward her, where it halted inches from her face. She slapped a hand over her own mouth, amazed before dissolving into bubbly laughter of her own. *She did this.*

"Wait—" Her hand dropped. "Does this mean *everything* is frozen in time right now?"

He pivoted toward the window, pointing out toward the

lights of a plane blinking outside, cutting through the night sky. "I think it's like a pocket. Everyone's limited in how much they can do, so you're freezing the time around you. Everything should snap back to normal once you stop it."

"And… what if I don't know how to stop it?" she asked, cringing.

Cade chuckled, taking her by surprise.

"I'm serious!"

"Just *will* it to stop. Do what you just did, but let it go this time." He motioned to the hanging water droplets.

Shifting her footing, she thought about the garage—that release once she heard the sound of the bullet hitting the concrete. The water fell, and she jumped back with a shriek. Cade doubled over, clutching his stomach and laughing harder when she hit him.

2:31 AM

A pass through the fence and a dizzying rush up the building later, they were back in the apartment. No Tarryn or Haven sitting, lurking in the dark to click on a lamp like a disapproving parent. Everything was just as they had left it.

"See?" Cade said, striding to the apartment's door. "It's like nothing ever happened."

"It… *was* sort of nice to get out," she said, fidgeting with the sleeves of her cardigan.

"I'm glad you enjoyed yourself." He pulled open the door, holding out his hand the second he was in the hall. "That'll be twenty bucks for the cab."

She bit back a retort, stepping up to stand face-to-face with him. With her hand on the door handle, she leaned forward and gave him a kiss on the cheek. When she rocked back, she saw his hand fall, stunned. She didn't bother waiting for his full reaction, opting for shutting the door and flipping the deadbolt. A quiet hiss from the other side sounded like a 'yes,' which she imagined was accompanied by a fist-pump.

Shaking her head, Evie rubbed at her smiling face. She was glad for tonight. Even if she did decide to give it all up, she didn't think she'd be able to part with tonight's memory. She hoped she would relive some of it in her dreams.

FIFTEEN

REN

THURSDAY, APRIL 9TH AT 5:27PM

Convincing Aiden of Ren's worth hadn't been as difficult as he anticipated when the opportunity presented itself. When he had mentioned that Cade and said mysterious new Trick would be at *Teal*, he'd gotten him inside. Granted, Ren had absolutely hated how loud it had been, and the sheer number of people packed into the space made his head spin. But he accomplished what he went there to do: win the loyalty of the Inked and stand face-to-face with the two major players themselves.

Ren jumped when a small box was slammed down on the table in front of him, the cheap, black surface vibrating on impact. Perhaps returning to the tattoo parlor after school hadn't been the best idea, but there was honestly something disturbingly enjoyable about talking to Aiden's boss. Honestly, he'd thought she'd get bored of him after a couple of visits, but her interest still seemed just as piqued as when he first stepped into this shared office-slash-storage space.

She took the seat across from him, smoothing down today's short dress over thick striped leggings tucked into black combat boots. Her long sleeves matched but with thinner bands. He assumed that this is how she hid her tattoos since the shirt was long and had thumb holes cut into the ends. Her nails were painted black and kept perfectly unchipped, contrasting her pale skin. Like Aiden though, she had a giveaway: the hair. Blonde streaked through with teal—the same color as her eyes that came with a devious twinkle at every twitch of her lips. She was young—maybe twenty-three or twenty-four, not all that far off from her assistant.

"So," she mused with a grin, her child-like demeanor slipping through. "Have you tried tarot?"

Ren frowned. "I don't do tarot, Lily."

Her features fell, eyes narrowing at him in disapproval. "Have you even *tried?*" She leaned forward, tapping the box. "Here I am, making beautiful cards that *you* won't even try to use."

He sighed, grabbing the box to escape her guilt trip. It was met with glee and a giddy round of clapping as he opened it. Soft, velvety black cardstock greeted him. Silver-foiled images printed in geometric shapes and patterns. He poured the contents out into his hand before Lily tisked, retrieving the box and pulling the stack of cards from his grip.

"Just the major arcana," she said. "We won't need the minor for the questions I have."

She split the deck into a small portion and a bigger chunk, dumping the latter back into the box before handing him the rest. He had no idea what to do with them now. Ren sort of understood that he was supposed to lay some cards down, but he wasn't quite sure of the mechanics to it. At least with his practice of palm-reading—the first trick he had performed for Lily when they met—he had always been able to feel it out. Not to mention that it often managed to mitigate some of the pent-up pressure that weighed on his mind as the next crushing vision threatened to break through.

He began to shuffle the cards, apparently not doing it appropriately since she slapped them out of his hands again. They spilled onto the table, and she leaned back, folding her arms over her chest. "Some need to be upside down when you draw them. Try again."

With the utmost patience, Ren tried again, collecting the cards and reshuffling so they faced whatever direction fate chose for them. "What's your question, Lily?"

"Keep shuffling until I ask," she said with a touch of annoyance.

He held back a grumble, waiting for her cue. Tapping a finger to her lips, she finally said, "Show me our options for the Custodian's Head seat. It'll undoubtedly come down to two or three like it always does." She waved a hand, leaning forward again. "You can decide to cut the deck if you feel the need to, and place three cards face down. It'll be one for each option."

Ren stopped, setting the stack down. He rested a finger on the top, feeling the energy pulsing from it. It told him not to cut it, so he didn't. He drew the three cards one at a time, placing them face-down between him and Lily.

"Have you done this with someone else before?" Ren asked as the last card snapped against the table.

"There was a guy I used to use for this sort of deal," she said nonchalantly. "But he was rather smug, so I quit using him."

"Is he still in the city? Maybe he could teach me a little more about this."

"I want him dead," she replied with a cheery smile.

Hesitating, he cleared his throat. "Never mind then."

She motioned for him to continue, and he moved to reveal the card on the left. Flipping it over, he revealed an upside-down High Priestess, triggering a flash of a man in his thirties with tanned skin, black hair, and sharp, dark eyes. Like most Spirits running for a top spot, he sported a well-tailored gray suit, driving home how everything about him was clean-cut. Ren recognized him, though it had been a while since he'd heard this man come up in conversation. The name was just on the tip of his tongue…

He started to flip the card the right way, but Lily slapped it. "Leave it." Her tone sharp before sliding into a purr. "Who did you see?"

"It was… David Sterling. I think that's his name."

She hummed, tapping the card. "The High Priestess in reverse could mean secrets, withdrawn, or disconnected from intuition."

"Well, I think he's been out of the public eye for a while…"

She clicked her tongue. "Yawn, let's move on."

He turned over the next card, where a reversed Hierophant appeared, along with the vision of a woman in her mid-twenties. Her dark eyes were far more determined than Sterling's. Her long, black hair was pulled back in a bun at the base of her neck, not a hair out of place. She, too, wore a blazer, only hers was paired with a pencil skirt.

"Emmaline Yuan," he said in a near-whisper. She'd been paraded just about everywhere during the past couple of weeks, a general favorite among the Spirits since her father, Carlton, had done well in the same position a few years ago.

"Freedom," Lily said. "And challenging the status quo. Interesting…"

Ren grabbed the last card, finding The Emperor there. A flash of an older gentleman—one in his mid-fifties—surfaced in his mind. His dark hair was graying at the temples, his eyes a soft gray-blue that didn't have the hardness the other two bore. "Waylon Frost."

"Finally, a card that's not reversed," she said, sounding pleased. "The Emperor represents authority, establishment, and structure." Her mouth tipped into a slight frown. "*Boring.* Why is it that all of them have to be so damn *bland?*"

Ren bit his lip, staring down at the options. Lily might consider them bland, but one of them could very well be the individual pulling the strings or working with someone else who was when it came to all this world-ending talk from his new friend.

"Well, that was rather lackluster," Lily sighed. "I'll have to think up another question for next time."

He tapped the cards against the table, straightening them out. "What would you like me to do with these?"

"They're yours."

He frowned. "But I told you I don't do tarot, Lily."

She grinned, tilting her chin up. "You do now. I suggest you brush up on your arcana meanings."

SIXTEEN
EVIE

THURSDAY, APRIL 9TH AT 12:38PM

As per usual now, Cade had appeared sometime before noon, only this time he came armed with one-liners and flirtatious passes. He was still riding that post-kiss high, leaving Evie with some regret. Fortunately, it was quieted some when Tarryn and Haven arrived with lunch, where they sat in a circle around the coffee table on the couch and the floor.

"I can't wait until you're allowed outside again," Tarryn mumbled. "I'll be overjoyed when Haven can take you some-where far, *far* away from me."

Haven set down his glass of water on the coffee table, grab-bing Tarryn's attention with a few gestures that devolved into sharp, intentional motions. Evie immediately regretted not taking sign language as one of her elective classes, though what-ever he said must've been funny from the way Tarryn was holding back a smirk.

"What did he just say?" Cade asked, pointing his sandwich toward him with a look in her direction.

"Nothing," Tarryn replied. "Don't worry about it."

Cade's eyes flicked over to the culprit, where Evie saw a smug, satisfied look pull at his features.

"Where did you learn sign language, Tarryn?" Evie asked, popping open her small bag of chips.

"Back when we first met." Tarryn dusted the crumbs off her hands, balling up the now-empty paper wrapping. "So... seven years ago? I was seventeen and Haven was eighteen when we were paired up at the Keeper training program. I sort of figured that I'd end up with a Crossover since that's just usually how they pair them. However, there are a few Keeper-Keeper assignments, and some of those go solo post-graduation because it's usually permitted with some proficiency tests."

She waved a hand. "Anyway, I took ASL in addition to all my training to better communicate with him since that seemed to be the main problem we struggled with. We probably beat the shit out of each other twice a week for the first six months."

"You two seem to get along pretty well now, though."

Haven sat up a little straighter with a prideful glint in his eyes.

"Yeah, well, our alternative to not getting along would be getting rematched and starting all over again, which is far from ideal. Not to mention that if Haven wasn't able to get accepted by another full-blooded Keeper, then he'd be dismissed from the academy or the force."

Evie's face fell, glancing between them with concern. "But... he's a Keeper..."

"It's the 'half' part that's the problem," Tarryn said. "There are general ideas that Crossovers aren't able to fulfill certain factions' duties to their fullest extent, which is bullshit, seeing how he's generally better at the job than I am. But I don't make the rules."

Evie's brows knitted together some, chewing thoughtfully before her next question. "Are all Crossovers half-Keeper?"

"Nope." Tarryn leaned back, stretching her arms out. "It's just the most common half to find in a Crossover since it typically stems from a… a guardian-charge relationship, I guess? It's a huge game of odds for how power splits. For example… let's say Haven's parents had another kid—"

Haven's head whipped around, scowling at her.

"*Hypothetically.* Don't be so selfish, you damn only child." She rolled her eyes. "It's possible that said kid could be full Mist, full Keeper, or half-and-half. And if Haven were to find a half-Tears Crossover or something, then it's possible their kid could be a Crossover combination just like one of them, one without the Keeper portion, or any one of the single options at full power." She shrugged.

Haven pressed his thumb and forefinger to his chin, tapping it twice with his mouth forming a thin, impatient line.

"Yes, I *know*. It was an example."

Huffing, he went back to his food.

"Honestly," Tarryn continued, "it beats the hell out of me how it all works, but it does somehow."

"Is there nothing you can do about the rules?" Evie asked.

Cade set his sandwich down, crinkling the paper. "Even if someone were to change them, it would take a hell of a long time before a lot more people started actually following them properly."

Silence fell over them as he lifted his glass to his lips, not making eye contact with any of them, even Evie.

"For once," Tarryn said, "I have to agree with him. It's hard to change people's minds around here unless you have such a large sway."

SEVENTEEN
EVIE

Evie stayed up late after everyone left, curled up on the couch with her rule packet to comb through any questionable rules regarding Trick. She hadn't found any, which led her to believe that they were sitting in the archives somewhere, waiting for her. Between the talk of how Shade and Inked were painted and now Crossovers, Evie was seeing far too many flaws in this hidden world.

Nothing made sense anymore.

Her head lulled back, hitting the back of the couch. With a sudden jolt, she sat up straight, the image of a faded yellow sticky note with the same words surfacing in her thoughts. Her grandpa's letter—the letter sitting back in her studio apartment in a lockbox. Exactly where she'd tucked away after finding it addressed to her in his old office. Perhaps that had at least *one* of the answers to her many questions, or hopefully it could point her in the right direction after flailing for nearly a week. If she had her phone, then she'd be able to text her aunt about all of this, but part of her was afraid to have that discussion.

Evie jumped at a quiet knock sounding at the door, immediately checking the time on the wall. 2AM. She soundlessly got up, creeping toward it, and froze at the thud coming from the other side. Mustarding up her courage, she peered through the peephole. A sigh escaped her when a blond head came into view. She unlocked the door and pulled it open for Cade to stumble inside.

"What…" she started, watching him sway a little. "Cade, are you drunk? Did you sneak out again?"

"What? *No*—What would give you that i—" He swerved, grabbing onto the couch for balance. "—dea?"

Evie shut the door and rubbed her forehead, murmuring, "I can't possibly imagine why I'd assume something so *outlandish*." When she turned around, he was falling face-first onto the couch. "Were you out playing with Inked again?"

"*Hell* no. Just some… random club run by a Custodian guy, but he lets normies in."

"And you're not afraid that your brother or another Shade might run into you?" she asked, rounding the couch with arms folded over her chest.

"I think Jay skipped town by now or found a really good hiding spot," he mumbled into the cushions. "I'll just be stuck here forever, or they'll toss me out on the street to fend for myself."

"You're being a sad drunk." She leaned over him, pulling the blanket off the back of the couch. "What you need is some sleep, and then we'll talk in the morning when you're coherent." She draped it over him, instantly rewarded with a content sigh. "Goodnight, Cade."

"You really are a guardian angel," he mumbled wistfully, matching that slight smile.

Shaking her head, she turned out the light and went to her room. She shut the door and crawled into bed, staring up at the ceiling for another half hour with a myriad of thoughts. But eventually, sleep took her.

9:12AM

When Evie woke, she wandered out into the living room to discover Cade gone and the blanket neatly folded over the back of the couch again. She tugged the handle of the sliding glass door before spinning around to find the apartment's deadbolt flipped. Frowning, she started for it, pulling it open to peer out into the hall. Empty. She headed for his door, gave it a knock, and tried the handle. It was locked.

Evie pressed her ear against it and knocked again, hearing nothing in response. Something about this felt… *off*. She took a step back with a frown and glimpsed a slip of paper poking out from the bottom of the door. She crouched down and turned it over to where a single number was written: a six.

Think of the numbers.

But why leave *his* number on it? Her stomach dropped. *Jay?* There was no way Cade would go with him willingly, right? She shot up, jogged down the hall to the elevator, and repeatedly pressed the call button.

"Come on, come on, come on…"

The doors opened, and she mashed the lobby and close buttons. The countdown was agonizing, and she pleaded with it to hurry up. She had to tell a guard. She had to tell *someone*. The doors opened, and she stepped out, immediately skidding to a stop. Cade stood in the lobby with a gruffer-looking, dark-haired man who chatted with a couple of guards. She darted into an alcove, locking eyes with Cade when she poked her head out. His head jerked away, flinching at the dark-haired man's voice rose in irritation, accompanied by his arms folding over his chest.

Six for Shade.

Whoever this guy was, he was Jay's replacement, and he was *removing* Cade from the Custodian's protection. The Keeper guards stepped aside, and the guy seized Cade's arm. He roughly led him out the double doors.

Cade didn't look back. Dread pooled in her gut, her fingers twitching at the idea of freezing time to rip him away from his captor.

The paper crumpled in her hand, echoing that sound of helplessness. She paced when she returned to her apartment, counting down the minutes until Tarryn and Haven arrived.

"Oh, thank God—" she breathed as the door swung open.

Tarryn eyed her hesitantly. "Haven, why don't you go get—"

"He's not in his apartment."

"*What?* What do you mean Hart's not in his apartment?"

"He left this under his apartment door." Evie handed her the paper, watching her unfold it as her own hands shook. "It was there when I went to check on him this morning. I ran down to the lobby and saw him there with some guy. He took him."

"Son of a bitch." Tarryn's voice dropped to a low growl, looking up again. "Evie, I need you to describe this guy to me, *now.*"

"Um, dark hair, grayish or maybe green or blue eyes? Tall, a little muscular? Late twenties, maybe early thirties—possibly around Jay's age?"

"Brown or almost-black hair?"

"Almost black."

Tarryn cursed, pulling out her phone. "And how long ago was this?"

Evie's eyes darted for the clock. "About fifteen minutes."

She held up a finger with her phone to her ear. "Finley? It's Fuentes. You remember that thing we discussed a few days ago? Well, it happened. I'm almost positive it's that bitch Liam Callaghan I brought in a couple weeks back. He took Cade about fifteen minutes ago. Look up my recent case file to get his info. Find and tail his damn car. Don't let him out of your sight." She paused, a muffled voice coming from the other end before she ordered Finley to keep her updated and hung up.

"Who was—"

"Another detective and his partner. They're going to follow

them. If Callaghan tries anything stupid, they'll catch him, and he'll go down with Jay. Assuming that happens, we're putting Cade back in a safehouse and the four of us will petition to have the next faction leader be overridden by the Head council seat to ensure he can testify against his brother."

Evie could've sworn her heart stopped. The urgency in Tarryn's voice caused the blood to drain from her face, fully realizing that Liam Callaghan might just try to kill him.

EIGHTEEN
CADE

Liam Callaghan taking Jay's place had been a less-than-ideal situation for Cade, especially when he discovered both Declan and Conrad waiting for him in the car. Naturally, it was some nondescript black sedan that Declan drove and glanced in the rearview mirror with every off-handed comment about how Cade had screwed them over. He wasn't sure if having Liam in the backseat with him was better or worse than two of Jay's former lackeys.

"So, where's Jay?" Declan asked. "Think he's going to save you now that he's decided you're fucking worthless?"

"Couldn't even follow instructions," Conrad scoffed, shaking his head with his cigarette held out the window. "The Custodians ain't going to suddenly respect you for being a hero."

"I don't think you quite realize the magnitude of your current situation, Hart," Liam said with a deadly calm, making Cade shift uncomfortably as his eyes moved from the windshield to pin on his new target. "You just sliced through your own life jacket, and now *I* finally get to claim the seat he fucking stole from me. I hope you certainly enjoyed your time at the top, because I'm about to send you right back down to the fucking bottom."

Three.

The car slowed as it approached the stoplight.

Two.

Cade took in a subtle, sharp breath.

One.

The car stopped.

Cade thrust his hand into the space where the child safety lock was, forcing it up with a shadowy hand and yanking on the door handle with the other. He tossed himself out of the car, bolting for the first alleyway in view, sliding across the hood of a car between him and his exit. Shouts followed him, even as he whipped onto the next street.

He ducked into the entrance to the subway, taking the steps down two at a time. Jumping the turn-styles, he threw himself into the first train he saw. The doors began to close, nearly clipping his jacket. Breathless, he turned to see Conrad and Liam on the other side of the station, features on the verge of rage. They cut away in an instant, leaving him with a view of the tunnel wall. Cade grabbed onto one of the poles, leaning against it on shaky legs as the adrenaline slipped away.

He'd gotten away. That's all that mattered. He considered going to Alyx's, but, then again, it was possible she might be newly allied with the Callaghans. There was also the Martellis, where maybe he could beg Emilio to take him in, though that ship might have sailed by now. They had to look out for themselves and turning Cade over to their new leader might just be their only reasonable solution.

His hand dropped into his jacket pocket, the feel of cardstock pulling a memory from the back of his mind.

When you finally decide you're done fooling around in little turf wars, I'll be ready.

His eyes fixed on the address there, still so very uncertain of what this woman had meant. But he was also pretty much out of options, and maybe she'd be able to help him with his current, bleak situation after proper introductions. He pulled out his phone and started typing in the address, wishing that he had Evie's number. Hell, even Tarryn's or Haven's would've been nice to have about now.

10:17AM

A station hop, and a few stops later, he was in front of a building on the wrong side of town, covered in old, worn-down tags, abandoned with signs and boards over most doors and windows. He walked around the perimeter, finding a door popped open around the back. It complained as he forced it free, and he cringed with every horrid, echoing, screeching sound that followed him inside.

After wearily eyeing the stairwell, he decided to keep his exploration to the first floor, weaving in and out of rooms. Old, dented filing cabinets, and the occasional desk made up what remained of this office building. No soul in sight. Not even the remnants of anyone squatting here.

Cade ran a hand through his hair, pushing open one final door to check before calling it quits. Once again, another desk, left diagonally in the center of the room, as if someone had used it to shield them against the spiderwebbing window, barely held in place through the protection of metal bars.

A shove.

He stumbled inside, smacking against the laminate tiles. In his scramble to get back up, he caught a glimpse of long dark hair, vanishing behind the door slamming to shut him in. His eyes widened as he took in the two black, overlapping diamonds on the back of the door, circled with a mark near each of the eight points. Eight symbols of the Custodians.

"Hey!" he shouted, trying to give chase. The door was locked, or maybe even jammed, and the symbol prevented him from passing through. He pounded his fists against it. "What the hell, lady? You told me to come out here when I was done fooling around, and I'm sure as *hell* done fooling around."

"Message received," came her sultry, sing-song voice.

His concern ramped up at the accompanying scent of something burning and jumped back at the heat licking at his shoes. "What the fuck—Let me out, bitch!" No reply. Only the sound of heels echoing down the hall. Smoke began to puff into the room, gnawing on the wooden door.

Why? Why had she asked him to come here only to leave him for dead?

"*Hey!*" he called out again, panic shooting through him. Nothing.

Cade bolted for the window, wincing at the consideration of passing through since he could shred himself with that. The metal bars were just another layer he'd have to manage, which left him with the option of phasing through the wall. It was *far* from ideal since he couldn't see the other side all that well. He cringed at the thought of dismemberment, but it was a far better alternative than death.

He backed up, bouncing on the balls of his feet. He could do this. He *had* to do this. The smoke was pouring in, the flames beginning to consume stray bits of paper and dust. Cade sprinted, hurling himself through the brick and falling into the alleyway. He coughed, his lungs temporarily screaming for fresh air. After several moments with his hands on his knees, he called the fire department without leaving his name.

Cade had just cheated death *twice*, and he decided he'd rather take his chances returning back to a couple of Keepers over most anyone else.

11:03AM

Standing at the sliding glass door, he heard Tarryn's muffled, "What do you mean you lost him?"

He tapped on the glass, sending Evie spinning on a heel and

running toward him. That relief on her face was both a welcome sight and a knife driven into his heart. She flipped the lock, sliding it free.

"Never mind, Finley," Tarryn said. "We just found him on the balcony. I'll call you back." Grimacing, she ended her call while Cade dropped down onto the couch, pulling the throw over him.

"I take it all back," he said, his voice likely muffled by the fabric and cushions. "I don't want to leave here ever again."

"All right." Tarryn ripped the blanket away with a sigh. "As unbelievably glad as I am to see that you've managed to survive Liam, you can't stay here, Cade."

"Like *hell* I can't. He was going to take me somewhere and kill me—you get that, right? Then" —he jumped up, digging his knees into the cushions— "to top it all off, some random bitch tried to off me in some run-down building."

"I'm going to go out on a limb and assume you likely deserved that for *roaming around* a run-down building. As for Liam, I had two Keepers following him until they reached the Callaghans' place, and you didn't get out of the car. I thought they already did something to you."

"I bolted when we were stuck in traffic and hopped onto a subway. Look, you have to let me stay here—"

Tarryn's hand went to her forehead. "Cade, *no*. It's against the rules to knowingly allow you to stay here, especially with Evie. You have to go. Is there anywhere else you can think of where you can stay? A friend with a couch until we figure something out?"

He slumped against the couch, Alyx the only person coming to mind. "I do, but I don't know if she's working for the Callaghans now. I don't have anyone else."

"We can work with that. I'll call Detective Finley back and have him and his partner take you over there. If she tries to turn you over to the Callaghans, then they'll follow you, pull you out, and bring you back here with a renewed reason to keep you here. Understood?"

He hesitantly nodded. It wasn't like he had a choice now. His eyes flicked over to Evie, who chewed on a thumbnail and watched Tarryn lift her phone back to her ear. She rattled off her instructions, peppering in some harsh words before hanging up.

Evie's hand dropped from her face. "Are you sure there isn't another way we can get him to stay? Can't we do something else?"

Tarryn shook her head. "If Liam finds out, he'll just come back and take him again. We literally can't do anything." Her phone buzzed. "They were already on their way over. It's time for you to beat it, Hart. Outside. Gray sedan."

He stood, hating how Evie's face uncomfortably dropped to stare at the floor on his way out. He wanted to tell her that he'd be fine, along with a quick hug, but none of it seemed appropriate in present company. He'd already been pushing that boundary a little further than he should. So, he opened the glass door, gave a short wave goodbye with a tight smile, and descended down the building.

Cade tugged up his hood on his way through the alley, beelining for the gray sedan pulled up along the curb. The sound of the power locks was his assumed invitation, so he climbed into the backseat. "Sorry to disappoint you, Mom," he started dryly, eyeing the woman in the driver's seat, watching him in the rearview mirror. "I got suspended again."

She clicked her tongue. "Yep. We got the right one."

Her partner passed a phone back to him. "Type in the address," he instructed. Taking it back when he finished, the guy partner happily continued Cade's joke. "So, son, what did you do this time?"

Cade snorted.

"Wes, I'm pretty sure you two are the same age," the woman said, pulling away from the curb. "It's kind of weird."

"Don't judge, Trinity."

Cade leaned forward, elbowing the seat's shoulder, unable to suppress a grin. "Would daddy be more appropriate?"

Wes threw his head back, howling while Trinity audibly wretched.

"That's a strike," she said, holding up a finger directed at Cade.

"Does that count for me too, or…?" Wes asked, earning a glare.

"Yeah, which puts you at two."

"When the hell did I get the first one?"

"Not-so-subtly threatening that other dumbass detective."

"He had it coming," he mumbled, absently opening the glove box.

She rolled her eyes, spinning the steering wheel onto another street. "While I'm not saying he didn't, I don't want to get slapped with probation for my idiot Animated partner."

"Things would be boring without me." He smirked, and Cade joined in with a snicker.

"I hate men. Speaking of—Where the hell is your brother, Hart?" Trinity's eyes focused on him in the mirror again, heaping on the discomfort.

"Smooth," Wes said, sighing.

"If he knows—"

"I don't know where he is," Cade answered.

"If you tell us, it would help save your ass," she said, continuing to press him.

"Drop it, Trinity."

"Grill me all you want," Cade said, "but I can't tell you what I don't know."

She quieted, dropping the car into uneasy silence. "Fine," she finally said. "But you should know that you're just hurting yourself."

"*Trinity.*"

"Wes, I'm just trying to emphasize that protecting his faction isn't going to help him here."

"Trust me, I'm aware," Cade ground out. "The Callaghans are pissed about Jay and that I screwed them on a job, despite me technically saving their asses by throwing my brother under the bus."

"Wait—" Trinity held up a hand, eyes wide in the mirror. "Wait, wait, *wait*—Are you saying that the *Callaghans* had a part in this?"

"Yes."

Her entire face lit up in a terrifying display that Cade hoped was excitement.

Wes cleared his throat. "I don't think Fuentes would appreciate us using Hart as bait to nab Liam Callaghan, Trinity."

She frowned, shooting him a glare.

"I'm going to second his statement," Cade piped up, "and if you could drop me off here, that would be great. It'd probably be best for me to walk the rest of the way."

The car slowed, coming to a stop against the curb, which Cade immediately took as his signal to hop out. That is, until the locks reengaged. His head whipped around to see Trinity twisted in her seat.

"Your number first." She had her phone at the ready.

"And we'll give you ours," Wes added. "That way everyone can get ahold of each other. You text us when you know it's safe in there. If you're in danger, call and put your phone in your pocket so we can hear what's happening."

The brief exchange was followed by Cade's escape to the sidewalk, the passenger-side window immediately descending into the door.

"Text us in ten minutes," Wes said.

"Or we'll come up there and break down the door," Trinity finished.

He sighed and jogged down the block, heading up the steps to the apartment building. The drab interior was familiar and sickeningly comforting. A home away from home with worn down, cheap carpet tiles in the halls and mismatched numbers occasionally stickered or nailed to the doors. He took the stairs, dreading dealing with the rickety elevator with all the jokes he and Alyx made about it being one ride away from plummeting to the basement. Today wasn't the day to test his luck.

Once he was in front of her door, he rubbed his hands on his pants. He was working up the courage to knock like a guy about to ask a girl on a date, rather than pleading to crash on her couch. His hand finally fell against the wood, sounding his request. It could've been ten seconds or an eternity before the door swung open, but her surprise and relief made it all worth it.

"Holy shit, Cade." A towel dropped from her hand, her hair damp. She'd just gotten up for the day.

"Hey, Alyx," he said. "I don't want to be forward, but are you working for the Callaghans?"

Her eyebrows shot up. "What? Fuck no. Cade, are you okay?" She stepped aside, grabbing his arm and pulling him through the threshold.

That was all he needed to hear, sending him collapsing to the couch.

"Seriously, where have you been? I thought you left with Jay, especially once I heard about Liam's takeover last night when I went to ask the Martellis if they'd seen you. Emilio was *livid*."

Cade grimaced, cupping his hands around his mouth to try to hide it. "Yeah, I doubt he'll be all that thrilled with me either once he hears I rolled over on Jay."

"You *what?*"

"Jay asked me to kill someone for a job last week. It was a girl. She's Trick. I found out after Jay shot me because she *unshot* me, and I've been under house arrest in a safe house ever since."

"Oh… oh, my God…"

He released a mirthless laugh. "Liam figured out where I was and dragged me out this morning. I ran from him, and then this psychotic bitch I ran into the other night tried to burn me alive."

"But you're not hurt, right?" she asked, dropping down next to him. "You're okay, all things considered? Like, there's not a bullet hole or anything I need to call in a street doc for, right?"

She grabbed at his jacket, pulling it back to check for a tell-tale dark spot.

"I'm fine." He pushed her hand away. "As long as you don't tell Liam I'm here, yeah, I'll be fine." Cade checked the time on the wall, realizing that he'd already eaten up seven of his ten minutes.

"Trust me, I want *nothing* to do with the Callaghans."

"Then… would it be okay if I crashed here for a while? I don't really have anywhere to go, considering my place is likely crawling with Keepers for the foreseeable future."

"Yes, of course." She squeezed his shoulder, concern mixed with pity reflected in her expression. "I'd rather have you around than sell my soul to the Callaghans. At least you seem to have one."

A bitter chuckle escaped him, and he pulled out his phone to give the all-clear.

SATURDAY, APRIL 11TH AT 10:05AM

A secret nook key and a box of small, various items later, Evie was officially allowed to step foot out of the building with supervision. The only problem was that her mind was elsewhere on the drive over to her studio apartment. The new key in her hand anchored her to the other night that she'd spent with Cade where they had stopped time to play with water like a couple of children.

"The Custodians will pick up payments for your unit," Tarryn said, breaking Evie's daydream-like gaze out the window. "It's too dangerous for you to use it without the proper security, and the safehouse is better equipped for that anyway. So, I put in the paperwork for them to cover the cost a couple of days ago."

They'd already made it back to the parking garage a block away. The persistent dinging sound of Haven opening his door while the headlights were on added to the eeriness of returning here. She said nothing, simply climbing out when Haven opened her door. The incessant noise stopped as Tarryn followed.

Instead of bolting away from Haven and Tarryn this time, she stayed safely between them the entire walk. No need to grab her arm or drag her elsewhere. When they reached the lobby, Tarryn took her keys to check her mail, as if there might be a bomb sitting inside. There wasn't. It was just a bunch of ads again, to no one's surprise.

Possibly the most disturbing part of the trip yet was how her apartment looked like no one had broken in. In fact, the studio looked cleaner than it had the previous week. It felt *wrong*. The entire room was more like a staged apartment to tour, rather than the place she had returned to every night. Her entire world had changed, tainting this space along with it.

Shaking off that feeling, she started for the bed and slid a lockbox out from underneath. It took her a moment to flip through her keyring, but she found the one that matched, throwing it open to find the few items she needed. A collection of important documents, her grandpa's still-sealed letter, and a small stash of emergency cash. If any time should be considered an emergency, she decided it was now.

She shoved it all in a crossbody purse that hung off a hook on her closet door, and gradually spun around the room for one final sweep of anything else she might want to take. She wished she could ward it for a little extra piece of mind, but the mention of Inked around Tarryn hadn't gone over so well earlier.

"Anything else?" Tarryn asked from the entry, arms folded over her chest while Haven's face panned along the wall of posters and sticky notes.

Evie shook her head. "I think that's all I need."

It wasn't until they were on their way out that she noticed the ad on top of her mail pile. Another advertisement for a tattoo parlor, called *Lily of the Valley, Ink*. The name and logo burned into her mind, telling herself that perhaps if she had the opportunity, she could check it out and run into Inked there. With enough money, she might just be able to convince them to ward her house, at the very least.

The door shut behind her, and they headed for the archives.

11:09AM

A frosted, revolving glass door transported them into a circular lobby. Black, marbled flooring was ringed in accented gray, like the yellow warning lanes lining the subway tracks. From there, it dipped down into eight recessed stairwells. Each of the domed archways above them boasted a small Roman numeral below an emblem. A symbol for each of the primary eight factions. It was a dim, moody place with a large, wheel-like, chandelier, its clouded lights bolted on like protruding spokes.

Tarryn nudged her, interrupting her gawking to nod toward the curved desk straight ahead. A woman busied herself there, shuffling around folders and files without paying them any attention. Tarryn placed her hands on the upper portion that acted as a shelf, like the ones in hospitals, banks, and hotels. It was received with a blank stare.

"We would like access to one of the archives," Tarryn said.

"Name?"

Tarryn grabbed Evie's sleeve, pulling her forward.

"Evie Thatcher," she said automatically.

Typing ensued, her fingers quickly dancing over the keys before returning her gaze to them, launching into a rehearsed spiel, "The door to your archive is behind you, the one closest to the entrance on your right. If you need anything, please alert the Keeper or Mist manning the door. Unless you have a general question or concern about the archives, you won't need to alert me of your visit so long as you have permission from your current faction leader. Seeing as you have none, and you're registered as the holder of one of the signifying timepieces, you are technically the one in charge."

Evie's eyes went wide, the room swaying slightly. Tarryn coughed into her fist, thanking the woman, and immediately steered her away.

"*What?*" Evie asked.

"I *was* going to tell you," she mumbled, "but we got a little busy. Each faction has their own leadership roles and setup, and *yours* is based on whoever has those pocket watches. There's twelve in all, making a miniature council of Trick. That means, by default, you have the One seat of the Custodians."

Evie's shoes squeaked against the tile, skidding to a stop. "Excuse me? Oh no—no, no, no." She waved her hands in front of her. "I'm *not* leader material—At least not *that* kind of leader material. I can help run something I understand, but I can't run *this*. I have no idea what the hell I'm doing, Tarryn."

"Relax, It's not permanent—" A pause. "I think."

"You *think?* What do you mean you *think?*"

"I mean, we're about to find out, but you have to let us in the damn room down there first." She pointed down to the bottom of the steps, starting to push her toward it again with Haven on their heels.

Evie glanced back at the receptionist, her voice dropping to a whisper. "Is she Mist? She just… seemed so stoic."

"Yes, Mist are in charge of the archives since they don't fucking talk." She shot Haven a taunting glare, and he cracked his knuckles with a tight-lipped smile back at her.

"What do I do here?" Evie asked when they were only a few steps from the bottom.

"There's a mark on the door to only allow Trick to open it. Once it does, you have to permit us to join you, or else the Keeper at the bottom will pummel us if we try to follow. The Mist on the other side is for you to consult if you need help. They'll also sick the Keeper on someone if they have to." Tarryn subtly gestured to the two small nooks on either side of the bottom of the stairwell.

The Mist woman looked up from her book, giving a graceful nod of acknowledgment while the Keeper sat vigilant, side-eyeing Tarryn and Haven.

Evie hesitated, looking back to Tarryn for help. "How do I…"

"Place your hand in the indent," came the Mist woman's

voice, calm and instructing with a motion toward the small curve cut in half by the seam of the doors.

So, she did, holding it there as a pulse thrummed through her. Mechanisms whirred before it shuddered and opened inward. The lights began to flicker on one-by-one overhead, revealing a sea of deep blue, elegantly patterned carpeting and crushed velvet curtains obscuring faux windows. Shelves upon shelves of books and rows of filing cabinets clustered together, breaking up the library-like long tables. Absently, she walked inside, spinning as Tarryn cleared her throat.

Evie tensed. "I permit you two to enter." She hoped that would be good or formal enough, so when they crossed the threshold, she breathed a small sigh of relief. Soon after, the doors slowly shut behind them.

"Well…" Tarryn said, whistling while she and Haven took in the opulent space. "It looks like we've got a lot of paper to sort through, don't we?"

12:35PM

"This says…" Evie mumbled, reading off a page from one of their many books. "There are numbers in each one of the pocket watches. They're labeled one through twelve with one as the leader by default. Only the previous owner of the watch can decide to relinquish their position to another Trick. It goes on to explain that this is traditional to pass down through family lines, though not required. Exceptions occur if the previous owner dies, then the lowest living number gets to choose a successor…" She lifted her head to see Tarryn and Haven staring back at her. "But I… don't know how to open it without smashing it."

"Call me crazy, but I don't think you're supposed to smash the watch, Evie," Tarryn said.

"Well, I don't know how else I'm supposed to open it when it's jammed." A low, frustrated growl tickled the back of her throat while she drummed her fingers on the smooth, dark surface of the tabletop.

The letter.

She sat up straight, twisting in her seat to rip open her purse and retrieve it.

"What are you doing?" Tarryn asked cautiously. "Remember that you can't take anything—"

"I'm not. I have a letter I got back at my apartment that my grandpa left me when he died. It has a note on it instructing me to open it when nothing makes sense anymore, so now's as good of a time as any."

She gently unsealed it, tugging the letter free of its housing. Unfolding it, a wave of shock fell over her. It wasn't written by her grandpa. Her hands started to shake, tears blurring her vision and slipping down her face, unable to progress past the first words.

My sweet Evie.

This was from her *dad*.

"Are you okay?" Tarryn began to rise from her seat on the opposite side of the table, an abundance of concern that Evie never thought she'd see from her.

"*No,*" she choked out, letting the paper fold onto itself again and swiping at her face. She could've stopped all of this somehow, couldn't she? After all, that was her talent—a talent that she'd been able to use all this time but *hadn't*. Something that she continued to wish away in favor of normalcy.

Tarryn paused, hovering there as Haven passed, rounding the table and sitting himself into a chair next to her. He pulled her into a hug, like he empathically knew she needed it. Evie buried her face into his chest, and she let out a stifled sob when the memories rushed to greet her. This time, they weren't plucked out by him but surfaced through her own grief.

"I can't do this. I…"

Haven pulled away, hands firmly on her shoulders. His eyes bore into hers, a firm yet gentle look that indicated otherwise. Letting go, he picked up the letter, handed it to her, and began to wipe the tears from her face, all with a small, warm, encouraging smile. After a shaky breath of her own, she opened it again.

My sweet Evie,

I hope that I've destroyed this letter by now, but I didn't want to leave you without some sort of message if we don't come back. I know my parents will take care of you, but I would hate to not be able to see you grow up.

I want you to know that you're very special, and so very, very talented, even if you don't realize it yet. This world can be a scary and confusing place, but you're never alone. There are so many more like us, and it's our task to ensure that we never forget the mistakes of the past. It's why I'm leaving you here.

There are people who will try to silence you to prevent you from stopping them in their conquest, even with their disregard for everyone else. Don't let them. Learn everything you can and realize your true potential. Don't be silenced. Don't back down. We're running to bide our time, so we can fight together, stronger than before when the time comes.

*It's okay to be scared, but you're not weak.
Always remember that.*

Dad

"They… were running from something…" she said absently. "Someone was hunting them."

"Was there some sort of record created?" Tarryn asked, beginning to shuffle through the piles of folders on the table.

"But don't the Custodians control everything? Why run? What's more powerful than one of them?"

Tarryn paused, biting her lip. "Well, the night we got you, you were attacked by Fallen and Shade. Cade mentioned the Callaghans, who were working for the Harts, but he made it clear that it was a job, which means that either Jay masterminded it, or…" she trailed off, eyes flicking up from the pile. "*Or* someone *hired* him. Considering the Fallen's involvement, it's becoming more evident that these two splinters of their factions were sent out as hitmen."

"But *why?* What would someone gain from getting rid of them?"

Tarryn half-sat on the edge of the table, tapping the edge of a folder against her leg in a chopping motion. "There's something we're missing…"

Haven suddenly sat up straight, rapidly signing to her with a sharpness to his gaze. Tarryn's eyes went wide. "Holy shit—"

"What? What's he saying?" Evie's head whipped between them.

"I'm so stupid… Back when Cade confessed—the timeline doesn't add up." She shook her head. "He mentioned that his brother had been given that job *hours* before we found you—*hours* before the Fallen failed whatever they were sent to do. It's documented that Jay told him that you'd be alone in the room. The only types of people that could possibly know that are Spirits. But what we don't know is why a Spirit would do that."

Evie chewed her lip. "Have I actually met any Spirits?" If she had, she certainly hadn't recognized it.

Tarryn raised a single finger. "Desrosiers. She's the Spirit in charge of the safehouses."

The blood drained from her face, realizing that she had handed that woman all of her personal information.

"But if she was involved," Tarryn continued, "she would have the perfect opportunity for an 'accident' to happen so someone else could breach the safehouse, which hasn't happened. The other issue is that she could easily be called out by any other Spirit unless they happen to all be in on it, which I highly doubt. There's no way they'd all be able to keep a secret this big."

"What about the leader of the Custodians?" Evie asked. "Cade said he's on his way out at the end of the month because he's going to be replaced, and if he's one of the culprits, then he wouldn't want me to end up back in the One seat, right?"

Tarryn tilted her head back and forth. "While that's a reasonable assumption, the current Head seat of the Custodians *hates* Fallen, Shade, and Inked. He's openly discriminatory of them, and he's discussed initiatives to find the Trick for the duration of his term, so I can't imagine him wanting them eliminated. Not when there are three other factions for him to aggressively go after like that instead. It's why some of the newer candidates have reached out to make amends with them. Hell, with all the olive branches going out, I wouldn't be surprised if Spirit candidates start showing up to talk to you in the next few days."

Evie swallowed down a lump in her throat. "And what would stop them from killing me?" She jolted at Haven's hand resting on her shoulder.

"Us," Tarryn replied. "We'd stop them. Not to mention it would look bad on them. Whoever's behind this is going to have to try a different tactic since you're in the spotlight now, and they'll likely make a huge show of the Trick's return."

"Oh, no—Nope, that's the last thing I want right now."

"I hate to break it to you, but you're sort of out of options, Evie. There's going to be a huge turnover at the end of the month with how all these terms are lining up." She began ticking off the list on her fingers. "So, we're getting a new Spirit, Animated, Tears, Mist, Keeper… and, well I guess a new Shade since Jay's gone. It's a power system: toughest at the top until someone knocks them down."

Evie rubbed at her face. "And what if I can open the watch and prove that I'm one of the other eleven? Would that be enough to get me out of it?"

"There aren't any other Trick. It would still default to you."

Oh, hell no, she thought. *Not when I am completely ill-equipped for something like this.*

"What if we found the other Trick?" she asked quickly, everything beginning to tumble out. "I can't be the only one in New Atlas, and whatever Spirit is hunting them won't be able to take *all* of us out if we're together, right?"

Tarryn pressed two fingers to her forehead, closing her eyes. "While that does make sense, it would also make it easier to eliminate all of you at once. We're also assuming that this someone isn't just using a Spirit as a hunting dog or a Fallen with some Spirit leftovers, which could be a bit of a stretch." Her hand dropped, flipping open one of the folders and cocking an eyebrow.

"What? What's in it?" Evie stood, leaning over the table for a better look. Haven joined her, bumping shoulders as the three of them peered down at *transcripts*. The only problem: Roman numerals replaced what should be names. One through twelve. Like a clock. She grimaced, and then brightened, a thought springing up. Evie pulled the folder away and began leafing through the documents.

"What are you doing?"

"There must be a key of names in here, right? So, if I find my dad's name, I can connect it to a number, which should be the number in the watch, right? As long as it's not the number one, I'm clear, and we can find the person who *is*." She picked up speed, grumbling. "There's got to be a roster somewhere…"

Haven shook his head, catching her attention.

"What? Are you saying that there's not a roster?"

He grabbed her arm, forcing her to abandon the transcripts in favor of leading her back toward the door. Shutters sat on one side, which she assumed must be for the Mist woman. He pressed a button next to it, and the shutters opened, replaced with a thick glass and a kind face. Haven motioned for Evie to continue, giving her a small nudge forward.

"Um—I-I'm looking for a roster of the previous twelve leaders," she said. "Where might I find that?"

"I can provide you with that," the woman replied, igniting a spark of hope. "I just need your number, Miss Thatcher."

Evie froze. Something told her she wasn't talking about her phone or social security number. "I—um—"

"The number in your watch," she continued uncannily, much like how Haven seemed to pry into her thoughts with so much as a glance. "Certain numbers are restricted from accessing certain records."

Of *course* they were.

"Well, I…" Evie said, exchanging an uneasy glance with Haven. "I can't open it because I'm not sure *how*—That is, unless you could possibly help me with that?"

A small, patient smile spelled doom for her. "Unfortunately, no. I'm incapable of assisting you in that fashion, Miss Thatcher."

"Sorry to bother you, then," Evie said, feeling no small measure of defeat. "And thank you anyway."

"No need to apologize. This is what I'm here for."

Haven gave a small wave and hit the button again, shuttering the window before releasing a bit of a frustrated huff.

"Well, that didn't work as well as you hoped, did it?" Evie asked, watching his shoulders fall. "But I guess it was worth a shot." She turned, leading the way back over to Tarryn, who continued pouring over documents. "I can't get a roster without opening the watch."

"Go figure," she muttered, slapping another folder shut. "I'm wondering if it's got anything to do with that makeshift closet over there." She jabbed her thumb toward the double doors in the middle of the room, jutting out from the wall. "The Keeper's archives doesn't have a room like that. It could be an additional record room for sensitive information."

"A dead end..." Evie mumbled, deflating.

"But we at least have a guess at what could be happening, which is better than nothing." She began to gather up the files to put away. "In the meantime, you have about three weeks to wiggle out of the One seat."

Evie gave a nervous half-smile. *Fantastic.*

TWENTY
REN

"Do you seriously do this every night?" Ren mumbled, hunched in on himself as he kept up with Carmen's confident stride. He shivered, regretting his decision not to wear a jacket over his hoodie. He wished he hadn't talked himself out of it since they'd only be walking a handful of blocks. The subway ride had shielded them from the dropping temperature for the most part, though it failed to keep the other passengers from ogling Carmen.

She kept to her phone, her expression drawing close to boredom until the speaker system had announced their stop in a distorted, near-incomprehensible voice. It'd still given Ren enough time to scrutinize her work uniform, which fell somewhere close to the outfits the women working in the perfume and makeup department in a Lacy's would wear.

A black top with capped sleeves was hidden under her jacket, transitioning to thick leggings—also black—and high heels. The problem? Everything looked uncomfortably *tight*, and the heels had those stupid, thin, crisscrossing straps that Carmen had mentioned were 'gladiator style' back when she'd threatened to kick Angelo's ass with them on. All that, along with her dark, glittery makeup left his stomach knotted. It'd never crossed his mind to ask about the details of what her job entailed until tonight. He'd always assumed that she'd solely used her talent like Angelo did—well, unless he was recruited for a territory fight.

"I'm forced to take a break after six nights of work," she said, "so that's why I take Sundays off most weeks."

He eyed her with his chin buried in the edge of his hood. "And… um… what does your job entail, exactly?"

She slowed as they turned the corner, the sound of her heels softening against the concrete. Her brows furrowed in the dim lamplight of the alley, giving way to a reinforced side-door up ahead where a couple of guys leaned against the brick exterior, waving around cigarettes in animated conversation.

"I feed clients the dreams they ask for," she said. "Why are you looking at me like that?"

"You… you don't put *yourself* in those dreams, do you?"

She jolted back slightly, her shoulders popping up with a tensity that made her flush. "N-no! At least—Look, Ren—" She grabbed at her jacket, pulling it closed as she glanced over toward the other alleyway lurkers and dropped her voice to a near-whisper. "*Sometimes* they describe someone that *looks* like me, but I always embellish it so it's some warped version that's off enough I can detach from it."

His jaw dropped. "*Carmen*—"

"And *this* is why I wasn't fond of you tagging along for something like this," she ground out. "But I'm a grown-ass woman playing the cards I'm dealt to my advantage. So, yes, it happens, but it's *rare*. As long as they pay me, and I can give a cut to Flynn, I don't give a shit. He keeps me and all the other dream-weaving Shade that work for him safe from being harassed by anyone looking for another escape, and I can sleep at night knowing Mom won't drown in honest work."

"You can work honestly too, you know—"

"For table scraps, Ren." She started forward, all business again. Cold and unyielding in her stride toward whatever sleazy client might be lurking inside.

He jogged to catch up with her, clenching his jaw as the two loiterers erupted into chuckles over some shared joke. All while he and his sister stepped into the back hallway of the MacGuinness's vice hall. A faded green carpet runner muffled their entrance, sending a shiver through him as Carmen led the way through dimly lit halls. The overpowering scent of wood-toned colognes mixed with alcohol choked him as they passed cracked-open doors. Clinking glasses didn't seem all that appropriate when they'd lost to Liam and the Callaghans, though perhaps they had cut a better deal than Carmen had anticipated. Either way, Ren's true reason for being driven here had yet to be revealed.

She wrapped her knuckles on the final door, rewarding them with a gruff reply to enter. The man inside stood over the desk with peppered, chestnut hair, a pale, lightly freckled face adorned with stubble, and a crooked nose. Flynn MacGuinness. It was a name that Ren had heard growing up, mentioned under his mother's breath with occasional disdain or despair. He'd retired as the Six at the age of thirty-four. Ren wondered if he regretted stepping down eleven years later or if he was relieved that he never had to deal with Jay and his rise to power.

Those amber eyes flicked up, framing a hint of curiosity. No malicious glint to be found. "Leoni? Someone bothering you?"

Ren's eyebrows shot up for a second, surprised by the smooth, gentle way he'd asked. All concern, like a parent, rather than an employer.

Carmen shook her head. "I just got here—" She hesitated, glancing over at Ren and taking a shuffling step in the doorway for Flynn to see. "I actually wanted to make sure it was okay with you if I had my brother follow me around tonight. He's a Spirit, but our family is all Shade, so he was interested in seeing how things work around here."

Flynn pinned his sights on Ren, his mouth tipping down in a scrutinizing frown. "And how old are you?"

"Seventeen."

He folded his arms over his chest, shoulders relaxing at Ren's answer. "Normally the only spirits I allow behind the counter are trapped in bottles."

"Would you make an exception for one that can rig a table?"

Carmen shot Ren a glare, but he kept his eyes forward, stuck to Flynn as he ran a hand over his scratchy-looking stubble. After a hum, his attention drifted back to Carmen with a nod, her mouth parting enough to reveal her surprise.

"Why don't I take your brother off your hands for the night, so you don't have to babysit?" Flynn asked, bringing no pulsing warning in Ren's mind. "If he'd rather hang out with sixes than twos, who's to deny him a taste of what that's like before he signs his life away? It can only bring him some insight since Callaghan certainly won't sign him over to us without a hefty price."

And Carmen wouldn't let Ren sign himself over to the Shade at *all*, regardless of who was in charge. Not if she had any say in it.

"I-I don't want to inconvenience—" Carmen started, cut off by the shake of Flynn's head.

A sly smile tugged at his lips. "It's no problem for me. I'd like to test a Spirit out in the main hall." He motioned for her to be on her way with a casual flick of his hand, and she took a shuffling step back. Ren felt her fingers dig into his shoulder with a warning squeeze before she vanished down the hall. Flynn was already at the door to fill that void. "All right, kid, you got a name?"

"Ren."

"Follow me, Ren."

He pushed open the door next to his office, holding it open for him. From there, he led the way down another corridor that emptied out into what must be the main hall. Warm, moody lighting fell over red-felt craps and card tables, roulette wheels, and backgammon boards. But the one thing that slowed Ren's pace was the sight of a woman snapping her fingers to summon a flame in response to the roulette wheel's attendant that called out black. The man next to her clamped a hand over hers with a hiss. There were Animated, Tears, and even *Keepers* playing the odds. Flynn didn't break his stride, weaving toward what Ren picked out as a blackjack table.

This was *normal*, despite how he'd assumed that they would've only catered to other Shade, Inked, and Fallen. Rumpled suits and wrinkled dresses marked the few Spirits lining the bar, adhering to the small signs posted at the tables that warned against use of certain talents—talents that Ren was about to use as the exception to amuse the owner.

He hovered along the wall, watching Flynn's gesture toward the blackjack table and leaned over to whisper, "Tell me what's about to happen."

On command, Ren's talent spilled forth like Flynn had called on a genie, pouring into every facet of the hall, greedily reaching into all the micro-moments about to pass. He sucked in a breath, unable to shove it all back in the bottle.

"He'll fold because he's afraid to bust," Ren said, nodding to a man at a table before redirecting to point toward the roulette wheel next, mid-spin. "It's landing on red." Then the craps table as the dice were being thrown. "She'll win with a four."

In rapid succession, the guy shook his head, folding, the roulette attendant declared red, and cheers erupted at the final destination. Flynn whistled, his eyes going wide. "And here I thought you'd tell me you only read palms or some shit."

"Did you want a palm reading?"

He chuckled. "Impressive, but I'll pass." All mirth vanished from his face in an instant, and Ren's head turned to find the source of Flynn's shift in mood. In the entrance stood a man that Ren recognized. That familiar form was no longer a ghost of a vision from a tarot card but an actual person in the flesh.

David Sterling.

"Excuse me a moment," Flynn mumbled, pushing off the wall.

He hurried across the room to meet him, weaving between guests in their rotation toward another game in search of better luck. A number was called from the entrance to a set of double doors at the far end of the hall, and a Spirit at the bar knocked back the rest of his drink before beelining toward it in answer. His stomach clenched when the guy vanished inside, deducing why any Spirits would hang around here if they were banned from playing games. It was because they were getting their fantasy fix from someone like Carmen.

Ren swallowed back that unease, ducking his head as Flynn guided Sterling through the side aisle with a hand clapped on his shoulder. He was backtracking to his office. Ren started after them once they were out of sight, slipping down the hall and waiting at the staff-only door, straining to listen.

"Don't waste your time with Liam," came Flynn's cold tone. Ren tensed, his pulse throbbing in his neck as Sterling's surprised expression emerged in his mind, the entire scene beyond the door spreading out like a watercolor.

"Why?" he asked, shifting his posture one too many times in a matter of seconds. "We had a deal that you could introduce me to whoever the new Six was—"

"Don't bother with this one," Flynn said, his voice hitting a near-growl, laced with disdain. "Liam is a rabid animal that needs to be put down. You offer your hand in peace to him, and he'll rip it off. You'll make an ass of yourself in the process and lose the race."

Sterling scoffed, his face turning sour. "I'm not here for advice, Flynn. I'm here to secure a meeting with Liam from a past Six that might be able to mediate a little for the good of the Custodians."

"And that's not something Liam or the Callaghans *want.*

You're trying to talk to someone who's power-hungry. I'll say it again: don't waste your time. Walk away."

Sterling threw up his hands. "Do you *want* this establishment shut down?"

Ren reared back, ripping himself away from the door, but not his vision.

"You wouldn't," Flynn snapped. "Not when it would cost you your damn dream-highs you're always chasing."

An image of Carmen flashed in his mind before it morphed into another girl—a blonde, tall, timid-looking creature. That was enough for Ren to force the vision down, sending bile rising in its place. He threw a hand against the wall, feeling the fabric-textured golden wallpaper with the other cupped over his mouth.

Keep it together.

He had to until Carmen's shift was over in a couple hours. He sure as hell wasn't going to cost her money for the sake of this little escapade. Plus, he'd gotten some new information— new information that could ruin David Sterling's reputation, at the very least.

TWENTY-ONE
CADE

Watching a weekend late-night drama with Alyx hadn't been how Cade had thought his night would end up, but since she'd ordered and paid for dinner, he didn't complain. He sank further into the couch, unsure if he was eyeing the Chinese containers littering the coffee table with the gluttonous urge for more, or with regret. Either way, he knew it was a war within him to try to keep his mind off Evie.

She didn't look at him like he was beneath her or like someone she could abuse the name of to get whatever she wanted. She had told him that he had a good heart. She'd actually *kissed* him—even if it was just a quick, playful peck on the cheek. At least it had been sincere in some way.

"You look like someone crushed your soul, dude."

He rolled his eyes, trying to play off getting caught. The show had vanished from the screen to the roll of commercials, which Alyx took as her cue to mute the TV.

He moaned. "Alyx… Can we just *not* talk about me for a while? I already know my life is in complete shambles."

"Wait—*wait*—" Her eyes lit up, nearly sparkling as her voice climbed with excitement. "Did you *meet* someone? Does Cade Hart have a *crush?* That would explain why this stupid show is making you so damn quiet. I usually can't get you to shut the hell up. Spit it out. What's her name? Or his name—their name?"

"*Alyx*—"

"Oh, no—*Sir*, if you're crashing at my place, I want to know if I'm ever going to come back to you having wild sex on my couch."

"Trust me on this," he said sternly. "That won't be happening."

"All right, all right—" She held her hands up defensively. "No need to get all snippy about it... I'm going to assume it's a *girl*..."

Cade cut her a glare.

"Is she cute? If she's not into you, can I take a swing at her?"

"No, no you can't. Back off."

"Cute, got it."

"Cut it out, Alyx." He groaned, trying to find some way to disappear into the couch cushions.

"Well, you're not denying it, so I'm on the right track. Not to mention that I've never seen you so torn up before. You're pissed at your brother, but my intuition says this is different... Maybe we can pay her a visit tonight?" She grinned, playfully punching him in the shoulder.

"Drop it. Seriously, Alyx."

"Give me one good reason—"

"Because she's Trick."

She reared back, eyes going wide. "*Shit*—Cade, you can't—"

"I *know*, Alyx, which is why I don't want to talk about it. I know that's a line I shouldn't cross, which is why I'm trying to tell myself to stop. I don't want to drag her down with me." He trailed off into a near-mumble, trying to soften the blow for himself. He knew that he shouldn't have pushed those boundaries to begin with, but it had just snowballed. She made him feel different, which made it that much harder to walk away.

"I'm sorry, Cade," Alyx said. "How about… we go out tonight?"

He scoffed. "You can't be serious."

"There's a place in Heaven's Gate I think would be fun, and it's a weekend, so…" She hopped up. "Since you're clearly feeling down, let's lose ourselves with a bunch of strangers, loud music, and copious amounts of alcohol." She put on a bright, dazzling smile.

"Pass."

Her face fell, changing to something a little more determined as she reached down and seized his arm. "My house, my rules." She forced him up, grabbing his jacket and throwing it at him while she collected her own.

"Alyx…" he said with a sigh.

"Shut the hell up. We're going."

TWENTY-TWO
CADE

Cade woke with a raging hangover, cringing while he tried his best not to move. The good news: he had made it to the couch. The bad news: everything hurt. He was nothing more than a ball of pain between his throbbing head and—for whatever reason—his back stung, almost like it had been sunburnt. The thought crossed his mind that perhaps he wasn't on *Alyx's* couch, but some random couch on a rooftop somewhere.

He cracked an eye open. Nope. He was in Alyx's apartment, face-down on her couch, all right. Groaning, he tried to recall what had happened last night, but could only conjure up a blur of colors and sounds. He had to have had a good time to completely forget how he had gotten back here. Cade propped himself up on his elbows with a grimace.

What the hell is wrong with my back?

He supposed that possibly his jacket had caught on fire, and this was the result of getting singed. Cade prepared himself to mourn the loss of his favorite article of clothing. Sure, he'd gotten some new stuff while he was in the safehouse, but it was all tee-shirts and jeans stuffed in a trash bag in the corner of Alyx's living room. A bunch of stuff that the lovely Wes and Trinity had dropped outside once they circled back to the safehouses with the all-clear. When he sat up, he saw his jacket crumpled on the floor, still fully intact.

A hand to his head, he winced and stood to start for the bathroom, swaying slightly in his trek down the hall. He fumbled for the bathroom light, flicking it on with a hiss and quickly closing his eyes. Grappling with the medicine cabinet, he pried it open and squinted at each of the bottles inside before finding the one he wanted. He unscrewed the cap and knocked back a pill with a handful of water from the sink. The mirror in the cabinet door wobbled as he haphazardly threw it back into place, the magnets keeping it from bouncing free again.

When he finally looked up, he had to do a double take, his eyes going wide at his own reflection. He wasn't sure he'd call his next reaction a *yell*, but it was definitely an outburst, or at the very least, a cry of surprise. "What the fuck?"

A thump in the hallway, and a shadowy figure emerged from the bedroom to peer into the bathroom doorway, her face lighting up with amusement. "Oh, my God." she choked out, clapping a hand over her mouth to poorly hold back a snicker.

"It's not fucking funny, Alyx!" He ran his hand through the section of his hair that was now dyed fire-truck red. A large chunk right in the front. "Where the hell did we go last night? And why does my back—"

Horror gripped him with the sudden thought that an Inked had gotten a hold of him. An *Inked* had gotten a hold of him, and his back felt *sunburnt*. He began yanking open the vanity drawers, ignoring Alyx's giggles. It took him far too long to find another mirror, but he found a compact. Snapping it open, he grabbed the back of his shirt collar and pulled it over his head.

Alyx's gasp sent a spike of anxiety shooting through him, fearing the worst. He dropped the shirt on the floor, turning around and angling the compact toward the bathroom mirror.

"Son of a bitch," he hissed. Sure enough, there it was. Unfurled, geometric angel wings with an embellishment of ink splotches, like an artist accidentally spilling on a canvas.

"That... actually looks pretty cool," she said quietly.

"Does it?" He snapped the compact shut, aghast. "Because I'm less than stoked about this when I don't recall consenting to this shit."

"I mean, it's better than the alternative."

"And what the hell would that be?"

"A tramp-stamp."

He had little doubt that his expression teetered on murder, flattening into borderline irritation. She gave a sheepish smile, and he dipped down to retrieve his shirt. "Well, say goodbye to the mural, Alyx."

"What? Why?" She motioned toward the mirror. "It's cool!"

"What's the name of the club we went to last night?" he asked, ignoring her pleas. "I need to hunt down a damned Inked."

She sighed, slumping against the doorframe. *"The Funhouse."*

"Great," he said, pulling on his shirt. "Sounds like a little too much fun."

"If it helps, I saw you disappear with some short, blonde girl. Think she had teal in her hair?" She tugged on a short, brown lock of her own.

Cade froze, hand on the doorframe. "Please say you're kidding."

"I'm... kidding?" Her smile turned uneasy and questioning.

He leaned against the frame, bumping his forehead against it with a groan. "This is the week from hell I just can't escape."

TWENTY-THREE
EVIE

Tarryn and Haven had stopped by to check on Evie early that morning, excusing themselves to deal with finishing up some outstanding casework. After Tarryn's brief reminder to text if she needed them for anything, they left. The moment the door had shut, Evie shot across the room, straight for her laptop, and pulled up a page to search for that tattoo parlor: *Lily of the Valley, Ink.*

Their website boasted a sampling of premade designs, customer reviews, and a portfolio of custom work. She tilted her head as she clicked on the company page, where she scrolled through a short blurb about its history before she scrolled back up, and her eyes caught on the top banner. The dynamic profile of a familiar face stared off somewhere past the edge of her monitor. It was the guy from the other night—the one who had been staring at her and Cade at the end of the bar.

That confirmed her suspicions. This shop employed Inked, which also gave her a destination for today. If the Inked could create wards, then perhaps she could not only commission one to add them to her property, but maybe they'd be able to help her break whatever kept her pocket watch sealed.

Evie snapped her laptop shut and grabbed her thin jacket and shoes. Wallet, keys, and phone tucked safely into her pockets, she tugged her hood over her head and crept out into the hall. It was empty, like she had expected since she was confident that no one else was staying on her floor now.

It was a nervous elevator ride down, her heart picking up speed as the numbers counted down the floors. Her mind kept skipping back to that sanctuary-like spa with Cade, flexing that mental muscle for what she needed to do next. When the doors opened, she ducked into the alcove she had hid in the day before and began to try to work her talent.

She took deliberate, even breaths, putting every bit of her concentration into forcing the pocket around her to stop. The guards' movement slowed, all of them facing away from the exit. Without another second to think, she ran, hurtling straight for the door, shoving it open and immediately shutting it behind her, praying it wouldn't leave any evidence of her escape. After she was out of view, she glanced back, letting it all go. No one followed.

Evie began to walk a little taller as she retrieved her phone, shaking slightly with how she'd managed to pull that off. But she didn't dwell on it, instead she pulled up the address for her destination, and headed straight for the parlor.

11:42AM

Lilies crowded around the looping, cursive script logo on the storefront window of her destination. Evie tucked her phone back into her pocket and grabbed the door handle, stepping into a deserted Inked wasteland of doodles posted along the walls and tiled out onto countertops under a membrane of glass and sleek, black décor. The place was empty, save one pale-looking, black-haired guy who glanced up at her entrance.

Surprisingly, he didn't greet her in a menacing or creepy way like she had anticipated, but more like the sound of a distant relative welcoming her home. "What can I do you for, sweetheart?" he asked, starting for the counter.

"I—um—I'm looking for a guy I ran into a couple nights ago," Evie said. "He's tall, brown hair, ear-cuffs… I can't recall his name, but I was wondering if he could help me design something."

"Oh, you mean Aiden? Sorry, but he's helping with some redecorating at one of his other gigs right now. If you'd like, I can take down your information for him to set up an appointment though."

"No- no, it's fine." She shook her head. "Actually… Would it be okay if I met him over there?"

He smirked, a strange, still-friendly glint in his eye. "Sure. I can't imagine he'd say no to a bright-eyed little thing like you." He grabbed a pad of sticky notes and a pen, jotting down an address.

"Thank you so much," she said, taking the note from him. He puffed up at the gratitude, giving a brief nod on her way out.

Fifteen minutes later, she stood outside an old factory, much like the *Teal* nightclub she'd been to the other night. The brick was painted over with a dark gray with checkered strips of black and white squares around the base of the building. Fuchsia tags and patterns were sprayed above it, much of it hard to read.

"*Hey—*"

She jumped, spinning on her heel to find none other than Cade. He looked just as surprised as she did.

"What the hell are *you* doing here?" he asked, looking around with furrowed brows. "Where's Tarryn and Haven?"

She barely heard him over the bright-red streak screaming at her. "What the hell happened to your hair?" She pointed up at it, and he gently slapped her hand down.

"I do *not* want to talk about that right now. You, on the other hand, should really be more careful because I thought you were

Inked, and I was *this close* to beating the shit out of you." He held up his thumb and forefinger, spacing them less than an inch apart.

It turned into a struggle to suppress a giggle. Her mouth twitched, and she ducked her face into her jacket collar.

"Stop that."

"I'm sorry, but didn't you say not to play with Inked after dark?"

"Oh, *ha-ha*. Look at Cade. He's a dumbass. Very funny, moving on…"

"Okay," she started, pressing a finger to his chest. "Then what are *you* doing out here?"

He scoffed, grabbing his hair. "To undo *this*. It doesn't come out. Trust me, I just tried using everything I could get my hands on. It's pretty fucking permanent, and there's no way in hell it's staying. But *you* better have a damn good reason for trekking out here by yourself, or else I'm throwing you in a taxi, taking you back to the safehouse, and telling your Keepers that you've been sneaking out. How the hell did you even get out in the first place?"

She gave a noncommittal shrug. "Oh, just… jumped off the balcony and nearly broke my neck." Her mouth quirked up in a smirk, which caused Cade to fold his arms over his chest. "Fine, I froze time in the lobby and made a break for it."

He raised an eyebrow, looking somewhat impressed now. "Seriously?"

"Well, I waited until they were turned and hoped for the best. It just sort of worked out, I guess."

He released a breathy laugh. "That doesn't quite answer why you're here, but I'll let it slide. After I'm done ripping a couple of Inked apart, we're going straight back to the apartments." He brushed past her, leaving her with no small amount of annoyance at his sudden, responsible attitude.

But Evie turned to follow him anyway, jogging inside though the wide-open doors. It was a plain space, the interior painted black with concrete floors and strung exposed lightbulbs. What little furniture there was had been shoved up against the walls. She frowned, her pace slowing as she tried to make sense of why anyone would want to come here.

She cut a glance toward Cade, whose face was angled upward. About two stories above them, a metal, grated catwalk bridged the concrete, where the guy from the bar stood with his back to them—glinting silver ear-cuffs and all.

"Aiden!" Cade called, cupping his hands over his mouth.

Aiden turned to peer down, looking rather annoyed until he took in the sight of Cade. He smirked, leaning against the railing. "Well, well…" came his velvety voice. "Look who's back for more."

"Where is she?" Cade demanded. "You two are going to fix what you did right *now*."

He rolled his eyes, which only served to egg Cade on. "Uh huh… That's not how this works, but feel free to keep yelling."

"I want to speak to the damn manager."

His request was answered with the sound of light, airy footsteps against the metal grating, matching a smaller frame that came into view. A woman with long, blonde hair, streaked through with teal, wearing a long-sleeved knee-length knit navy dress with a black suit vest overtop and leggings. Her face lit up when she saw Cade, which gave Evie an uneasy feeling in the pit of her stomach.

"You're back!"

"You bet your ass I'm back, Lily," Cade said, fuming. "Now get the hell down here and undo whatever the hell you did to me last night. You can start with the hair."

Humming, she tapped a pen to her lips. In her sweet, girlish voice, she finally replied, "No."

"Excuse me?"

"I said no." She grinned. "Request denied. Bye-bye." She wiggled her fingers at him.

"I don't think you understand—"

"No, I don't think *you* understand, little shadow." Her voice began to teeter on the edge of dark as she threw her arms wide. "This is a game of chess, and I'm playing two steps ahead." Her fingers formed a V holding them up next to her eye like some sort of magical girl in a cartoon. She spun the pen with her other hand, leaning forward when her gaze caught on Evie.

"What the hell are you on about?" Cade asked, pulling those greenish-blue eyes off of her.

"You'll get it later. Maybe—Eh, it doesn't really matter." She waved a dismissive hand. "All that matters is that you got a new tattoo, and I got to make something really cool."

Evie's eyebrows shot up, her face unable to contain her amusement. "A *tattoo?* Is it a tramp-stamp?"

"Why are you not the first person to say that?"

Lily's fist slammed against the railing. "Now why the hell didn't *I* think of that?" She pouted in Aiden's direction, who rolled his eyes. "Bah, I guess there's always a next time." She shrugged.

"No, there will *not* be a next time, Lily. Especially when I don't appreciate that there was a first time."

"All right, I'm done with you." Lily made a motion to shoo him away. "You're a broken record. I'm more interested in your girlfriend."

Evie and Cade exchanged glances, both denying the statement simultaneously.

"I'm not—"

"She's not—"

"*Sure,*" Lily crooned with a smirk. "What are you here for?"

"She's not here for anythin—"

"Can you open this?" Evie held up her pocket watch from around her neck, feeling a chill run down her spine at the way Lily's eyes went wide and excited. Even Aiden cocked his head in interest. Cade was the only one of them that shuffled forward hesitantly.

"So, you're the Trick that's suddenly thrown the Custodians

into a frenzy," Lily said. "Interesting that you'd be so bold as to waltz on in here with a lowly Shade, no less. My, *my*... What would the other upper levels think?"

Evie tried to stand her ground. "I don't really care what they think or say. I'm here because I don't know what I'm doing, and I'm hoping that one of you can help me open this. That's it. I can pay you—"

Lily tisked, scowling. "I don't want money, *Trick*. And I don't think you realize who you're talking to, either."

The blunt transition took her off-guard, Lily's tone no longer playful like she had been with Cade. Evie was beginning to think that she had misstepped somewhere in her request, but she was completely unsure of *where*. Aiden pushed away from the railing, walking past Lily to somewhere out of view, his predatory gaze unwavering.

Lily snapped her fingers, sending a jolt through Evie as the doors swung shut behind her. Evie stifled a yelp, grabbing onto Cade's jacket, despite noticing how he'd jumped a little too. A cat-like grin appeared on Lily's face, leaving Evie with that horrible sense of regret. Her only saving grace was Cade pushing her part-way behind him to shield her.

She proudly threw her arms wide. "Bow before the Queen of the Inked. The Seven of the Custodians."

Evie's heart dropped. There wasn't a single visible tattoo on this woman, yet Evie had just hit two for two in the bad impressions department for the Custodian seats. First Jay had tried to kill her, and now Lily might very well do the same. After a moment of cowering, Lily pouted, like it wasn't as much fun as she had hoped it would be.

"It seems I have two players in a game where all the pieces are painted black on the board to hide that some are white underneath..." She squinted at them. "You two, however..." A finger pointed in the air, her face brightening again. "Quiz time! What are the two most important pieces on a chess board for a single side?"

"Lily," Cade started, "We're not here for a damned qui—"

"The king," Evie said quietly, shutting Cade up as Lily pointed toward her. "And… the queen."

"Correct! Educate yourself, Hart. So, little Trick, what happens if someone takes out the queen?"

Evie shifted uncomfortably, not particularly fond of where this metaphor was going, especially if it was in reference to *them*. If she was implying that Cade was the strongest piece in her twisted game, then once he's out of the way…

"You leave the king vulnerable," Evie answered, *really* hoping that she wasn't referring to *her*.

"And what happens when the king's knocked over?" she asked, her grin going a little more impish.

Evie swallowed. "The game's over."

The entire building went dark, ripping a surprised gasp from Evie's lungs. Lily let out a long, maniacal giggle from above, resulting in Cade squeezing Evie's arm.

"Make it to the exit at the other side of the room," echoed Lily's sing-song instructions, "and I might let you leave. But I call this place *The Funhouse* for a reason."

Evie wasn't entirely sure that Lily was still above them now, her voice no longer seeming to carry the way it had before.

"That's enough, Lily!" Cade shouted. "We're not playing your stupid gam—"

"Three, two—"

"*Lily!*"

"*One!*" she cheered.

The lights turned back on, flooding the space with an eerie, pinkish glow. Where the concrete had been, large black and white tiles sat, almost like a chess board. Red, velvet curtains draped over the walls, and gold, classical chandeliers hung from the ceiling. The grated catwalk was gone. The *doors* were gone.

"It's all fake," Cade breathed. "Just ignore everything between here and the other side. If we run, she can't mess with our minds. Ready?" His face turned toward her, looking for confirmation.

The comforting grip of her hand in his allowed her to nod, briefly looking him in the eye. *This* wasn't something she expected the Inked to be capable of. And when they bolted forward, the traction and the squeaking of her shoes on the tiles sent a shiver through her.

None of this is real. It's an old factory. None of this is real.

Flickers of triggered illusions fell out of her peripheral vision. She swore she could hear Lily giggling somewhere behind them. Evie pushed herself to go faster, and Cade did too, keeping pace until someone grabbed the back of her jacket. She gasped, her hand ripping free of Cade's. That horrible déjà vu feeling of coming face-to-face with Jay stopped her heart.

"Oh, no you don't—" came the voice of her captor.

She stumbled, helplessly watching Cade turn back for her and smacking straight into some invisible barrier. She managed to catch herself in the backward progress, finding Aiden between her and the exit now. The sound of Cade and Lily's voices clashed behind him in a shouting match while Aiden mumbled something she tried to make out. He seized her arm, deftly drawing something on her hand with a pen.

The room fell quiet, muffling the bickering behind him like everything was under water. Her hand fell to her side as he capped the pen, and she tried to bend her knee to run. It didn't budge. Nothing moved, despite her push to escape. Her full attention was stuck on Aiden, unable to pull away from it. Minus that sense of urgency, her senses were so... *dulled.*

"What's your name?" he asked, leaning forward. His tone smooth and coaxing in an inviting way that unnerved her.

"Evangelina Melody Thatcher." It had slipped out automatically, sounding emotionless to her own ears. "But I go by Evie."

"Pretty," he said, smirking. "All right, Evie. Now what is your worst *fear?*"

This question gave her pause, not so much because she didn't know, but more of the fact that she wasn't positive of the correct word. She had lost nearly everyone she had ever cared about through the years, so she almost answered that she was afraid of being alone. Though, the problem with that is that she lived alone, but she was never lonely. She had always had someone a phone call or text away, even if there weren't that many people she talked to. It was something deeper than that.

"Isolation." She supposed that was one of the reasons she had left with Cade that night they snuck out. She was overwhelmed by stacks of papers with foreign rules and having no way to contact the last or her family or the friend she thought she knew. She'd been separated from the life she had known before this. She'd begun to feel less afraid of that until this very moment, noticing how white walls appeared to build themselves up around them.

Aiden glanced down, gently lifting the pocket watch away from her neck. In his other hand, the pen turned over and over again in a fluid, infinite motion. He twisted the timepiece around, checking every millimeter of its surface, his face dipping into a thoughtful frown. Rubbing his thumb over a spot in the middle of the backing, he tilted it toward her. A faint, flowing mark stared back at her—the same mark that sat over the Trick's archives.

"I'm afraid that you are the only one who can open this," he said. "If it wasn't marked, I could, but clearly the Trick have made good use of Inked in the past, haven't they?" He hooked a finger at the top of her jacket zipper and dropped the watch inside.

Strangely, it was comforting that he even bothered to examine it since it meant that he and Lily weren't trying to kill her. There wouldn't be a point in any of it if they were. This was just a game to him—a way to feed off her fears for amusement while he obliged her request.

"Are you afraid of me?" he asked in an even, slightly bemused tone.

"No."

He raised an eyebrow, tapping the pen to his lips. "Interesting… You do realize that I could do whatever I wanted to you right now, and no one would be able to stop me, right? We're alone."

But the white walls were fake. Cade's reminder that none of this was real rang true in her thoughts. "You could, but you won't. I think you like to play the part, but I don't believe that either of you are the people trying to get rid of me."

He let out a short, sharp laugh. "You're *very* lucky that we're on the same side of the board, Miss Thatcher. But I have a feeling you're mixing up your pieces, and if you want to properly play this game, you should consider re-examining the situation before you proceed." He hummed for a moment, eyeing her. "Though, I am curious as to why you're bothering with Inked and Shade to help you when your best bet is to stay near the top with the more *civil* levels of the Custodians. They'd say you're treading dangerous waters. You might as well be isolated then, wouldn't you?"

"Maybe I'm ignorant of how all this works, but… I don't really care what anyone is. I don't see how it matters because I could be just as destructive, right?"

A chuckle. "So, since you're relatively new, haven't you thought about just… *forgetting* all of this? You could walk away. You don't have to deal with any of us if you really don't want to." He was baiting her. She could see right through that with his smug smile.

As much as she had thought about it, did she really want a normal life now?

"Is there something you've discovered that you don't want to forget now?" he mused, gauging her reaction with mischief sparking in his eyes. "Or, rather, *someone*."

Fear surged through her, bringing back that sense of urgency to break free. Cade was still somewhere dealing with Lily beyond Aiden's fake white walls. She guessed Aidan was losing his grip based on how the dullness was drifting away from her.

"I'm sure we'll be seeing more of each other. If not me, certainly Lily, considering you're the only Trick for the council seat. For now, try to stay out of trouble. I'd hate to see you killed before Lily's done with her game."

He uncapped the pen, grabbed up her hand, and struck through the mark, snapping her free of her haze. The illusionary white walls crumbled as she tried to back up, only to be ripped forward and past him. A shove sent her colliding with Cade, sending him against the wall, where a panel fell away.

"Until next time!" Lily called cheerfully, sending them plummeting down a ramp.

They screamed on the rapid descent to the bottom, echoed by Lily's giggles somewhere beyond the chute. Foam chunks flew out from under them, and Evie gasped, scrambling up at Cade's groan.

"Shit…"

"Sorry—Sorry!" she said, trying to crawl off of him, her head whipping around to cinderblocks and cement outside the foam bin with a few stacked tubs propped up along the walls. The basement. "Are you okay?"

"Yep," he said, grimacing as he sat up. "You might as well have slapped a target sticker on your forehead though. Why the hell would you ask them to open that watch?"

"Because if I can't open it, then I can't access the special records section," she said. "And if I can't access the special records section, I can't find another one of the Trick with a watch that has a number lower than mine, which means I can't find someone to take the council seat that I *really* don't want."

"Wait, there's numbers? Like, numbers other than the ones on the clock face?"

"Yes. And there are twelve watches."

"And what if your watch has the number one in it? Then what?"

"It better *not*." She pointed up the chute. "You saw how great that went. Do you really think I can handle myself around the rest of the Custodians?" She sighed and rubbed her forehead.

Cade pushed himself up, standing unevenly in the pit while he offered her a hand. "Come on."

She took it, teaming up to climb out of the pile. A set of stairs led them up to a door, which emptied them outside to an alley. She pulled her hood back up, and Cade tucked his hands into his pockets, as if nothing in the building had happened. The two of them walked in comfortable silence to the street, and eventually strolled until the waterfront came into view somewhere in the distance.

"So," she started, "are you going to drag me back to Tarryn and Haven now?"

He came to a stop, his head dipping down and away slightly, giving her pause.

"Evie, I think you should really consider keeping your distance from the Shade and Inked."

She hesitated, narrowing her eyes some with confusion. "Um... why?"

"I... I get that maybe I encouraged it before, but—" He shook his head, his expression somewhat regretful. "But it doesn't look good for you to be seen with people like me. It's the fastest way to get yourself painted as an outcast."

She scoffed. "Seriously? Why does that matter? Outside of Haven and Tarryn, you've been the one to help me the most so far. You act like I care about some weird social system that you guys have—"

"Maybe you should start caring. Once new people begin filling in those council seats, you'll have to deal with them, even if you're not sitting in the One's chair. It'll determine the allies you make, and the Inked and Shade aren't good choices, especially with Liam running things. When it comes down to it, I *have* to defer to him, even if I don't want to." He tapped his chest. "I don't want to see you caught up in that."

"Cade, I don't care about their stupid politics and how they categorize people. I'm not just going to cut you out. You've answered so many of my questions and explained things that Haven and Tarryn skirt because they don't want to approach it. I don't want to assume that everyone in the 'upper-levels' or whatever is my ally because it's likely that someone from this is orchestrating getting rid of me."

His eyes went wide. "You're serious? You honestly think one of them is coordinating this?"

"What reason would the Inked and Shade have, Cade?" she asked, motioning back toward *The Funhouse*. "The Shade were hired as hitmen, and the Inked seem to do whatever because no one really needs them anymore, right? Lily and Aiden could've gotten rid of us back there if that's what they really wanted."

He tilted his head from side-to-side before begrudgingly nodding.

"Plus, I trust you." She watched how his eyes awkwardly darted away, unable to face her sincerity. She worked up a smug look, trying to lighten the mood. "Or is all this your way of telling me to get lost after hitting on me for a week? You no longer interested now that you're a free man?"

"What? N-no—" he sputtered. "I just—I didn't want Liam to get any ideas."

"So… are you just going to hide from him forever?"

He leaned against the walkway railing with a sigh. "Either that or wait until someone who doesn't care about me knocks him down."

She rested her arms on the railing next to him, glad to stay out with him a little while longer.

"Hart!"

Evie went rigid as Cade snapped to attention, his head swiveling toward the woman's voice.

"Oh, shit—" He blocked her view, grabbing the edge of her hood to cover her face a little more. "Keep your head down and pretend you're Shade. These are the two Keepers that picked me up the other day."

Evie's eyes went wide as Cade turned, hunching over in her jacket with a prayer that they didn't have a picture of her or something.

"You're supposed to answer your damned phone," the woman continued as she approached. "Not flirt, so let's start with who the hell this is—" She casually pointed in Evie's direction, shock taking over her features and bringing her to a stop mere feet away.

It was only then that Evie didn't bother trying to obscure her face anymore, her hand falling away from the edge of her hood while a guy jogged up behind this Keeper. An old friend. The one who gifted her a flimsy little friendship bracelet that year her grandpa gave her the watch hanging around her neck. Trinity Avery.

"Is this your roommate, or your girlfriend, Hart?" her partner asked as he slowed next to her.

"Neither."

The answer hadn't come from Evie or Cade, but Trinity, who stood there in stunned bafflement. Cade cleared his throat, eyeing her uneasily. "Well, uh—my friend probably needs to get going now—"

Trinity shot forward, grabbing Evie's arm and yanking her away from him. "Oh, *hell* no. She's not going anywhere. Stay away from this loser, Evie."

"Wait—what?" Cade's eyes went wide.

"You know her?" her partner asked.

"Yes, but—" She stared at Evie with uncertainty, the blood draining from her face after a moment. "I'm... so incredibly stupid...."

"You're a Keeper..." Evie whispered.

"Wes," Trinity said unsteadily, "this is Evie. She's an old friend, and... I guess she's also Trick."

Her partner took a step back, surprised. "I don't und—" He shook his head. "Wait, how did you not know—"

"Because my parents never mentioned Trick, dumbass. By the time I started hearing things, we were in the academy, and I never considered…" Her free hand went to her forehead.

"You're *friends* with a Keeper?" Cade asked, motioning between them.

"I didn't know!"

"Don't talk to him," Trinity snapped.

Evie reared back in shock. "Excuse me?"

"He's Shade, Evie."

Evie's jaw set, her features hardening. "Yeah, I'm aware, Trin."

"Where's Fuentes and Bennett? Why the hell are you running around with *him?*"

She bit down on her tongue, getting a stern look in the process. "They're doing casework," she said sheepishly.

Trinity's eyes nearly bulged out of her head while Wes cleared his throat. "It sounds like someone snuck out."

"Wes, grab dumbass and throw him in the car. I'm calling Fuentes."

"What?! Wait, Trinity—" Evie said, trying to wiggle out of her grip. She was *way* stronger than she thought, remembering back to how Cade had tried to bolt from Haven back in the garage. Haven had acted like he was a squirmy child, but he and Tarryn must've been dialing it back with her. "Let's just talk about this for a second—"

"Absolutely not."

Trinity pulled open the rear passenger door, pushing her forward. Instead of climbing in, she bolted, hurtling back toward Wes and Cade before being lifted a foot off the pavement with arms wrapped around her.

"Put me down!"

"Just get in the damned car!"

She shoved her inside, shutting the door immediately. Evie tried the handle. When she found it safety-locked, she opted to bang on the window while Cade and Wes rounded the car. They climbed in as Trinity messed around with her phone in the driver's seat.

"Wes," Trinity said. "Call Fuentes while I drive."

"Can we talk about Hart's hair first?" he asked.

"Can we *not* talk about my hair? Like, ever?"

Trinity did a double-take in the rearview mirror, twisting in her seat for a better look at him. "Good God, what in the hell happened?"

"Lily. Now let's agree to never bring it up again."

"Noted…" she mumbled, turning back around and starting the car. "Good to know that my childhood friend has also been turned into a safehouse-escaping delinquent because of you too."

"*Hey*," Evie said, her voice rising. "I *chose* to sneak out because I had questions that Keepers don't like to answer, so don't pin this on him. He didn't help me. I did it on my own."

Wes tapped on his phone, putting it up to his ear with a brief back-and-forth that resulted in some shouting from the other end. Evie shrank down into her seat until he hung up, and they pulled into the garage.

"We probably shouldn't bring Hart through the front," Wes said.

"Then how the hell else are we going to get him up there?" Trinity asked, the two of them glancing back at Cade, who smirked in amusement. Her head whipped back toward her partner. "Oh, hell no, Wes."

"You're the main Keeper here, so you get Hart, and I'll take Evie."

"No, no—*You're* taking Hart."

"Rock, paper, scissors?"

Trinity narrowed her eyes at him before readying her hands. They counted down, and Wes let out a curse.

"Paper beats rock," she cheered, hopping out of the car.

"Have fun with Hart." She opened Evie's car door with a nod to get out, seizing her arm the second her shoes hit the concrete.

A long, awkward, uncomfortable silence stretched between them during their trek across the garage. It wasn't until Trinity talked with the guard and they gained access to the elevator that she finally spoke, "I'm sorry I didn't come looking for you when I came back to New Atlas. I honestly didn't know if I'd be able to maintain a well-grounded friendship with someone I thought could never know about… all *this*. I should've anyway though."

"You don't have to apologize," Evie replied, staring at the lit call button.

"But you should also be careful here, Evie. These people can be dangerous."

"I understand, but I'm also not completely helpless either." A half-truth that quieted Trinity, at the very least. The resounding chime of the elevator broke that silence, taking them all the way up to her comfortable cell. The sound of their footsteps on the hallway carpet filled her with dread, knowing that Tarryn and Haven would be waiting to reprimand her on the other side of that door.

Trinity gave a light knock, answered by Tarryn swinging it inward. Haven shook his head with a look of stern disapproval off to the side. Evie shrank down, staring at the floor.

"Thank you, Avery, for returning our charge," Tarryn said flatly, shutting the door behind them just as a second knock sounded from the glass door.

On the balcony, Cade grinned and waved. Wes's hand was pressed to his own forehead as he half-hung over the railing, looking pale. Haven popped the sliding door open.

"What the hell happened to his hair?" Tarryn asked.

"Lily." Trinity waved a hand. "But that's not what I want to talk about. Jay's gone, like *gone* gone."

"Financial records?"

Trinity shook her head. "No activity. He hasn't been back to his apartment or seen by anyone that's been interrogated either."

She eyed Cade as he, Wes, and Haven drew near. "Either he's completely ditched New Atlas, or he's… well, *dead*."

"Have you talked to any of the Shade?"

"A couple, but they were too afraid to actually say anything that might help us."

"I don't understand," Evie said, glancing between them. "Why wouldn't they help? I thought they didn't ever really like Jay?"

Cade's eyes moved to a different part of the room, shoving his hands into his pockets while the others gave each other uneasy looks.

"Well…" Tarryn began. "The problem is that they're still very much afraid of him. The only ones bold enough to out him probably won't do it because they'll want to hunt him for sport."

"But he's not in charge anymore…"

Everyone looked toward Cade, who shifted uncomfortably.

"Cade," Tarryn said, Evie watching him close his eyes at his name, wincing like he knew what she was about to say. "Tell Evie what he can do."

His gaze shifted to the floor, biting his lip and slightly hunching in on himself. "He um… his talent is that he can puppet people through their shadows."

Evie could almost feel the blood draining from her face.

"It's… *really* rare. He only used it on me *once* when I was younger because he thought I might get in the way and end up hurt. He promised he wouldn't do it again unless he absolutely had to. He could've used it back in the garage, but… That's how I knew he'd given up on me."

MONDAY, APRIL 13TH AT 3:54PM

After the excitement of yesterday, Cade had been glad to be left alone in Alyx's apartment. The only downside was him being stuck with his ever-growing collection of thoughts concerning what might be happening with the Shade and if they actually knew about Jay. So, he left around four in the afternoon for a walk while mulling over where to go for dinner.

Cade tucked his hands into his pockets, rubbing his thumbs along the smooth lining of his leather jacket as he ducked in and out of his less-utilized information gathering spots. Like he predicted, no one paid him any mind as he kept to the exposed-brick walls of bars and pubs filled with chattering Custodians. He tugged on his hood and fidgeted with his phone as rumors floated through the air, giving him little or nothing to wield before he pushed out of his booths and barstools to his next haunt. Always in and out of shadows, smooth as silk.

He would've been lying if he said stopping by the Martelli's hadn't crossed his mind, though he talked himself out of it shortly after. Instead, he strolled down the alleyway of the MacGuinesses casino, latching onto whispers on his way by since he didn't dare duck inside. Cade slowed when he turned down another alley, weaving past overflowing dumpsters and scurrying rats when a dark stain of a graffiti tag caught his eye—one marked with a small Fallen logo with its eight downward shards under the word 'RISE' with a backward 'E'. His brows furrowed, but he shook his head and moved on to the small restaurant up ahead, beckoned by its neon sign and his growling stomach.

The retro fifties and sixties theme put him at ease with the retrofitted jukebox sitting in the corner and puffy blue and pink-red booth cushions. The waitress's tennis shoes squelched against laminate tiles when she brought him a greasy basket of a burger and fries, calling him 'sweetie' or 'sugar,' like she was worried about a young man sitting by himself in a hole-in-the-wall diner's corner. Despite his now-limited funds, he tipped her extra before he left.

Dark closed in by the time he dragged his feet down the sidewalk, defeated by the lack of progress. Nothing about Trick. Nothing about Jay. Nothing about anything connecting the two to make more sense of why Cade's life had been turned upside down in a single night. He wove between streets, taking his time to think about everything he knew. He absently clapped his fists together, swinging them at his sides as another shadow pooled along the wall next to him.

Cade stopped to turn, but his legs kept going. Sweat broke out along his neck, and he lurched into a sprint, snapping back with a slight stumble in his forced march. The glow of a taillight from a car parked around one of the dumpsters filled him with panic just as Jay stepped up next to him.

"Jay, *stop*," he ground out, his voice quieted by the snap of the car door being ripped open. Cade's hand automatically slipped into his jacket pocket, closing around the silicone phone case and holding it out to him. Jay plucked it out of his hand, powered it off, and tossed it into the cup holder.

"If you're going to kill me, then at least give me the chance to defend myself."

Jay narrowed his eyes at him, patiently puppetting him into the car. The car door vibrated straight through his soul when it slammed shut. His brother, however, unhurriedly climbed into the driver's seat.

"Let *go*," Cade said through gritted teeth as the car started, pulling out onto the street.

"Quiet."

"You fucking shot me. The last thing I'm going to do is be quiet, Jay."

"You didn't leave me with much of a choice with the Callaghans right there. I told you just to fucking do the damn job. What part of me telling you I can't protect you forever did you not understand? You're too damn soft, Cade. You're so damn lucky she was Trick."

Cade scoffed. "You're telling me you didn't know?"

"Of course I didn't fucking know," he snapped. "If I knew she was Trick, I wouldn't have taken the job in the first place. I'm not that damn stupid."

"Let me out of the damn car, Jay."

"So you can get the shit beat out of you? How about no."

"Just leave town. Everyone else thinks that you already have because the rest of the Custodians want your ass. Just let me go and get lost. I'm done taking the fall for your shit, and I'm done being your puppet."

The car jerked to a stop, filling Cade with alarm at the sight of dozens of storage unit doors along the alley-wide swatch of driveway. Jay got out, Cade mirroring the movement to follow against his will.

"What are you doing?" Cade asked nervously, watching Jay pull a lock free from one of the doors.

"I have a couple of loose ends I need to deal with before we leave, and I can't have you running back to Alyx's place."

"*We?* Jay, I'm not going with—"

"Oh yes, you are."

"What? So I can be your spy somewhere else? Go fuck yourself."

Jay drew uncomfortably close, making Cade wish he could shrink down. "I think you're forgetting just how much I've done for you over the years. You're going to do what I ask. You're going to wait here until I come back, and then we're leaving."

"Where? Tell me where we're going then."

Jay slid the unit door open, a jolt of terror ripping through Cade as he began to walk inside.

"Where?" Cade demanded, trying to tamp down his panic.

"You'll see once we get there."

He shoved him the rest of the way in, sending him stumbling to the floor. His palms struck the concrete, shadow blending into black spray paint of interlocking shapes among a circled star. Fear rippled through him as his head whipped around to the door closing. He shot to his feet and threw himself against the door just as the lock snapped into place, leaving him in the chilling dark.

"Jay!"

Bile rose in his throat as he listened to his boots scraping against the pavement, wordlessly walking away. The car started again and drove off, leaving him there. Alone. Trapped. Stuck in the confinement of a warded, five-by-five prison.

Cade cursed and paced, rubbing his arms until his ears perked at the sound of tires tracking asphalt again. A shining beacon of hope. He shot toward the door again and pounded his fists against the metal, echoing through the unit.

"Hey! Someone—help!"

Car doors opened, and relief spread through him in the instant voices and scuffing shoes started toward him.

"I'm in here!" he called, hearing the sweet sound of the lock being jostled outside.

The door flung open, and he was immediately grabbed by his jacked. The world blurred as he was yanked forward.

"Hey!" he yelled, losing his balance as he was dumped into the back of a car—the trunk. The top of it was decorated with that same symbol in the unit. His eyes widened at the sight of a smug Conrad before it slammed shut. His hands flew to the top of it. "Let me out, you bitch!"

Conrad wrapped his knuckles on the trunk with a laugh. "Glad your brother did us the favor of nabbing you for us."

"Oh, shut the hell up, Hart," came Declan's irritatingly familiar voice. "Save it for when Liam breaks every bone in your body. I'm sure Jay will lose his shit when he snaps your neck in front of him."

Cade threw himself against the trunk lid, earning a dark chuckle from Declan before he spouted off orders to get in and drive. He gritted his teeth, feeling around for something that might aid him. The minutes stretched by. His fumbling resulted in nothing before the car parked.

The trunk flew open again, and he was ripped out of the back, dragged into the back of the Callaghan's pub, roughly jerked down a couple of hallways, and shoved into an office, falling to his hands and knees in front of Liam.

"Turns out we just needed to wait for Jay to grab him for us," Conrad said, a grin in his voice. "He locked him up in a storage unit, like a present with a bow."

Cade's head lifted to see Liam's snide smirk. He scrambled to his feet, his knees wobbling in the face of the man who was going to beat him senseless.

"Guess that answers my question if Jay will take the bait," Liam said. "Leave me to deal with this one for a while. You two keep an eye out for Jay."

The resounding *click* of the door shutting sent ice flooding through his veins, face-to-face with his worst nightmare.

"Now what are you going to do, Hart? I've heard you've been playing with Inked in your free time, but they certainly don't give a shit about you. They won't come running. And by the time your brother shows up, you'll be just a few breaths shy of your last. I would go ahead and say your final prayers to save your miserable soul."

"I thought your problem was with Jay, not me," Cade said shakily.

"You two *nobodies*," he spat, taking a menacing step forward, "stole what's mine. *I* was the one who was supposed to take charge of the Shade in New Atlas—not some jackass and his idiot little brother. You're just collateral at this point. I know you've cleaned up for him, so don't bother denying it because I've been watching to poke holes where I can. But, turns out, all I needed to do was just drop the hint of a job so important that Jay would want to take it himself. Hook, line, and sinker." He gave a mirthless chuckle. "I just had to sit back and wait for your house of cards to collapse. So now I plan to finish the job, starting with you."

Cade took a step back, his mind working on if he'd be able to make it to an exit before getting caught. He made a small attempt to shift, his shadowy form not giving.

"Maybe I would've given you a chance if you had decided to come to me for assistance in dismantling your brother's empire, but that ship has sailed. You're a traitor, and I don't have room for traitors in my faction."

Liam lunged, and Cade dodged but not quick enough for Liam to avoid grabbing his jacket. He pinned him against the wall, pressing an arm to Cade's throat. He gasped, grappling to push him away. His body repeatedly attempted to phase through the wall, screaming in pain that accompanied a horrible burning sensation from his back. The corners of his vision darkened, and his head swam before he saw Liam's eyes go wide. Cade's arms fell, and everything went black.

The next thing Cade knew, he was swaying in the middle of the room. Doubled outlines took over his vision and dulled echoes of shouts pulsed in his ringing ears. He wasn't sure if he was staring at two or four people in the doorway, along with the form on the floor, but his body buckled, and the darkness pulled him under again.

TWENTY-FIVE
EVIE

Evie drummed her fingertips against the keyboard. She pressed her lips into a thin line, shoulders falling as she shut the laptop. Her head tipped back toward the ceiling in her stretch against the arm of the couch, eyes searching for unwritten answers in each imperfection of the paint.

She pulled the pocket watch over her head, turning it over and over while she mulled over Aiden's words. Maybe there was something else back at home that she'd missed with instructions on how to open it? Maybe she was forgetting some important clue her grandfather had left? Evie worried her lip, contemplating if her aunt would know, but it had belonged to her father and his father. Asking her would snowball into a flurry of questions and panic that neither of them needed right now, landing her straight back to square one.

She dropped the watch onto her chest, hands clapping over her eyes with a groan. Muffled voices sent her upright, grabbing onto the back of the couch to witness Tarryn burst through the door.

"Get your jacket," she ordered. "Cade's in the hospital."

"What?" Evie shot up, feeling the blood draining from her face. "Is he okay? What happened?"

Haven pushed past her, huffing on his march to Evie's room.

"Trinity said that he and Liam got into a fight, but I don't have any details."

Haven reemerged from the bedroom doorway, jacket in hand before starting toward her. The urgency of his expression was amplified by the grip on her arm, forcing her into the hall.

"I don't know what condition everyone's in," Tarryn continued, "but Haven was insistent that we come get you before we headed over."

His hand tightened on her arm, eyes dead ahead as he jammed the elevator button and shoved the jacket into her arms. It slid in her uncertain grasp, too busy staring at Haven with a mix of emotions settling in her gut. Trembling, she tugged it on and tucked the loose strands of hair behind her ears during the ride down to the garage.

Evie watched him from the backseat of the car as Tarryn weaved through traffic, starting and stopping with slight, hiccuping jerks of the seatbelt. Haven didn't look back at her. His brows stayed furrowed with a hand on the dashboard, peering out up ahead at the kaleidoscope of city lights before they pulled into hospital parking.

Tarryn muttered something under her breath as she pulled out her Custodian-only key to access the fourth floor. Four for Tears. Exactly like the spa Cade had taken her to, but instead of therapeutic healing, this was for literal healing. The thought made Evie's heart work a little harder, stealing her breath with each push closer to panic.

So, when the elevator doors slid open, and she saw Trinity and Wes, she jogged toward them. Trinity did a double-take, the sound of Evie's sneakers squeaking against the white tiles tore through the corridor's silence. But her sights ripped away from Evie in favor of targeting a Keeper behind her.

"Fuentes, I didn't mean for you to—"

"Evie was worried, so we brought her. Deal with it, Avery."

Wes put a hand on Trinity's shoulder. "Don't turn this into a big deal."

"*I'm* turning this into a big deal? I think you're forgetting—"

"Avery—"

Haven seized Evie's arm again once he caught up, ignoring them all in favor of one closed room. Her eyes widened as they passed the window, taking in Cade's prone form on the hospital bed. Eyes closed.

Oh God.

The nurse caught sight of them in the middle of capping her marker, leaving a note on the whiteboard under 'HART, CADE'.

"What are you doing?" Trinity demanded, reaching for Evie as Haven spun on her. His face contorted into something almost feral, causing her to recoil with a sudden step back.

"Why can't you leave well-enough alone?" Wes hissed as the door opened, puffing out air that tickled Evie's skin from its weight.

The nurse stood on the threshold, her scrubs rumpled and hair falling loose around her neck. "He's still unconscious, but he'll be fine," she said. "I just can't tell any of you when he'll wake up. I'm not exactly sure what caused the trauma, and it's not like he can tell me. But he'll recover with enough rest."

"Can we see him?" Evie asked, fidgeting with her hands since she wasn't sure what else to do with them.

She hesitated, starting to shake her head as Haven waved Tarryn forward to sign something to her.

"He doesn't have any family to check in on him," Tarryn said on his behalf, melting away the urgency in Haven's hand gestures. "And we know you're only supposed to allow Keepers, but Miss Thatcher is… a close friend of his."

Evie's head whipped toward him as his hands fell to his sides, though his gaze was pinned on the recipient of his words, rather than her.

"Well… as long as there's a Keeper accompanying her, then it's not technically against the rules."

"Thank you," Tarryn said before Haven even lifted a finger.

He gave a short nod as she stepped to the side and guided Evie inside with a firm hand resting on her upper back.

"Thank you, Haven," she whispered in the short walk over to Cade's side, her hands dropping to the bedrail where a fingertip grazed something cool and hard. They jerked away, and she peered down to find him handcuffed to the railing. She grimaced, mumbling, "Is this really necessary?"

Haven nudged her a little further up, despite standing vigilant, looking over his shoulder toward the window with narrowed eyes. She guessed it was a borderline dirty look at Trinity since he was pushing so hard for her to see Cade. Every protective and aggressive reaction coming from him became an empathic nod to every comforting feeling she'd ever experienced around this foolish Shade.

Evie bowed her head over Cade, her shoulders relaxing at the sight of his face. His stupid, *reckless* face, even though he appeared unharmed. No bruises. No blood. Just him laying there, resting like he had in the back of the SUV when they'd first met—for real, that time.

"Hey…" she whispered, reaching out and giving his arm a brief squeeze—nothing too horribly intimate that would send Trinity in here to rip her back into the hall or start a fist-fight with Haven. "I need you to wake up, okay? I need someone to be an example of what not to do before I start doing it myself." She huffed out a short, humorless laugh to mask the wobbliness of her voice.

She shouldn't be getting choked up, but her heart hurt. It pressed heavier with each passing second he didn't answer, throwing her into a deep, dark chasm of dread. Of loss. Of loneliness. Aiden had been right about all of it, but Evie swallowed down that sentiment in favor of focusing on walking away.

But could she?

TUESDAY, APRIL 14TH AT 12:37AM

"I don't think he's going to jump up from the bed anytime soon…" Tarryn mumbled, halting her slow pacing in front of the window with a frown. She turned her head toward Evie and Haven sitting side-by-side on the bench across from it, where Evie's began to buckle to that thought.

Her fingers curled under the seat as she worried her lip, pitching forward slightly. She found it funny that her mind decided to grasp for her talent—thinking that it might somehow be able to jolt him awake long enough for them to talk. Something just long enough for her to tell him he was an idiot while she forced back all concern that would work its way into every gesture, every word, every *look* they shared. And Cade would probably just grin because he'd somehow won, even though he was cuffed to a hospital bed.

She stood, shuffling toward Tarryn to peer inside for herself. Haven brushed up against her shoulder, leaving her perfectly framed between her two guardians in the faint reflection on the pane.

"When do you think Trinity and Wes will be back?" Evie asked, her arms slipping into a cradling self-hug that did little to comfort her.

Tarryn hummed in contemplation, ignoring how Haven rolled his eyes.

"I would think another few minutes. I'd like to see if they were able to talk to Liam at all before we head out."

Almost on cue, the elevator chimed at the end of the hall and two figures emerged. Trinity's brows were furrowed, her expression one of distorted contemplation while Wes forced an unconvincing smile. There was a nervousness to his eyes that became increasingly more apparent as they drew closer.

"Well?" Tarryn asked, frowning.

"Er, well…" Wes gave an uneasy chuckle, stopping short

with a hand on the back of his neck. "Liam's fine, fortunately—or *unfortunately*, depending on how you look at it."

"Yeah," Trinity rounded on him, her expression shifting to a scowl, "and you heard what he said—"

"Let's not jump to conclusions—"

"*Conclusions?* Wes, something isn't right here—"

"Which," he started, his voice gentle yet stern as he leaned forward, face-to-face with her, "is exactly why we should wait to hear what Cade has to say first."

"That's not—" she began, triggering a wave of Tarryn's arm.

"Hold on for a second," Tarryn said, shaking her head. "What happened? What did he say?"

Wes hesitated, clearing his throat while Trinity narrowed her eyes at him. She rocked back expectantly, folding her arms over her chest.

"He, um… said some things that don't quite add up…"

Trinity's head tilted back with a groan, turning to the rest of them. "Liam said that some weird shadow attacked him and that it came from Cade."

Evie's eyes went wide, glancing between Tarryn and Haven to find… *confusion*. "Um—I'm sorry, but I don't understand. Cade never mentioned he could do anything like that. I mean, not to me, at least…"

"Because it's not possible," Wes explained with a roll of his eyes.

"Then how do you explain what he said, Wes?" Trinity shot back.

"How?" Evie asked, catching Tarryn's short, frustrated growl that indicated she was growing impatient with Trinity's interruptions.

"It's exceedingly rare for Shade to have more than one facet of their talent," she said, ignoring the bickering between the other two. "Each of the Custodians have their own caveats, and that's just one of the limitations they have. If Cade had something like that, it'd be on his record, and it's *not*. I checked. He can't manifest shadows like that… Hell, I'm not even sure that I've ever heard of another Shade being able to do that before…"

Haven tapped his foot softly against the tiles and lifted a hand to his chin in contemplation.

"Something definitely doesn't add up here," Tarryn mumbled, following his gaze to where Cade slept.

"I'm sure Cade will have an explanation," Evie breathed. "He'll clear it all up." She pulled her hands into her jacket sleeves to pick at the seams.

"I sure hope so. But if he's been hiding something, then it could potentially hinder parts of our investigation—specifically anything that roots back to Jay or the Shade. The *new* council could end up getting involved in the next week." Her eyes slid back to Evie. "Which will include *you*."

Evie found it hard to swallow, deciding to bite down on her tongue instead with another stolen glance toward Wes and Trinity. An echoing series of questions volleyed between them, barely registering in her mind like drifting leaves coursing through the river of her thoughts. Everything poured straight into that dam that was the pocket watch, keeping all those answers stuck on the other side.

TWENTY-SIX

CADE

TUESDAY, APRIL 14TH AT 6:02AM

"Detectives, he's starting to wake up."

Cade's eyes popped open with a wince, and he jerked his arm up to shield his vision from the harsh light. The bite of metal against his wrists turned his wince into a grimace as he ran a knuckle along the edge of the bed railing where it met a thin blanket.

What the hell happened?

The sound of two sets of footsteps made him squirm just before the shadows of Trinity and Wes loomed over the bed.

"Took you long enough," Trinity said, folding her arms over her chest.

He started to prop himself up before abandoning the idea. "Did you shoot Liam?" he rasped.

Trinity exchanged a hesitant look with Wes.

"No…" Wes said slowly with a frown. "He was already on the floor before we got there. We were waiting for you to wake up and tell us what happened."

Cade opened his mouth, pausing for a second.

Trinity tapped the bedrail. "What did you do to Liam? We need to know. He just got out of the ICU."

What? "I… I didn't do—"

She smacked it, and he jumped. Wes grabbed her elbow. "Trin—"

"*Yes*, you did. When we arrived, Liam was already on the floor, and you collapsed in front of us. The two of you were the only ones in the room. We had to subdue the other two Callaghans to get to you, but there was no one else around."

He swallowed, shaking his head. "I don't know. Conrad threw me into his office, Liam attacked me and pushed me up against the wall… I started to black out… and then he was on the floor. I thought you two had to have shot him because he was going to kill me. I don't remember anything else—"

Trinity set her jaw. "Tell the *truth*."

"I *am*—You're just assuming I'm lying because that's what you want to hear," he said, his tone dropping low and defensive, just on the verge of anger. "Just get the fuck out of here and leave me alone. You have the truth. I can't give you anything else. My head's pounding, and I just want to sleep…" He sank into the pillow, closing his eyes with a sigh.

He felt her hovering anger through the thudding in his skull, but she stomped out of the room with Wes on her heels. The shift of her soles tapping against the room's floor to a squeak of the hallway finally let his body relax into the mattress.

8:57PM

Wes patted the bed rail on his way out for the day, leaving Cade alone with his aches, pains, and longing for sleep among his patchy memory. Every time he closed his eyes, he replayed the moment when Liam pressed his arm to his throat, felt the throbbing in his back, and tried to peer past the black before he woke to the blur of the doorway.

He sank into his pillow, letting the pain medication lull him to sleep for an hour until the nurse checked on him. The process repeated into the night until his patience finally hit its limit.

The nurse left, and the door whooshed open maybe five minutes later. Cade gritted his teeth and turned his head over to take in a woman in a pantsuit hovering next to his bed. Long, dark hair framed her pale face, complete with her smokey hazel eyes and blood-red lips quirked up in a small, smug smile. The woman from the bar.

Damn they'd given him some good drugs.

"I'm not really in the mood for ghosts or whatever," he mumbled. "So, if you could just see yourself out, that would be great. Or you could change yourself into a different girl to keep me company. I'm cool with that too."

Her form didn't shift into the smaller, cardigan-wearing girl he'd rather be staring at. "Glad to see you too, Hart," she said smoothly, leaning against the bedrail and jostling his restraints. Fear slithered down his spine. He hadn't given her his name, had he? His eyes flicked over to the whiteboard, where it was written out in bold, blue marker. *Oh.*

"What the hell are you doing here?" Cade asked. "I don't know if you were the one who tried to kill me back in that building you gave me the address for, but I don't appreciate being lured somewhere under false pretenses."

"Consider it a gunshot at the start of a race. We've officially started."

"Started what, exactly?"

She leaned a little closer, and he instinctively pulled away, swallowing. The cuffs bit into his wrists.

"Our infinite game of cat and mouse."

A nervous chuckle tumbled out. "I... don't know you. We haven't met outside of the bar, have we?"

Her eyes narrowed on him, her smile something hard and mirthless. "You've been a pain in my ass for *years*, Hart. I know you all too well, but you don't know me. At least, not yet."

"What... are you talking about?"

She sighed, playing with the corner of the thin blanket. "After all the time we've spent fighting each other, this is our last dance. I intend to get it right this time to end your miserable existence." He could feel the blood drain from his face as she casually continued with, "Did you know I've lit this room on fire before? It would've worked too if you didn't have so many damn people trying to keep you alive."

"W-why are you doing this? I haven't done anything to you…"

She chuckled. "It's like I said. You've been a pain in my ass… But don't worry about my lighting your room on fire tonight. Consider this a final goodbye since the next time we see each other will be your last." She patted his cheek and pushed off the railing. "It's been fun, Hart, but I can't say that you'll be missed."

WEDNESDAY, APRIL 15TH AT 7:36AM

"I don't think you understand—" Cade said, trying to sit up in bed. "A woman snuck into my room last night and told me that she knew me, even though I don't even know her name. She threatened me and said that she's lit this hospital room on fire before."

Trinity scowled, turning to the nurse. "Is he on any hard drugs?"

"No, I'm no—"

"Hart," Wes started calmly. "It's possible that they drugged you to help you relax yesterday."

Cade shook his head. "I'm not making this shit up."

"No, Detective Avery," the nurse finally replied. "He's just on a saline drip and took some acetaminophen for pain."

"I'm not crazy," Cade said. "I need out of the damn hospital before she comes back and kills me."

"Uh-huh…" Trinity said, glancing over to her partner. "Look, I want you to know that Liam is being held until tomorrow morning after some torn stitches and sketchy blood counts, so you're stuck here until then for observation since I guess they were questioning some of your results too."

Manic laughter bubbled up from Cade. "Oh no—No, I need out of here. I know you don't like me, but you can't just let me *die*."

"You're not going to die, Hart," came Wes's gentle but firm response. "It's just an extra night, and no one else is on this floor anymore."

"That's even worse!"

"Could we get him something?" Trinity asked the nurse, pointing to Cade like a misbehaving child. "Like, something to calm him down, or…?"

The nurse started for the locked cabinet, and Cade immediately yanked on his cuffs. "Wait—Just—I'll stay put as long as you take these off, *please*. I seriously just need to be able to defend myself—"

"Just *relax*." Wes held his hands up, trying to placate him. "You're getting yourself worked up over a hallucination. We can't remove yours or Liam's cuffs until everyone's cleared and sorted, which will be tomorrow, okay?"

"I might need one of you to hold him down for a moment," said the nurse as she rounded the bed. "He'll need to hold still while I inject this into the other line."

"Do *not*—" Cade growled, slipping into panic. He yanked on the restraints, and Trinity pushed his shoulders down into the mattress.

"You're clearly losing it," she grumbled.

He jerked away for a second, his heart racing and his back starting to burn again just before feeling that warm, fuzzy sensation. His body relaxed, sinking into the cushioning, and Trinity lessened the pressure before she lifted away.

"How long will this last?" she asked, her voice starting to sound far away through the haze of the medication caressing the edges of his mind.

"A few hours. We can give him a little more throughout the day and into tonight to keep him relaxed if you think it's warranted."

Cade tugged on the cuffs again, his arms starting to feel impossibly heavy.

"That's probably for the best. Wes, can you keep an eye on him while I go ask Liam a few more questions? Fuentes should be stopping by in a few minutes to join me."

"Sure." He patted Cade's leg as she left, a reassuring gesture that only made his heart sink. "You're fine. It's just one more night."

And then Cade surrendered to sleep.

WEDNESDAY, APRIL 15TH AT 8:23PM

Ren tugged up his hood and kept his head down on the subway, rocking back and forth at each stop. His thumbs ran over his phone's keyboard every couple minutes when he faded out into a trance, sending people on and off the train in a blur like he'd accelerated the scrubbing speed on a video. A muffled call warbled out of the speakers, bringing him back to reality with just enough time to see the street listed on the last line of his notes matched the current stop.

He jumped up and bolted out the doors, spinning around to find the exit while his sneakers popped against the sticky linoleum. The second he laid eyes on the stairs, he froze, swallowed by a sea of people as a woman jogged up to the street, her red-soled designer heels clicking in her wake. Ren's hold on his phone tightened, and he brought a hand to his hood to pin it in place on his way out after her.

A waterfall of dark, wavy hair poured down the back of her blazer jacket, bouncing with every purposeful step toward the crosswalk. Ren tucked his hands into his pockets and trailed after her. That nagging urge to check his phone was silenced by that need to follow his new quarry to the ends of the earth, despite his friend's warning in that café nearly two weeks ago.

"See her?" A fingertip had tapped against the window, pointing through the generic, etched glass coffee cup logo.

Ren ran his spoon through his cup of tea again and scowled at the sight of the designer red-soled heels matching her blood-red lips on the other side of the street. "You mean the vampire lady?"

A breathy chuckle. "You could say that."

"What about her?"

"Keep an eye for who she mingles with but try to avoid her. She's working for whoever's at the top of all this."

Ren tore his gaze away from the street. "You saying you haven't been following her? Wouldn't she be able to lead us straight to our guy?"

"Right now, she's leaving her meeting with her boss, but I don't know from where. She's switched it up a couple times too."

"I'm sorry… You've lost me," Ren said flatly. "Shouldn't she be coming from the same place each time?"

"There are two types of players here, Ren. We have our constants, like you, and our variables, like her and I. The constants keep moving in a linear fashion while the variables aren't tied down to the same events. They can move freely and independently of the current situations because they've seen other outcomes, which means that they can adjust to what's coming next. The constants *can* be diverted off their tracks, but they tend to snap back toward the original timeline in the end. They just end up taking the scenic route."

"O-kay… But how is *she* a variable?"

"She followed me here, and now she's trying to manipulate things to her advantage. Fortunately, she'll be limited in what she's able to do."

"Then why not just go straight for you and be done with it? Why bother continuing to play this game?"

"The issue is that if she goes straight for me, then everything will start to collapse. Imagine me as a tent pole, and the fabric of reality is the rest of the tent. I'm the one thing holding it up right now until certain events play out. Otherwise, I shouldn't be here. She's waiting for the wheels of progress to start before she strikes, and even then, she'll opt to go for someone else before she bothers with me. She'd like to eliminate *two* problems, instead of one."

"So… is she going to take care of said problem now?"

"No. She's headed to a few different places in the past, but she can't deal with her number one problem yet."

Ren snapped back to the present, keeping close to his reflection in the storefront windows. Block after block, turn after turn, he kept out of her line of sight, hanging back whenever she stopped to cross a street. It wasn't until she turned a corner after about fifteen minutes of tailing her that he whipped around to find her *gone*.

He spun on his heel, checking the other side of the street. Kids his age in nylon jackets and hoodies with boba tea playfully shoved each other on the way to the crosswalk, followed by a couple guys in suits readjusting their messenger bags while they talked.

No vampire lady.

Ren got out his phone again and pressed his back against the wall. His notes app was filled with jibberish—street names, shops, restaurants—like he'd been following someone doing errands. He typed the last name into his map search and cursed.

She'd messed up his notes.

The pinpoint was marking a bougie-looking restaurant two more stops away. Ren turned back and ran to the station, panting after the four-block trek to the subway stairs. The second his hand grazed the railing, he cringed, immediately regretting it, and wiped it on his pants as he hurtled down the steps two at a time.

Turnstile. Rumble strip. Subway car.

His hands hit his knees with mere milliseconds separating him from the next train, doubled over with relief that he'd made it. He hooked an arm around the pole and swayed in time with the dizziness he felt until the speaker garbled out his real stop this time.

Shaky legs turned his next stairwell into a bit of an ordeal since the adrenaline had abandoned him, but he climbed his way up to the street, where the station was poised right across from *Vino Compreso*. In the window, shaking hands and about to take their seats, were Emmaline Yuan and Waylon Frost. He unrolled the black napkin from his silverware. She untangled her pearls from the bun at the nape of her neck. Nervous, warm smiles all around like they weren't a couple of competitors in a race to the top.

Ren kept his head down and pushed open the glass door to a coffee shop. One black coffee later, he stole a seat from a girl wearing a baggy NAU sweatshirt after she packed up her laptop. He settled onto the bar stool at the window, readjusted his hood, and got out his phone again, readying a new notes page with his sights set on his targets.

They handed their menus to the waiter, signaling the real discussions were about to begin. His thumbs began moving to match the words pouring from Frost's mouth while he brushed some of his hair aside—the color of pepper with a little salt mixed in from the gray.

Sorry for such short notice, but I'm glad you could make it.

Emmaline's hands fell into her lap. *It's no problem at all. I wanted to talk anyway.*

Oh? Frost pulled from his ice water.

I figure I should check up on my competition.

Ren caught Frost covering his mouth to stifle a laugh. *Just like your father, aren't you?*

Her mouth didn't move as he typed out the words: *I am nothing like my father.* A chill ran through him, and he knocked back some of his coffee before continuing.

Actually, she said, *I wanted to ask you about why you're gunning for the Shade and Inked. It's rather odd that you've been seeking to bring them back to the inner circle from the start, but Sterling hasn't bothered until the Six changed.*

Frost tapped his glass. Ren could almost hear that velvety chuckle from where he sat. *I know I'm not exactly the bright, young thing we need right now, but I'd like to think I have a decent shot because I've seen how twisted things have become. No one within our sphere is our enemy—not unless we make them to be.*

That's a rather bold claim, all things considered with Jay Hart.

He shook his head. *I'm sure even that has an explanation that we can't quite understand. Nothing's black and white, at the end of the day. I know Carlton voiced his own opinions when he was the Head, but he was short-sighted. Whether or not he sees that now...* He shrugged.

He doesn't see things the way you do. I would call him old, *but you're not much younger than he is. It's all a matter of perspective. There's a lack of respect that's come with whatever rift came between the 'upper' and 'lower' levels over the years. It's... unfortunate. But I do have to say that if I do end up losing this race, I'd feel much better losing it to you.*

That's very kind of you to say. I have to admit that you're not quite what I expected, Miss Yuan. You have a good head on your shoulders. You could take us to brighter places, should they give you the opportunity.

The waiter returned with dishes in hand, and Ren set his phone down with a sigh, watching the cursor in the notepad remind him where he'd left off. He rotated his coffee cup against the wooden bar top, losing himself in the black surface like he was staring into a scrying mirror.

His phone buzzed, tossing a notification onto his screen.

Any progress?

Ren's eyes flicked back to the restaurant as Emmaline cut into her meal—distorted through the strips of frosted glass. Then back to the line of text in his notes she hadn't said. He high-lighted it in blue and drummed his fingers against the table before jumping back to his texts.

Maybe.

TWENTY-EIGHT
CADE

When Cade finally roused, still muddled by the medication after the shift change, he saw her standing next to his bed, lips pursed as she read a label off a vial.

"Great," he rasped. "You're back."

She smirked without so much as a glance in his direction. "I have to admit that was easier than I thought. Getting you to panic was probably the best decision I've made in a while." She angled a syringe into the vial, filling it just like the nurse had with his other poison.

"Can't we just… I don't know… *Talk?*" he asked. "I'm sorry if I made you mad, but I can't help if I don't know what I did in the first place…"

"It's a little late for that now. I'm not here to try to be friends." Her heels clicked as she rounded the bed

He tensed, his hands gripping the thin blanket while he tried to pull them out of the cuffs again.

"Don't waste my time, Hart. Just hold still, and you'll go to sleep. It'll be over before you know it." She gave him a warm smile that chilled him to the core. "Plus, it'll be much nicer than all the other things I've tried to do. It was fun while it lasted." She reached for the short line, and Cade winced, sucking in a breath.

"*Freeze!*"

The woman's head swung toward the door, her face crumpling into a mixture of surprise and fury. Cade flinched at the sudden, whirling blur of movement, sending taped papers fluttering and his hair standing on end before the woman stood in the hall the door slammed shut behind her with Trinity and Wes stuck inside with him—almost like she'd teleported past them.

Wes sprinted after her, ripping the door open and tearing down the hall while Trinity stood there, stunned. His cry for Trinity to stay put came as an after-thought with the pounding of heels and boots thundering through the floor. A nurse and security guard rushed into the room a few seconds after.

"Told you so…" Cade mumbled, collapsing into the mattress.

The nurse started for him, checking the equipment, his vitals on the screen, and began prodding at his arm near the taped drip lines until Cade squirmed, hating how the guy manipulated the fluids under his skin during his examination. Cade twisted his arm some from his grip to show his discomfort right before Wes stumbled back into the room, scratching his head and giving Trinity the short run-down of how he'd lost her.

"You're *sure* he wasn't given anything else?" Trinity asked, gripping the railing.

"No," the nurse said. "Nothing other than the drip and the sedative that's beginning to wear off." He finally let go of Cade's arm, and his head lulled back with relief.

"Who the hell was that?" Wes asked.

"I don't know," Cade said, a slight whine to his voice.

"I'm more interested in *what* she was," Trinity said.

"I would say Shade, but they don't move like *that*, do they?" Wes said wearily, looking to Cade for an answer. He shook his head.

Trinity folded her arms over her chest, narrowing her eyes at the window before something lit her gaze.

"What?" Wes asked.

"I hate to even consider it, but I think there's only one real possibility… Trick."

6:43AM

Wes shuffled back into the room right as the nurse took the last of the paperwork from Trinity for Cade's discharge, baring a grimace. "Apparently Liam left about a half-hour ago."

"What?" Trinity rounded on him. "You're kidding—Please tell me you're kidding."

"He by-passed us and contacted the chief, who gave him the go-ahead to leave after a few threats. When I contacted him about it, he said that we couldn't keep him here anymore."

Cade pulled on his restraints, making an irritating jingling noise to get their attention. Trinity narrowed her eyes at his held-up wrists and dropped her shoulder, plucking the keys from her pocket. The *click* of the cuffs coming free was the sweetest sound he'd ever heard.

"Thank God," he breathed, rubbing his wrists. "But holy hell does this stupid thing itch." He moved to touch where the IV was taped down.

"Give the nurse five minutes to deal with that," Trinity said. "Then we'll get out of here."

"I believe it's also warranted to admit him back into the safe-house," Wes said. "Two people have tried to kill him in about forty-eight hours, so…" He shrugged, rubbing the side of his head.

Cade sat up, picking at the tape on his arm. "Oh, so in the chaos of all this attempted murder business, it slipped my mind that there was something else since I was being accused of *lying*." He pointedly stared at Trinity, who bit the inside of her cheek, averting her gaze. "I was in the process of being kidnapped by Jay."

Her head whipped back around. "What?! Holy shit, where? We have to go—"

"Trinity, hold on—" Wes said. "He's probably long-gone by now." He turned to Cade. "Did he say anything? Where was he planning on taking you?"

"He wouldn't tell me. I just figure he realized just how screwed he was without me and decided he needed me in order to start over somewhere else. I kept telling him to let me go and leave me alone, but… Well, he took my phone and locked me in a storage unit. The Callaghans followed him and picked me up to use as bait."

"Anything else?" Trinity asked.

Cade hummed, biting his lip. He tilted his head back and forth and snapped his fingers when the rest floated back to the surface. "Liam baited Jay into taking the job to go after Evie. He had no intention of taking it himself, and he probably had some inkling it was something to do with Trick, which he omitted to get Jay and I out of the way for his takeover."

"We need to corner Liam," Trinity said, seemingly more to herself than him or Wes. "If Jay didn't know, but Liam *did*, then that's our lead. That is, unless Jay's coming back for you."

Cade sighed, peeling the edge of the IV tape. "Well… there's only one way to find out."

9:24AM

Trying to find the storage unit, even in the daytime, turned out to be more of a challenge than Cade expected. Trinity rolled past dull red door after dull red door until Cade spotted the broken lock and leaned past Wes, pointing out the window. They pulled over, and both Keepers readied their guns before ripping the unit open. The lock hit the metal outer wall with a clang, vibrating through the yard while flashlights swept over the spray-painted ward along the floor. And in the center, sat Cade's phone.

Cade's heart sank as he stepped inside and crouched down to flip over the rubber case. The screen didn't light at his touch, still powered off. It stung to realize that Jay had abandoned him yet again—a tool for him to use and nothing more.

"A phone?" Trinity asked when he stepped outside.

"Yeah. My phone," Cade said quietly. "I probably should get myself a new one just in case he did anything to it though…"

She pulled it from his grip. "We'll get you a new one on the department's dime."

He blinked, his hand frozen in place like it was still holding the weight of his brother's clear message: he was only useful until he became too much of a hassle.

Trinity shrugged, staring down at it while she fidgeted with the silicone sides. "Well, I… I should've believed you back there."

Wes cleared his throat. "I believe what my partner is trying to say is 'I'm sorry,' but she's too prideful to say it."

"It's okay," Cade said. "I forgive you."

TWENTY-NINE
EVIE

"Okay, let's back up for a second," Tarryn said, holding up a hand. She leaned back against the safehouse kitchenette counter, crossing her legs with her brows knitting together. "You're saying that a *Trick* tried to kill him while he was in the hospital?"

Evie paled, her head snapping between her and Trinity, who nodded. Haven scowled, looking lost in thought with his thumb running under his chin and staring at some arbitrary spot on the floor.

"Which is why Wes is letting him take a nap down the hall," Trinity said. "It's been… wild, to say the least."

Tarryn shook her head. "That doesn't make sense, Avery."

"Oh, trust me, I wouldn't have believed it either, except for seeing it myself. This woman was *fast,* and there's no way she could've done it unless she was manipulating time. Plus, every-thing she told Cade—"

"It's impossible," Tarryn finished, pushing off the counter. "Trick can only manipulate a small portion of time. What you're saying is that she's somehow spun back... I don't know, weeks? Months? Possibly longer, depending."

"It works like a pocket," Evie said, shifting and playing with the chain of the pocket watch around her neck as all eyes in the room moved to her. "So that sounds sort of... farfetched unless there was some way to do it on a larger scale."

"Exactly." Tarryn motioned to her. "It has its limits, and something like that would be bound to get noticed."

"Unless there's something in the archives about it?" Evie asked. "Something that maybe we've overlooked?"

"Sounds like if there were anything big like that, it would be locked in that smaller room, which we can't access without opening that watch of yours." Tarryn pointed to her chest. "So we're sort of stuck until then, it seems."

Evie's hand fell to her side, bumping against the back of the scratchy canvas of the couch while she chewed on her lip.

"You said you already went to the archives," Trinity said, "but there were only three of you. Maybe it would be beneficial to have more eyes on things in there so we can find a way to open the watch and get into that other room? We could go first thing tomorrow with the six of us."

Tarryn raised an eyebrow, huffing out a laugh.

"What?" Trinity asked, frowning.

"Nothing, just... You really seemed to do a three-sixty with Cade and the apology you gave Evie."

She rolled her eyes. "Do you want our help or not?"

"Yes," Evie blurted. "Yes, *please*. I'd like nothing more than to start getting answers to this ever-growing list of questions."

THIRTY
CADE

The crinkle of a shopping bag filled the car when Trinity threw it back to Cade. She clicked her tongue and started the car as he dug through the bag to find a new phone and SIM card. He smirked and tore open the packaging before trying to stuff the trash in the car door, earning a motherly complaint from Trinity while Wes chuckled.

Cade sank down in his seat with a grin and played with his new phone, thinking of Evie during the rest of the drive. Seeing her over a fancy pizza dinner in her safehouse apartment had been the highlight of the past few days, and he was looking forward to spending the rest of the day with her, even if it was in the confines of an archive room with dusty books and dull documents.

Before they knew it, Cade was standing between Trinity and Wes near the bottom of the stairwell to the archives, his eyes pinned on Evie as she unlocked the door and allowed them inside.

The archive's Mist eyed him with a tilt of her head, giving him pause when her Keeper counterpart glanced between them, furrowing his brows. Cade swallowed and kept his head down, repeatedly telling himself not to act suspicious, which probably made him look even *more* suspicious since the Mist woman stood, and her Keeper mirrored the motion.

"One moment, Mr. Hart," she said, her tone pleasant but firm as the rest of the group turned around with quizzical expressions. "Miss Thatcher, are you certain you'd like to permit him in the archives?"

He hesitated and tucked his hands into his pockets, sweating a little since he supposed he was the only non-Keeper among them. Though he'd seen Shade permitted into the Inked archives before without the Mist at that door batting an eye.

"Um, *yes*," Evie said with a hint of irritation, scowling at her.

Haven eyed his fellow Mist as Cade stepped through the threshold, and the group began to make their way toward the center cabinets.

"Okay," Tarryn started. "Haven, you go with Evie just in case she needs any assistance in the far left corner, and Wes, you babysit Cade in the far right. Trinity and I will split off to cover the other corners near the front. Sound good?"

A sea of shrugs and nods before Cade wandered after Wes to a shelf when his phone buzzed—a notification from his chat app.

Can I call you? We need to talk.

"Something wrong?" Wes asked.

"Oh, um, I think Alyx—sorry, my roommate, I mean—she might have some questions. Mind if I call her?"

He shrugged. "Go for it."

Cade gave a quick appreciative smile and jogged past the tables, ducking near a set of cabinets near the middle of the room. He popped open the app again.

I have a new phone. Let me call you.

Then Cade put the phone to his ear, bouncing on his heels until the soft vibration through the speaker ended.

"Hey," he said. "What's going on? You okay?"

"Cade, where are you?" she asked, her voice low and urgent.

"Are you somewhere safe? What's with the whispering?" He glanced over his shoulder to Wes, afraid that he might need to signal for him and Trinity to go find her.

"Yes—Yes, I'm fine. I'm at my apartment, but the Callaghans showed up a little while ago looking for you."

"Those sons of bitches. Did they threaten you?"

"No, they didn't—Cade, they told me Liam's gone, and…"

"And what, Alyx?"

"You were in the hospital, right? Liam too?"

"*Yes*, because he attacked me the other night. Wes and Trinity said they stopped by and told you, didn't they?"

She hesitated, her breath catching through the receiver. "Cade, I… um… I think the Callaghans are trying to figure out what to do next. Everyone's gone weirdly quiet, even the Martellis and a few other louder families. A couple other people have shown up asking for you, and I don't know what to tell them."

"Why the hell are they harassing *you* about me? Why can't these people just leave me the hell alone?"

Another pause.

"What?" Cade asked. "What are you *not* saying, Alyx?"

"Cade, I don't think you heard me when I said Liam's *gone*."

"No, no, I heard that part quite a bit already."

"Liam *attacked* you, and he *ran*, Cade," she said sharply, emphasizing each word.

The entire world shuddered to a stop, the phone feeling like a brick in his hand. "I got to go," he rasped, ending the call. He grabbed at his shirt collar, pulling it away from his throat as he turned to make his way back toward the rest of the group, now huddled around a table with a new discovery he pinned his eyes on. The phone buzzed in his hand, and he fumbled to ignore the call. His slick fingers moved across the screen's keyboard.

Later

He jostled against one of the filing cabinets and hissed as it bit into his arm.

A playful smirk danced across Wes's face as his head jerked up, and Haven snorted. They were the only two bothering to look up at his mishap while the others began pulling out leaflet papers from a filing folder with chatter he couldn't decipher.

"Careful," Wes teased.

Haven's amusement faded as his eyes went wide. Cade's stomach lurched. He figured it out with a single look—that damning, uncanny Mist way of picking up on whatever infinite knowledge had been tossed into their collective ether. Something the Mist woman at the door had realized even before Cade had.

"So, um—" Cade gave a nervous chuckle, rubbing the back of his neck as he stood at the edge of the table. "You guys remember how that lady checked with Evie if she really wanted to let me in here?"

Annoyed, Trinity looked up first. Evie followed, but Tarryn didn't bother until Haven tapped on the table to get her attention.

"I... may have just figured out who the next Shade leader is..." He shifted uncomfortably.

"Yeah, who?" Trinity asked.

Haven's hand went to his face with a silent groan before signing something to Tarryn, her face paling from the explanation Cade hadn't gotten to quite yet.

"It's a power-grab system, Avery," Tarryn said in a rush. "Liam turned tail and *ran* because he got the shit kicked out of him. You're looking at the next Six."

Trinity jolted upright, her jaw dropping as she fixed her gaze on him again, everyone else staring in stunned silence. "Is he even *allowed* to be in here, then?"

"Well, Trinity," Wes began. "I assume that's probably why he was stopped at the door to be double-checked first, or else she would've outright denied the request."

Cade shuffled backward, his hands on his head as if that would keep it from spinning. "Can't I just—I don't know—*give* it to someone? There's no way in hell I'm going to be able to hold onto it if someone challenges me. I shouldn't have been able to beat Liam in the first place. I don't even know *how* I did..." His arms dropped onto the back of a chair, and he tugged it out, collapsing into the stiff cushion. His shoulders crumpled, feeling the weight of it all finally sinking in. "I'm a dead man... Wait, could I get Alyx to kick the shit out of me and take it?"

Trinity made a noise of disapproval, rolling her eyes. "I don't think having your friend beat you up to pass it off like an unwanted family heirloom would work all that well."

"In case you haven't noticed, *everyone* that's Shade seems to hate me with the exception of—" He halted, realizing that Alyx wasn't the only person he might be able to hand it to. There was someone he knew that might just be willing to trade.

Emilio.

"Did... he just short-circuit?" Trinity mumbled, a muffled sound to Cade's ears.

Wes snapped his fingers in front of him, pulling him from his thoughts. "All right, so you're going to sit here and not look at *anything* until we've read it. No names, no personal information or data of any Trick. If you see it, you say something, and we'll decide if Haven needs to remove anything. We can't risk you knowing if you're a major player that could be a larger target than Evie right now."

Cade twisted toward him, throwing an arm out to the files. "I don't *want* to be a major player!"

"Too bad," Tarryn said. "That ship has sailed, so sit down,

shut up, and we'll deal with that mess after a little more digging, okay?"

Frustrated, Cade slid down into his chair, folding in on himself.

Trinity dropped a handful of papers back into a folder. "Well… out of all the power shifts we're about to deal with, this is by far the one I least expected."

"One that can also bail himself out of the safehouse whenever," Wes added.

"Oh, hell no," Cade said. "You can bet your ass that's not happening any time soon." He hesitated at Evie's expression, pinned between a document and some portion of the table in thought. "You okay?"

"Hm? Oh, no, sorry—I was just… thinking of something." She reached for a file from the stack. "I guess let's just focus on opening the watch first and see what else we find along the way?"

FRIDAY, APRIL 17TH AT 2:38PM

Typed meeting notes upon meeting notes obscured whatever chance Evie had to pick out her father's contributions to the documents on other factions. Each dated page discussed seemingly arbitrary complaints and newly imposed rules like a homeowners association meeting in which Trick moaned about how their Spirit neighbors aren't picking up after their dogs. And there were a *lot* of concerns about Spirits, contributing to the possibility that there might've been some truth behind the suspicions they had, despite any solid evidence.

Evie rocked back in her chair and fidgeted with her watch, turning it over in her hands much like how Aiden had. Her thumb traced where that mark had glowed along the back with his touch. She peered at it, narrowing her eyes and tilting it in the light to try to make it out again. Nothing. Evie tugged the chain over her head and flipped it over a couple more times, her fingers catching on the cover's intricate design.

She cupped her hands around the back, squinting into the small, dark cavern she created with the hope she'd catch sight of that glow again. She didn't. She blew out a breath and dropped it into her hand, pressing her thumb against it like how she pressed her hand into the recess of the archive door. The device warmed, letting out a ticking hum with a subtle pulse under her skin, followed by a sharp, resounding *click*.

It slipped from Evie's hands with a clatter against the table. "*Shit!*" She shot up from her seat, her eyes wide and her heart stopping before she scrambled to scoop it back up.

Opened.

"What?" Trinity asked, her head whipping toward her past the short stacks of books. Everyone else stood or craned their necks, the entire table fixed on her.

She twisted it around in her hands and prayed not to find a one, feeling guilty with Cade's blue eyes peering over her shoulder, stuck in a position she desperately wanted to avoid. There it was. Her rank. Her fate.

II.

"Two," she breathed. "It's the number two."

"You opened it?" Trinity shot up, her chair scraping against the carpet in a muffled push.

Evie couldn't help but look to Cade then. He smiled at her—an expression that echoed her relief, though there wasn't that soft twinkle in his gaze that she'd seen when they snuck off to try out her talent.

Haven tapped her shoulder, guiding her away from the excitement of the others and over to the window to stand face-to-face with the archive Mist.

"Two," Evie answered this time, angling for her to see the inside of the watch. The woman smiled, sliding her a key through the small slot. Her heart sang, realizing that not only could they finally get the name of the individual to take over the Trick as a faction, but maybe some answers as to why this was happening. "Thank you."

She stared down at the keyring, where the Roman numeral two rested. Her hand closed around it as they hurried to the far side of the archives, falling into the mob marching toward the ominous double doors.

"How much you want to bet it's all filing cabinets?" Wes said with a wry smile.

"If that's the case," Trinity said, "then they better have *everything* in them."

Evie pushed the key into the lock and turned. A satisfying *click* of the bolt, and she shoved the doors wide open. Inside, books lined every inch of the walls, and a small island of filing cabinet drawers sat in the middle with a solid, marbled countertop over it. A small box sat on top, directly in the center.

"Oh, *good*," Wes mumbled, "it's a fuck-ton of books."

Evie slowly stepped inside, her eyes roaming over the cabinet labels. A couple were blank, but next to them was a drawer labeled what must've been the final year they stood in these archives with a dash that led to no end date. She tugged it open. Thick, marked folders that ran all the way up until fifteen years ago.

She plucked out the most recent one, flipping it open to find a list posted inside. A list of Roman numerals. Her father's name was listed in the slot next to the two, and just above it was the name Kenneth Belmont.

4:57PM

"What do we got?" Trinity asked as Wes returned to their huddle table.

His phone was still dangling from his hand after a check-in with the Keepers' records office. "Good news or bad news first?"

"Bad," came Tarryn's reply, dropping another folder onto the tabletop.

"Belmont's kid isn't in our system. He must've bypassed noting that he even had a kid in our records because I searched public records—and here's the good news—he did have a son. Master's student at NAU by the name of Leigh Belmont. He went to a college out of state until a couple years ago and transferred into his other program right here in the city." He tapped his finger against the stained wood. "I checked up on his social media, and he's updated it recently. He's stuck around."

"We need to get to him before someone else does," Tarryn said. "Let's pack up—"

"Let me talk to him," Evie quickly said, earning an uncertain hum from Trinity. "Look, it was a lot for me to handle coming from two people who I wasn't sure were real detectives or not. He might be a little more relaxed if I approach him and show him that I have a matching watch."

"Haven and I are still going with you," Tarryn said. "It's out of the question to go by yourself."

"And that's fine. I'm just asking that you two keep your distance while I approach him."

"Only under the condition that you call me and let us listen in."

Evie stood a little straighter, almost unable to believe what she was hearing. "Yes—Of course. Deal."

Trinity wrapped her knuckles on one of the books. "So, what should we do in the meantime?"

Cade cleared his throat. "I, um… I think there's somewhere I'd like to go, but I'd rather not go alone after everything that's happened."

"And where would that be?" Trinity raised an eyebrow.

Wes folded his arms over his chest. "Trinity, you act like we have the option to tell him *no*. We can't make him go back to the safehouse now that he's in charge of the Shade. He outranks us."

"Wes, if you say that again, I'm going to lock you in here and leave you."

"What? That he *outranks* us?"

She glared at him, slowly pulling one of the books off the table, bouncing it in her hand like she was considering hitting him with it.

"Are you two going to help me out here, or am I on my own?" Cade asked sharply.

Trinity rounded on him. "If it's the Callaghans, no, I refuse to take you."

He shook his head. "They're the last people I want to see right now. Just trust me on this. I need you two to take me and wait outside for maybe ten minutes."

"Only if you call us and mute your phone too," Trinity said without hesitation.

He scoffed. "What? *No*, that could get me killed."

"He's got a point," Wes mumbled.

Her lips pressed into a thin line. "Fine. We'll go, but if you get your ass beat, then that's on you."

Tarryn's fist hit the table a couple of times. "Okay, we'll track down Leigh. You three deal with whatever Cade needs. Before we leave, let's try to split the list of names and run them so we have something to go on in the rest of our search." She grabbed Evie's shoulder. "Could you grab the list of names real quick since that section is warded?" She jerked her head toward the small archive room.

Evie nodded and jogged back in, pulling open one of the cabinets and tugging the list back out. She nudged the drawer shut and paused when she stood in front of the box sitting on the cabinet island. Twelve Roman numerals surrounded the lock like a clock face, and her hand went to the key resting in her pocket. She glanced over her shoulder, the paper crinkling in her grasp.

Later, she thought. *Later*.

THIRTY-TWO
CADE

Trinity threw the car into park across the street from their destination and stared at the curving, gold-painted letters above the door that spelled out, *Martelli's*. "Why are we here, Cade?" Trinity demanded, twisting in a seat with her lips pulled back in a snarl.

"Because I asked you to drive me here," he replied, reaching for the door handle. The power locks clicked, and he jumped, swiveling back to her.

"I am *not* letting you walk in there to get yourself killed after all the shit we just went through," she hissed, a low guttural sound that strangely held a kernel of empathy.

"Just fifteen minutes. If something goes wrong, and I don't text you, you can bust down the door with my full permission."

"You have to let him out, Trin," Wes said.

She continued to stare at him for a moment, her jaw working until she unlocked the doors again. *"Fifteen minutes."*

Cade scrambled to get out of the car, tugging up his hood before jogging across the street. He wasn't a fan of how his hand shook when it pulled open the door nor did he enjoy the workers milling about to get prepared for the shift. He kept his head down, acting like he belonged there—like he was walking with a purpose as one of Roman's little informants or Marco's straggling thugs.

Navigating down the hall, he stepped into the lounge, circumventing most of the Martellis surrounding the card table who emitted cheers in the heat of their game. His pace picked up, along with his heart, in that final stretch toward Emilio's closed office door. It swung open just as he reached it, and Angelo backed up with some goofy, apologetic grin directed at whoever stood inside.

"*Move,*" Cade ordered, dropping his voice to something hard like Jay would use. It sent him stumbling backward into the wall with wide eyes. Cade didn't hesitate to step inside and rip the door shut behind him. Emilio simply stood there, his brows raised in surprise as Cade removed his hood.

"What the fuck happened to you?" Emilio breathed.

Cade winced as he remembered the vivid, horrific red he was staring at. "It's been… a very long week, Emilio. I honestly don't have the energy to even begin talking about *this* again." He motioned to his hair.

Emilio moved ever-so-slowly, planting his hands on his desk as the surprise slipped from his features. "Let's start with a different question then… *Where* the hell have you been?"

"Oh, you know…" He let out a nervous chuckle, bordering on the edge of hysterics with how they were both dancing around a certain question—assuming that Emilio actually knew and wasn't fooling around. "Cheating death left and right because that's my new normal now."

Emilio scowled, seeming to re-examine him like he'd missed something. There was no mention of why or calling in Marco and Roman to witness his execution in some duel. *Nothing.* Alyx had said that the Martellis were being quiet, but was that because they were just laying low during Liam's wild ride, or was Cade being baited?

"Do… you not know?" he hesitantly asked.

"Know what?"

"About Liam."

Emilio scoffed. "What, that Liam's running things now? Yeah, it's a travesty. Everyone's pissed. If you're here for sanctuary, Cade, you need to know I can't give it to you now. Not with Liam's warpath. I have to look out for my own, I'm sorry." His gaze softened with remorse.

"I—" Cade forced out, a little more worried now that he had to explain his predicament. "I'm not asking for sanctuary from Liam."

Emilio sighed, rubbing a temple. "Then why are you here, Cade?"

"Well, um… Liam's… He's *out*."

His head tilted, confusion consuming his features.

"Liam's not in charge anymore. He… left town."

"All right… So, who's in charge now? I don't remember hearing a declaration yet. I'm not stupid enough to think that Liam just ran for no reason since he's salivated over that damn seat for years."

Cade swallowed. "Um… because that someone has no idea what the hell they're doing, let alone how they beat Liam."

It took a horribly long moment for Emilio's face to light with understanding and disbelief. "*You?*" he whispered.

"Look, Emilio," he began, clapping his hands together in a pleading gesture. "I don't know how it happened because I was trying to defend myself, and now he's gone. So now I have the Callaghans and a couple other families visiting Alyx like she's my assistant or something. I don't know what I'm doing, and I'm freaking the hell out because I don't know where to go. I wasn't even sure coming here was a good idea because I feel like you're about to snap and beat the shit out of me." He released a breathy laugh, watching Emilio begin rounding the desk. "Are you?"

He halted, confused. "Am I what, Cade?"

"Going to beat the shit out of me?"

"What? No!"

Maybe it was something in his voice or the fact that he'd continued to advance toward him, but it sent Cade's heart racing. He shot backward, his back colliding with the door as he grappled with the doorknob, his palms feeling impossibly slick.

"Cade, *stop*—I'm not going to hurt you." Emilio held up his hands, slowing his pace.

It didn't do much to bring down his heart rate, but he pressed himself against the door, hoping that it would open the moment he'd need it to.

"You're here to take me up on that offer I gave you, right?"

Cade nodded, bracing for the worst.

"You have to *promise* me that you won't go back to Jay. If you do, I'll have Marco hunt you down, got it?"

"There's no way in hell I'd go back to him willingly," Cade breathed.

Emilio reached into his pocket and slid something free, holding it out to Cade in offering. Cade stared down at the metal casing in his palm, realizing it was a pocketknife, and swallowed. His fingers twitched, but he gently picked it up from Emilio's hand. Emilio shifted, rolling up his sleeve a couple times, completely unbothered that he'd just given Cade a weapon. "I'll protect you," he began, "so long as you promise to do the same for the rest of the Martellis with your seat. Like brothers. And I promise not to push you down to better myself like Jay did. I'd expect you to do the same."

Like *brothers*. He understood where this was going now—allowing Emilio to fill that void as someone who actually seemed to care about him. Someone who saw what he could do and contribute. Cade pushed away from the door, standing straighter as he tugged up his own sleeve. He pressed the blade into his own hand before handing it back to Emilio, who did the same. A handshake, and it was done.

"Welcome to the family."

"Does, um… this mean I have to change my name now?" Cade asked with an awkward laugh. "Like marriage or something?"

Emilio rolled his eyes, smirking as he rounded his desk and pulled open one of the cabinet drawers for a first aid kit. "We have plenty of other members who are Martellis without the name or blood." He set out a couple of bandages, flicking his wrist in a silent instruction for Cade to take one.

"Now what? Some sort of family initiation ritual?"

"Just an announcement."

"Like… an email newsletter?"

Emilio chuckled, shaking his head as the kit snapped shut. "I'm going to lead you out into the room over there and make an announcement to the rest of the family."

"Marco's going to piss his pants…" Cade mumbled. "Do you think that maybe we could skip the introductions and let me be like that weird, elusive cousin that everyone just ignores and occasionally shows up at family gatherings?"

Emilio stared at him, a single eyebrow raised. Cade put on a sheepish grin, hesitating as Emilio grabbed his arm and wheeled him toward the door. "We're also going to officially announce you as the Six."

Cade blanched as Emilio opened the door, and he lurched into the hall in a dead-sprint, gagging from Emilio's grip on his hood. His feet dragged against the carpet on their way to the back room. Cade's stomach twisted.

"I *really* don't want to do this right now," Cade hissed through gritted teeth.

"That's too bad, seeing how you just walked into my office and surrendered yourself to the Martellis."

"Would you have let me go if I'd declined and ran?" The hesitation made Cade's heart drop. "You *bitch*—"

"Hey!" Emilio shouted as they crossed the threshold. "Everyone listen up!"

Cade subtly tried to slide from Emilio's grip, freezing up in fear when every head in the room swiveled toward them. He tried to tamp down his panic, but the glances Roman and Marco exchanged gave way to more fear.

"As of now, Cade Hart is a member of the Martellis."

Marco's jaw dropped like someone had hit him over the head with a frying pan. Roman's eyebrows shot up, though he appeared more impressed than completely shocked. Emilio released his arm, slapping a hand to grip his shoulder instead. Cade wobbled, just as shocked as everyone else.

"I'd also like to make the formal announcement that Liam Callaghan is no longer the leader of the Shade. The title has been won by Cade." The corner of Emilio's mouth quirked up. "Which means that the Martellis run things around here now."

5:47PM

"I want you to be my second-in-command," Cade said. He watched Alyx's eyes widen, like it had been the absolute last thing she expected to hear from him in the middle of her living room.

Begging Trinity and Wes to take him here to talk in person had been a bit of a struggle, especially after skirting the explanation of selling his soul to the Martellis. However, it was something he very much had to dump on Alyx in order to make this request of her.

"You want a former *runner* to be your second-in-command? You realize we don't have anyone to back us up or defend us outside of your cop friends, right?"

He held up his hand, showing off the bandage. "I made a deal with Emilio. I'm officially with the Martellis, which means, by association, you're with the Martellis if you take my offer. I won't force you, but I'd want it to be you since you've stuck your neck out for me more times than I could count. I want you to be there at the top with me."

She gaped. "How? I—" She shook her head.

"Emilio offered me a deal back before Jay ran, remember? I took it. He made me promise to help him take care of the Martellis with my seat in exchange for their protection."

"So… wouldn't you want Emilio to be your second-in-command?" she asked wearily, folding her arms over her chest.

"We're going to be more like partners or equals. He's still running the Martellis, and I'm a part of that. That means that I still need someone to back me up like how Roman and Marco do for Emilio."

He waited for her response, watching her bite her lip as she considered what he was really asking of her. He couldn't think of anyone better suited for the job, so if she told him no, he wasn't sure who else he could ask.

After an agonizing moment, she let out a breath, nodding. Cade threw his arms around her, lifting her off the ground. "Thank you!"

"Put me down, you dumbass!" she exclaimed, hitting him until he did.

THIRTY-THREE
EVIE

Evie pushed open the door to the main campus library, scanning the students in NAU hoodies, sweatpants, and sloppy buns. Some stifled yawns on her way past or bobbed their heads to music floating from their earbuds as she shuffled to the stairs, climbing up to the next floor. That's when she saw him with his last tutoring appointment of the day.

She instantly recognized the clean-cut dark brown hair and bright green eyes from his pictures. Dressed in a pullover with a casual dress shirt underneath, he looked like the model master's student next to a hoodied undergrad twirling her hair whenever his mouth opened. He didn't really seem to pay her any attention, instead pointing to lines in her textbook before jotting things down in the notebook between them. Either he didn't notice her flirting or simply didn't care.

Evie turned to fake-hunting for a book, running her finger down the spines with a concentrated frown until the girl began to toss things back into her bag and dragged her feet some before she left. Leigh pulled out his own textbook, pushing aside his pre-packaged cafeteria sandwich and chips. His mechanical pencil tilted back and forth in his hands, jotting down a few things in his notebook as Evie started toward the round table, nervously trying to get his attention. "Leigh? Leigh Belmont?"

He looked up, giving a cordial smile. "Yes. Sorry... have we met?"

"Uh, no, but... There's something I want to talk to you about..." She tugged the chain of the pocket watch from under her jacket.

His forehead wrinkled with confusion until the watch fell free, and then he shot up from his seat with a flicker of fear in his eyes. He quickly rounded the table, and Evie tried to take a step back before he seized her arm. "Put that back," he hissed, glancing around the library.

Stunned, she nodded, dropping it back into the cover of her clothes. Once he let go of her arm, she realized that he had been trying to shield anyone else from seeing it.

"You have to go. *Now*," he told her. "Don't tell me your name or anything that can identify you. Just *leave*."

"I don't understand. Why—"

His voice dropped, low and urgent. "Because there's someone following me around that is very interested in people like *us*. If she sees you have a watch, she'll come for you too." He motioned for her to leave, still checking around them like someone might be watching.

"You—you *know?* Who told you?"

The question appeared to take him by surprise, giving him momentary pause before he began packing up his things.

A surge of panic shot through her. "What are you—"

He zipped up his bag, tossed it over his shoulder, and grabbed his sandwich container. "Follow me. Be quick and keep your head down."

So, she did. She kept as close to his side as he allowed with his pace back-tracking through the library. "Where are we going?" she whispered.

"Grad housing. We can talk there."

Leigh checked over his shoulder before they stepped outside into the gray afternoon, jerking her sideways toward one of the campus streets, where they awkwardly waited at a crosswalk. He tapped his foot, glancing up and down the sidewalk until the signal chirped, and he ducked into a building doorway alcove. One keycard tap later, and they were inside, riding the elevator up to his room and locking the door behind them.

Only after dumping all the stuff on his neatly-made bed did he reach into the pocket of his jeans and retrieve a watch identical to her own.

"Were you not told when this was given to you?" Leigh asked.

"No—No, I assumed it was just another gift from my grandpa because he worked on clocks. I didn't know any better until maybe two weeks ago when a couple of psychos busted down my apartment door."

His eyes went wide. "But… you know now, right? Someone's told you?"

"That I'm Trick, *yes*. Did your family tell you?"

"Yes, and they told me to stay away from New Atlas, but I foolishly thought I could fly under the radar while I finished school. Considering you're the second person in the last week I've encountered that wants to talk about it, I've made a mistake."

"Who else talked to you?"

Leigh paused, his mouth working for a moment as he glanced back toward his studio apartment's window. He rubbed his cheek. "Look, if you know what's good for you, you'll get the hell out of New Atlas. I'm not sure what's going on, but I have a feeling we'll want to be as far away as possible and *soon*. I'm just here to finish my damn program and book the next flight out."

"Leigh—"

He put his hands on her shoulders, his eyes boring into hers. "I'm telling you for your own safety. The moment *I* stop being useful to this woman, I'm almost positive she'll try to get rid of me. If you don't know how to control what you can do, then you don't stand a chance, which is why you need to stop asking questions and *leave*."

"I'm not leaving." She clenched her fists and pushed his arms off her. "Who talked to you?"

His lips pressed into a thin line, irritation clouding his features as he took a step back. Then his face fell, accompanied by a sigh. "Vivian. She followed me to the library last week and wanted to make a deal. I assumed she was a university worker who wanted to offer me a post-graduation job until she mentioned the watch. She said that she needs someone like me to help her, and she also alluded to something I'm not… super comfortable with…"

"Like?"

"I-I don't know. Maybe I was reading too much into it? But it sounded like if I told her no, she might kill me so I couldn't get in the way."

"Then come with me," Evie said, offering a hand. "She won't be able to touch you if you come back with me to the Custodians."

He reared back in surprise, shaking his head. "You seem like you mean well, but you should probably cut yourself loose and run. My family told me not to go back for a reason. They made it clear that something big was going on when they started hunting us down."

"But you're saying that they're doing that because we're the only ones that can stop them, right? Is Vivian the main force behind this?"

He released a nervous laugh. "No, I don't think it would be her because she *is* Trick. I don't even think her talent is all that strong from the way she talks."

Evie's mind snapped back to the woman who'd threatened Cade in the hospital. This wasn't the same woman, was it? But what were the odds that there were *two* rogue Trick threatening people? "Leigh, if you sit back and do nothing, what will happen to the rest of us? What if we can stop whatever this person has been trying to do? They clearly already assume we can, which is why they're trying to get rid of us, right? You're just going to give up and walk away? Won't they come after us later?"

A noise of frustration. "I don't *know*, okay?"

"What was she possibly alluding to?"

He ran a hand through his hair, shifting uncomfortably. "Exposure," he whispered. "I… don't know why anyone would want to expose us to the rest of the world, but it could cause mass hysteria. The entire reason the Custodians exist is to quietly keep things on track with our talents, not openly flaunt that we're doing it. It wouldn't turn out like some dumb superhero movie where people just accept that some of us can do bizarre shit. People will panic and try to resist. Imagine how you felt when you found out about all this and amplify it because you don't have any sort of talent to defend yourself. It leaves people vulnerable and scared. It turns into fight or flight, almost like if aliens showed up one day."

"But couldn't Mist, like… make everyone forget? Why aren't they being hunted?"

He gave a harsh chuckle. "Not on that scale, no. I don't even think Trick could just… *reverse* an entire announcement and have people forget either though… It would take an absurd amount of talent."

"We're still clearly being hunted for a reason though. You can't seriously think that we won't suffer the consequences if it really does happen, do you? We can't hide forever—"

"Vivian is going to come after me if I try to ditch her, and you might become collateral damage. Are you sure you want to put yourself in harm's way like that when you're clearly new to all this?"

The degree of concern written on his face struck her deep. He was trying to be brave and protect her, but the problem was that Evie was done hiding.

He buckled. "I don't suppose this shit can wait until my

master's program is over, can it?" Leigh half-joked and scooped his bag off the floor.

"You can think about it when we get you somewhere safe," she said. "I have a couple of friends waiting a few blocks down in case I needed help. They'll get us there."

"No offense, but I don't think anywhere is safe. Not while there's someone among the Custodians slowly dismantling everything brick by brick."

THIRTY-FOUR

CADE

FRIDAY, APRIL 17TH AT 6:26PM

Cade's legs bounced slightly in his chair while he watched Leigh shift on the couch, seated next to Evie. She tucked a lock of hair behind her ear and he fidgeted with his rolled-up sleeves, making sure his dress shirt tucked under his sweater vest didn't get wrinkled in the places where it stuck out. Watching him made Cade squirm, originally assuming that whoever they'd bring back would be some sloppily-dressed student he'd passed on the street a million times, rather than a guy who seemingly had his life more together than Cade ever would.

But instead he was staring at a pair of matching, studious Trick. He sank a little further into the armchair, the heel of his hand digging into his chin.

"Why, exactly," Tarryn said, slowly passing in front of a blank TV screen, "would this woman go about exposing us and backstabbing her own faction?"

"While I'm not positive what stakes Vivian has in all this," Leigh replied, "it's logical to come to the possible conclusion that if one doesn't want the Trick to reverse a potential outcome, then you eliminate them. It's like… burning history books to allow history to repeat itself. If you know the past, you can prevent something in the future, right?"

"Let me guess… history major?"

He slid her a begrudging look, his cheek puffing out like he was biting down on his tongue.

"I have a question about Vivian," Evie said, ripping the attention away from mister pretty boy. "Is it possible that this is the same Trick that went after Cade in the hospital?"

There was a hint of distaste in Leigh's weary gaze in his direction. "That seems… rather odd for her to confront a Shade…"

"She tried to kill me," Cade said flatly. "And she mentioned that she'd tried it before but failed."

Leigh's mouth parted in surprise. "What? What the hell would she have to gain from killing a Shade? I could understand another Trick or maybe a Spirit with a decent glimpse of the future, but…" His hand moved to his mouth, his brows furrowing as he stared at some arbitrary spot in the room.

"Has she threatened you at all?" Tarryn asked, stopping in front of him.

"Not directly, no," he mumbled. "So long as I continued to help her."

Cade watched Haven start over to Leigh, tugging off his glove. Watching Leigh scoot closer to Evie made Cade's hackles rise, forcing himself to start to sit up.

"What are you doing?" Leigh asked nervously.

"Oh!" Evie exclaimed, her eyes lighting up. "Wait, Haven can compare who Leigh's seen against Cade's memory, couldn't he?"

"I'm not sure that I'm all that comfortable with—"

"Leigh, it would be beneficial to know who we're looking for," Tarryn said. "Not to mention it would allow us to come to any conclusions about what you've seen that you might've overlooked." She turned her attention to Cade, and he grimaced, finding Haven's sights locked on him. "Cade…" She snapped her fingers, pointing toward where Haven hovered near Leigh.

Grumbling, he pushed himself up, taking a seat on the edge of the coffee table as Haven perched on the arm of the couch. Haven already began signing something to Tarryn, which she began to translate, "All three of you will enter into those sets of memories…"

Haven paused, as if he was contemplating before signing something else.

"Chronological order would be best," Leigh said, Cade whipping his head around to find him focused on Haven's signing. Haven, too, looked just as surprised. Leigh cleared his throat, rubbing his hands on his jeans. "I've… taken a few ASL classes."

"Chronological order, it is," Tarryn said, gesturing for Haven to begin.

Haven held out a hand to Cade, who took it with a sigh, and the other to Leigh, who hesitated. Cade was a little annoyed that Haven didn't push him into getting this over with, instead waiting patiently for him to come to his decision.

"What's the worst I could see?" he finally said. It was a comment Cade would've laughed at had he not been immediately pulled under by the Mist.

———

The first memory was one of Cade's own. He was at the bar. The mystery woman slid into her seat, sending a shiver up his spine in real life. That sense of déjà vu never left and was further amplified when she handed him that damn card. An omen of a bad time and worse things to come. But it was over in an instant, and the bar dissolved into a library.

This couldn't have been him, that conclusion further confirmed by the hand that reached for one of the books, showing off a dress-shirt sleeve capping a sweater rolled up to his elbow. This was Leigh. His eyes tried to roll, but instead they were pinned to the book he flipped open.

"Quite a dull place to be spending a Saturday, isn't it?"

Cade knew that sultry tone, a little pissed that she'd gone out of her way to hand him a death warrant the night before. She stepped into view then, standing next to him along the massive row of books.

"It's not all that boring when you have a goal," came Leigh's reply, adding a soft chuckle in her direction.

"It's funny how you mention goals… I think that perhaps you can help me with my own, specifically in regard to a certain problem I've been having."

"If you're looking for a tutoring session, I usually refer people to my calendar to set an appointment—"

A breathy laugh from her cut him off, taking him off-guard.

"Oh, Leigh, I'm not here for tutoring."

His grip tightened on the book, echoing that realization that he hadn't given her his name. His voice dropped to something low and defensive. "Who the hell are you?"

"A friend. I believe we have something in common." She casually slid the book from his hand, examining it. "Time is quite a funny thing, isn't it?"

"I'm not interested." To his credit, Leigh turned and started to walk away from her, but he wasn't fast enough for her not to step in front of him again.

"Oh, Mr. Belmont, I wasn't asking if you were interested or not. I'm suggesting that you help me. It would be a shame if you were to decline." She gave a razor-sharp smile that held just as much malice as the look she gave Cade back in the hospital, spun completely differently in terms of what she stood to gain.

"What do you want?" he ground out.

"To offer you safety in exchange for helping us."

"*Us?*"

A smirk. "I'm not a one-woman army. I have many friends, and I'd be more than happy to share as long as you do as I ask."

She held the book out like a peace offering, and Leigh took it without breaking eye-contact.

"I don't even know your name," he said evenly.

"Vivian." Her eyes crinkled slightly around the edges, pleased with his answer. "Don't wander off campus. I'll be back soon."

The world tilted, setting Cade—*Leigh*—at a table in the same damn library, Vivian sliding into the seat across from him with a pleasant smile. He barely glanced up at her, keeping an eye on the text in front of him while rubbing his temple like it might make her go away. "What do you want, Vivian?"

"Don't you ever grow tired of hiding?"

He choked out a laugh. "What's that supposed to mean?"

"You've been hidden away for so long, wasting your true potential. Reduced to a glorified librarian when you know you're above those you study alongside."

"That's rather presumptive, seeing how I actually enjoy what I'm doing. Maybe I want to live a normal life."

She casted her eyes down on his open book with a look of disdain. "Why read history when you can make it? Isn't that what you want—to be known? Be a name that gets written in the history books, rather than just some nobody that organizes shelves and writes dull, meaningless contributions. It's all a waste when you consider the real history no one else really knows about."

He ignored her, though his eyes stopped catching on the letters printed on the paper.

"You know," she said, leaning forward with a slight edge of remorse to her tone. "I've hid for a long time too. I've wasted so much time pretending I was someone I wasn't. I was robbed of my talent and the life I deserved, and there are plenty of others who feel the same way too."

He sighed, meeting her gaze then. "Vivian, I… I'm hiding because I was asked to. I don't want the years spent protecting me to go to waste because I decided to make a foolish decision."

"How noble of you, but have you ever asked yourself what *you* want?" She raised an eyebrow, and Leigh didn't have an answer. There was only a void between them. "I don't think you're really content wasting your life with these trivial books. I think you'd rather get your hands on the real history locked just out of your reach. You could even bend and shape it to your will. All you have to do is help me, and I can give it all to you."

A blink, and Cade was himself again, standing on the subway with a card in his hands. That scribbled address on the back of it slipped into smoke from under the door of that abandoned building he'd followed it to. He fell back into Leigh as he crossed the college campus, catching a glimpse of Vivian watching him. Cade during his two terrifying nights in the hospital with her nonsensical threats—her promise to finally get it right after so many tries to end his miserable existence.

———

Cade ripped his hand away the second he regained control. "That's her," he breathed.

Leigh slowly pulled his hand from Haven's, shaking his head with a frown. "But what she said to you doesn't make any sense —back in the hospital, I mean. If she'd actually lit the room on fire before, you'd remember it. Just because we can manipulate time doesn't mean that we can manipulate memories like that. It would have to be on a global scale, which I've never heard of. The most I've ever done is undo something from breaking, but someone else knew it had been broken because they saw it happen moments before. They didn't just… *forget*…" He bit his lip, staring down at the carpet. "It would mean that Vivian's rewriting entire *timelines*, which is… honestly impossible."

"Or…" Wes leaned against a wall, a thumb tapping his lips. There's *one* possibility, but…" He tilted his head back and forth with a grimace. "Back when I was eight, my parents decided it was time to tell me about the Custodians. Out on the west coast

—where I grew up—the Tears are in charge. They typically take on an advisor. That was my dad. An Animated counterpart to the Tears Head of the Custodians in the city.

"They let me listen to some of their talks here and there, but I admittedly snuck out of my room late at night to eavesdrop on some other things. It was mostly political shit, but one night they discussed a… *story*, for lack of a better word. It was specific to the Tears, but my dad made it sound like there was an Animated one as well. It's the sort of thing that's off-limits to everyone but those who were granted permission by the council…"

"Oops?" He shrugged, giving a sheepish grin. "Now, I don't know if this is real or fictional, but it was a tale about some sort of world-altering disaster. In the story, a Tears stepped up to petition the Custodians to undo the damage that had been done. Somehow, she began to draw power from the world around her and became an embodiment of water.

"She could heal anything that ailed a person and bring life to everything around her. She could push back tides and calm waters, but… The problem was that it wasn't infinite. It was a concentrated, finite power. Once she'd finished her job, her talent or whatever she'd manifested ran out, and she… she died.

"She was one of the first of the original eight to be called 'Fallen', and to honor her and those who stepped up after her, they designated an honorable ninth faction for those who sacrificed for the greater good."

Trinity gave a nervous laugh. "But… that's sort of a *huge* speculation, isn't it? Like, we're assuming that this woman had managed to get ahold of that sort of information in the first place."

Leigh leaned back into the couch, closing his eyes in what appeared to be deep concentration. "If she gave her real name *and* had access to that sort of information…"

"You don't think she has a watch, do you?" Evie asked.

"She did act like she no longer had access to the archives

though, which makes me reconsider how or when she would've been able to get ahold of it."

"Her name wasn't on that roster either," Tarryn mumbled. "But we could see if there's a Vivian connected to any of them."

"Worst case, we'll need to head back and pull an earlier list," Trinity said. "Maybe check her picture against some of the people we have on file or seek out to see if we can find a match?"

"Maybe... I guess let's get to running and see what we get."

Cade locked eyes with Evie for a mere moment, folding his arms over his chest before his gaze flicked to Leigh.

FRIDAY, APRIL 17TH AT 7:02PM

Ren lifted his chin and stared at his reflection in the mirror-glass windowpanes across the street, his face peering from under the shadows of his dull, white hood. Every misting water against his skin sent goosebumps rising along his arms, though he wasn't wholly convinced it wasn't from being in the proximity of the building itself.

The logos posted along the side and hanging off of signs mounted to the corner spouted insurance and marketing offices for their respective levels, taking up one to three floors. Nothing lined up on the fifth floor because that had to be for Mist's little headquarters. He'd caught enough of them heading in and out during the past fifteen minutes while he posted himself at the street corner, pretending like he was waiting for someone to pick him up that he'd almost thrown his phone into the street with the lack of proper notes.

Useless chatter about where to get dinner or excitement about the weekend filled the lines of space instead, leaving blanks where the enigmatic Custodians bypassed his talent. Ren leaned against the brick, huffing and playing with the edge of his phone case. What was he supposed to find here? He wasn't supposed to go inside, was he?

Ren chewed on the inside of his cheek, considering the weight of the tarot cards in his backpack until a man in a pinstriped suit pushed through the revolving doors, his slicked-back black hair and sharp eyes filling Ren with immediate recognition.

Carlton Yuan.

He pushed himself upright as Carlton tucked his umbrella under his arm and stepped up to a car rolling against the curb, its little pink logo glowing on the dashboard making Ren scramble to tap into his notes app again. Carlton's confirmation of the address filled in one of the empty spaces, and Ren bolted to the subway.

The stops blurred with the minutes of Ren bouncing his shoes against the sticky tiles until he emerged from the station and walked the two blocks to the hotel marked on his map. Ren shoved his hands in his pockets and bit his lip, craning his neck to peer up at the towering suite windows looming overhead. He strode through the automatic revolving door into the lobby, warmed by the overhead heater dusting off his puddle-drenched canvas sneakers.

Golden light flooded the lower floor like he'd stepped into a sepia-toned film with the star of this show patting his son on the shoulder while his daughter folded her jacket over her arms with a tight-lipped smile. All three of the Yuans started into the restaurant after the hostess, and Ren ducked in after them, slowly pacing along the mirror-backed bar until they took their seats. He climbed into a stool, and the bartender stopped at his seat.

"Are you meeting someone, kid?" she asked hesitantly.

"My dad's busy with a meeting upstairs, so he told me to get something for dinner and charge it to the room." Ren smirked, but the woman flashed him a warm smile, eating it up with an offer to get him started with a water and a menu.

Ren's grin dropped the second she had him situated, and he fished out his phone, pouring his focus into the trio in the corner of the mirrors.

…concerned about your asking into the current Six, Carlton said.

Emmaline shook her head, Ren nearly hearing her breathy, exasperated laugh. *Out of all the times to oppose this—now? Dad, we need to be a united front, and leaving anyone out of that—*

They're almost definitely the ones behind all our recent problems because they do nothing but stir up trouble. There's division for a reason. The ranks are tightening for the better. This is the natural progression of things—

Dad—

Enough, Emmaline. He jammed his finger against the table. *This is precisely why I thought you shouldn't be the one to run for this seat.*

Excuse me for a moment… Elliott mumbled, dropping his manilla napkin on the table with Carlton's permissive nod and pressing his phone to his ear on his way to the lobby.

You're being unreasonable, Emmaline hissed.

Ren's phone clattered against the bar top.

"You okay, honey?"

His vision swam as he looked back up at the bartender, her caramel-colored eyes filled with concern.

"Y-yeah… Just getting a little headache…" he breathed. He winced and rubbed his forehead, the quiet pulse slowly spreading across his skull.

"There's medicine in the gift shop—"

"I should go," he rasped, sliding out of his seat. "Sorry for the trouble." He dropped a couple bills on the counter and fumbled with his phone on the way out.

You should've left this race to your brother. He'd be better suited to this than you.

Emmaline threw her napkin down, scooped up her clutch, and marched through the restaurant. All the patrons turned to stare in the bar wall's eerie reflection, and Ren ducked toward it before her heels echoed through the lobby.

Ren swayed as he followed, skirting past modern art with black, white, and yellow shapes dabbled on canvas.

"Em, where are you going?" Elliott's voice cut through Ren's skull, amplified ten-fold. Ren stumbled, glancing back to see his hand on Emmaline's shoulder, ducking into a whisper. A faint ring pierced Ren's ears, growing louder with each word.

"He doesn't respect me. I've had enough. I do nothing but try my hardest, and it's never good enough. I'm doing what Mom would've wanted, and he's pissed—"

"Em—"

Ren bit down on his tongue, trying to shove their voices away as he followed the revolving doors. The street screamed with blaring horns and sirens. Bile climbed up his throat as he staggered toward the crosswalk, and his knees buckled.

Holy shit.

His phone almost slipped from his hands, shaking as he scrolled through his contacts and half-collapsed against the building. Every ear-drum-shattering pulse made his vision blur, so he squeezed his eyes shut and pressed his sleeve across his face.

"Hello?"

"Angelo," he gasped. "I need you to pick me up."

9:38PM

"You really need to stop sneaking out, Ren," Angelo muttered as he helped him up the stairs.

"Sorry," Ren mumbled, his head bumping into his shoulder with every shaky step. "It's never been this bad… Usually I can make it home." Cold sweat beaded along the back of his neck, sending shivers through him. His closed eyes squeezed tighter at the hint of light shining red through his lids.

The creak of Ren's bedroom door was a sweet melody to his

ears, filling him with relief as Angelo guided him across his haphazardly strewn clothes and dumped him onto the mattress.

"Water? Meds? What do you need?" he asked while Ren focused on the rattle of his pain medication rolling around in his nightstand drawer. "This it?"

"Probably," Ren said, grimacing as he held out his hand. Two pills dropped into his palm before his ears perked at the fumbling of the cap clicking into place.

"I'll be right back. Hold tight."

No footsteps. The tap kicked on downstairs in the kitchen, and then a rough, damp hand took his free one.

"Spilled a little in the rush, but here you go."

The smooth glass intertwined with Angelo's fingers as he helped Ren knock it back with the pills—a gesture he was thankful for since he swore he would've tossed water all over his sheets with how badly he was trembling. The cup scraped against the nightstand, and Ren fell back into the pillows with a sigh.

"Does it actually help?"

"Knocks the edge off sometimes," Ren breathed.

The side of the bed sank down, taking his heart with it. He was sticking around out of pity when he could be doing something else more productive than babysitting Ren's dumb ass.

"You don't have to stay, Angelo."

"Maybe I want to chat a bit. You okay with that? Something to maybe keep your mind off the pain. Or, wait—does it make it worse?"

"We can talk. As long as you whisper."

The mattress shifted, and Angelo patted his leg. "So… the Martellis are in charge now."

Ren heard the slight smile seep into his voice. "Yeah?"

"Yeah." He chuckled. "Cade Hart beat Liam somehow, and Emilio took him in under our banner. I was talking to him about other possible ways to help out where I can right before, and he pulled me aside right before I ran out, saying he might have something in mind for me. Might be getting a promotion." He shook Ren's leg, half-singing, and Ren rasped out a laugh.

"I'm glad to hear it. What do you think of him?"

"Hart?" Angelo hummed. "I'm… not sure yet. Jay was pretty damn scary, but I don't really get that vibe from him, you know? I'm hoping that means things will be a little better with him in charge."

Ren half-nodded, mussing up his hair against his pillowcase. "Yeah… Me too."

THIRTY-SIX
EVIE

"Vivian Greene," Tarryn announced, dropping a packet of papers onto the coffee table. In the corner sat an image of a girl with freckles and rosy cheeks.

"What…" Cade mumbled, staring down at it.

Leigh pulled it toward him. "That's her, but… it says she's thirteen?"

"Yep," Tarryn said. "She's the daughter of one Abigail Greene, the former holder of the twelfth watch."

Cade's head jerked up, his mouth falling open. "The woman we saw has to be in her thirties, not—"

"There's two of them," Leigh said in a breath, his hand moving to his mouth.

"So, she really did it, didn't she?" Evie asked, staring down at the bright-eyed girl. She bit her lip, her thoughts obscured by the jingle of Trinity's keys on her belt as she paced.

"Why? I don't understand…" Trinity said, throwing her arm toward the document.

"She's *thirteen?*" Wes cut in, leaning over the back of the couch past Evie.

"According to this, yes," Tarryn said.

"Then, assuming she managed to find whatever's in the archives to master time, she had to have done it in the future." He drew back, folding his arms over his chest with a thoughtful gaze pinned on the coffee table. Humming, he tilted his head. "So, she jumped all the way back here from fifteen or twenty years from now…"

"She said we hadn't met *yet*," Cade mumbled, his face pale and his fingers digging into the knees of his pants with his blue eyes distant and haunted. Evie wished he would've looked at any of them then, but he didn't.

Leigh frowned, tugging at his collar. "And she acted like she knew me."

Tarryn lifted her head, staring Wes down. "You believe that she Fell, but what's the motive?"

Haven's sharp motion caught Evie's attention. A near-fist went to his lips, arcing downward and out to meet his other hand.

"Revenge?" Tarryn asked, her tone somewhat dismissive. "For what?"

"She's the twelfth watch-holder, right?" Leigh asked. "That puts her at the bottom of the totem pole."

A flurry of hand motions from Haven in answer, slowly sending both Tarryn and Leigh's expressions into a slackened state.

"If a Spirit wanted to destroy the Trick," Tarryn said, "then they could manipulate her into going all the way back to shove them out of the picture."

"B-but," Trinity stammered, "there's a way to—I don't know —*undo* that, right? Isn't there a way to stop her before she decides to possibly jump back again?"

Evie heard a hiss from Wes. "*Maybe…*"

"*Maybe? What do you mean maybe?*"

"Look, the only way I know to stop it is for her to run out of fuel, which is time in this case. She might be rationing it because she knows it's finite, but I don't know how much she could have left."

"I do."

Evie's head turned toward Cade, along with the rest of the room. All eyes were on him, everything still, as if the room were on pause.

"She said this was it, remember?" The question was aimed at Trinity, striking true with how her hands fell to her sides.

"We have to reverse it," she mumbled, her voice rising immediately after. "We have to reverse it. She needs to know that she's on the wrong side of all this. We can't let her die for nothing just to shield some spineless asshole."

"And we won't." Leigh stood from his seat on the couch, his green eyes hard. "I'd like to go to the archive. There should be a solution there too if it holds the problem."

"Did we even see a special book that might have anything like that?" Tarryn asked with furrowed brows, bouncing that question off of Wes, who shrugged.

The stark image of that box sitting in the cabinets. Evie shot up next to Leigh. "I did. It was in the secondary room."

"Well, then." Tarryn fished out her keys. "Let's get the hell out of here."

The rush of movement began to sweep Evie toward the door. She skidded to a stop in front of Cade's chair when she noticed he was still staring down at the documents, no sign of him leaping up to join them.

"Cade?"

His head jerked up. "Oh, um. Go ahead. I… think that maybe I should stay here."

The door creaked, everyone stopping just outside or on the threshold of the door. The excitement fizzled out like air escaping a punctured balloon. Trinity glanced back at Wes, clearing her throat. "You go with them. You have a better idea of what to look for than I do. I'll stay back with Hart for a bit and catch up with you tonight."

Evie forced a smirk, tucking her hands into her cardigan pockets. "Talk to you later?"

His gaze flicked back to the door. "Yeah. Yeah, I'll talk to you later."

Her smile faltered slightly, but she gave a brief nod and started after the others. Even though she looked back before Wes began to pull the door shut behind them, Cade didn't. He sank down into the chair, angled away as Trinity watched them leave.

11:37AM

Having Cade on her mind when she stood side-by-side with Leigh in front of that ornate box wasn't helping. The feel of three sets of eyes on her back only served to make the matter worse, especially when Leigh pulled his hands away from it.

He shook his head. "This isn't right," he whispered. "We shouldn't open it. There's got to be another way—"

"Leigh, we don't have the luxury of time," she said, forcing herself not to meet the gaze of their Keepers. "If you don't open it, I *will*."

"I don't think you understand the risk involved."

"Clearly, I *do*, or else I wouldn't even be standing here right now. I would've turned in my watch and asked to forget everything."

"We can't *unsee* what's in here," he snapped, finally looking her in the eyes. "Once we know it, we can't just have Haven or someone else remove that because then *they'll* know."

She rocked back.

"This is the equivalent of opening Pandora's box, Evie. We won't be able to put it back."

Her fists clenched and unclenched. He may have been watching her, but she was watching the box. "Are you afraid of it?"

There wasn't an answer. Just a bob of his Adam's apple.

"If you're worried about knowing it as the leader of the Trick, then let me read it. We can check the rest of the archive based on what I find if the answer isn't in there."

His hands gripped the edge of the cabinets, worrying his lip. There was a moment of stillness before the tension in his shoulders slipped. "Are you sure you'll be okay?"

She reached over, pulling the box in front of her. Her palms pressed against the sides, feeling that hairline fracture where it would split apart. "I can take it." Strangely, she believed those words—a truth knotting in her chest, keeping her from fraying.

"Okay. I trust you."

12:03PM

The dump of information that followed sent Tarryn belting out a list of orders, orchestrating the divide and conquer of the sections to hit first. It hadn't been all that surprising to not find a way to reverse it in that book, though the new knowledge that weighed on her mind pushed for an alternative answer. The feel of the bound pages was too slick between her fingertips in comparison to the rough, worn pages of the one in that box. The cover was ornate and encrusted with metal that the leather tomes shelved around her lacked. Deep in her soul, she already knew that none of these books could march back time or bring it to a shuddering halt.

Evie snapped the book shut, sliding it back into its slot. As much as she wanted to tell Leigh to have a hand in thinking it through, she might at least be able to pick his brain. She strode toward the other side, passing Tarryn sorting through a stack of thick volumes at one of the tables and noting Wes thumbing through a section further ahead. Vaguely recalling that Leigh had vanished into one of the recesses of shelves book-ending the special room, she made a sharp turn, skidding to a stop.

Her brows shot up, possibly reaching her hairline when she found Haven shoulder-to-shoulder with him. Heaven's head was turned slightly, grinning and mouthing words to go along with his hidden hand-gestures, barely noticeable by the jostling of his arms. Leigh gave a breathy giggle, finally glancing toward him with a, "Would you stop? You're being distrac—"

Evie recognized the moment he noticed her. His body snapped up straight, along the thud of a book shutting. He shoved it into Haven's hands—the quickest way to shut him up, though Tarryn was the only one here able to understand what they were conspiring about. Leigh cleared his throat, smiling nervously as he started toward Evie. She hadn't ever recalled seeing Haven's eyes darken like that, especially in her direction, but she supposed there was a first for everything.

"Evie," Leigh said curtly, tugging on his collar before clapping a hand over the flush creeping up his neck. "Um—Is there something you needed?"

"Oh, um—" She awkwardly pointed away from the nook, not all that sure where else to go other than away from Leigh's *distraction*. "Mind if we talked in private for a sec?"

He grabbed her elbow, guiding her away several paces to the edge of the next set of shelves. "Did you find something?"

So that's how he was going to play this. "You don't want to talk about—" she started, starting to point toward Haven's shadowy corner.

"*No*," he hissed, his face turning a darker shade of red. "I'd *prefer* to discuss whatever you retrieved me for."

Her hand dropped, sliding into her cardigan pocket, her eyes catching on that damn forbidden box. "Leigh, I don't think we're going to find anything out here."

"We have to." He started shaking his head.

"But we haven't yet, and we're running short on time," she said, dropping her voice to a whisper. "We might be better off going after the Vivian that's… er, I guess the *current* Vivian—not the one hunting people."

"I understand where you're coming from, but…" A low, agitated hum. "*But* the flow of time is… ugh… *tricky*." He cringed.

"How… so?"

He chewed on his lip, bouncing slightly. "Well… there are several theories of how time can work, but it's honestly hard to know how it functions because none of it can truly be properly proven. Let's say that we do reach out to *our* timeline's Vivian, we talk with her, and she sides with us, but the other Vivian doesn't disappear. It could be that said second Vivian isn't hooked into this timeline anymore, or she's somehow from another timeline that resembles this one but was disrupted. It could be fractured already if she's gone after me and Cade more than once."

Her lips pressed into a straight line. "I don't follow."

He sighed, running a hand through his hair. "They could be the same, but different somehow. It's the conundrum of if you were to go back in time and kill a distant relative, would you still exist? Would you disappear on the spot? Or, because you came from a reality in which said relative didn't die, would you continue on like nothing happened? A second you may or may not exist if you carried on through that timeline."

Her shoulders fell, staring at the edge of a table with a thumb to her lips, searching for answers that weren't there.

"The other issue is sequencing," he said, stepping into her view to lean against that spot. It forced her to look up, taking in his contemplation. "If Vivian's done this for at least a dozen iterations, she knows what buttons to push and levers to pull. Things that happen out of order could cause everything she *wants* to happen—or I guess, her puppet master wants to happen —to crumble, rendering everything around us unusable, and triggering a reset."

She grimaced. "That doesn't mean we can't at least try it, right? It's got to be worth a shot."

"Fair…" he forced out through slightly gritted teeth. "However, if she's barely a teenager, there's going to be a parent or guardian standing in our way that might be rather pissed to find a couple of Trick and some Keepers on their doorstep to talk to their soon-to-be-wayward child. It might not even be an option. Plus, there's no saying what triggered Vivian to take the bait in the first place, so it might all be for nothing."

Evie's hands went to her head, fingers interlocking overtop of it with her chin tilted toward the chandeliers.

"We can *try*," he said, sighing. "But I personally feel it would do us more good to find a way to stop future Vivian instead."

"Then we'll keep looking," she mumbled, closing her eyes.

But instead of seeing young Vivian's face, she only saw those typewriter-printed letters on old paper, taunting her with all their secrets.

THIRTY-SEVEN

CADE

SATURDAY, APRIL 18TH AT 2:27PM

Cade fake-napped on his couch after Trinity brought back a bag of Mexican food from down the street. It wasn't so much because he didn't want to talk to her, but that wasn't *not* the reason either. He'd called for sleep to take him, but the bastard never came. The vibration of his phone also ensured that it wouldn't be happening any time soon once he read the message it had delivered.

> Got some stuff I want to discuss. Swing by tonight.

The name at the top read, 'Emilio'. Cade picked at the rubber case, tilting his head back to glimpse Trinity busy with her laptop.

> I might be a little busy. I'll let you know if I can slip away.

It turned into a waiting game after that. Every tap of her

fingers against the keys became some indication of whether or not he'd be left alone. That solid, final *click* perked up his ears, cueing him to shut his eyes before she could tell anything was amiss.

"I'll be back tomorrow," she mumbled, patting the back of the couch on her way to the door. The soft sound of it catching behind her became his signal to begin his count. Five minutes. Ten.

He sat up, his phone screen brightening in his hand.

I'll be there soon.

2:59PM

No one stopped Cade on his way to Emilio's office—an odd thing to get used to. Sure, a few of them followed him with their eyes, finding something else to stare at when he acknowledged them, but that was the extent of it. No Marco sitting around with his cronies playing cards. No Roman tossing out orders or keeping peace. Only a few Martellis milled about, mumbling about the bar staffing and filling in. Cade was just… *there.*

So, once his shadow fell across Emilio's desk, and he was greeted with a grin, his heart almost broke. That horrible, familiar feeling of being welcomed. That's what he hadn't been able to place.

"Glad to see you made it," he said, rising from his seat. "Got a bit of a surprise for you."

"I, um… don't really know if I'm all that fond of surprises anymore."

A firm, gentle pat on the shoulder guided him back out of the office, sending him lagging behind Emilio down the hall. He laughed, causing Cade's feet to drag a little, despite the light-hearted amusement it echoed. They stepped out the backdoor together anyway, where Emilio pulled out his keys and motioned to his car. "I would've had you meet me there, but I wanted to show you myself."

Cade's flashback to the last time he'd gotten into a car with a brotherly figure didn't exactly help in this case. He let the back door squeal on its hinges, slamming as Emilio started to climb into the driver's seat. No extra coercion outside of a slight frown when he did a double take at seeing Cade still standing there. Finally, he followed his lead.

The small talk that commenced on the way to, well, *wherever*, eased him into pulling his hand further away from that red buckle button after maybe five minutes. Once they hit a secured parking garage under a newer-constructed apartment building, Cade relaxed. At least it wasn't a storage unit.

The ride up to the top floor left him staring at the little security card tap in the elevator. His heart squeezed, and his arms moved to fold over his chest—the closest he'd dare come to hugging himself in front of the Martelli leader. 'Brother' or not, this whole mess was still very much a transaction. So, when they stepped into a sleek, contemporary-styled hallway with cylindrical lights illuminating large, over-simplified number plates next to the doors, he was a little surprised that Emilio was unlocking one.

"Er, um—Look," Cade said with a slight chuckle, "we're *brothers*, right?"

Emilio paused, raising an eyebrow before breaking into a laugh. "No offense, Cade, but you're not my type." He rolled his eyes and shoved open the door, motioning for him to go ahead.

Though he had the urge to wipe his hands on his pants, he took a step inside. He wandered into a two-story loft with floor-to-ceiling windows lining one wall and a freestanding electric fireplace parallel with it—the only thing obstructing the view. Leather furniture and dark wood was broken up by steel and exposed industrial components.

"Nice place," Cade said, his eyes roaming up the stairs to the second-floor walkway.

"It really is. It was a bit of a bitch to throw together on such short notice too."

Cade spun around, frowning. "Short notice?"

"Yeah. It's for you."

He blinked, jaw dropping slightly before he started shaking his head. "I—"

"Cade, I'm not just going to leave you to fend for yourself after all this. You're one of us now."

"I'm not sure that I can accep—"

"I said I'd look after you. I'm keeping my word. This is your home. Well, unless you'd prefer something else, which I can arrang—"

"No!" Cade said, his words tumbling out in a rush. "No, no! This- this is fine—great, even."

"Good." That damn charming smile again with a hearty clap on his shoulder. "This is Martelli property, so no one's going to bother you here. I'm sure it's a far-cry from crashing wherever you've been anyway."

He jingled keys, teasing Cade to hold out his hand. The feel of that smooth metal and textured plastic reminded him of the unless set still on his own keyring. Emilio's hand fell away, strolling on in to *Cade's* apartment—a weird thought—his face angled upward toward the hanging bulbs. "I also lured you out here to discuss the chain of command."

Cade's hand balled around the keys, turning toward him. "I asked Alyx to be my second-in-command. That won't be a problem, will it?"

"Oh, no. She seems fine to me, but I was thinking more about resourcing. Like someone you can use for errands and things that you should steer clear of."

"I'm… not sure I follow."

"You're the *Six*, Cade. I know I can't exactly stop you, but I can at least offer a body in your stead for running out to check on something and the like. Jay had you and the Callaghans mostly. You shouldn't be running around doing house calls because you have bigger things to deal with—*we* have bigger things to deal with."

"So, what? You're going to give me a lackey?" He snorted.

"You want one?" It took Cade a moment before he realized he was serious. Emilio leaned up against the edge of the kitchen island countertop. "How about Angelo?"

"N-no, absolutely not—"

"He's not as good as you when it comes to networking and intel-gathering, sure, but he's got potential."

"Emilio—"

"It's about an *image*, Cade. Jay had his—the unyielding hardass that got his hands dirty because he was a lone wolf. If you're going to be a Martelli, you're going to *act* like a Martelli. Hold yourself in a higher regard. Only deal with the high-level things that warrant your time." His arms fell to his sides, standing face-to-face with him now. "What do you say? Are you ready to command respect?"

Cade stared down at the keys in his hand, his thumb tracing over the keyring while he bit down on the inside of his cheek. "Yeah… I think I am."

8:54PM

Cade bounced on the balls of his feet, his arms swinging back-and-forth in front of the fence. Evie's apartment light was on with faint shadows dancing along the walls. Eventually, everything settled, and he worked up the courage to make his ascent. A light tap on the sliding door caused her head to jerk up. She fumbled with her laptop, shoving it away at the sight of him, and ran over to let him in.

"I was getting worried," she said. "They said you checked yourself out of here, but…"

"Yeah, I… Wait, you were worried?"

"Um, yeah? Cade, people have been trying to kill you, of course I'm worried. Plus, you were acting weird when we left."

His hand went to the back of his neck, glancing away. "Well, I didn't want to get in the way since I'm the Six and Leigh's the One, so…"

She frowned, folding her arms over her chest. "Hold on… Are you *jealous?*"

"Oh, please," he said, shoving his hands in his jacket pockets. "I'm not the jealous type."

"Uh-huh… So, you didn't decide to stick around and see me just because you wanted to say goodbye for your dramatic, brooding exit?"

"*No*, it's a friendly, strictly-platonic goodbye. No drama."

"Finally gave up, huh? Thought you could push through the whole Shade business, but realized you couldn't compete with another Trick?"

His eyebrows shot up, letting out a laugh. "I mean, you two would certainly pair well together with your college educations and cardigans."

"Yeah, that's a real shame, considering I caught him flirting with Haven."

"O-oh…" He cleared his throat.

"Yeah. 'Oh.'" She shook her head, grinning. "Regretting checking out yet?"

"Now? A little."

She playfully punched his bicep—an action that sent an unexpected jolt through his body. All amusement faded then, his face falling as she turned away and started toward the couch.

"Wait," he said, grabbing her arm.

When she spun on her heel, catching her stride, she gave him a puzzled look. "What?"

"Do that again?"

"Do *what* again?"

"Hit me."

A scoff. "What?"

"Just—" He released a low, uncertain hum that bordered on a

growl. "Just humor me, okay?" He let go, her arm dropping with a glance at his own.

Evie repeated her action, lightly hitting him. It was enough. Enough for the blood to drain from Cade's face at the realization his back tingled. Exactly like it had when Trinity had held him down in the hospital bed. Exactly like it had when Liam had shoved him against the office wall. Exactly like it had when Cade had first woken up with a damn tattoo plastered across it.

"Holy shit..."

"What? Are you okay?"

"No, I got to go."

"Cade—" Evie's voice hit a sharp note as she grabbed the edge of his jacket sleeve. "What's going on?"

"I just figured something out, and I need to talk to Lily."

"Wait, what? Alone? Cade, no—"

"I'll bring a friend if it makes you feel better, but I have to see her."

"Fine, but I'm coming with you too."

His eyebrows shot up. "What? No, absolutely—"

"I'm *going.*"

The ferocity of those words snapped his mouth shut. There was worry there. Concern for his well-being that punctured his heart. "Okay," he said, crescendoing from a whisper he thought he might not be able to force out. "Let's go."

THIRTY-EIGHT

EVIE

Much to Evie's relief, Cade hadn't lied about asking a friend to tag along. She considered it a bonus that Alyx was also a little bubbly and friendly, grinning at her during their walk while Cade shot her sideways looks. She asked Evie about school and hobbies like the three of them weren't en route to a psycho's lair but out for a fun time.

"Have you met Lily before?" Evie finally asked, derailing the personal questions causing Cade's frown to deepen.

"Er, not exactly?" she said, shoving her hands in her pockets. "I know *of* her, but we've never been introduced or anything. I didn't even know what she looked like until a few days ago."

"Jay took me to meet her," Cade said, his features softening as his stalk ahead turned to more of a stroll. "It was back when Alyx wasn't around yet. He said that we should try to make friends where we can, but she doesn't actually give a shit about diplomacy."

"What about Aiden? Can't you talk to him? He seemed a little less… intense."

He guffawed. "No, I think if I had to choose between the two of them, I'd pick Lily. Aiden's far more manipulative."

Evie's shoulders fell, her gaze drifting over to the brick-and-mortar walls framing windows papered over with advertisements. She opted not to object. Though, in her opinion, Aiden appeared far more reasonable than Cade believed. Her vision traced the windowsills and doorways, absently mulling over how to re-approach the topic until she snagged on a graffiti tag. A tag with a familiar symbol.

"Hey, isn't that..." She pointed to it, slowing down.

"Huh..." Alyx mumbled. "Weird someone tagged a Fallen logo out here."

"Looks like the one I saw a couple nights ago," Cade said, giving a half-shrug. "I don't know what this weird 'RISE' shit is all about, but they need to learn to spell. Leave the Fallen to do whatever cryptic nonsense they do. We got bigger problems to worry about."

So, Evie forced herself to keep up with his pace, taking in one last look with her ever-present question of belonging stuck on repeat. Like a song she knew every word to but refused to sing along.

10:37PM

The Funhouse looked nothing like it had the last time they'd stepped foot inside. A myriad of violent colors had been splattered against the white brick walls. Tall, standing tables attracted patrons holding drinks, where they laughed and bounced on their heels to the thumping music.

"Stick together," Cade yelled. "I'm going to hunt down Lily."

"By yourself?" Alyx gaped.

"Preferably, *yes*. Keep an eye on Evie, and if anyone asks, she's a Spirit. I'll be back in a few."

"Dumbass," she muttered once he was swallowed up by the crowd. Evie's breath caught when her eyes drifted up from where he'd been. Straight up to where Aiden stood on the catwalk overhead, surveying his makeshift kingdom before fixing his sights on her.

"Well, we might as well gather some intel," Alyx said, breaking her stare-down with Aiden. "Maybe we'll find out who's hunting you. Come on."

She led the way, only allowing Evie to glance back up for a brief second to find him gone. The irony of potentially being hunted by him in the midst of tracking down a deadlier hunter wasn't lost on her, but she jogged forward anyway, knowing full-well there was no hiding in this crowd with her cardigan and loose blouse. She cursed herself for not asking Cade to wait so she could've changed—not that she really owned anything ripped, black, or vibrant enough to fit in.

Ten minutes later, she and Alyx had somehow melted into a small grouping that didn't recognize either of them, despite the off-putting looks they gave her. Alyx cranked up the charm, leading the conversation into the Fallen, getting balks and eye-rolls from them before the floodgates of complaints let loose. The memory of Wes's story caused their harsh words to bite a little harder, making Evie's nails dig into her palms.

When she couldn't take it anymore, she asked Alyx where the restrooms were. Her reply came with hesitation and a caveat to be quick, but at least she was able to step away. That was enough. She began cutting through the crowd, heading for where Cade had gone when she'd placed enough bodies between the two of them.

"Lost, Miss Thatcher?"

She spun around to find Aiden there, a bemused expression plastered on his face.

"No. I'm looking for Cade."

Instead of discouraging her, he motioned for her to follow, heading in the complete opposite direction. She bit her lip, taking one last look toward her original destination before she complied. Even if Aiden wasn't taking her to Cade, she might be able to get more answers from him than what Alyx was fishing for.

He pulled open a door tucked into a shadowy corner, taking the two of them into a dim, bare hallway that gave way to a metal stairwell. The music muffled with the *click* of the door behind them.

"Awfully brave of you to come back here again," he said on his way toward the steps.

"I want to know more about Lily's game."

He glanced over his shoulder with a hand gripping the wood railing. "It's not really so much *her* game than one she *feels* is hers. A little Spirit has been whispering things that have certainly piqued her interest." He began his ascent, a swift jog that Evie mimicked until they hit the upper landing. She assumed the doorways further beyond must've been offices since the entire side wall boasted viewing windows, though she hadn't remembered mirrors or anything when she'd been down below.

"A Spirit?" she asked, her mind catching on the potential connection there. "Aiden, have you met a woman named Vivian?"

"Can't say that I have."

"Are you lying to me?"

"Miss Thatcher, I don't have any reason to lie to you."

"But if you wanted to get rid of the Trick, you could lie and say we're on the same side."

"Then tell me," he said, leaning his shoulder into a window-pane, "have you encountered hostility from any Inked outside of Lily and I?"

Her composure wavered. She hadn't. At least, none that she could recall. It'd only been Shade and Fallen. "No... I haven't."

"The Inked have nothing to gain by getting rid of the Trick. We're already considered to be at the bottom, so why bother adding more negativity to that? However..." His head turned back to the pit of bodies, tapping a finger to the glass. "If you're looking for someone with a motive, I'd consider having a little chat with your Fallen friend from *Teal*."

Sure enough, when she peered down, Serina stood at the bar, bottle in hand while she laughed next to some guy who grinned ear-to-ear.

"Wait, she's *Fallen?* And how do you know that they were some of the ones to attack me?"

"Word gets around quick here. Everyone knew about Jay and the Fallen the day you were brought into the Custodian's care."

"And do you have any idea why'd they want to get rid of me?"

He hummed, shaking his head. "If I knew, I'd tell you. Though I have a feeling Lily's new Spirit is withholding *some* information."

"Who, Aiden?"

His eyes glittered with amusement as he released a chuckle. "If you believe that her little Spirit somehow masterminded this whole ordeal, I'd reconsider since he's seventeen. I doubt a two- or three-year-old managed to do all this."

She shifted uncomfortably, the tips of her fingers digging into her cardigan sleeves.

"So, perhaps you should start asking a Fallen who might lead you in the right direction, should you decide to seek out the answers yourself." He pushed off the wall, starting down the hall again. "Our time is limited. Tick-tock, Miss Thatcher."

Staring down at the crowd, Evie worried her lip. Oh, the risks she was taking. She started back down the steps, shoving open the door and slipping through the crowd like a thread through the eye of a needle. When she made it to the bar, Serina was gone. She spun around, her eyes searching for the streak of blue, catching it nearing the exit.

"Serina!"

She bolted for her, pushing past irritated patrons as she called out again. Serina's head whipped around, her eyes wide and searching before landing on her. She broke into a wide, excited smile as Evie skidded to a stop. Before she got another word out, she was pulled into a hug. "Another club?" she asked, shouting over the noise. "Damn, you're really breaking out of your boring ways."

"Can we talk outside?" She tried not to sound desperate, attempting to tamp down her emotions as Serina pushed away. It'd been too evident in her voice from the concern on her friend's face.

Serina took her hand, giving it a squeeze on their way out into the crisp night air. The oppression of all the distorted noise fell away with each step, along with the tense feeling knotted in Evie's shoulders.

"Is something wrong?" Serina asked, slowing to a stop once the music eased into a soft pulse.

"Um… Are you Fallen, Serina?"

"Oh, actually… yes…" She bit her lip as she dropped Evie's hand. "I didn't really know how to bring it up back at *Teal* after hearing you're a Spirit and all. Honestly, I was starting to think you were avoiding me."

Evie shook her head. "It's been a little bit… *busy* lately. Nothing to do with you, but—I… actually was hoping I could talk to you about something. I'm considering Falling." Saying it as a way to bait her into possibly giving her answers to all of the links to the Fallen floating around, paired with Aiden's nudge, left her stomach in knots—though, on the other hand, it felt like a weight lifted off her shoulders after bottling up that idea for so long.

Cade had encouraged her to stay the course. Everyone else reassured her this was right for her. Serina was the only person who didn't fully understand the weight of her situation but had known her the longest—the one member of the Custodians to give her an honest opinion in this entire mess since she sat in the place Evie envied the most: one sitting on the outskirts of expectations.

Instead of excitement that Serina was possibly gaining a

closer friend, her expression darkened, closing herself off with arms folded over her chest. "Are you sure, Evie? It's not at all something you should take lightly—"

"I understand that. Trust me."

Her head dipped toward the pavement, sighing. "Okay, well… ask away."

"Why'd you do it?"

A breathy, humorless chuckle. "Because I was afraid of hurting someone."

"Because you were Inked?"

Her eyes went wide. "What? Oh—" Her hand went to her hair with a snort. "No, I was Animated. I really struggled with keeping any fire under control. I turned into something I feared. I was depressed and anxious about slipping up in front of someone that didn't know or not being able to contribute to, well —*everything* to help keep things in order. Not to mention that I always felt more at home with the Inked, so… They set me up with a therapist for weeks to make sure I was in the right frame of mind before giving approval."

Serina slid up her sleeve, revealing a small flower tattooed on her wrist. It looked like a simplified textbook botanical sketch. "People say the Inked don't have much of a purpose anymore, but they're just treating them like a dirty little secret for handling stuff like this." She tugged her sleeve back down. "At least I got to pick something I liked. The downside is that I'm stuck carrying around this stupid little token."

"So… you have a normal life now?"

"Sort of. I guess? I'm still a part of things, but I'm an outsider like I always felt I'd been in the first place. At least I'm comfortable being who I am now… Do you… Do you not like being a Spirit?"

Her chest tightened as she tucked her hands into her sleeves. It was like looking in a mirror, only the disassociation with being Animated translated to Trick, and Inked had been replaced with Shade. "I don't feel like I belong." A hollow, horrible truth. A sad reality that she didn't have to tell a lie in the hopes that Serina might offer her more.

Her face crumpled into sympathy. A slight, knowing smile tugged at the corner of her mouth. "That's okay. I know how you feel. But you know this can leave you pretty vulnerable, right?"

"I already feel pretty vulnerable, Serina. I'm not exactly *great* at what I can do. It's more of a burden than a gift. So, do you... do you think you could help me figure out where I need to start?"

"Of course." She grabbed her shoulder, giving it a comforting squeeze. "I'll help you through it."

She could've cried then, hating how relieved she felt that someone wasn't trying to talk her out of it. That horrible tug-of-war within her finally began to calm, satisfied with her solid answer that weighed heavy on her heart. The entire reason why she'd really wanted to talk to her almost slipped her mind until that moment.

"Oh—I um... I also had a question about this graffiti tag with the Fallen mark on it I saw around town. What is that, exactly?"

She frowned, looking puzzled until her eyes lit with recognition. "Oh! I actually asked some Fallen friends about it recently. They said it's a group meeting on Sunday and Wednesday night. I made a joke asking if it was some sort of alternative Fallen church-cult thing, but they said I should join them at some point. I'm... not sure what it is, exactly, but I guess the tag is a coded address to get there? If you want to come with me, I don't think anyone would mind since you're considering Falling anyway."

"I don't want to intrude, but..."

"We should go tomorrow." A firm decision Evie was relieved to hear. "I'd feel better having a friend come with me, and the others aren't nearly as level-headed as you are."

"Okay..." she started. "But what if someone asks to see a token?"

Serina waved a hand. "Trust me, they won't. Fallen don't typically ask for private things like this. Not to mention I can just flash mine, and they'd assume you're good since we'd be together."

"Thank you, Serina."

"Anything for a friend, Evie. And even if you decide not to Fall, I want you to know I'll always be here to talk."

SATURDAY, APRIL 18TH AT 10:39PM

Cade pounded a fist against an office door, rattling it in the frame.

"I'm *busy*," came the sharp, snappy reply.

"Yeah, well I'm busy too, Lily. Open the damn door before I kick it down and beat some answers out of you."

It flew open, Lily glaring at him with a hand on her hip. "*What?*"

"What the fuck did you do to me?"

All irritation fell away, sliding into angelic innocence that made his stomach twist. "I don't know what you're talking about—"

"Cut the shit, Lily."

Now wearing a smug smile, she turned to lead him inside. It reeked of a trap, but it was for something he was already committed to pursuing. He stepped inside, shutting the door behind him as she leaned against the edge of her desk. "I *may* have taken it upon myself to… manipulate the board to my advantage."

"How so?" Cade asked, tamping down a growl.

"Well, there are lots of fun things that Inked aren't allowed to do, but I simply don't care. I honestly *hated* your brother, but you… You're *different*."

His back started to warm, threatening to bead with sweat at the way she'd said that.

"So, I brought it upon myself to eliminate Liam and put who I wanted at the top of the Shade instead."

His eyes widened. If he wasn't sweating before, he sure was now. "Explain," he forced out through gritted teeth, itching to smack that smirk off her face.

"I think you've realized by now it's not a normal tattoo, right? I added a protection ward to it, and that dumbass Liam made the mistake of triggering it."

That's what he'd been afraid of. "Get rid of it, Lily."

She threw back her head, releasing a tinkling laugh. "I don't think you understand that I'm doing you a favor. I'm keeping you *alive*. No one can attempt to directly harm you now, and I get to reap the reward of having someone who isn't a completely useless piece of shit sitting next to me in the council chamber. I suggest you treat me with a little more respect."

"I'm not here to be your damn puppet."

"Then allow me to extend an olive branch instead. If you refuse, at least I could say you had a choice. You can either work with me willingly, or I'll use you to get what I want, whether you like it or not. Not to mention that if you try to get someone else to remove it, it'll be rather painful. I made sure of that."

His hands curled into fists. "What did it do to Liam? How does it work?"

"It pulls on your talent, that's all. It temporarily cleaves it from you to eliminate the threat. A living shadow—a guardian angel."

"But I can't control it!"

"That's the *point*," she growled. "If *you* could control it, then you wouldn't *use it*. You're too afraid to fight back because you're too damn nice to be a Shade. You actually have a" —Lily giggled, causing the room to sway— "*heart.*"

So many mistakes. He'd made so many mistakes along the way for one reason or another. He'd unknowingly traded his freedom for malicious safety.

"Well?" Lily asked, her eyes shimmering in a way that could've been mistaken for joy if it weren't for the hardness there, combined with that twisted smile. "Are you going to work *with* me, or will you be working *for* me?"

A bitter tang settled against the back of his tongue. That wasn't so much of a choice as it was the illusion of one. All of his tensity collapsed into defeat, his hands uncurling with a shaky breath.

"With."

Her features softened, beaming at him. "Good. Then remember that your vote is now mine. It's best you don't forget I'm your guardian, Hart."

11:09PM

When Cade found Alyx hovering near the bar, bouncing on her toes to peer over the crowd, his stomach dropped. "Where's Evie?" he yelled.

"She said she was heading to the restroom, and I haven't seen her since."

Grabbing her arm, he began to lead her through the bodies, eventually letting go in favor of sticking close in their search. It wasn't until they passed by the door that a wave of relief fell over him, glimpsing her standing outside with that girl from *Teal*. He tugged on Alyx's sleeve, and the two of them jogged out the doors.

"Oh, thank God," Alyx breathed. "Cade, I am so sorry."

"It's fine," he said, dropping to a mumble. "She's not exactly fearless. I probably should've warned you of that."

Evie didn't appear to notice them until they were a few yards away, her head turning in their direction with a hand flying to her hair. "Oh, shit—I'm so sorry. I ran into Serina, and I'd thought I'd be back before you were done—"

"We were just saying goodbye anyway," the girl—*Serina*—said with a hesitant smile. "I didn't mean to steal her away from you. I'll see you tomorrow night, Evie?"

"Oh, yeah. Tomorrow night."

With that, she left, throwing back a small wave in her departure.

"You okay?" he asked, forcing his hands into his jacket pockets to muffle his shaking.

"Yeah, I'm really, *really* sorry. It just sort of happened and—"

"It's okay, Evie. As long as you're okay."

"What about you?" she asked. "Did you get what you wanted from Lily?"

No, the exact opposite, actually. "Lily… wasn't very helpful."

Alyx ran her hands up and down her arms, shifting as she glanced back to the pinkish glow of the club. "Looks like this trip might've been for nothing then," she mumbled. "The Inked I talked to didn't seem to have anything valuable to spill… I don't suppose you got anything, Evie?"

"No, sorry… I got a little side-tracked."

"Then let's get the hell out of here," Cade said, placing a gentle, guiding hand on Evie's shoulder. He refused to look back, despite that horrible, creeping feeling that told him they were being watched.

FORTY

REN

SUNDAY, APRIL 19TH AT 11:29AM

Lily's child-like hum filled the tattoo parlor's back room, the melody bouncing off the linoleum-checkered tiles as she shut the small locker and wove through the small towers of cardboard boxes. She hopped up onto the stool across from Ren, dropping a small black box onto the table.

"A gift," she chirped, patting it.

Ren frowned as she nudged it closer, and he plucked it up, prying off the lid to take in the sheen of the circular token resting inside. A token with a curving line bisecting it until it reached a thin, triangular shard—like a pen or brush inking out an artist's design. His thumb bit into the corner, turning white at the sight of the Inked logo on Lily's offering.

"I… don't know what to say," he finally whispered, thinking of Angelo and Carmen's hard work to help fund his college tuition—thinking of all the hopes and dreams his mother had placed on him as her only Spirit son. To give himself a better life off the blood, sweat, and tears of the family who'd been denied what he'd be happily given.

Despite how strong his talent was, it wasn't enough to

exempt them from the damage. That was something he only prayed Cade could fix. Which would take time. And accepting this would throw all that hard work away.

Lily rolled her arm in a motion for him to continue. *"Thank you, Lily,"* she offered.

Ren popped the lid back on the box. "Thank you, Lily, but I can't take it." He slid it back across the table.

Her mouth turned down in an irritated frown, and she slapped her hand over the token's container, shoving it back in front of him. "It's for *you*. If you change your mind before you sign your life away, the Inked would welcome you with open arms. There's still time," she sang.

She tapped a teal nail against the black-papered lid, and Ren sighed, cramming it into his hoodie pocket.

A predatory smile tugged at her lips, and she tilted her head with hands folded under her chin. "So, tell me, little Spirit, do you *really* enjoy your faction, or is it all just an obligation?"

He loosed a chuckle, shaking his head. "That's personal, Lily. I'm not here to spill my guts about my home life."

"Your home life filled with Shade, hm?"

Ren bit his tongue, watching her eyes dance.

"I think we both know what you think of the Custodians as a whole: as broken and fractured as the ninth faction and their forcibly limited involvement in it all." Her sympathetic half-pout vanished with her palms slapping against the table, turning into a carefree smile. "But who gives a shit, right? We're all useless little troublemakers needed less and less with each passing day in their utopia. If you want to reap the rewards, I can't blame you. Have fun. Enjoy the ride." She half-shrugged, her chipper mood bleeding through in its fully disingenuous haze. "But things can change if you break them enough. And I plan to break as much shit as I can before my replacement comes for me one day. So should you."

Ren worried his lip as Lily slid back off the barstool, her hum taking back over the room in her activities as he felt around his hoodie pocket for that box. He gently hit the floor, whispering his goodbye to her as she raised a lazy hand in farewell, not bothering to turn back around.

1:44PM

The circular auditorium stage was crammed with bustling election workers when Aiden escorted Ren past the Mist and Keepers guarding the doors. For once, Ren actually felt like a child in the midst of the Custodians with their suits, blouses, and ties. Aiden tapped his rings together in the depths of his peacoat's pockets, his half-lidded eyes scanning the attendants passing along scraps of paper and tallying votes.

"So damn tedious," he mumbled.

"Do you think the Inked will have a vote like this one day?"

Aiden snorted. "Hopefully not in my lifetime." He settled into one of the blue-velvet flip-down seats, leaving an empty chair on the end for Ren, who dropped down next to him.

"I have to ask… Is your goal to eventually overthrow Lily?"

Aiden's sharp bark of a laugh cut through the frenzy, earning a few annoyed, disapproving looks from nearby Mist. "Hell no. There's no way I'd be able to juggle all the shit I deal with and keep the Inked happy. I'm a pillar of order in a pit of chaos. Lily needs me as much as I need her." His head tilted back, sinking into his coat collar. "I'd prefer to keep it that way, so no, I would fight tooth and nail to keep Lily as the Seven."

Ren leaned back, shifting the box still loose in his pocket. "You don't sound like you feel like you fit with the Inked all that well."

"I sort of don't." Aiden shrugged. "But I still enjoy it here because of the people I've fallen in with. You find your own niche within the Custodians or carve out your own place as you go. It's the reason why we all have different strengths and weaknesses—to balance each other out. Trick and Spirits, Animated and Tears, Mist and Shade, Inked and Keepers. They're all two sides of the same coin when it comes to their talents, but not a single one of them are molded the exact same way. I'm no exception."

Ren spun the box around in his pocket, mulling over Aiden's words as the tallies climbed higher on the screens. Names shifted around in a blur of changing seats like musical chairs, the mere equation to a game making him uneasy.

"Not sure why I bothered bringing you here when all these people getting elected probably want my ass out of this auditorium the second they take their bow on stage," Aiden muttered.

"Well," Ren breathed, "maybe you're wrong. Maybe most of them are just like you: a weird puzzle piece that doesn't quite fit but doesn't quite belong anywhere else."

"That's some wishful thinking, kid."

"Yeah, but that's how we've all managed to work together so far, right?" Ren turned to him, watching his brow lift before a smirk danced across his lips.

"Fair enough."

FORTY-ONE
EVIE

The day that had followed Cade's departure was relatively quiet, especially once Trinity and Wes said they'd follow him. At least that prevented Evie from wearing down a path in the carpet from all the pacing that could've ensued. She watched the clock instead. Every minute passing on her phone or laptop became another milestone—another minute closer to when Tarryn and Haven would leave, taking Leigh back to his apartment. The four of them putting an end to their day of agonizing over possible ways to halt Vivian's progress.

Almost on cue, her phone buzzed mere seconds after her apartment door shut, sending her heart leaping her chest. Cursing, she pulled it from her pocket.

> You need help sneaking out tonight?

She winced down at Cade's question, her thumbs hovering over the screen.

> Thanks for the offer, but I can manage.

Adding a smiley face for good measure, she collected her darker hoodie, and made her escape.

The rest became a blur of lights reflected in street puddles and the slight bite of spring night air. She tried to tell herself that was why a chill slid up her spine at every other corner on the way to the subway, squeezing her phone at every sudden noise. It wasn't until she met Serina at the next station that she allowed herself to relax. They strolled side-by-side down a street that gave way to a diagonal intersection, chatting about the dreadful weather and exchanging nervous giggles.

When Evie set her sights on the opposite end of the street, she saw it split off like a Y. Tilting her head with a frown, she caught a glimpse of the number printed on the glass door Serina pulled open.

153.

RISE—it *was* a secret code like Cade had complained about. Evie recalled a map of the area as she followed her inside, cobbling together that strange collection of streets that resembled an R. And the ISE portion with that backward E wasn't backward at all—they were *numbers*.

She bit down on her tongue as they navigated the interior of the shop, passing by racks upon racks of comic books and heavy hard-backed game manuals. A few rooms were sectioned off with people shuffling in and out, their voices ramping up with dice clattering against the wooden tables. Some of the patrons leered on their way from the restrooms while others pursed their lips, stuffing their noses deeper into books they had little intention to buy.

But no one stopped them from slipping through the door in the far corner that descended into a basement. Framed posters of superheroes, fantasy creatures, and people dressed in steampunk outfits lined the walls. The black, foam tiles padding every inch of free space muffled rubber soles against business-grade carpeting. She swallowed. The soundproofing must be to keep anyone not in the Custodians from eavesdropping, right?

Everything's fine, Evie. A blatant lie, but one that she decided to continue rolling with for sanity's sake.

Other Fallen mingled near the other end, some sitting around the rickety card tables while the rest stood. A small, red-felt-covered platform sat on the far side, where a guy in his mid-twenties with a sharp grin and honey-colored shifty eyes perched on the edge. The water bottle in his hand beaded with sweat, dripping onto his ripped jeans with every sip between his comments to a reedy, bored-looking woman leaning against the wall.

Nudging Serina's arm, Evie mumbled, "Is this a lecture deal?"

"I'm… not sure…" Her head whipped around, frowning. "I'm not seeing any of my other friends here…"

"Maybe we're early? What time is this thing supposed to start?"

"*Welcome*, fellow outcasts!"

Evie almost jumped out of her skin at the bellowing voice that filled the room, sounding as if it were projected through speakers when there weren't any to be seen. Her heart started to thud a little harder in her chest as she bumped shoulders with Serina, who'd gone completely rigid. Water bottle guy was standing up on his makeshift dais now, his hands clapped together like a mafia member about to make them all an offer they couldn't refuse.

"I'm sure some of you are here with friends and skeptics, but the rest of you are probably here without a clue about what our message means. Curiosity always manages to win us over, doesn't it? After all, that's our nature as those who are still privy to the wide expanse of knowledge the others occasionally drip-feed us. But I digress—allow me to introduce myself: I am Sinclair, the one who will open your eyes to the truth of our *unfortunate* situation—"

Serina sucked in a sharp breath. "Oh *boy*, it *is* some cult shit..."

"As all of you already know," Sinclair continued, "we are the leftovers. The *nobodies* of the Custodians. When a problem arises within our faction, the council simply ignores it or pushes it off on each other until it's finally dealt with or dropped entirely. We are not equals. They don't wish us to be. *However*, do we not still contribute toward the well-being of the Custodians? We've been left to keep an eye on the criminals tossed into our faction, bridging the gap between them and the rest of the general population. We do what's asked of us, despite what little we're able to do in our Fall. Some of you may have felt that you were born into the wrong talent or wrong faction altogether, but does that mean we *deserve* to be punished for it?"

Evie felt Serina's hand tuck into hers, giving it a squeeze. She was rooted to the spot, unable to move her legs and drag Serina out with her. That urgency was still there though, her heart ramping up, her mind throwing every warning to go because of her adrenaline spiking.

"What if I were to tell you that we could *rise* to a new height? Imagine the Custodians *without* the split of upper versus lower. I know a lot of you think it's a ridiculous notion, but we could be the gatekeepers of a new era."

Evie's eyes went wide. If she were sitting, she'd be on the edge of her seat, drinking in every word that flowed into the crowd. There was something here that she'd been searching for —an answer that she didn't quite know the question to.

"Imagine a spot at the adult table. A fledgling faction accepted as a newly inducted member of the Custodians. 'But *how*, Sinclair?', you ask. It's simple: we need a lower rung on the ladder. For *years*, the Custodians have wasted their time keeping these miserable people from the brink of destruction while we bicker and fight amongst ourselves. It's time for us to stand together and reign the world in by *force*. We need to show them that they have never really been in control. The *Custodians* are their masters. They are *gods* among men. And we, the Fallen, are their messengers. Their angels, saints, and evangelists. It's time we rise and take our proper place to the right hand of the Custodians—as the angels to gods over men. *Who's with me?"*

Evie's jaw dropped. *Gods?* They couldn't be serious. Why would anyone—

She rocked back at the realization, dizzy because she'd forgotten to breathe. Serina yanked on her arm, sending her stumbling as she dragged her toward the stairs.

"We have to get the hell out of here," she hissed, gasping when she almost smacked straight into a woman blocking their path.

The woman wore a cat-like smile, folding her arms over her chest. Long, dark hair. Deep, crimson lips. Porcelain skin. Evie's blood ran cold.

"How nice of you to join, *Evangelina*."

Vivian.

The muddled ring of an alarm clock echoed somewhere in the back of her mind, bubbling like it was underwater until she plunged in to retrieve it. The world silenced with it—the cheering cut mid-chorus, and Vivian paused like she was stuck in a photo.

"We got to run," Evie ordered, taking the lead past Vivian.

Serina gaped, stammering as they jogged up the steps. "H-how the hell—"

"I lied about being a Spirit. I'm Trick, and if we don't make a run for it, that woman is going to kill us."

Her eyes nearly bulged out of her head, but her legs picked up speed as they moved from a jog to a run through the store, throwing open the door to the street. Wherever that pocket ended, it had to have been somewhere along the way, vanishing in their frantic hurtle toward the station. Only once they stood on the yellow warning strip of the platform did Evie let go of Serina's hand, throwing them to her head to catch her breath.

"You're *Trick?"* Serina hissed, glancing around at the other pedestrians bobbing their heads to the music blaring out of their earbuds or yawning while they scrolled through their phones. "You were just talking to me about *Falling*— Was that a lie too?"

"No, that was the truth. I couldn't tell you the first bit because I was the only one until a couple days ago, and I'm pretty sure they would've tossed me in a padded room or something if I mentioned Falling."

Serina's hands went to her face, rubbing at her forehead. "What the hell…? Evie, you know I wouldn't have taken you there had I known *that's* what they would've been talking about, right? You have to believe that I don't want anything like that. I'm not—"

"It's okay. I know, Serina—I know," she whispered, prying her hands away like she was helping her rip off a mask.

The subway tore into the station, screeching to a stop and unleashing a torrent of bodies. Shoving their way inside, Evie turned back toward the platform before the doors closed, her mouth going dry at the sight of Vivian staring from its center. Serina's grip on her arm tightened, along with their pursuer's gaze of fury. A brief eternity, and then the train sped off, shooting them through the tunnel.

"Holy shit," Serina whispered, refusing to let go for the entirety of the ride to the safehouse.

11:02PM

The following sequence of events turned into an elaborate dance to get Serina checked into the safehouse without throwing Evie under the bus. She'd snuck back up to her room, making a show of meeting Serina in the lobby, where she had also gotten on the phone with Tarryn. Granted, it was a *pissed* Tarryn for being interrupted just before bed, but she and Haven drove all the way back to hear what Serina had to tell.

While most of it was modified to omit Evie, Serina's tears and trembling were far from fake. She ripped up each tissue she'd been given into little strips, refusing to make eye contact for most of the questions. Her description of Vivian had Evie holding her breath when Haven brought in Leigh, but he must've shown an image from his memory, rather than hers from the way none of them turned to shoot her aghast looks.

Ms. Desrosiers took all of this in stride, calmly jotting down notes on her clipboard as Tarryn continued her questioning. Once everyone had seemed satisfied, out came the stack of papers.

"I'll petition for an extension," Tarryn said. "Seeing how you're a friend of Evie's, it's not that much of a surprise you've ended up being targeted too. However, I'm not sure how far we can push the graffiti case since it's being labeled as non-violent, and we're having to keep this fairly under-wraps. I'll have to talk to the detectives involved, and they'll likely want to talk to you early tomorrow."

All Serina could manage was some nodding before they headed upstairs, where she was taken to Cade's former unit. Evie's heart sank.

"I can't believe it," Leigh whispered, stopping next to her in the hall.

"There's a reason why they wanted to get rid of the Trick, Leigh," she said, staring him dead in the eyes.

Despite her resolve, the flicker of surprise in Leight's gaze from the mere implication of Falling simply to stop Vivian might as well have been a slap in his face. "It's *suicide*. You don't fight fire with fire because that's how you go up in flames. We're better off finding another way to combat this."

Haven's abrupt stop behind them kept her from arguing, her hand twitching as it closed around her door handle. Refusing to break his gaze, she stepped backward inside, closing her eyes once she heard the quiet thump against the frame.

Tonight, she'd stood face-to-face with Vivian, a puppet strung up by a mastermind that had the Fallen under their control. Someone who'd hired the Shade as backup. Someone who was a

Spirit lurking in their midst, wishing the Custodians would stand as gods in front of the world.

Exposure.

Equality.

But not really.

It was just a warped reflection of it that Vivian had bought into—what Evie refused to let go of as the real thing. The longer this nightmarish game drew on, the more she realized that perhaps it wasn't *her* that was being dragged down by Cade, but that it was possibly the complete other way around. All of this could've been brought on by her, sticking him in the crossfire. She'd begun to dismantle the lives of everyone around her when she had the knowledge to fix it.

Aiden had said she'd been getting her pieces mixed up. The memory of her standing next to Cade in the stripped-out building of *The Funhouse*, unprepared for Lily's little magic act resurfaced. Lily hadn't hurt Cade. She'd only antagonized him in the glimpses before and after Aiden had Evie cornered. She could either chalk that up to Aiden's claim that they were on the same side, or she could remap the roles Lily had listed specifically to them.

So, would she?

FORTY-TWO

CADE

MONDAY, APRIL 20TH AT 1:44PM

Marco's cards pressed down against the felt of the table, a finger tapping against it with a snort. "You want to shake down the Callaghans?"

Cade didn't budge from where he stood in front of him. His arms folded over his chest, his shoulders tense, his fingers hidden and digging into his jacket with every dread-fueled thud of his heart. This was a test he didn't enjoy—a test that Angelo clearly didn't enjoy either from the way he shifted from foot to foot, fidgeting. However, to his credit, when Cade had ordered him to follow on his way down the hall to meet his nemesis, he had, just like Emilio had said he would. Well, maybe not without stumbling out of his chair first and almost eating the carpet, but he could still work with that.

"Yes," Cade forced out in the hardest, most commanding tone he could muster. "Liam fell off the map without ratting someone out. I need their name."

Marco raised an eyebrow, leaning back in his chair. The cards slid from his hand, snapping against the table. There was a thoughtful gleam in his narrowed eyes that made Cade's stomach clench. It was the type of look he'd expect from meeting a future father-in-law for the first time—a look bearing the full weight of judgment.

"Huh," he finally said, a bit of amusement lacing that puff of a word. Cade felt his pulse in his fingertips now, his body giving a small jolt as Marco's chair scraped against the floor.

I'm in charge. I'm in charge. I'm in charge.

Who the hell was he kidding? Emilio may claim Cade was in charge, but that meant jack shit to someone like Marco—a man who towered over him and caused Angelo's eyes to bug out of his head like he'd chosen the wrong team.

"Gianni, Omar—" Marco called out, his voice booming to rattle Cade to his core. He was certain that he was about to get the shit beat out of him as the lackeys rose to their feet with Marco's lip curling into a menacing smile. That is, until he said, "How would you two like to visit some friends at a pub?"

2:37PM

"L-look, Hart, it was just business—" Declan said, backing up into a desk.

Both he and Conrad had been plotting something in an upstairs office—fortunately not Liam's, so Cade wouldn't have to relive that hell—evidenced by the scattered documents that jumped up with Declan's collision. Conrad still gripped a marker in his hand, his scowl deepening with each step into the room.

"*Save it,*" came Marco's growl. His emergence from the double-wide entry changed Conrad's tune—eyes going wide and wild with horror.

Conrad's voice pitched in alarm. "If you're looking for Liam, he's long gone—"

"I'm aware," Cade replied with far more confidence than he felt. "But since he's gone, that leaves me with you two dipshits to give me some answers, so here I am. I want to talk about the night we hit up the hotel."

The hesitant exchange between both Callaghans tightened Cade's jaw.

"If this is about you getting shot—" Declan said with a nervous laugh.

"Oh, I'm still pissed about that, but I'm talking about *why* we were there. When Liam was trying to kill me the last time I stepped foot in this hellhole, he mentioned that he gave the job to Jay. So, who hired Liam?"

Declan flinched, feeling around for the papers behind them to busy his hands, which stuck to each sheet. Good. He was sweating. "Liam never said his name or anything—Just called him the 'old man'. S-Some old Spirit piece of shit."

As much as Cade had wanted a name, it was at least *something* more than what he'd already had. It confirmed everyone's original suspicions of it being a Spirit, but now he could narrow it down to an older, male member of the faction. He chewed on his lip, swiping a thumb against it before he nodded to Marco and his goons. Angelo's eyes darted between them, quickly filing behind Cade as Marco led the slow, menacing charge toward them.

"Wait—" Declan's eyes went wide, throwing his hands out. "L-Look, we were just following orders before, Hart. We would never disrespect the Six—"

"But you tried to get rid of Jay, who favored the Callaghans when he was in charge," Cade said, his voice cold and unforgiving. "I don't fucking trust you or Conrad. I don't give a shit about the Callaghans. You've all done nothing but try to screw me over or have me killed. So, let me be *abundantly* clear: you're either going to leave town or disband. If Liam ever shows his face around here again, I'll have every Shade on his ass in a heartbeat. And if Jay reappears, I'll do the same for him. They were both pieces of shit who did whatever the hell they wanted, so long as they sat at the top. But do you know what *I* want?"

Conrad's throat bobbed, and Declan dug his fingers under the lip of the desk for support, neither of them brave enough to speak out of turn. It was a strange, empowering feeling between having Angelo, Marco, and his underlings at his back and watching the Callaghans' cower. It was something too easily abused that Cade cupped in his hands—the fragility of the word he used as his new weapon:

"Justice."

10:47PM

Cade stared up at Evie's apartment, comparing the movement in the light to the unit next door with the dark shapes bleeding through the blinds. So, a small party in Leigh's apartment, which either meant Evie was alone or her unit was empty. He hoped for the former, especially after handing off his newfound information to Trinity and Wes earlier in the evening by jumping into the backseat of their car like some snitch.

He'd planned on going home once that was done, but when Trinity mentioned Serina's run-in with Vivian, his mouth had dried up. He knew without a doubt that Evie had come face-to-face with her too, not that he would tell on her until he'd gotten a chance to talk with her first. So, here he was.

Sighing, he went for it, merging into the building's façade and creeping up to the balcony where he found her curled up in a chair. She was chewing on a thumbnail, hand tangled in her hair with her eyes pinned somewhere on the other side of the room—a point where the carpet neared the wall. She didn't even see him—or if she had, she was doing a damn good job of ignoring him.

A gentle tap on the glass caused her to jump in her seat, her face shifting from surprise to something he couldn't quite place. Concern? Stress? Anxiety-driven contemplation? He tried to puzzle it out before the door slid open, but he wasn't given enough time.

"Hey," he breathed.

"Hey."

"You okay? From earlier, I mean. I heard about your friend, so I assume…"

She cringed, nodding as she stepped to the side. An invitation inside that he took in favor of privacy, rather than lingering on the balcony.

"You could've called me, you know."

"Cade, the chances of you being recognized there were too high," she said, wrapping her arms around herself. "Despite however unlikely, I thought it was safer for me and Serina to go alone."

"But why?" he hated the hurt that seeped in his tone, unable to carve it out. "You didn't have to go at all. You could've talked to someone else about what you thought, and—"

"So I can sit around and do nothing again? Leigh might be working on some sort of plan, but it's all taking up time I'm not sure we have, and I've tried to bring up other ways, but—" There was a sheen in her eyes that caught his breath, ripping through his heart worse than that damn bullet. "I just… I feel so *useless*."

He wrapped his arms around her, tucking her head under his chin. His fingers dug into the fabric of her shirt like she might slip away if he let go. His eyes squeezed shut at her shuddering breath against his chest. "You're *far* from useless, Evie."

"I don't belong here. I can't do anything right. I'm being told to sit on my hands and *wait*, so I can't help *save* anyone—"

His soul cried out when he pushed her away, his hands cupped around her shoulders at arm's length. "So how am *I* here right now?"

"A fluke." She sniffed.

Cade released a breathy chuckle, wiping the tears from her face. "You don't give yourself enough credit. You've already done so much, even if you weren't *supposed* to. You're brave, smart, and… well, super pretty, so the only thing you're truly useless in is getting rid of me."

His smirk earned him a chortle.

"Even though I'm Trick and you're Shade?"

That smirk lessened, giving him pause. She waited expectantly, her eyes searching his face for an answer, though he wasn't sure which to give: the truth or a lie. Danger or safety. He regretted not realizing how his hands squeezed her shoulders at the contemplation—an action Evie didn't miss.

"It would be easier if I wasn't Trick, wouldn't it?"

It was a blow he didn't expect. His heart dropped. "No—" he rasped. It didn't even sound genuine to his own ears, but he pushed forward anyway. "You shouldn't have to give up part of who you are for anyone—*especially* me. I couldn't live with myself if you did. I believe that you could be a *really good* Trick if you keep at it. Don't throw that away for the sake of someone else."

Her shoulders slid down, her hands swiping at her face with a deep, shuddering breath. "Can… can you stay for a little while?"

"Of course."

FORTY-THREE
EVIE

Evie had fallen asleep on the couch, tangled up in Cade's arms. His soft, rhythmic breathing sent calming waves rippling through her, anchoring her to that moment. Stretching to check her phone turned into a challenge of not waking him, but when she saw it was encroaching on Tarryn and Haven's arrival window, her heart began to crumble. She closed her eyes and pressed her forehead to his chest, taking in the feel of his encircling warmth, the scent of worn leather and the faint notes of driftwood, the light thrumming of his heart.

Could she really sit back and hope for the best? Wait for the others to figure out some plan to fix everything when there was already a clear solution to try to undo everything that'd already been done? It wasn't like Evie truly felt like she fit here anyway, not when her family had kept it all a secret, and she felt more at-ease with Cade—with Serina—with anyone lingering near the bottom of this totem pole, where expectations fell so low she could breathe. Where she could save the people around her and finally embrace that piece of herself she always craved but never indulged.

She gripped the edge of his jacket when he shifted, silently pleading for him not to sit up. But he did. Stretching with a groan, she pushed herself up too. That annoying grin shot her back to when they'd first met—when he'd asked her if she was his guardian angel in the back of that car.

"Good morning, beautiful," he breathed. The glitter of those blue eyes might as well have been hands around her throat with how she felt like she was choking. When she couldn't reciprocate his teasing amusement, his face fell. "Guess I… should probably go before the wardens arrive, huh?"

Her hand flew out, grabbing his wrist like he might suddenly disappear. "No, please—Not yet."

Cade jerked back a little in surprise, catching his balance with a confused look. "O-okay, okay." He chuckled, though his eyes were searching and uncertain.

So, she let go, chewing her lip. "I… um… I think I figured something out, but I think Tarryn and Haven will want to hear it without a little more proof it could work."

He twisted his wrist in a motion for her to continue.

"Will you take me back to the archives?"

Blinking, he gave a hesitant nod, like he had anticipated something more than a trip to that secret library.

She grabbed her phone off the table, pushing off the couch. "Give me a second to get ready, and then we'll head out, okay?"

No argument. He only nodded again, sinking into the couch as she slipped into her room. Her heart beat a little quicker in her chest once the door shut, her free hand curling and uncurling with a few short, deep breaths to stave off her unease. She tugged out clean clothes from the closet, quick about each movement until she eyed her cardigan thrown over the arm of her cushioned desk chair.

She was no longer a cardigan-wearing college student. She wasn't sure she'd ever go back to that. But that wasn't what snagged her attention: a yellow, folded sticky note scrap lay on the floor near one of the chair legs. Navy ink indented and smudged, but still legible. Evie knelt down, turning it over in her hand after reading the string of numbers there. The back, however, held far more weight.

You know what to do.

And indeed, she did.

10:21AM

People definitely knew Evie was gone by now, but it didn't matter. Not when she was hand-in-hand with Cade, descending down the archive steps with a cryptic sticky note in her pocket and a watch hanging heavy around her neck. Every phantom tick it cried kept her pulse in even time, despite the fear coating her throat. She'd been afraid that Cade would find her hand dripping with sweat when he took it earlier, but if he did, he hadn't declared it.

No alarms rang out once they stood in front of the doors, though the Mist woman watched her with that eerie, all-knowing gaze. Guilt tugged at her as the doors parted, leaving her with that pinpricking sensation at the back of her eyes. She rounded on Cade, taking his face in her hands for a kiss—a real kiss. Sweeter, happier, and more painful when it ended.

The confusion in his eyes gave way to alarm the second she felt a single, warm tear slip down her cheek. If there was anything that she wanted to remember, it was this moment. A time where she finally had stopped burying herself in the future, learned from the past, and lived in the present.

So, her next words hurt her as much as they undoubtedly shredded Cade's soul: "Close the doors."

The whirling mechanisms began to groan back into place in her retreat, leaving Cade stuck on the other side.

"Evie, wait!"

Blood pounded in her ears while she grabbed the key left for her on the window tray. It dug into her palm as she started toward the back room, swiping at her face in defiance of Cade's cries. The resounding collision of the doors shutting sealed her fate with only one person left to open them. One person left to find the remnants of her actions.

So, for her final trick, she'd cleave through time and space to fix whatever the hell Vivian had done.

FORTY-FOUR
CADE

"**O**pen the damn doors!" Cade shouted. He managed to get in one swift kick before the Keeper shot up from his seat with a snarl. Lurching back with his hands up. "J-Just hold on—You don't understand—"

"*You*—"

Cade whirled around, peering up to find a small cluster of people at the top of the steps. One of the men pointed down at him, a scowl creasing his features with a glance back at the rest of his crew.

"*Carter*," came the stern, warning growl of a petit woman next to him. Her straight, black hair swung over her shoulder, cascading in front as her face scrunched up.

"No, Emmaline, we're dealing with this *now*. He's warded by Lily—"

Cade's stomach dropped. *Oh. Shit.* These were the new representatives of the Custodians. And somehow they'd found out that Lily was rigging the system.

"That's enough," Emmaline snapped. It wasn't enough to stifle Carter's rage, though the others kept themselves reigned in, either examining him with varying degrees of disdain or hesitation.

"*Enough?* I don't think you quite grasp the ramifications of her actions—"

"If this is about *experience*, then you can shut your damn mouth right now, Carter. Know your place."

Every second they argued was another second Cade began to shake, wanting nothing more than to spin around and pull open a door that was sealed shut. But that would be what this Carter guy would want—a damn demonstration of Cade's tattoo on a Keeper. An excuse to toss him in a warded room until they could rip everything away from him. Part of him screamed for it since his heart was tearing open anyway.

His saving grace was the sound of echoing footfalls and the sight of Leigh rushing past them. That flicker of disbelief he gave hardened into something commanding and authoritative as he jogged down the steps, ignoring Carter's protests. Trinity did the same when she hurried behind him.

"I said *stop*," Carter roared. Wes was the only one to comply, glancing between him and his partner. All it took was a glance back from Trinity to unroot him.

"Evie locked herself in," Cade forced out.

Leigh mumbled a curse, pressing his hand to the indent.

"Emmaline Yuan, tell these Keepers to stand down—"

Cade's heart leapt into his throat at the sound of damn over half the council converging on them. "Where the hell is Tarryn and Haven?" he hissed.

"Right behind us," Leigh said, dragging Cade inside.

Sure enough, when he looked back, the two of them were weaving through, forming a wall just inside the archive's threshold at Leigh's command for them to come in. "Now back the hell up," he snapped. "Move, or I'll have you forcibly removed from the entrance of *my* archive."

After some shifting and mumbling, they did, giving a thin buffer between the council and the Keepers, including the archive's guard that hovered near the edge. With that, Leigh jogged to the back, Cade watching him slow as he rounded that center counter. He didn't see her there. The floor began to fall out beneath him with each step Leigh took on his way back, disintegrating completely when he noticed the gleam of a necklace chain dripping from one hand.

No.

Leigh's grim expression told him everything. He was going to be sick.

"Do you know who you've let into your archive, *Trick?*" Carter said, hell-bent on continuing his tirade.

The cords in Leigh's neck tightened, narrowing his gaze on their aggressive opponent. A silent challenge.

"He's *warded*. Lily tattooed him so none of us can directly cause him harm. That means he can do whatever the hell he wants, and we can't stop him."

Every word sounded muffled with the world collapsing around him. He wasn't sure if he should laugh or cry. There was a surreal numbness to it all—a disbelief that he'd just been curled up with her in his arms on a couch that morning, and now she was *gone*. If she'd done what Vivian had, then where the hell was she? Why wasn't she *here?*

"I'm not… I'm not going to…" he whispered, unable to get the rest out before the room started to sway.

Leigh grabbed his shoulders. It was something that should've bolstered him, but the horrible press of the pocket watch into his arm pushed something in him to the verge of breaking.

"I believe you, Cade. We're going to find her. We'll fix this."

That harsh *click* of heels sent a chill down his spine, turning his head toward the door. Emmaline stood at the front of the pack, testing the boundaries of Leigh's order with her head held high. "I want to talk to Hart."

Leigh's arms dropped, he and Cade locking eyes. "It's up to you," Leigh whispered. "We can either walk you out of here without another word or you can entertain whatever she has to say before we go. I'm on your side."

Cade wiped his hands on his pants, swallowing with another glance back at Emmaline's commanding presence. With a hesitant nod, Leigh gave the word for her to enter, plus another to shut the doors. That latter statement came with an uproar, arguments breaking out while she strode toward him, undeterred by the fact they were locking her in. That didn't even include the four Keepers flanking her the second the archive was secured.

"A word of warning, Emmaline," Leigh said, wielding each word like a weapon. "If you try anything I don't care for in this hall, I don't care if you're the Head of the council, I *will* order these Keepers to stop you."

"Understood."

That was it. Like it was a simple business transaction and not the New Atlas Custodians' leader attempting to wheel and deal with one of the most despised factions.

"What?" Cade asked, the word coming out in a croak, rather than something fierce.

She cleared her throat, puffing out a breath with a hand extended. "I'd like for us to work together."

He eyed her with disbelief. His mouth was trying to work, but no words poured out.

"I talked to Lily," she continued. "She mentioned she had something over you, but I didn't know to what extent. It doesn't matter though since I don't care about the tattoo. I want a better future for New Atlas, and I think you want that too."

A bitter laugh escaped his lips. "How can you be so sure?"

"Because there wouldn't be four Keepers and a Trick protecting you if you weren't someone worthy enough to shield as the Six. So, please, let me walk you out of here to somewhere safe, and we can discuss a little more in-depth about what I can do to help."

Cade couldn't stop himself from stealing a glance at Leigh, lobbing him that unspoken question of if he should take it.

"Leigh can only do so much, Cade," she said. "But I outrank *everyone*."

"And where will you be taking him?" Leigh asked.

"My apartment. It's secure, but I'll give you the address if you're worried."

Cade swallowed as he fixed his sights on her hand again.

"Please, Cade. I don't want to be your enemy."

It at least *sounded* genuine. Not to mention that perhaps she could lead him straight to this son of a bitch that was ruining his life. So, he took it.

11:32AM

The car ride to Emmaline's apartment came with uneasy conversation. It was specifically because he hadn't expected another passenger riding with them. Elliott kept Cade quiet with his sly smirks and mischievous glints in his eyes. He couldn't help but wonder if maybe Liam had lied or been mistaken about the age of his employer with the sheer presence Elliott carried—a wrongness he couldn't shake.

However, he somehow managed to make it into her sleek, plant-infested dwelling in one piece, despite his body tensing at every snicker or giggle from Elliot in their light conversation. He'd gone straight for the wine rack, much to Emmaline's audible displeasure before Cade was led to the dark-stained oak dining table. The chairs had that elegant, classic feel in their design, matching all the white marble and thin, gold trimmings of the place, merging old with new.

"I don't want any more barriers within the Custodians," she said, wasting no time getting to the point.

A nervous chuckle slipped out. He had to keep his sights pinned on Emmaline to avoid revealing his uneasiness over having Elliott lingering nearby. "That's great and all, but... You just learned I can accidentally kill people, which means all my cards are on the table, and yours aren't. I don't know if I can trust you."

She hesitated, exchanging looks with her brother, resulting in an uncertain smile. "And why wouldn't you be able to trust me? I'm the Head of the council. I'm a Spirit."

He had to stifle a scoff. Like that somehow still meant something in all this. "Because there's a Spirit that used the Shade to put a hit out on the first Trick that the Custodians found."

The shattering of glass against tile sent Cade bolting upright in his chair, eyes going wide in his search for the noise's source. Elliott's wine glass. The man stood stock-still on the edge of the kitchen, his face pale. "What?" he gasped.

"Why would you say that?" Emmaline asked, her voice climbing in horror.

"Because I confronted two of Liam's lackeys about the job yesterday. He left town, but they admitted it was some old Spirit guy. And if it weren't for me, this guy would've gotten away with it. So, forgive me for not being all that eager to play trust games with you."

He cut himself off, his frustration coming to a choke point with the mere thought of Evie. They should've heard something by now, right? She should've shown up like Vivian hopping around town. Unless maybe it didn't work, and—

The intercom buzzed, releasing all the tension knotted up in his shoulders. The sound of Elliott's shoes against the tile heading for the entry signaled that at least he wasn't being kept here against his will. Well, that's what he hoped as he dropped his elbows to the table and pressed the heels of his hands to his forehead.

The good news: he'd been right. Mere minutes later, Leigh was admitted with all the Keepers. Trust had been flung out the window when Leigh took over for him, going all-in on the truth.

1:28PM

"There should've been something by now," Leigh mumbled in his slow pace across the white, fuzzy rug. The thing looked like one of those Samoyed dogs had been shaved and glued down to the damn hardwood.

That was probably why Cade opted to keep his eyes fixed on the potpourri bowl sitting on the coffee table. The twine-woven, hollowed balls with rose petals or some other floral bits that his fingers twitched to pick up and hurl across the room one-by-one. But he acted like a civilized human being in a near-stranger's home, keeping his ass on the couch, tethered by Trinity's hand against his back in unspoken support.

"We'll find her," she said. The same thing she'd said each time any of them skirted saying the worst possible outcome.

Emmaline hummed, her hands steepled together from her seat on the jutted L of her pristine, bright-white sofa cushions. "We need to keep this quiet. If anyone else in the Custodians discovers this, then it'll speed up the culprit's plans."

"And who's to say that isn't happening already?" Elliott asked. He pushed off the entryway's frame, halting Leigh dead in his tracks. "If they're a strong enough Spirit, then they could already know—"

"While that's true," she continued, "as long as we don't prematurely expose them, they'll have no reason to panic and push their plans forward. If we throw everything out into the open, it'll force their hand, which will result in dire consequences—mass hysteria."

Cade's stomach lurched, his eyes falling shut with a shallow, shaky breath. Only Trinity seemed to catch it with how her thumb began to move in small circles.

"It's something potentially reversed," Leigh mumbled, his hand moving to his mouth with a concentrated, downward stare, "should Evie manage to succeed and reappear. If not, I'm inclined to agree with Emmaline."

Elliott scoffed. "This is ridiculous. With more people aware of what's happening, there'll be more of the Custodians on high alert. Regardless of whether or not your friend has ripped through time, time is still of the essence, is it not?"

"*El—*" came Emmaline's stern reply.

"*No*, Em." He plucked out a slim, black notebook from an inner blazer pocket with a pen.

"Oh, my God," she whispered, her hand going to her head.

Cade's shoulders fell as he glanced over to Trinity with the hope he'd get her attention. After a brief argument between the Yuans, she noticed. Her mouth dipped toward a frown.

"Can you take me back to my apartment?" he asked quietly. "I don't think I can handle any of this right now."

He ignored the stares when she helped him off the couch. Whatever she'd said to excuse them hadn't impressed into his mind. The elevator's decent, the car ride across town, the slow walk through the parking garage felt simulated. There was no sudden cry of his name or familiar face rushing to greet him with triumph. Everything he imagined grew dim and more outlandish the longer it dragged on.

"You going to be okay by yourself?"

He hadn't realized he'd ended up in the elevator bank. Just a few steps away from where he'd asked her to take him. He cleared his throat, nodding since he couldn't bring himself to speak—at least, not without his voice cracking.

"If you need anything, call, okay? I got to get back to Wes, but we'll stop over later to check on you and discuss what we're doing next." A brief, comforting squeeze of his arm sent a rippling sorrow through him.

They parted ways, the sound of her echoing footsteps in the garage only outmatched by the obnoxious chime of his escape skyward. The card tap for his floor had hurt, like a lingering burn of his brother, but the fire department-like keyhole marked for his special key twisted a knife in his gut after sparing it a mere glance. It spilled over into a memory of taking her to that secret nook—that stolen, private moment to show her she was special. Maybe that was where he'd failed her. By not giving her a good enough reason to love who she was.

Cade's walk down the hall stretched onward, taking longer than he remembered. His keys clinked together as loud as a wind chime on a gusty day. The entire floor gave off that eerie sensation of morning solitude in the early afternoon. So, when his apartment door swung open, the drop of his keys against the wood floor might as well have been a shriek of an alarm.

Because sitting on his couch was some kid he vaguely recognized and Evie.

If Evie were being completely honest with herself, then she would've admitted that she didn't quite know what to say in this instance. What made the situation even worse was that she and Ren had been sitting or milling about the place for the better part of an hour, which should've been plenty of time to come up with *anything* to say.

Those wide, blue eyes stole whatever was left of her thoughts. The swing of the door behind him became her cue to stand, though she tried to throw her arms out to stop him from the impact that would follow. But, exactly as she'd anticipated, he hugged her anyway. Instead of reciprocating it, she went rigid. Her thoughts looping like an old, skipping soundtrack: *not the same, not the same, not the same—*

"Where the hell have you been?" he breathed, still refusing to let go.

How had she gotten so good at predicting, yet so terrible at getting through this part? It never mattered where she met him, it always managed to pry every word away.

"It's… complicated."

"A *huge* understatement," came Ren's reply, muffled by a fist over his mouth.

She cut him a glare as Cade pulled away. Simultaneous relief and dread pulsed through her, knowing she'd have to look him in the eyes again. Her breath caught when she did, sent backward through time—back to the Cade she'd likely never stand face-to-face with again. No more flirtatious winks, stolen looks, or shared giggles in private. This one belonged to another Evie—an Evie who was stumbling into a new reality to start down an off-kilter path so similar yet so vastly different from her own. He was a copy, just like his Evie was—not that it had made either of them any less important.

"Who's this...?" Cade asked, his brows furrowed in Ren's direction.

He hopped up, wearing a near shit-eating grin. "That 'damn kid' from the club. Angelo's brother. Call me Ren."

His jaw slackened, attention snapping back to Evie. She sighed, pinching the bridge of her nose.

"You brought some Shade kid to my apartment?"

"Some 'Shade kid?'" Ren demanded.

"He's not Shade. He's a Spirit," Evie said, her hand dropping from her face.

"I don't understand—He said he's Angelo's brother, but why did you go get him instead of coming straight back to the archives? What does he have to do with any of this?"

She gripped his shoulders, holding him at arm's length. "Cade, lov—" She swallowed down that pet name, though it went down like a jagged pill. "I'm not your Evie."

He blinked, his features revealing nothing, but that didn't mean she didn't intimately know his inner most thoughts. Confused, upset, distraught, overwhelmed, *hurt*. He choked out a laugh—a joyless, hollow sound bubbling up from desperation. "But—"

"This reality is paralleled to the one I come from, but it's splintered off at a different point *years* from now. Each iteration

I've stepped into is the same but skewed, and it's further distorted and accelerated by Vivian's presence. I'm not sure if *I* created the split, or if it's been there since the Trick disappeared, but it's possible that everything can reconverge. It might line back up again if we can finally nail down the Spirit who set this in motion and put an end to this."

He took a step back, tearing free from her. The disbelief in his eyes was amplified by the shake of his head. "I- How—" he started, glancing over to Ren with hands tucking into his own pockets, patiently waiting. "Prove it. Prove to me that you're actually from the future." Cade folded his arms over his chest, giving a poor attempt at playing heartless.

Undaunted, Evie retrieved her thin, worn wallet, unzipping it to hand him a business card. The paper was soft in her hand, her fingertips almost unable to let it go as he plucked it from her grasp. The sight of those now-rounded corners made it hard to swallow.

Promise you'll always find me.

She had. It wasn't like she could've allowed herself to say no with his hands cupping her face like that. Not with the way his thumb had crested her cheek, feather-light like it had been wiping away a phantom tear.

Cade's features twitched, his fingers pressing into the card before meeting her gaze again. "How?" he whispered, sounding lost and confused after reading off each printed word.

"Because you have a good heart, a kind soul, and a firm hand. Emmaline was the one to endorse you when her term was up. She said it was time for a change, and you changed everything for the better. It's why you have to live." She told herself the smirk on her face was to make him feel better, but her memory tugged at the joy sparking from the first words he'd said to her. "So, future Head of the Custodians, I guess I am your guardian angel."

5:47PM

The arrival of the rest of them had been a little easier for Evie to handle than Cade, who continued to steal looks throughout the evening. Leigh brought his breathy awe and admiration. Trinity welcomed her home with a warm embrace. Wes pasted on a brave, respectful smile that shone as regret in his eyes. Tarryn tried to hide her stricken expression with neutrality. And Haven simply took a seat across from her, peering into her soul like he always did—pulling apart the lifetimes she'd spent and refused to speak of. The weight of it all became evident with each passing minute.

However, the one thing they all agreed on was approaching Ren with the utmost caution. They either eyed him with suspicion or gave him a wide berth. She could see from all the little ticks that they were trying to determine what to make of him, ignoring him during their initial questioning that she had little doubt they'd circle back to later.

"So, the Vivian from your timeline keeps jumping back with you? Is she Fallen too?" Leigh asked, teetering on the edge of his seat.

"No, she's not, but she's… time-bound to me, I guess? That's why she's left me alone. If I go, she goes. If I throw us into another timeline, she gets forcibly pulled in with me. My guess is because when I jumped the first time, she grabbed onto me, so we're sort of fused." She interlocked her fingers. "Though, if something happens to her, it shouldn't affect me. It's one-way. But that means that she's been able to track down her Spirit cohort and accelerate it each time."

"Sorry if this seems a little off-topic…" Trinity said, making a circular motion toward Evie. "But how do you still look twenty if you and Vivian are from the same point in the future?"

Evie bit down on her cheek, sighing. "Well… in my parallel timeline, when *I* Fell, I didn't travel backward. I did it with every intention to conserve what I had, gather clues, and unmask the culprit. At that point, I would have all the evidence I need to send myself back and undo it all, which is something I discussed with all of you, but mainly Leigh and Cade. We had about a dozen suspects by the time Vivian intervened. She had let it slip that we were minutes away from exposure, so I used my trump card. We fought. I took her with me."

"Why not play it out and rewind everything to just before?" Tarryn asked, frowning.

"Memory tampering," Leigh said. "It's possible that it wouldn't work."

Evie nodded. "That, and we were almost positive that whatever Spirit was being things is also Fallen like me."

"*Shit,*" Wes hissed, rubbing the side of his face.

"Is that why you have a little Spirit tagalong?" Tarryn tilted her head toward Ren. She didn't bother looking at him, treating him more like a decoration or accessory. He sank further into the couch, brooding.

"He's a damn talented Spirit, which makes him a strong asset. Each time I've ran into him, I've been able to narrow down my list. Ren's the reason why we've made it down to two: Carlton Yuan and Waylon Frost."

Cade sat up straight at that, his eyes widening. "But you said Emmaline—"

"Emmaline and her father don't see eye-to-eye. Elliott's always been a bit of a weird guy, but unless *he's* the Fallen Spirit doing his father's bidding, I can't imagine him being involved. He may be a little secretive and shifty, but from what I've gathered, he's not *that* strong of a Spirit unless he's hiding it really well."

"I think it's Carlton."

All heads turned toward Ren, who shifted to sit up straight.

"He has the most motive out of everyone I've followed," he continued with a shrug. "He hates the lower levels, but he'd be willing to overlook it in favor of power. That's just the sort of guy he is."

"This isn't exactly something we should base off of a gut feeling, even if the motive is there," Trinity said, rising from her seat. She began to pace across the room, tapping a finger against her lips. "Do we have any concrete admissions? Would Emmaline be able to get one from him if we really think this is our guy?"

"Possibly," Ren said. "If she really respects Leigh and Cade, then she might be convinced to pull it out of him."

"Maybe Trinity and I should stake out Emmaline's place until Elliott leaves?" Wes suggested, leaning back with a sideways glance at Evie. A flicker of nervousness danced in his eyes that she wanted to extinguish. Too bad she couldn't.

"Do that," she said, adding a little more confidence than she felt. "I'd like it if Tarryn and Haven could drop off Ren at his house anyway. After that, they should be able to take over so you two can keep an eye out around here, just in case Vivian decides to take another swing at Cade."

Despite Tarryn's pause in regard to her request, her features smoothed to neutrality. "My only concern is who's going to watch Cade right now?"

"I will," Evie said. She didn't miss the weary, heartbroken look he gave before resting his chin on his palm, finding another arbitrary point in the loft to examine.

"But the safehouse—" Leigh started.

She shook her head. "If I go back there now, it'll trigger a ripple effect. It's better I stay hidden. The only people who know I'm here are in this room, Vivian, and Vivian's Spirit. We need to keep it that way."

No argument came, only varying degrees of nods. So, Tarryn stood, jerking her head toward the door in a silent order for Ren to follow. With a brief look at Evie, he did, shuffling behind Leigh on their way out a little slower than Haven approved of. It was enough to indicate he hoped she'd call him back, but she wouldn't. Haven rolled his eyes when Ren finally stepped through the entry, clicking his tongue as he gripped the back of his sweatshirt to drag him down the hall.

"We'll be around in a couple of hours," Trinity said, awkwardly hovering near the seating area as the remaining few began to stand. "One of us will text Cade when we're back."

"Okay."

Trinity fidgeted with the zipper of her jacket, all that pent up energy unleashing in her sudden advance for another hug. It was a gentle, comforting thing that Evie hated, feeling sick with guilt each second it drew on.

"You may say you're not her," she whispered, "but there's at least a small part of you that is. We'll fix this. I love you."

It might as well have been a punch to the gut—one that she tried to appear unphased by when Trinity released her. This was grief talking. That's what the blurry look in Trinity's eyes said. That's what Evie told herself.

No goodbyes. No apologies. No tears.

She left with Wes, and Evie and Cade were alone. Neither of them spoke right away, a quiet understanding to let everything sink in. In those moments, Evie considered telling him this would be the last chance they had. That there wouldn't be any do-overs or restarts, and if there were, it wouldn't be done by her but a copied Evie—maybe even *his* Evie, even though he'd cease to exist. The pulsing tick at her wrist indicated that horrible reality. Her stomach knotted at the thought that it would cascade into a loop of never-ending destruction.

He ran his hand through his hair as he cleared his throat. "So… where have you been staying?"

Her arms folded over her chest, and she casted her eyes downward. "Been sleeping at a few safe havens here and there… Just keeping my hood up and head down."

"Ones I showed you?"

Her head snapped up, opposing how her stomach dropped. "The other you." It came out too harsh and clipped, but if it hurt, he didn't show it.

"But it was still me, right? I just haven't become that version of me yet."

That *yet* sounded like the smooth introduction to a song before it ramped up to the chorus. She forced out a huff of a laugh, laced with disbelief. "It's not like that."

"Even though you said everything will converge again, which could make us the fractured people we've been in all those other lives?"

"I said it *might*."

"But you can't go back to that me, can you?"

Her answer had to claw up her throat, though it still didn't feel like she was given enough time to smooth out how it'd sound: "No."

He'd been thinking on this the whole time they'd been strategizing, rehashing a familiar yet ever-unique dance of questions. Always at a different point but never without his rationale. Another copy to find everything she missed in, all so she could abandon him for another. And another. And another. Jerky starts and stops. Shorter and shorter until there would be nothing left.

People were right when they said time is fleeting. It was like digging your hands into sand at the top of an hourglass, trying to hold onto as much as you can before it fell away. The only way one could actually stop it was to smash the thing to pieces, at the price of sacrificing everyone you loved.

"So…" Cade said, biting his lip. "What were we, exactly?"

"What do you mean?"

That lighthearted breath of a short, nervous chuckle gripped her heart. "You know—Like, do we drive each other crazy? Are we friends? Engaged? *Married?*"

Evie scoffed, narrowing her eyes at him.

"Do I still have a shot?" A *wink*.

The absolute audacity.

"First off, *no*. You do not 'have a shot.' Second, I'm not disclosing my relationship status with *you*. And finally, I already told you that I am not *your* Evie."

She'd somehow let him slide up next to her, the light bump of his shoulder against hers sending sparks shooting through her soul.

"It's *us*, Evie," he said, his voice a gentle sound like the soft edges of that business card in her pocket. "Who's to say you just haven't come full-circle to the same reality you started in? Who's to say that you're sifting through copies of the world you love and not phantom memories of what could've been? Who's to say you're not tired from the long journey you've been grappling with for so long that you don't recognize home?"

She couldn't blink away the tears welling up in her eyes. Her throat tightened with every word—every searching look he gave. It reignited that familiar feeling, but it wasn't one that she recalled from all the other rousing speeches he'd given before. Each iteration had come closer and closer, but never as close as *this*.

"I know what I would say if I knew you had to travel this path on your own. I would make you promise to always find me so I could be there to help keep you going."

Against her better judgment, she grabbed his face and kissed him.

FORTY-SIX
REN

It had taken Ren a little longer to get out of bed than usual. He stared at his alarm clock as the minutes changed, buried in his thoughts and blankets. No calls up the stairs, down the hall, or next to his door that he would be late. Not that it would've mattered to him. With a sigh, he pushed himself up, relieved that no pounding in his head caused him to sway.

A quick change later, he hurried down the stairs, hopping on the landing. A grin broke across his face when he saw the small stack of envelopes on the counter. His name scrawled on the front of each one.

The first one was thick cardstock, adorned with splashes of blue over penned birds carrying green clovers. His heart tugged at the handwritten message jotted down inside, each looping letter so deliberate, delicate, and heartfelt. It was signed by his mom with a little heart. The four five-dollar bills tucked inside may have been faded and crumpled, but there was a clear effort that she'd tried to straighten them out.

The second was a thin card with a joke about the money inside. A printed message within finished it off with an added hand-written smiley face and Angelo's sloppy signature. With a snicker, Ren moved onto the third, which boasted a kitten wearing a party hat. Shaking his head, he read Carmen's appended note to the card's text, waxing on much like his mother had to a less sappy extent. It, too, was signed with a heart.

He slid the final card from its envelope to find one of those embellished, expensive ones with intricately cut paper decorations layered to create party hats and balloons. Ren's smile faded, his stomach clenching as he flipped it open to see the generic, elegant script printed inside, followed by 'Love, Dad'. The crisp one-hundred-dollar bill in his hand dredged up a bitter taste in his mouth. So, he folded it into the other bills before dropping the card into the trash.

The sound of jogging down the stairs forced him to shove the cash into his pocket, pasting his smile back on as Carmen came into view.

"Happy birthday!" she cheered, grinning. She tousled his hair on her way to the kitchen cabinets. "How's eighteen feel?"

"Little strange," he said with a chuckle. "But I think it'll grow on me."

"You say that—" She half-turned, wagging a finger at him. "But just wait until you have to fill out all that paperwork. I'll take you this weekend since Mom's going to be busy and Angelo will likely be doing some Martelli bullshit." She waved a hand, returning to her search.

"Thanks, Carmen."

"Anytime. Have fun at school today."

He gathered up his bag with a brief goodbye before shoving open the door. He cringed to see the sidewalks growing empty, way past the time he should've been well on his way now. Too bad he had other things weighing him down now, including the cash heavy in his pocket. Maybe he should've dropped it in his room instead. Then again, he could get rid of that hundred in exchange for a nice dinner tonight. Something to treat his mom as a thank you that both Angelo and Carmen would be teasing about but deeply respect. His declaration that he would help take care of her like they had been.

A shout ripped him from his musings, sending him stumbling at the sound of his name. He spun around to find Carmen jogging toward him, holding up his brown paper lunch bag. Ren started toward her, gasping at the sudden jerk back. His heart caught in his throat and dropped like a rock at the sight of Carmen's face going slack for the flicker of a moment. The paper bag fell from her hand, spilling onto the sidewalk in her dead sprint toward him.

"Ren!"

He tried to force out a shout as he was shoved into a car. Someone pressed his face into the leather interior, gritting his teeth as he tried to squirm free. The hum of the engine thrummed through him, matching the sound of blood pounding in his ears that muffled the gruff orders of his captors.

Flailing led to his arms being seized and pushed into his back. *"Stop—"* he choked out, his throat dry from panic. One of them barked the instruction not to hurt him, which resulted in further panic. His body screamed in agony with every attempt to tap into his talent. A shiver worked its way down his spine at how much effort it took. Something was so very, *very* wrong.

Even before the car rolled to a stop, Ren knew he was about to come face-to-face with his Spirit opponent—one that was out-maneuvering him with sudden twists and turns he couldn't keep up with. How long would he be kept alive for? Would he be used as bait for trapping Cade and Evie? Would Vivian be tasked with making an example of him?

They dragged him from the car, his legs shaking so bad that he was positive the guy restraining him had to be a Keeper from how he kept him upright without so much as a sweat. Another searched his pockets, confiscating his phone and not bothering with the cash. The upward climb of the elevator floors turned his stomach, and he closed his eyes while he repeated that wish of not wanting to die. Not at eighteen. Not on his birthday.

Down a hall basked in soft light and modern art spread along the walls to break up the unit doors, they turned off to one where the number posted outside ripped the floor out from under him. They hauled him inside, and he tensed at the sight of Vivian in the entry.

"*Ren*," she purred, making his blood run cold, "I've heard so *much* about you."

The sound of dress shoes on the blue-patterned tiles followed, rolling into the slow, dramatic reveal as his opponent emerged from around the corner.

"Good morning, Ren," came that smooth, familiar cadence.

He couldn't breathe. His vision started to wobble. Ren had made a mistake. He'd pointed the finger at the wrong Spirit. The man standing in front of him wasn't Carlton Yuan.

It was his father.

FORTY-SEVEN

EVIE

WEDNESDAY, APRIL 22ND AT 8:54AM

Evie woke to a muffled pounding drifting up to the lofted bedroom. At first, she'd thought it was her imagination piecing together bits of a dream, only to realize that it refused to quit. Once she propped herself up, she found the source of the problem: Cade's arm hooked around her body. Her mouth twitched, unsure if it should break into a smile or a frown with how easily he'd lulled her into a sense of security. But that wasn't even the worst part.

She grimaced, ripping the sheets up over her chest, reddening. A fool high on love. That's what she was. "*Cade*," she hissed, giving him a shove.

He jolted awake. "Huh? What?"

"There's someone at the door."

"Who?"

Her hand went to her forehead. "I don't *know*, which is why you have to go check."

Cursing, he scrambled out of bed, and she tugged the covers over her face. Whether it was to hide her creeping blush or to prevent her from staring as he threw his clothes back on.

Hearing his feet padding downstairs allowed her to drop her makeshift shield to quickly find her own clothes.

"I was trying to call you, but it kept going to voicemail and—"

Evie stopped at the top of the steps, frozen to the spot when Angelo's sights fixed on her.

"O-Oh—I'm so sorry, I didn't mean to—"

"It's okay, Angelo," Cade said. "Just get to the point."

Angelo's eyes jittered between them, his breath hitching. "I-I need help, but I don't know if—" He shook his head, squeezing his eyes shut. "No, I just need today to deal with something—"

"With what, Angelo?" Evie asked, resuming her descent. Icy fear began to lace through her.

"Um…"

"You can tell us," she said, calm and coaxing while she tried to tamp down that gnawing dread.

"It's my brother. My sister told me that our asshole dad kidnapped him this morning."

Evie's eyes went wide. "Ren?"

He hesitated, nodding. "How did you—"

"I need his name, Angelo. What's your father's name?"

"Waylon—Waylon Frost."

10:36AM

Cade ran a hand through his hair after hanging up his phone. "Okay, Alyx just made it to the Leoni house. She's looking after them for the time being."

Evie chewed on her thumbnail, pacing as the last of their Keepers trickled in.

"What the hell happened to us believing it was Yuan?" Trinity asked, bafflement slipping through.

"Ren had too much faith in our other suspect to be a better person," Evie mumbled, slowing to a stop. "I think I figured out what happened though."

Wes leaned forward against the back of one of the chairs. "By all means, enlighten us."

"Going back to before when the Trick disappeared, Frost was an outcast. He fell in love or maybe something he *thought* was love with a Shade. This snowballs into resentment at the status rift, and he manages to get ahold of what he needs to dismantle the system and remake it to his liking."

"He Falls," Tarryn said with a grimace.

"Right. By then he's had two kids, he's begun to plot out a better future for them, and then he discovers he's having a third —one who turns out to be a powerful Spirit that's ended up with the residual effects of his deeds."

"Oh God…" Trinity's hand went to her mouth.

"And he realizes that he won't be able to get away with anything unless he eliminates the Trick from the picture. They're the counterbalance. They'd be the only ones to stop him. So, he clears them off the board, rallies the Fallen, and figures out that his son has that echo of his stolen Fallen talent. He knows he's running out of power, so he's taken Ren to help him finish the job without destroying himself in the process."

"Holy shit…" Leigh mumbled.

The sad, remorseful shake of Haven's head twisted Evie's gut.

Cade folded his arms over his chest, his face going sharp and serious. "So how do we want to do this? Bust down Frost's apartment door?"

Trinity scoffed. "If they have Keepers around, that could turn into a problem."

"I think I know how to handle them," Evie said. "So, leave that to me. Our focus should be on retrieving Ren to force Frost's hand."

"And try to save Vivian," came Leigh's firm decision, rising from his seat.

Evie's mouth worked, her face twitching at the solemn determination there. "Leigh, I don't know if—"

"We're going to try. She's one of *us*. We owe it to her to do that much, especially after whatever Frost has told her to pit her against us."

Tarryn blew out a breath, putting her hands on her hips with a glance toward the ceiling. Like some higher power would come through for them now. Too bad that was the job of everyone here. "Okay, so how much time do we have to strategize?"

With a shake of her head, Evie's shoulders fell. "Days? Hours? Minutes? I don't know."

"Then let's be quick about our plan of attack and strike," Cade said. "This ends today."

Ren had never been to his father's apartment before, and now he wished he'd never seen it. The cozy nooks and crannies of his mom's townhouse may have been old and worn, boasting yellowed laminate tiles or fraying, stained carpet, but at least it carried love. That couldn't be found here. Everything was open, cold, and sterile. Bright white with clean lines and a touch of refreshed antique design. The sofa he had been perched on was stiff—whether it was intentionally made this way or from disuse didn't really matter since both caused his blood to heat. Where everything had a purpose at home, there were a number of things that served as decoration here, including Ren.

Well, at least that's what he was determined to be.

"You don't want to talk?"

Vivian's lilting tone from the matching chair across from him sent his fingertips digging into his arms—crossed over his chest like a sulking child. The fact that his father had temporarily abandoned him to entertain this monster wasn't winning him any favors.

"Why are you doing this? You're *Trick*—He wants to get rid of all of you."

Those scarlet lips tipped downward in a mock frown, pouting. "Oh, honey. Have you never experienced what it's like to not matter?"

He bit down his immediate reply with the sudden weight dropped on his chest. As much as he was told he'd do good things—that he'd do well in life with his talent, he never truly believed it. Not when he was the reversed black sheep. The golden child. Both an outcast by the Custodians and accepted with open arms, should he shrug off the burden of his attachments. Much like how his father had with the supposed intention of making this *right*.

But he'd had a choice. Ren *hadn't*. He'd grown up torn between both factions. And no matter how hard he tried, he couldn't quite make himself fit into either. Now, to make it all worse, here he was, unraveling the horrible secret that he was *different*. The mere thought of it caused his stomach to twist.

"Yes," he said quietly, wanting her to keep spilling as much as she could, but praying she wouldn't pry further for an admission.

She threw knee over knee, tilting her head to rest on her propped-up hand, scrutinizing him. "I'm the Twelfth Trick. The bottom rung of their little hierarchical ladder. Shoved to the side over and over and *over again*. Never quite good enough to be included in anything that truly mattered." She picked at a piece of lint on her skirt, sighing. "Leigh did try, though. I suppose that's why I had the tendency to reach out to him during all these failed attempts. But he'll never see me like your father did. At least with Frost I'm part of a balanced set. A proper partner and counterweight instead of dead weight. No longer a nobody."

"You're not nobody, Vivian." It pained him to think how many lies his father had told to reinforce that idea. "You don't have to go through with this. The Custodians can change—"

"Oh, Ren." That mirthless smile reappeared, as hard as the glint in her hazel eyes. "I know how it changes, and I'll still be a nobody unless Frost changes things *now*."

"I won't help you."

"You will. Your father will see to that. Together, the three of us will stand as the leaders of the Custodians. The new conductors of the world. You have such a vibrant future ahead of you—such an incredible talent that's been wasted on foolish little games."

The airy noise of the door gliding open made Ren stiffen. The light, casual humming that followed sent a chill down his spine, rather than a sense of comfort. When he finally came into view, Ren caught sight of assorted envelopes and folded magazine flyers in his hands. He was shuffling through *mail*. As if today was just another Wednesday in which he wasn't kidnapping his son on his birthday and declaring war on the Custodians. Ren's jaw slackened briefly before the rage welled up in him again, his hands balling into fists.

When he stopped at the edge of the oversized area rug, he lifted his head with a dazzling smile. "I see I've come back without incident."

Something in Ren snapped in that moment. Maybe it was the sheer greed dripping all around him, or perhaps the blatant disregard for what his mother had always looked him in the eyes and reminded him of as their greater purpose. Either way, he couldn't bottle it up any longer because the cork was about to shoot as true as a bullet from a gun.

He stood, shoving down all the childish fear that gripped him—telling him to know his place. But he *did* know his place, and it wasn't here—nor was it among Spirits or Shade. The slight narrowing of his father's eyes didn't deter him from letting the words fall out either.

"I'm not helping you. Take me home."

His face creased in annoyance. "Sit down, Ren."

"No."

The slow clench of his jaw flipped Ren's stomach. "I said—"

"What do you think Mom would say if she was here right now?"

He knew he'd hit his mark when his father's face slacked in disbelief. It'd only lasted for a split-second, but it'd been enough to bolster him. That is, until he had marched over, thrown the mail down on the end table, and seized Ren's arm. A jerk forward, and his other hand clamped his jaw.

"You will *not* disrespect your father like this—"

"*My* father didn't use his family against their will and actually gave a shit about other people. You're not him, you're just some *bastard*."

He reared back, shocked before Ren saw stars. Stumbling, he tried to catch his balance, fumbling to grab anything to slow their progression down the hall. When he found nothing, he used his weight, sending them to a near-stop with his body going full-limp.

"Get *up*."

Like hell he was going to budge with the taste of blood in his mouth. A frustrated growl later, and Ren was being ripped to his feet. A Keeper had emerged from one of the rooms, lifting him so the toes of his sneakers barely skimmed the floor. He threw his head back, missing his opponent's face as he kicked.

"Let go of me! *Help!*" He stopped caring about getting hit again, hoping that one of the neighbors would call the police. Ren beat on every wall they brushed up against until he was tossed inside a room, falling face-first into the high-pile beige carpet. His head whipped around to see the door closing, and he launched himself at it, unable to stop it from latching in time.

"That's enough, Ren."

"I'm not helping you!" Ren screamed, pounding his fists against the door. "You've done nothing but make me a *monster!*"

The lack of reply turned into the worst weapon to be used against him, cutting deeper than anything his father could've said then. A sob caught in his throat at the soft mumblings and muffled footsteps trailing away. No denial. No correction. Simple, silent reinforcement of what Ren had always suspected: that there was something wrong about him.

He slid down the door, tears spilling down his face.

A tool. That's all he was. His stomach knotted, bringing fresh pain with it. His heart ached for the familiar, throbbing pain of visions in the dark embrace of his room—cool, tranquil, and safe. A place where he could settle into his misery like the embrace of an old friend. So, Ren closed his eyes, imagining he sat on the floor near his bed, and waited for someone to comfort him. All while knowing they'd never come.

WEDNESDAY, APRIL 22ND AT 1:26PM

"Ready?" Cade breathed, squeezing Evie's hand.

"Whenever you are."

He picked up the pace as they rounded the corner. But while his attention fixed on the route to the building's side-entrance, Evie's face tilted toward the sky and how it reflected in the window panels climbing to greet it. It fell away from view when Cade dropped them into the pavement, folding into the dark corners in their smooth hurtle toward the door. Right on cue, it popped open for a new wave of staff escaping for a late lunch.

Cade shot them through the threshold and up the wall, zipping along the ceiling to the service elevator before it shut. She gasped at the rapid decompression, her head spinning from the shift back to something corporeal.

"Sorry," he panted with his hands on his knees. "That could've gone a little smoother."

"It's fine." She pressed a shaky finger to Frost's floor. "We made it. That's what matters."

"You sure Leigh can manage getting everyone through the front?"

"Once we let them know the Keepers are being handled, I'm confident he can walk them in with a short pause. As long as Vivian's preoccupied with us, it'll buy them enough time to reach us."

"And who's going to handle the Keepers? I don't recall discussing that bit…"

The elevator chimed, accompanied by the thudding of footsteps on the carpet. Evie shoved her hand back into Cade's, and the two of them melted into the carpeting right outside the doors. Three Keepers passed, barreling into the stairwell at the opposite end of the hall. A jerky slide in the opposite direction, a whip around a corner, and a gasping pop up in front of a door later, Evie saw the gleam of the hall light on the engraved number plate.

Cade's hand tightened in hers, their pulses pushing back against one another's as he rasped, "On three. One, two—"

The world collapsed one last time in their crawl under the door, the feel of carpet shifting to tile sending a cold shock through her. Cade's flip of the deadbolt rang out like a gunshot at the beginning of a race, calling forth the snap of heels as Vivian hurried to greet them. Her eyes were wide and child-like with something akin to surprise or horror until they landed on Cade. At that point, her mouth twisted into a snarl.

"Hey, Viv," Evie said with a smirk that she hoped portrayed more confidence than she felt—especially since her heart was speeding up with every echoing reminder of the time ticking away between them. "Miss me?"

"You dumb bit—"

She didn't get a chance to finish hurling her insult. The door burst open behind them at top speed, a gust of air ruffling Evie's hair over her face and knocking her off-balance into the wall. Leigh stood between them, hand-in-hand with Haven, who wasted no time shoving his elbow straight into Vivian's chest.

But the sound of a body hitting the polished ceramic never came, only another flash of movement straight into the living space that left the crystalline shards of the chandelier clinking above her. However, Evie no longer cared about her in that moment, not when she'd laid eyes on her new target.

Frost stood a little further behind her, his back to a line of glass panes overlooking his would-be kingdom. His posture straight, elegant, and commanding, even with his arm hooked around his son's neck and a letter opener in his other hand—the closest defensive item in his arsenal. He turned it over and over in his hand at his side, not raising it to Ren's neck as he gripped Frost's blazer sleeve, squirming to free himself.

Evie forced her hands to uncurl, telling herself that he *needed* Ren for this to work for the foreseeable future. "Let him go, Frost."

Even the clattering of Trinity, Wes, and Tarryn filing in behind her didn't deter his scoff. He shook his head, pitying in a way. "I don't think you realize what you're doing."

"Do I? Because I'm thinking the same about you. Throwing the Fallen down as your buffer to even out the playing field is only going to cause more problems."

A snarl. "And you honestly think that someone like *him* is going to be able to change the minds of *all* the Custodians?" He thrust the letter opener toward Cade. "Sure, maybe it'll work for New Atlas for a time, but it'll lose steam. We'll end up right back where we started. Divided. This is the only way."

"So that's your justification for driving out the Trick? A short-term sacrifice for the greater good? That makes you no better than the rest of those who look down on your own children—"

"*Enough,*" he spat, his voice creeping to a growl. "You will *never* understand how much I surrendered for the betterment of the Custodians—What I had to *become* for anyone to listen to what I had to say by walking away from everything I loved."

"Selflessly for the Custodians? Or selfishly so you could have everything you wanted and then some?"

"Shut up!"

Ren recoiled, his face creasing with how tight he'd shut his eyes, shrinking down against Frost's chest.

The small shifting movement from the corner of Evie's eye came with Leigh's coaxing voice, calling Vivian's name. Her head swung toward him, her crimson lips giving a nervous twitch.

"You can still walk away from this," he pleaded.

She bared her teeth. "Oh, *please*. Don't start acting like you actually care. You don't get to try to mend things now. Not when there was nothing but injustice in the corners you refused to look before."

And with that, Evie called out to the clocks. She lunged forward, past Vivian, and let go of that frozen time as she flung herself against Frost. He gasped, the letter opener clanging and Ren stumbling away. Vivian shouted behind her, the whip of time crackling through the air as her and Leigh's energy clashed, shoving back and forth in the midst of Keepers.

Evie took a swing at Frost, his eyes a white-hot glow in a flickering instant before she collided with the floor.

"That's enough!" Ren yelled, throwing himself between them as Evie's shield. "Walk away. Walk away before you do something you'll regret. There's no justice in what you're doing. You're not helping anyone but yourself."

"Listen to your son, Frost." Evie shoved herself to her feet, wobbling to the horrid sound of distant ticking. "This is your last chance to step back and do the right thing."

He stepped forward, reaching for the one thing she refused to let him have. She sucked in a breath, and the world screeched to a halt at her command so she could shove Ren aside. He caught his balance on the edge of the sofa and his eyes went wide the second light in Frost's eyes winked out, giving way to confusion —then horror. That last glimpse into the future to offset her had finally burned him.

Frost clawed at his sleeve, pushing it up to reveal a mark of stars, fading in and out like the night sky. Growing dimmer by the second.

Ren swayed at Evie's side, his shoulders dipping with that too-familiar look of regret. Loss. Remorse. Glassy eyes and a brave face when facing his father as he was slowly consumed by pinpricks of starlight. She saw the resemblance then with Frost's face mirroring his son's. His hands held out like the statue of a saint.

"No!" came Vivian's cry, allowing her only a glimpse of Frost's final sigh into shimmering light.

She sprinted toward Evie, slamming her against the floor. Every grasp for time turned into a pause Vivian would be ripped into, filled with rage and defeat in the form of yelling bubbling over to near-sobs and hands being wrapped around Evie's neck. The pressure released with a scream, Vivian rocking back to fight off another assailant—one that she'd smacked and had fallen to the floor like a stone.

Cade.

Vivian's hazel eyes widened as a shadow pooled across the floor, seeping onto the rug, eating up curtains, rippling through the air. One final cry rang out, cut off by the consuming mass pulling her into its dark, quiet embrace. When it left, Vivian was gone, leaving a void of silence in its wake.

Evie's head lulled back, bumping against the floor. Her vision faded in and out as the ticking grew louder—closer. An army of footsteps started toward her and Cade. Ren dropped to his knees at her side while Cade was hoisted up. He held a hand to his head before he pushed everyone away in favor of heading straight for Evie.

"Hey," she breathed, pushing up her sleeve out of habit. Cade grabbed it, staring down at the mark there.

With a stricken expression, he met her gaze. "You didn't— No, no—" He cupped her face, shaking his head. "Stay with me. I need you to stay with me."

Ren cursed, his head swiveling toward their now-growing

audience, though Evie blurred them all out. It was her and Cade. Her hand went to his hair, the color tickling her soul with how it'd gotten there.

"It's okay," she whispered, unable to suppress a small smile.

"No, it's *not* okay—"

Ren stood out of the corner of her vision, pulling something out of his pocket and holding it up. It'd looked like it was directed toward Tarryn until she turned, stepping aside for someone else.

"You can't leave," Cade begged. "*Please.*"

"I always found you, Cade." Her thumb stroked his cheek, her heart slowing with every motion. "And in every instance, there wasn't a single time you and I didn't make our way to each other."

"Then *stay.*"

His hand grew tight around her wrist, his voice pained as the tears began to slip free. Her eyelids began to droop, obscuring the figure taking Ren's place at her side. A figure that took her arm. The person to finally release her from all this.

FIFTY
CADE

Cade put a fist over his mouth to cover a yawn, pushing through a half-hearted stretch before his arms dropped to his side. The Custodians' meeting hall lobby busied with chatter; each faction fragment tucked into its own recess around a leader. Last-minute deliberations before the monthly New Atlas council meeting. He shoved his hands into his pockets, sighing with a weary glance at Trinity, Wes, and Angelo. No Emilio this time since he'd said there was business he needed to attend to.

"You ready?"

He jumped, breaking into a sly grin at the sight of Evie at his side.

"I think I should be asking *you* that after your casual brush with death," he said. "But I admit that it'll be a little weird to have a full council of nine factions, rather than eight at the helm for once."

"It'll be for the better," came Leigh's confident remark, strolling up next to them with Tarryn and Haven in tow. "I don't think there's anyone better suited for the job than someone who's sacrificed so much for them."

Evie huffed out a modest laugh, tucking a lock of hair behind her ear. "Thanks, Leigh."

He patted her arm with reassurance before the sound of a throat clearing demanded their attention behind them. They turned in unison to see Lily, who folded her arms over her chest and tapped her foot against the black-marbled tile. At her side stood Aiden with a hand on Ren's shoulder, who bore a lazy smirk. Still the same old brat he'd met mere weeks ago, though the main difference now was the small tattoo on the side of his neck, barely hidden by the collar of his hoodie.

A mark that sank Cade's heart knowing the sacrifice it stood for. Whether Ren was putting on a brave face or not didn't matter when he saw Angelo's tight smile that didn't quite reach his eyes. The decision hadn't been his, but Cade knew he'd feel that same regret if it was his own brother who'd thrown himself to the Inked for someone else.

Cade's recollection of cornering Ren once they'd moved Evie to the hospital pooled at the surface of his thoughts regarding that deal—his attempt to reason with Ren when he'd started with: "Let me talk to Lily—"

"No." The reply had come with such a strong conviction that Cade had rocked back in the hospital's hallway, the two of them left alone while Keepers lingered at the far corners of the waiting areas and by Evie's room.

"I- What? *No?* Ren, you're about to sign your life over to the Inked. You don't have to act brave because you're saving Evie's life."

He sighed, shoulders falling with arms wrapped around himself. "I don't belong with Spirits. Shade? Maybe. But you know I'm closer to Fallen than anything. If the wrong people find out, I'll be used as a weapon."

"And Lily *won't?*"

"Lily might be a nuisance or a rival to you, but she's not a villain. She wants change too, which is why I did what I did. We can fix things if you trust me on this because we both know Frost won't be the only person to stand in your way."

Cade closed his eyes, his hands clenching into fists at his side before letting all that tension slip away. "You don't deserve this."

"And you didn't deserve any of the shit you've gone through either, Cade." Ren had given an uptick of a smirk. "But here we are. I think you're forgetting the main goal."

He'd huffed out a laugh. "You'll have to remind me since it's been a long few days…"

"When the king's knocked over, the game's over."

Cade snapped back to the present—hospital corridor traded for the Custodian's meeting hall lobby. Standing here now, Cade saw through Ren's guise of amusement to that terrifying fragment of Frost underneath. Always a step ahead—working out how to potentially play Lily before she gets the chance to sink her claws into him. Though, when he returned his focus to Lily, impatience outweighed the favor of her new toy. Her lips were pursed, waiting for some sort of acknowledgment that Cade wasn't sure he'd ever be able to willingly give.

"Thank you, Lily," Evie said with a slight chuckle, "for giving me such an opportunity."

Lily rolled her eyes, releasing a dramatic sigh. "Well, that wasn't what I was referring to, but you're *welcome*. Now hurry up and get inside. *I'm* supposed to be the last one in for a grand entrance."

Leigh shook his head, leading the way, and Cade slipped his hand into Evie's. He laced his fingers through hers, the two of them walking in time past the confidants left in the council leaders' wake.

"So, Lily," Cade said over his shoulder with a prayer that perhaps Ren was wrong, "is this little game finally over?"

"Oh, we're just getting started, my little shadow friend." She wagged a finger at him, a devious, twisted grin plastered on her face.

Evie gave his hand a quick squeeze, her eyes dancing with excitement in that promise of a new adventure. "Then let the games begin."

ACKNOWLEDGMENTS

I have to thank my sister for helping me build out some of the characters for this tale so many years ago: specifically Lily and Aiden. Cybil, thank you for being this story's absolute biggest fan—it meant so much to me to see such support for this twisty urban fantasy when we barely knew each other, and I'm looking forward to seeing your stories come to light as one of my awesome writing buddies. Melissa, thank you for all the gushing and hype over these characters, even when I was floundering trying to flesh out Evie more on paper. Dominique, I appreciate you so much for helping validate my accidentally writing a neurodiverse main character from my own life experiences and views. Katya, thank you for the additional emotional support and for being another project enabler.

And, of course, thank you all for reading this little book of my high school heart.

It's so strange to finally see my first fully fleshed-out concept brought to life after all the iterations it's gone through. I sincerely hope that all of you enjoy these little episodic adventures and spin offs in this off-beat urban fantasy. So if you're looking forward to more of Evie, Cade, and Ren's adventures, know that I'm also just as thrilled to dive back into it between my other stories.

ABOUT THE AUTHOR

Cara Nox is an urban and science fantasy writer, combining their love of magically-inclined chaotic idiots and modern/futuristic tech. They also love mysteries, thrillers, and anything that draws inspiration from stars. Cara works as a web developer by day, holds BA in Japanese Language and Literature they occasionally use to read video game announcements, and resides in Ohio with their younger sister and two black cats.

For more information on all of their books, visit **caranox.com**.

To find some of their newest works-in-progress, bonus content, serialized stories, where they're at on social media, how to get deals on their current and upcoming works, and where to preview the first few chapters of their other books, visit **caranox. com/links**.